MORE PRAISE FOR *Ice Fire Water*

"Like Saul Bellow and Stanley Elkin before him, Epstein writes an energetic, full-throated prose that finds maniacal vaudevillian comedy in both everyday absurdity and historical catastrophe. . . . [Leib Goldkorn] is a delightfully outrageous creature." —*Newsday*

"An expertly balanced mixture of hilarity and pain. . . . [Goldkorn] is surely one of the liveliest nonagenarians in fiction, detailing the decay of impoverished old age with a kind of ridiculous dignity." —*San Francisco Chronicle*

"Fantastical, wickedly funny." —*Elle*

"A wise, heroically funny novel . . . [a] masterful linguistic and critical performance. . . . Earthy, resourceful, and wistful." —*Publishers Weekly*

"A masterly blend of the plangent and the preposterous. . . . *Ice Fire Water* abounds with inspired confusions and illusions." —*Los Angeles Times*

"Successfully mixes real characters with imagined ones, the beautiful with the ugly and aspects of goodness and unspeakable evil. . . . A delightful romp through Goldkorn's century." —*The Forward*

"The voice of Leib Goldkorn . . . combines a carnival barker's campy energy with genuine moral urgency and a poignant evocation of human longing. . . . One of the most exuberant and underappreciated voices of American fiction is back." —*Boston Review*

"Meticulously crafted. . . . Disarming and moving, an always hilarious 'cocktail' of three novellas that manages to adroitly fuse the past with the present as well as the beautiful with the profane." —*Houston Chronicle*

"*Ice Fire Water*, in its ribald episodes and philosophical agitations, fits on that very small shelf with Gogol's tales. Leslie Epstein conducts the tragic and the comic with epic grandeur." —Howard Norman

"Extremely funny and touching." —John Bayley

Ice
Fire
Water

a Leib Goldkorn Cocktail

Leslie Epstein

W. W. NORTON & COMPANY
NEW YORK • LONDON

Portions of this work have appeared in somewhat different form in *Harper's Magazine* and *TriQuarterly*.

This is a work of fiction. Although some characters may bear some resemblance to historical and living figures, the narrative is not intended in any way to be a depiction of any real events.

Part title illustrations: Pablo Picasso, *L'Aubode* (details) © 1999 Estate of Pablo Picasso / Artists Rights Society (ARS), New York

For information to reproduce selections from this book, write to Permissions, W. W. Norton & Company, Inc., 500 Fifth Avenue, New York, NY 10110

The text of this book is composed in Sabon and Futura with the display set in Panorama and Liberty
Desktop composition by Justine Burkat Trubey
Manufacturing by The Maple-Vail Book Manufacturing Group

Library of Congress Cataloging-in-Publication Data
Epstein, Leslie.
Ice fire water : a Leib Goldkorn cocktail / by Leslie Epstein.
p. cm.
ISBN 0-393-04804-7
1. Jews—New York (State)—New York Fiction. 2. Miranda, Carmen, 1909–1955 Fiction. 3. Henie, Sonja, 1912– 1969 Fiction. I. Title.
PS3555.P655 I28   1999
813'.54—dc 21   99-30719
CIP
ISBN 0-393-32090-1 pbk.
W. W. Norton & Company, Inc., 500 Fifth Avenue, New York, N.Y. 10110
www.wwnorton.com

W. W. Norton & Company Ltd., 10 Coptic Street, London WC1A 1PU

1 2 3 4 5 6 7 8 9 0

For Fred Busch,
Leib's friend

Ice

Cast of Characters

IN EUROPE
The Family Goldkorn
Leib Goldkorn, Graduate of the Akademie
Mutter, his mother
Vater, his father
Yakhne, his manly sister
Minkche, his beautiful sister

at the akademie
Hans Maltz, Second-Place Finisher, flute
Willi Wimpfeling, young violist
Pepi Pechler, young woodwinder
Professor Pergam, Instructor in Classics
Professor Lajpunger, Instructor on Woodwinds

Rabbi Goldiamond, a childhood religious advisor
Dr. R. von Krafft-Ebing, a noted author
S. Umin, American ambassador to France
Jacques Warner, American cinema producer
A. Hitler, German Reichschancellor, Olympic enthusiast
Esther, a heroine of Jewish folklore

IN NEW YORK CITY
At 130 West 80th Street
Clara Goldkorn (formerly Litwack), L. Goldkorn's spouse
Martha Goldkorn, 6/7/43-6/7/43, their daughter
F. Fingerhut, *père*, his former landlord, friend to Madam Goldkorn
F. Fingerhut, *fils*, his current landlord
Madam Schnabel, an eager neighbor
Bowser, a boxer

Miss Crystal Knight, a model

IN HOLLYWOOD
Miss Candace Kane, a producer's assistant
Miss Sonja Henie, Norwegian skating champion
D. F. Zanuck, chief of production, Twentieth Century-Fox
Irving Cummings (also Katz-Cummings), a cinema director
Jack Warner (see Jacques Warner)
E. W. Korngold, cinema melodist

Others: A chauffeur, a French telegraph boy, Austrian sharpshooters,
studio personnel, crowds, etc.

1

H*APPY BIRTHDAY TO YOU! Happy Birthday to you! Happy Birthday, Leib Goldkorn!* The words to this famous melody I sing in my basso profundo. *Happy Birthday to you!* Music has charms, so speaks the poet, to calm the savage beast—and there lies the boxer dog, once so fierce, with a smile on his liverish lips. Such an animal has been known to eat small children and tear the seat from the postman's pants. There once was a time when to appease this hellish hound I had to perform a complete *Tannhäuser* overture, with multiple selections from *Der fliegende Holländer.* A Wagnerite, this watchdog. But victory is mine. I have outlived him! Not in the literal meaning of the word, since, behold, the stump of his tail still wigwags: but if I am this day turned ninety-four, poor Bowser is now— here we must multiply by seven the number of years, fifteen, since he was a pup—one hundred and five. No teeth. No eyes. No problem. There he lies, under the spell of this folkish tune, in what Americans call a dog's daze.

Therefore the way to the cabinetto is clear. I speak of the public necessary just down the hallway from the door of my own apartment, 5-D. *Hello? Hello? Anyone there? Madam Schnabel? Mr. Fingerhut, fils?* Empty! Inside, the small bulb casts no more light than that of a Frigidaire. Nor is this closet any larger than the inside of such a machine. Nor warmer! A chill breeze—we are now in the month of November—blows through the crack in the window and under the crack in the door. Heavens! There is a frozen film upon the water of the johnny! Overhead, on the wall, the tank for water has frozen into a solid cube of ice. Not even Scott, not Admiral Peary, would in such conditions have dropped their pantaloons. Time now for the first of my birthday treats, permitted on an annual basis by Dr. Goloshes. TWA bottle of potato vodka. *Salud,* Akademie Graduate Goldkorn! Ninety-four years young. Ah, in my throat such a burning, like the man in the Roumanian Circus who swallows fire.

Have we reached the moment for the second treat? No, no, a *treatment*, prescribed, like the schnapps, as a tonic for the system. Here it is, the happy holiday issue, behind the clouded cellophane. How was I to obtain it? This was the thought I faced upon waking this morning at dawn.

Waking? I had not once through the long night of anticipation closed my eyes. I heard, from my corner of the Posturepedic, the snores of my wife. In a glass, formerly containing seedless jelly, her dentures lay like a mollusk under inches of water. On the pillow, her wig. From her nightdress a breast protruded. This was reminiscent of the Zeppelin IV I had seen in my youth: length 140 meters, filled with inflammable gas. Even if this exposure had provoked in me a modicum of libertinism, the fact that Clara and I had not exchanged any but the most essential of words—*insulin, sweetheart? A potty perhaps?*—since the debacle with Father Fingerhut, would have driven from my mind any entertainment of erotics.

I knew that the newsstand of the Broadway local opened at 5:30, *ante meridiem*. I also knew that the gay holiday issues, in their semi-transparent sanitary jackets, did not go on display until eight or nine, during the hour of the morning rush. Nothing to do but lie under the bedclothes: see how the four walls about me slowly turn from black to gray to a fly-specked white, much like the screen of our Admiral TV; hear the coo-cooing of the pigeons upon the sill. On the Avenue Columbus the traffic unceasingly flows, like the thoughts of a neurasthenic patient. From the flat on the left the gargling of Fingerhut, *fils*. And on the right Madam Schnabel, a hefty coloratura, utters her runs and trills. At last: the laughter, the high-pitched cries of children on their way to the public Schule.

That was my signal to, as Americans say, rise *und* shine. Clara was still in the land of nod. Stealthily I moved about, stepping into trousers, shirt, and red and black lumberman's jacket. Also Thom McAns. At the kitchen sink, ablutions. Facial rub with unsinkable Ivory-brand soap. Into the depths of the same receptacle, with its faucet drip, I emptied the contents of my bladder. This took seven minutes. No need for at least four more days to think of number 2. Time for departure. I doffed the Panama-style hat that old Fingerhut had left on the bedpost and walked to the window.

The window? Why not, good friends, the door? Here, in a nut's shell, the answer: books. And more books. Stacked here, stacked there, they formed a blockade against exit or entry. In the middle of the room these paper pillars stretched from floor to ceiling, like the columns that, as Professor Pergam taught his younglings at the Akademie, held up the temple of the Philistines. And if some modern Samson should pull them asunder, it is not unlikely that the whole rooftop of 130 W. 80th Street might collapse upon our nightgowned Delilah as, with her wig, her whiskers, she calls out one last time in spite of expense for Campbell's corn chowder and jerky made by Slim Jim.

You have without doubt guessed the secret: these are the thousands of volumes of my memoirs that, at 88 cents a copy, I saved from the machines that threatened to reduce them to illegible pulp. This venture I financed by depositing my instrument, a Rudall & Rose–model flute, bestowed upon me by the Emperor Franz Joseph himself, into the Glickman Brothers shop of prawns. I thought that by selling each book for two dollars and sixty-four cents a copy, a tripling of my original investment, I would thus secure my golden years. How could I fail? Was not my building filled with bespectacled Jews? What of the postman, the gas man, the brown-clothed messenger from UPS? Think of the hungry masses that crowd Herr Greengrass the Sturgeon King and Williams Bar-B-Que chicken. Friends! Acquaintances! Neighbors! All of them subscribers to Book-of-the-Month.

Not only that, the *Goldkorn Tales* possessed a cover design by the modernist Picasso, on which an unclothed woman is serenaded upon the flute by an unclothed man. Visible display of the privates. Above all, had I not an excellent review by Miss Michiko Kakutani of the *New York Times*, in which she speaks of the author's "artistry and ambition." End Quotation. No question, ladies and gentlemen: Goldkorn was sitting upon a gold mine.

Kakutani? Kakutani? Michiko? What kind of name is that? Javanese? Japanese? Like the place mat weaver, Marimekko, perhaps a Finn? A person with such insight is not likely American born. Naturally I wrote a brief note of appreciation, suggesting a small luncheon, an hour of pleasantries, the exchange of photographs. Yes, a blond-headed Finn! There was no reply. Even worse: the prawn ticket from Mr. Ernie and Mr. Randy Glickman remains hidden inside one of these innumerable books, of which through all these years I have sold not a single copy.

Bᴜʟᴏᴠᴀ ᴡᴀᴛᴄʜ ᴛɪᴍᴇ: 9:07. *Ante meridiem.* There can be no further delay. *Presto! Prestissimo!* And so, with a smart shoulder shrug, I slip off my braces. If there is in this city of eight million souls a single loyal reader, he will recall that my trousers belonged at one time to the late Vivian Stutchkoff, a man who weighed nearly three hundred pounds. That is why this garment drops so easily from my waist zone, forming about my ankles a lake of gabardine. S. Klein drawers soon follow. Immediately the goose flesh erupts upon my gale-swept flanks. There, awaiting, is what the poet calls the wooden O. The liquid within has frozen as firm as the winter waters of the Bodensee. In these few weak watts the oval ring seems to float like a life preserver over the hidden depths. Sinking upon it, I stifle the cry of dismay that rises to my lips: both bums have adhered to the chilled surface, the way, in ferocious February, a boy's tongue will become glued to the metal bars of a fence he has unwisely licked. Thus seated I am able with more comfort to view my prize. What do I see, in a blur behind the cocoon of cellophane? An open mouth. Red-painted lips. A tongue tip that licks—what do Americans call it? A peppermint pole?—ein Pfefferminzstück.

Through the window, onto the fire escape. A chilly November morning. Wind gusts threatened to remove the Panama hat. Overhead the clouds played tag me, a schoolyard game. I am not at present as agile as I was in my eighties. Down the ladder, eyes averted from the window glass of Madam Schnabel, lest I see unawares the bozom zone and bustier of the unclothed contralto. Goloshes, M.D., has warned of the consequences of just such unattainable provokements. Already we have seen the difficulty in making peepee. The gland of the prostate is now the size of an apple from Washington State. My birthday has come not a day too soon.

Terrible the things that occur when we catch heedless sight of others. Once, in a jungle-hot summer, I descended this same ladder from the rooftop to our window and surprised Father Frank Fingerhut in the very act. *Mein Gott!* The pinkness of his backside. The size of that shlong. And Clara? No sign of dropsy as she performed the scissors and somersault. Do not think this was an hallucination. Or a false interpretation. Leib Goldkorn is not, in the matter of abandoned morals, a mere rubbernecker. On at least one occasion I have achieved a definite penetration. New York City. November, 1942. The dressing room of the Tivoli Jewish Art Theater. Clara, the youthful stage star. Her athletic chests. The smell from her, like paste of anchovies. Unmentionables. Garter trolleys. In my mind, there played a scene from Schnitzler. In my body, sauciness surged. *Miss Litwack! Honey!* Thus my voice as I approached the climactic: *Tivoli! This is in reverse I lov it!* A swoon of pleasure, a blankness. There is no doubt of a congress because in the June month, in what had become the Tivoli Cine Palace, our dear little mistress, the blue-faced Martha, was delivered by young Dr. Goloshes.

Onward! Downward! The last little leap to the ground. Hurry. I had to hurry. First, the Avenue Amsterdam. Then Broadway. Then the block between 80th and 79th. So much, on this morning, to accomplish. I had to make my purchase, retrace my steps, and climb the inner stairs, five flights to the cabinetto. There I would sing the canon to the canine. My goal was to achieve a paroxysm in time to administer the noon hour injection to my wife. Did you, at that early hour, see the elderly gentleman at the trot? Note how, from his nostrils, the breath poured visibly onto the winterish air? Or hear the coin hoard as it jingled within his copious pockets? At last: the entrance to the chasm of the former IRT.

FROM AS FAR back as memory takes me I have been upon the johnny a reader: tales of Old Shatterhand, for example, in the works of the author Karl May; ofttime stories by the Brothers Grimm; in my teen years the account of Peary and other Arctic explorers, or the novels of romance that my sister Minkche kept furtively under her pillow; also the newspapers that my father brought back from

Prague, Vienna, Berlin. This early exposure to the literary life has led to consequences unforeseen: first, I cannot now enter a library or a book emporium without, after but a moment of perusal, a telltale pinch in the zone of the bowels; second, I have learned that if I should in forgetfulness step into a water closet without a supply of relaxing reading materials, I cannot hope to experience from my labor the fruits.

Mistake not: I have not purchased this holiday issue as a digestive aid. It is other organs that must achieve on doctor's orders an evacuation. I can delay no longer the examination of this birthday boon. Time to discard the frosty cellophane. Why this hesitation? The task is no more difficult than removing a raincoat. One, two, and three: off we whisk the wrap. Here are the bright Christmas colors: Santa suit red, mistletoe green. Now we see clearly the feminine lips, the feminine tongue, a hint of incisors in mother-of-pearl. Healthy pink gums. A syrup of saliva. And into this inviting cavern there is introduced the what-do-you-call-it? White as a bratwurst, with, like a barber's pole, red ribbon stripes. Ah! Ah! The word yet escapes me. Am I suffering from the disease that Goloshes calls Uncle Al? A sugar stick? *Nein!* For this Fräulein and her friends I have paid the Indian gentleman five American dollars and ninety-nine cents.

"Birthday fund," I explained. "One year of savings."

It took some minutes for the Sufi or Sikh—note the turban and the lips stained with betel—to sort through the quarters, pennies, nickels, dimes. I stood in mortification as the impatient crowd of travelers pressed close behind me. A train, the New Lots Avenue Express, came hurtling along the interior rails of our local station. In such a tantarara I could not at first hear what the dealer of news cried out. Then the linked wagons went rocking away into the distance. In the ensuing silence his words echoed across both the platform for the north and that for the south.

Hindoo: "*Hustler*, huh?"

NOVEMBER 9, 1901, the day on which, in the empire of the late Franz Joseph, in the town of Iglau, L. Goldkorn was born. *Happy birthday to you!* Will this day be remembered like February 12, the birth date of A. Lincoln, who walked miles through the snow to pay the one penny fine on a book; or like February 22, the nativity of G. Washington, who hurled a larger coin across the Potomac? We cannot yet say. Perhaps if the score of my *Esther* should, at the Metropolitan Opera, receive a premiere. Then might the musical world recall a ninth of November the way they do a twenty-seventh of May or a fifth of September, the birthdays of Halévy and Meyerbeer. Let us turn our gaze from the gazette cover to its rear. Here we see a full female form, platinum-haired, in a dickey too small to contain the mams. With one hand she holds the base of a telephone, with the other she presses the receiver to her ear. So that we might know her thoughts, we see the printed words *I'm Waiting for You* and the following number: 1-800-666-HOTT. I was not, as they say, born overnight. If one accepted this toll-free proposal, one could engage in frank discussions. Alas, I have been by the Bell Company for many years non-connected.

Of course November 9th is well known as the day of the abdication of Wilhelm II and the founding of the Weimar Republic. Also for the anniversary of one of those days so infamous that—as with the assassinations of President "Jack" Kennedy and the Archduke Ferdinand—one can never forget precisely where one was or what one was doing.

11/9/38. Where was, on that fateful date, the birthday boy? In Iglau, with its bending river and its factory for Trabucco tobacco? In Vienna, upon the Türkenshanzplatz, at the Akademie für Musik, Philosophie, und darstellende Kunst; or at the Wiener Staatsoper, in whose ranks Goldkorn had played the glockenspiel? No, no. No, no. I was that November night on the banks of a different river, the Seine, in the City of Light. There was, over my head, no rooftop. With my shepherd's panpipe I had not been able to earn a single sou. For warmth the score of my *Esther* was tied with string bits about my body. On what then did I live? On air, on water, on the pale yellow sunshine of Paris. Not like a person, like a plant. Not living! Dying. Oh, how seductive the Seine! How enticing its susurration, like the soft smack of a lady's lips. With the lap-lap of its waves and wavelets, it called to me: *Venez! Venez, Monsieur Goldkorn! Come to my embrace!*

TEMPUS, AS PROFESSOR Pergam would say toward the end
of each class at the Akademie, *fugit*. Why, then, do I continue procrastinations? Open, sir, the rotogravure! Ah, but what if the object I
seek, my own dear Venus, should be marked absent? I speak of the
maiden whose acquaintance I first made in these pages, decades
before. The hair on her pubes had hardly sprung. *This Crystal is
sweet, petite,* such was the printed message, *and ready to eat!* Exclamation. Yes, she was then, my missy, no more than thirty, or at most
thirty-five. Hands clasped to the rear. No lip rouge. No kohl for the
eyes. Upon her brisket her bosoms resembled the two complimen-
tary *Makronen*—macaroons, yes? Almond delights?—upon the
plates at Demel's. Each with its adorable maraschino. But what
caused in my nether zone a certain peppery feeling was the glimpse
of Miss Crystal's feet. One was unshod, but the other, her left one,
was encased in a boot of red leather. Heel like a stiletto. Toe like a
trowel. This foot was raised in my estimation some ten inches from
the ground. Printer's legend: *This Tramp Will Walk over You!* Exclamation.

Question: why was Leib Goldkorn celebrating his birthday in La
Belle France? Answer: because Herr Hitler was now in Vienna.
At that thought I reached up to the lump of silver, Yakhne's
medallion, that lay on my breast. A similar lump formed in my
throat. My poor family! Their fate awaited every Jew. Mutter;
Vater; sister Minkche, the minx; the aforementioned sister
Yakhne: all, together with 150 musical Hebrews—of the Orchester der Wiener Staatsoper, the Wiener Philharmonic, *Die kleine
Wienerwaldphilharmonie* the crème de la crème—had embarked
immediately after the Anschluss upon a barge, the *Kalliope*,
named for the mother of Orpheus. That craft was to drift eastward, with the Donau current, some forty-five kilometers, to the
safety of the border with the Czechs. This was an arrangement I
had made with Hans Maltz, former Akademie classmate, and
now, in his brown shirt and brown pants, a natty Nazi. I paid the
Goldkorns' ransom by placing into that Gauleiter's hands my
Rudall & Rose. Farewell, Papa! Farewell, Minkche! Chins up!
Surely all would be well: had they not pickled cucumbers? And

tins of liver pâté? Instead, a trick! A hoax by the Huns! The engines roared. Smoke came out of the smokestack. Huffing, puffing, the barge sailed westward, *against* the current, into the land of the beast: from blue Donau—in English blue Danube—to gray Isar, from the Isar to the Amper, all the way to Dachau. This was a hillside village, well known for ceramics and textiles and picturesque views. But judging from what one heard from those aboard her—silence, only silence—the good ship *Kalliope* might have sailed off the ends of the earth.

D o   I   n o t   sense, now, at the memory of the youthful Crystal, a definite titillation? In order to view my zone of reproduction it is necessary to overcome two obstacles. *Primo*, the barrier posed by the growth of my abdomen. By expelling oxygen from the lungs and contracting the ventral muscles, this obstacle may be temporarily overcome. The second difficulty is not so easily dealt with. Those who have read my earlier memoir will recall that I do not possess a religious nature. Even so, the teachings of the fathers present a psychic barrier no less formidable than that posed by the flesh. Forbidden to look. And to touch, heaven forfend! It is true that in Iglau Rabbi Goldiamond had made an exception for married men, who during urination were permitted to hold the organs from below. Piffle! We are now only five years from the twenty-first century. My Philco-brand radio is a non-starter, but I have heard on the audible portion of the Admiral that Jupiter is about to reveal the secret of her moons. At the public Schule the young boys and girls are taught through practical demonstrations how to engage in harmless fornication. Away with the cobwebs of the past! So: an exhalation. So: flexion of the musculature. *Voilà!*

Here is a disappointment. The sac of the scrotum has in my golden years tended to surrender to gravitational forces, so that my spheres hang at this moment no more than an inch above the frozen surface of the johnny. The masculine member, however, is nowhere in view. It is almost as if there were at work here the principle of the fulcrum: the weight of the stones descend, the organ of generation retracts. Also, cool breezes, like those that now blow through the cabinetto, cause fickleness in this part—just as, at the icy blast, the hedgehog and woodchuck, the bear and the beetle, will return to their hollows and dens. But my putz, pardon this folkish expression, has been in hibernation an entire year! Wake up, Mr. Winkle! Alas, the little birdy has—a constant shock, the whiteness of the nether hair, as if, protected from the elements, it should have retained its sable luster, along with its youthful abundance—fled the nest. To work! To work, friends! We must now, in the pages of this carnal cornucopia, seek out my inamorata.

Yes, from Dachau a deathly silence, until one night—I am speaking of the end of the month of April in the year 1938—a rock flew through the window of what had been the Goldkorn Vienna estate, Rennweg 30, smashing the panes to smithereens. I sat up—not in bed, since all our dear Biedermeiers had been sold at bargain prices, but from my spot on the floor. All about me lay jagged fragments of glass, like knives surrounding the female target in the Roumanian Circus. In moonlight they glistened. Yet one piece among the shrapnel glittered more brightly than all the rest. Across the sharp shards I picked my way with caution, until I came to what appeared to be a silver schilling: no, this was larger than any coin, thicker, and with more heft. What were the words printed upon it?

GARMISCH-PARTENKIRCHEN

IVTH OLYMPIAD

DIE WINTERSPIELE

MDCDXXXVI

SILBERMEDAILLE

Yakhne! It was Yakhne! Her *olympische* medal! Instantly I dashed across the glass bits as heedless as a Hindoo upon his bed of nails. I leaned from the window. On the street all was quiet, all was still. Only then did I note the half-open scrap of paper that must have been wrapped around the silver disk. I seized it. Those same beams of moonlight were more than sufficient to make out the familiar hand:

> *Leib, Mein Liebchen:*
> *All hope for us must be abandoned. Here we have noth-*

ing but torture. Mama is no more. Soon Papa will follow. Minkche is used for the pleasure of the men. We must beat each other. We must bury each other to make a joke. My first wish is to kill myself. My second wish is that you flee. I beg you, brother. Run! By the time this reaches you—brought by a guard whom Minkche has bewitched—the winner of the silver medallion will have reached her goal.

Run? I ran. Across the still-frozen Bodensee and, after many adventures, to Paris. Gay Paree!

P AGE ONE. P AGE two. Page three. Here are visions indeed. I will not, of this harem, in detail describe the inhabitants. This is not from shyness. During my student years Professor Pergam sought, in our illustrated texts, to cover with small silver stars the enthusiasm of the satyrs, half men, half goats. The rascal Pepi Pechler peeled these paper undies away. Crystal? Where is my Crystal? Not among these sporting ladies, who are from their posture apparently followers of Sappho. Let us turn a new page. And yet another. As I wander, like Orpheus, through the underground of this colorful journal, the sight of these contortionists and hermaphrodites and gymnasts with double joints reminds me of nothing so much as the poor creatures—two-headed men, ladies with whiskers, or the pitiable fellow with the hands and feet of a seal—of the Roumanian Circus. *Eurydice! Eurydice!* Oh, my Crystal! Speak! Answer me! Can you be here?

If only I had in my hand my Rudall & Rose. The Glickman boys, Ernie and Randy, are good-hearted chaps. Perhaps they would have lent me the instrument for my jubilee. Then might I accompany myself, as did Orpheus on his lyre, during this journey through Hades. Look! Do not look! Males and females amok. Ah, if I cannot have my flute then I wish I could be accompanied by my most loyal of readers. No need to fear maidenly shyness. Surely Madam Kakutani has from childhood peered through the steam bath vapors to see the beet-red Finns strike their unclothed bodies with branches and twigs. Here, Miss Michiko, take my hand.

Eurydice! Eurydice! Squinting, squatting, we hurry past activities that I have not experienced even in the pages of R. von Krafft-Ebing. *Eurydice!* Answer your Orpheus! Now I see why the first of musicians was forbidden by Pluto to look at his underground kingdom. Goloshes, M.D., has given me a similar warning. For reasons of hygiene it is necessary to empty annually the prostate of its contents. However, these glandular hydraulics present a certain risk. Stimulation of the organ that is not followed by a purge might aggravate the very condition it was meant to heal—just as, by voyeurism, the act of looking, Orpheus lost his paramour forever. Soon, for number 1, I will have to rise from my bed six, ten, fifteen times times in a night! Now we understand why the rabbis have ruled that when making water a Jew must look always upward, in the direction of heaven; and that Jewesses, so as not to draw our lively glances, must avoid cosmetics and Chanel and furthermore shave their heads until they are hairless.

Do the popes and vicars require that female Christians shave similarly the zone of reproduction? Is this a covenant, like the loss of foreskin I underwent as a child? The majority of the ladies before me seem to have undergone such a ritual. This does not produce in my body the effect of peppercorns. *Au contraire,* instead of spiciness and warmth I feel a chill foreboding: only four pages remain. No Venus, no Eurydice—in short, no Crystal. Only the portraits of concubines: Cherry Tarte, June Bugger, Diva Evian. Also Amber Waiff. Turn the page. Here are more comely Misses: Syd Chemisse, Lucy de Quiff, Blossom Wydde. One with an *Afrikaner,* one with a horse. Such unseemliness! The penultimate page. Here are the Fone Fancies: Miss Anatola Boudoir, Miss Bitch Adder, Miss Trixie Cox. Only a single page left. Alas! Nothing but the announcement of a new vacuum tube—not the kind now defunct in my Philco, but one that guarantees virility in the organ of procreation, with augmentation in height and width or your money back. *Accept no substitutes!* Exclamation. The end. Happy birthday, Leib Goldkorn! Ha! Ha! Ha! Five dollars and ninety-nine cents! No Crystal. No teenage temptress. Outrage! Swindle! The despair!

Sans Espoir. I removed my laceless shoes. Also stockings. Into the syrupy Seine went my toes, my ankles, my fleshless calves. Dark, dark the water, broken only by the reflection, like glowing butterscotch balls, of the lights on the Pont Alexandre. About my torso I felt the pages of my opera, like the grip of a life preserver. *Esther: A Jewish Girl at the Persian Court*. It would be sung by a chorus of minnows! Thus I stood, one hand raised, the other clutching my nostrils. Farewell, Paris! *La vie!* Farewell!

WAIT. WAIT. HOLD on to horses. Either I am in error or that was in my manly parts a feeling of epicureanism. There! Again! Is the sleepy hedgehog about to peek from his hedgehog hole? What is the cause of such lustiness? Let me, like poor Orpheus, look backward to Madam Boudoir, Madam Adder, and the other Fone Fancies. Ah, ha! Who is this woman at the lower left? Could it be? But where is the waif of yesteryear? That nubile nymph? The faun of forty. Where have flown the *Makronen*, those delicate cherries of spring? Now, on the bust zone, are bolsters in the Biedermeier style. Is this, too, the result of a vacuum appliance? Painted eyes, painted lips, and on the cheeks a painted blush. Paint on the nails of the right-hand toes. Where is the artlessness? The schoolgirl's virginal charm? It is true that from year to year, one holiday issue to another, I could not help but note that my little spindleshanks was putting on avoirdupois. But this representative of the weaker sex is, not to mince meat, quite strapping. Clever birdy! It had recognized her with its one eye before Leib Goldkorn had with his two. This is she! One thing that could not be disguised, or altered by time, is my lady's eyes—or eye, since one of them, rimmed in black and with mascara on the lashes, is screwed up in the act of nictitation. A wink for Mr. Winkle. But the other, a watery blue, stares unchanged into my soul. My Venus! My Valentine! Look: in her hands, a cat-o'-nine. Around her hips, a system of straps, prettily strewn with metal studs, of the sort favored by motorcyclists' associations. Also chains of steel, of iron. Let us be thankful that her single boot has not changed. It is as red as her glossy lips. Red as the Titian tones of her hair. And the heel is as sharp as a knife blade. As is the custom, we are allowed to read her hidden thoughts: *You'll Be My Prisoner*. 1-800-525-POON. Now I grasp the meaning of the wanton wink. The lip curled in a beckoning smile. In response my machinery of fruitfulness begins an extension. Above my darling, the following legend: *EXPECT NO MERCY FROM CRYSTAL KNIGHT!* Capitals. Exclamation.

"Figaro! Figaro! *Demandez Le Figaro!*" What was that cry? A newsboy! A French newsboy! *"Pluie de verre dans les rues de Berlin! Une mer de cristal! Dernières nouvelles! Les Allemands en guerre contre leurs Juifs! La vérité vraie! La grande synagogue de Berlin en flammes!"* What was he saying? Ah: in the capital of the German Reich it was now raining glass.

This was the night, the dread ninth, the November navity, that all the world still recalls. One hundred Jews murdered. Thousands sent off to the camps. Two hundred synagogues burned to the ground. How many businesses destroyed? Seventy-five hundred. The broken glass! Equivalent to half the output from Belgium for an entire year. Believe it, says Ripley, or not. The cost: five million marks. And who would bear this expense? The insurance companies of the Reich? The brown-shirted perpetrators? Do not force me to laugh. The answer is—and here we see, in the master race, diabolical cleverness—the victims themselves! For creating a public disturbance. Special tax: one billion marks. The Jews would pay for their own pogrom! *Kristallnacht!*

Of all the inhabitants of Paris only one at that moment was filled with joy. It was Leib Goldkorn. At once I pulled my wrinkled feet from the river's watery embrace. I danced on the embankment, to the accompaniment of my penny panpipe, a Scottish-style jig. Why such callousness of feeling? It was because I realized that at long last the world would be forced to listen. All these Frenchmen, and Frenchwomen too, with their berets and baguettes, and on their lips cynical cigarettes: they all would have to admit that this wretch, in rags, possessed the truth. My *Esther* would make the pariah a prophet. *Aux armes citoyens!* Or, in the words of "A Loud and Bitter Cry," the solo of Mordecai from Act One:

> I throw off my sackcloth!
> I wipe off my ashes!
> I must speak in spite of ten thousand lashes!

Then, as the Hebrews press closer, so as to hear:

In each man's life there comes a moment to choose.
For him in the heavens there shines but one star.
—On the thirteenth day of the month of Adar,
—Haman will cause to perish all of the Jews.

Strings; trumpets; celesta; the beat of the drum.

For one giddy moment I forgot that I had not, in my pockets, even the point of a pencil with which to finish my musical score. What did it matter? Was I not, like Mordecai himself, a stranger in a strange land? Would not my rags, like his sackcloth, be replaced with royal apparel of blue and white, and with, as it is written, *a garment of fine linen and purple?* A triumph at *L'Opéra! Esther,* my masterpiece, *A Jewish Girl at the Persian Court,* might yet change history's course. Surely the subtle French, so wise in the ways of the world, would understand the association of Haman with Hitler. Both begin with the letter *H. Formez vos bataillons!*

I put on my stockings. I put on my shoes. I climbed to the upper embankment and made my way down the Quai des Tuileries and the Quai du Louvre. The United States embassy was then on the Boulevard Bourbon, in the shadow of the Bastille. By the time I arrived the sun had risen high enough to cast, over the expanse of the boulevard, the swath of open lawn, and the steps of the building itself, a dark shadow. I blinked. I looked again. Not a shadow: a crowd, in black coats and black trousers, with black hats on their heads. Jews! Hundreds of Jews! Enough for three Philharmonics. Or for my chorus, the multitude of the City of Shushan:

Woe to our menfolk, our women, the old and the young.
The trials of the Jews have only begun.
For Haman has persuaded the good king Ahasuerus
To smite us, confound us, kill us, and harry us.

These might have been the words of the refugees, who now besieged the six-story embassy. In some magical fashion—perhaps, like ants, passing an invisible substance from member to member—the news from the Third Reich had reached them even before the newsboy's shouts had rung in my ears. They were lined up around the block's four corners and part way down the Rue St. Antoine. I took my place at the end. The time went slowly by. An hour. Another hour. We seemed, my co-religionists and I, to move forward invisibly, like the minute hand of a clock.

What these Jews wanted from the embassy was a visa. So did I. But what was required was a relative in America. In New York City alone there were millions and millions of people. More Jews than in Warsaw, more than in Kiev. Alas, not one Goldkorn, a cousin or half-cousin, among them. Never mind relations! Never mind New York! In all of the forty-eight states, was there not a single person willing to guarantee a woodwind player, also skilled at the percussion group, piano, triangle, glockenspiel, employment? *Gott! Gott!* Surely there must be kindly souls who would assist the multitude who were heeding the warning of the Jewish Queen:

> *Flee on horseback, on mules, by dogsled, by camel*
> *The sword of cruel Haman will strike each living mammal.*

I looked up. On the Place de la Bastille the shadow from the Colonne de Juillet no longer stretched westward, over the Rue de Tournelle and the Place des Vosges; indeed, the dark finger pointed now to the east, toward the Porte de Vincennes. In other words, according to the needle of that great sundial, the whole of this day had gone by; it was now almost, *post meridiem*, five o'clock. A different newsboy passed by, with issues of *Paris-Soir*. The crowd passed the papers from hand to hand, groaning as they learned of the noose that was tightening about their necks. Now they broke ranks. They pushed forward, toward the embassy steps. There they milled, shouting and waving their arms. It was almost as if, taking courage from their surroundings, the masses were once again about to storm the Bastille.

The embassy staff appeared in the open and attempted to reason with the mob. The desperate refugees were weeping. Their wails and curses rent the air. Clearly they had no relations in America, nor prospects of employment. Finally, one of the undersecretaries shouted over the tumult: "Business hours are

over. We must close. We have only these left. Here—take them!"
With that the diplomatist hurled a dozen slips of paper into the
air. Oh, terrible lottery! The exiles hurled themselves forward,
struggling each against each, their hands clutching at the precious documents.

"Pardon," I said, addressing one of my co-religionists. "Are
these the visas? Or steamship tickets? To America?"

"Quoi? America?" returned my companion, thrusting his copy
of Paris-Soir into my hand. "Crétin! Imbécile!"

I glanced down at the journal. There, in a boxed announcement, I saw the following:

GALA AMÉRICAIN-FRANÇAIS
LA PREMIÈRE EN NOTRE LANGUE
Monsieur le Premier de France, Édouard Daladier
et
Son Excellence S. Umin, Ambassadeur des États-Unis
Avec la participation de Monsieur Jack Warner, producteur
exécutif du
STUDIO FRÈRES WARNER
Aussi en attendance
Messieurs:
Paul Muni, Erich Wolfgang Korngold, William Dieterle
Et la très belle Anita Louise comme "Annette"
en plus
les musiciens et LA CHORAL DES JEUNES FILLES DU MOULIN
ROUGE!
Venez!
Faîtes Tribute au plus grande héro de France
et à l'Amitié franco-américain
Ce Soir!
le dixième Novembre!
A huit heures!
Au Théâtre Égyptien!

I had, it seemed, been mistaken. These were not exiles. They
were not even Jews. Here were theatergoers, mummers, and lovers
of film. Also a claque for Anita Louise. In their disappointment they

surged up the steps. The diplomatists had retreated behind their closed doors. Undaunted, the crowd beat upon the heavy panels. And I? I was among them. The ambassador himself would be at the gala. And the premier of France. The renowned Jacques Warner, as well. Who better, with a single stroke of the pen, to secure me a visa? Who better, with the aid of his magic lantern, to send my message to the world? With my fists I beat upon the wooden portals. All about me the cinéastes were pounding as well. We would be heard. We would not be denied. Nothing could stop us from attending the premiere of *The Story of Louis Pasteur*.

K*NOCK! KNOCK-KNOCK-KNOCK!* The blows fall upon the fragile door. In the eyelet the hook shudders and jumps. Who could the invader be? Boxer dog? Gentleman from Consolidated Edison?

"Who the fuck is in there? It's been over an hour. Goldkorn! Goldkorn! I know it's you. You're five months behind on the rent! Five months!"

Fingerhut, *fils*!

I sit, like a forest beast, a yearling, caught in the grip of a bear. The hammering persists, as powerful as stones of hail or balls from a cannon. Surely this thin beaver's dam, the door of the cabinetto, will give way in the torrent. No: with abruptness, the thunder ceases. There is only the rumble of Junior's footsteps, fading away.

I remain atremble upon the johnny. In my ears the heart fibrillations echo almost as loudly as the landlord's fists. On my knees, I note, the holiday *Hustler* remains open at the Fone Fancies. Here is Madam Knight. My Crystal. With red lips and apparatus of straps. Unfortunately, there has been a disruption in the mood of romance. Manual assistance, therefore, will be required. Easier to say than to do. It is necessary to lean forward, in order to anchor the rotogravure between left elbow and left knee. Next, an exhalation, to facilitate the withdrawal of solar plexus. Right-hand fingers must now blindly grope in the nether parts. *Gott!* This is a task for the rubber man of the Roumanian Circus.

Is Fingerhut truly departed? He believes I killed his father in a jealous rage. But with my own eyes I saw that F.F. *père* had expired from unnatural exertions. Let us hope my own contortions will not bring on a similar spasm. Crystal. From between her lips the protruding tongue tip. On her foot, the red-colored boot. Leib Goldkorn does not ask for mercy. Let this sweetheart walk, with her pointed heel, her pointed toe, upon his back. Back and forth, like a conquering army. *Mach schnell!* The quickstep. Like a Cossack. Oh, that stiletto! We now begin, not unlike the idiot of Iglau, a friction-polka.

Black stockings. Thigh flesh. White petticoats held up for view. In short, the saucy can-can. This, too, is a kind of polka, under the influence of the gavotte and the military trot. From my position in the orchestra pit I counted fifty ballerinas. Times two equaled one hundred feet. One hundred heels. *Five hundred toes!* Half of these limbs were hop-hopping on the lip of the stage. The calves of the others were oscillating, like so many admonishing fingers—naughty, naughty Nanette!—in the air. The froth of undergarments! The pungent perfume! *Gott im Himmel!* The way they kicked! And held their anklebones up to the sky! This was athleticism. This was art.

Tra-tra-la-la; la-la-la-la-la-la-la!
Da-da-dee-da; da-da-da-da-dee-da-da!

Even as I rendered, upon my penny whistle, the gay themes of the Israelite, Offenbach, I looked up toward the box of honor. There, behind the tricolor bunting, the dignitaries were straining forward for a garter glimpse. The premier of France had a chin twitch. Decadent Daladier! And Monsieur l'Ambassadeur? Mr. Umin? He licked his lips. The others, Jacques Warner, producer; E. W. Korngold, musical score; Dieterle, director: all of them seemed—and I include here Monsieur Paul Muni, leading actor—drenched in perspiration, as if it were they, and not the fifty *filles*, who were performing the exuberant dance.

How, this is what the world is asking, did L. Goldkorn procure in this pit a woodwind position? Yakhne! My strapping sibling! With her boy's Adam's apple and, in her teeth, a Trabucco D.D., a *Doppeldezimeter*. Her wire glasses. Sailing suit. Bosomless breast. Even now, almost sixty years later, if I were to employ the hand that is engaged in a chafing to touch instead the spot on my breast where her *Silbermedaille* once hung, I would experience a feeling of sadness and shame. Confession: I traded this Olympic treasure to the gatekeeper, who plucked me from amidst the stage door Johnnies and ushered me backstage. Forgive! Oh, forgive, beloved sister! A *Doppeldezimeter*, by the way, is a cigar of eight American inches.

Immediately I encountered a colony of naturists. These were, in a state of undress, the Moulin Rougettes. "*Pardon*," I declared. "I am not a Nose Parker. See? Here is my panpipe." At once I was taken through an escape trap and down a short flight of steps. This was the pit, where my colleagues were already engaged in sounding an A. With my back to the stage I ran through the scales. Then the conductor, a thin man, elegantly dressed, switched on the electrical bulb at the end of his baton.

Dee-da-dee-da-doodle-dee
Da-da-dee-da-tree-tree-tree
  Tootle-oo, o, tootle-oo
  Tum-tum, tum-tum, doodle-do

The moments sped quickly by. Why did I remain playing these dance hall tunes? Had I not come to bring my warning to the world? Could I not leap from this pit onto the stage? And with my basso sing forth Mordecai's message? But I sat as if in a hypnotic trance. Oh, the tramp-tramp-tramp of the terpsichordians! The thud of their heels! The heat waves of their thighs! Swish, in my ears, went the sound of their silks. The fine spray of their zest fell over my head, my shoulders. In truth, I could no more interrupt such a performance than I could, with the flat of my hand, stop the flow of the Seine. Suddenly, on its own, the music ceased, the dervishes departed and *Monsieur le conducteur* extinguished his beaming baton. Now, amidst the thundering ovation, was my chance. I clutched my panpipe. I girded my loins. And then, just as I was about to hurl myself upward, the lights went out and *The Story of Louis Pasteur* began to play upon the screen.

An excellent drama, in which, though the actors moved their lips to speak words in English, their voices came out in French. At the start, Louis—he had a black hat, pince-nez type spectacles, and a black beard, through which, in the manner of a rabbi, a plump lower lip protruded—was under attack for suggesting that diseases like childbed fever could be caused by little animals—in the vernacular, *les petits animaux*. His chief enemy, one Charbonnet, asks the Royal Empress, "Is it not preposterous to think that a human being can be destroyed by an animal no bigger than a flea?" Excellent dialogue. And excellent logic, to which even the audience in the Théâtre Égyptien sagely nodded. Thus was the great Pasteur and his entire family, including his daughter, played by Anita Louise with genuine mammilation, banished from Paris.

While this action took place on the screen, Leib Goldkorn had not been sitting, as the saying goes, atop his hands. Quietly, in the darkness of the pit, I unbuttoned my peacoat and blouse. While the projectionist's beam played above my head, like a ray of light from a divinity's eye, I removed from my torso the sheets of my operetta and began to distribute them among the strings, the woodwinds, the brass.

Meanwhile, a crisis has befallen France. The livestock of the nation have been dying in astounding numbers. Dread anthrax! But in his exile Pasteur, with the help of the cream-shouldered Anita Louise, has developed a vaccine. Once more the doctors and Academicians heap scorn upon him. They propose a test. Fifty sheep will be injected with the pestilence, but only half will be given the vaccine. The disdainful Charbonnet, whose name sounds so much like an aperitif, hurls down the challenge: "I dare him to try."

From Pasteur: "*J'accepte!*"

A tense forty-eight hours. The French nation trembles. Headlines of newspapers spin before our eyes. Scientists in every nation await the results. During the anxious night before the fateful dawn, we see Monsieur Muni atoss in his bed. From her own distant bolster, Madam Pasteur comforts her husband: "Try not to worry, Louis." Up comes the sun. First the Academicians drive to the pen of the unvaccinated sheep. Of course the unhappy creatures are stiff and unmoving. *Moutons Morts!* Now the carriage moves off to the treated animals. *Hélas!* These sheep, too, are stiff. They, too, are unmoving. Even Pasteur is nonplused. Then a sheepdog barks, and the lambs and lambkins jump to their feet. *Baa! Baa! Baa!* Only sleeping, the darlings! How bright their eyes! How frisky their gambols! Now they, and the citizens of France, and of the whole world, too, are awake!

Did I now, while everyone was caught up in this moment of celebration, spring at last into action? *Pas du tout.* Leib Goldkorn, like the thousands who sat about him, wanted only one thing: to know what would happen next.

Free at last, Pasteur returns to Paris, where he sets to work upon a treatment for the scourge of rabies. The injections work well upon poodles, but now the scientist is confronted by a cute-as-a-button boy. Dare he dare test the vaccine upon this infected child? If he does nothing the lad, bravely asmile, will surely die. "But if I fail," thus muses Muni, "it will mean prison—perhaps the guillotine!"

"You must do it! *Das is ihr Menschen-Servize!*" That cry came from the orchestra pit. From the throat of the panpipe player.

The result was a triumph for reason and for Louis Pasteur. He risked everything and found the cure for rabies. Not only that, but, by overcoming the hostility of the medical establishment, as well as the effects of a numbing stroke, he brought healthfulness to the entire world. Could I, with such an uplifting example before me, dither longer? Was it not my duty, my *Menschen-Servize*, to destroy the German microbes who were at that very moment infecting the continent of Europe? In three strides I moved to the front of the pit and, with a lightning stroke, plucked the baton from the hand of *Monsieur le conducteur.* Then, with a running start, I hopped, skipped, and executed a gambado onto the stage. Silence. Stillness. Only, directly above me, the elongated forms of the Academicians as, with accolades and laurels, they welcome Grandpapa Pasteur, his beard now streaked with gray, into their midst. Close view of Charbonnet, thirty feet tall. A changed man. A germ enthusiast. Close view: Anita Louise. Breasts the size of mattresses. A three-meter tear in her eye.

"Pssst, fellows!" Leib Goldkorn addressed his fellow musicians. "On your stands. *The Wrath of Haman.* Let us play it. Measure one-thirty-two."

No one moved. Not a note sounded. Now the premier of the nation greets the half-paralyzed Pasteur, "In the name of France and of all humanity." While the academy applauded, I flicked the switch on the baton.

"Ready, chaps? An *eins. A zwei. Und a drei!*"

Whether it was because the glowing bulb at the end of the stick had entranced them, or simply from force of habit, the Moulin Rouge band struck up the melody, *con agitazione e abbandono*. What a thrill for an artiste! To hear, for the first time, the sharps and flats, the whole and the half notes, the do-re-mi and la-ti-do that had, until that moment, existed only in his head.

At once the auditorium was filled with cries of amazement. The lotus-shaped lights in the house came on. The projectionist's beam fell full upon the perfidious Persian. With one foot forward and arms outspread, Leib sang the spine-chilling *Lied*:

Fall on your knees and pray, Amen! Amen!
You see before you the all-powerful Haman.
I won't be sated with the people of Israel.
My crimes shall not cease until all men are mis'rable.
Greeks, Turks, the French and the Dutch—
Even then I shan't have done much.
Arabs and Esquimaux, whomever I choose—
The whole world—Oh, hear me!—will be turned into Jews.

What happened next was almost a miracle. For week after week, with patois and panpipe, I had not been able to earn so much as a single centime. Now, so powerful was the message of *Esther*, the French people responded with all their hearts. Coins of many dimensions, five-franc pieces, ten-franc pieces, rained down upon me. A guinea flew straight at my head. A silver dollar—from the munificent Muni? From Director Dieterle?—struck me upon the collarbone. Pennies from heaven! Not only that, root vegetables plummeted from the balcony boxes. Also tomatoes. Also boiled eggs.

"No, no, dear friends. I am not singing, as they say, for supper. Ouch! Ha! Ha! Ha! I wish to warn you. The Germans! It is the Germans! They have killed Minkche! An intimate of Franz Joseph. Known for her beauty spot. And all the musicians of Vienna. Also the Jews! Heed my words! The words of Haman! Next they will be coming for you!"

A howl went up through the Théâtre Égyptien. "*Arrêtez cet homme! C'est un fou!*"

Mr. Jacques Warner stood up in his box. "What the hell is going on here?"

Ambassador Umin rose as well. "Gendarmes!" he shouted. "Remove this idiot!"

Now all was pandemonium. The orchestra broke out in the Offenbach reprise. From both wings the Rougettes strode shoulder to shoulder across the whole of the stage. Meanwhile, in the Academy of Science, the Tsar of Russia was putting a Medal of Honor around the neck of Louis Pasteur. Immediately I reached toward the newly created void at my breast. "You! Daladier!" I cried out in anguish. "You should give me a medal. I shall save France!"

The premier heard my words. "*Quoi?*" he responded. "*Mais c'est insupportable! Ce fou se prend pour Jeanne d'Arc!*"

Then the police fell upon me. With a grip of iron they seized my arms. The dancers, with high-pitched shrieks, broke ranks. I could see, that's how close to them I was, the marks of lipstick on their incisors and the mascara that crumbled beneath their eyes. "Bravo! Bravo!" cry the Academicians as Pasteur, with the light dimming about him, makes a last oration about the nobility of man.

FIN

Just then, as the lawmen hoisted me into the air, there was another interruption. A disturbance at the back of the auditorium. Everyone turned in that direction. A little old man in a blue uniform was making his way down the aisle. He also had a blue cap with a red ribbon, and thick spectacles in plastic frames. "*Télégramme!*" he shouted. "*Télégramme!*" It was a Western Union boy. A silence fell over the multitude. The old gentleman, he had chin whiskers sprouting from his chin, stared myopically at the document in his hand: "*Un télégramme pour Monsieur Goldkorn!*"

"Present!" I declared, from my state of levitation.

Down the red carpet the messenger tottered, all eyes upon him. At the edge of the pit he halted.

"*Monsieur Goldkorn?*" he piped.

"*Oui.* Me."

Then the old man handed the canary-colored missive to the conductor, who handed it to the tuba player, who in turn passed it up to one of the chorines. She, not a full breaster, and with a long nose as well, started to open the telegram with the sharpened nail of her thumb. But the nearest gendarme took it from her and opened it himself. He gave a Gallic-style shrug. "*En anglais,*" he said.

I seized the pale paper and read out the words upon it for myself:

DEAR MAESTRO
ESSENTIAL YOUR PRESENCE NEW SONJA HENIE VEHICLE STOP CURRENT
SCORE UNACCEPTABLE STOP STAR INSISTS NO ONE BUT YOU STOP ALL
MUSICAL DECISIONS YOUR HANDS STOP WARNERS AGREES TO LOAN
OUT STOP MONEY NO OBJECT STOP TICKET PARIS-LISBON-LISBON-
NEW YORK-NEW YORK-LOS ANGELES ENCLOSED STOP MALIBU RESI-
DENCE FOR DURATION STOP ALL CONVENIENCES STOP EXPECT
ARRIVAL UNION STATION 11/23/38 STOP NEED COMPLETE SCORE
END YEAR STOP NO LATER STOP

YOURS FAITHFULLY
DARRYL ZANUCK
HEAD OF PRODUCTION
TWENTIETH CENTURY-FOX

The famed Zanuck! The famed Malibu! And—the ice dancer! The Olympian!—Miss Sonja Henie! My own first love. Could this be true? The words were attached to the paper with paste. I shook it to see if they would fall off. No. The message was real.

"Mr. Ambassador!" I cried. "A visa, if you please. I have employment! Yes, employment guaranteed!"

Then, still floating above the stage, like a fakir, a phantom, I folded the paper and pressed it to my chest. It burned there, as ice will burn. Here was, to replace the old one, a new silver medal. A gift from the tsar? No, the star!

2

"WAKE UP! WAKE up! You sleepy head!" Such are the words of the folkish tune. And what little robin, at the sight of such leathers, of a boot with a stiletto-type heel, would not come bob-bob-bobbin' along? These breasts! Like loaves of Wonder-brand bread. Who does not know the wrapper in its gay polka pattern? My own polka has achieved an amplification of one American inch. Two point five four centimeters, or twenty-five and four-tenths millimeters: far from a Trabucco *Doppeldezimeter*, perhaps, but enough to grasp firmly by forefinger and thumb. To work, Leib Goldkorn!

I'm just a kid again
Doing what I did again—

In medieval times, which of course have not entirely ended, self-stimulation was thought to be the work of the devil, leading to pustules, softening of the brain, and growth of hair upon the palms. Such tales did not inhibit the lads at the Akademie für Musik, Philosophie, und darstellende Kunst. We passed from hairless hand to hairless hand whole chapters of R. von Krafft-Ebing, in particular the account of the woman who suckled her own nipples, as well as case 123, a man, initial B, a melancholia victim, who felt such warm sensations when smelling roses that he experienced a pollution. Case number 230 was also a best-seller: here W, a shoemaker's apprentice, upon being caught in a passionate embrace with a waterfowl, responded, *So? Was ist los mit der Gans?* For years thereafter we woodwinders, upon being reprimanded by Professor Lajpunger for a missed musical note, would reply: "So? What's wrong with the goose?"

Ah-choo! Ach, from trouserlessness I am at risk of a catarrh. Why is there, from this steam pipe, no hint of warmth? Fingerhut, *fils*, counts his pennies. Then berates his loyal tenants for rent arrears! I have perhaps made a mistake in leaving the state of California. In such a subtropical zone, one can take sunbaths even in the month of November. Indeed, it was in that month, more than a half century ago, that I arrived in the Golden State. Ah, the sunlight! The palm leaves sighing. The exclamation of the passing gull. Listen: do you hear the thump and thud of the wave break? And then the soft sizzle as, like the white of a frying egg, the ocean's remnant creeps up to the toes of Leib Goldkorn as he lies upon the Malibu Beach?

1938. The Super Chief. The Union Station. I was met by a limousine and driver provided by Twentieth Century-Fox. In the back seat of this vehicle was a cooler filled with ice and a bottle of French champagne. A basket overflowed with native fruits and nuts. On top was a box, wrapped with silver ribbon and a silver bow. Inside I discovered a Bulova watch. *In Time with Your Music*— thus the inscription, signed with a *D* and an *F* and a *Z*. The mighty Zanuck! And more: a box of cigars, of Cuban manufacture. "Ha! Ha!" I laughed, tap-tapping on the partition glass to draw the attention of the liveryman. "I am from Iglau, home of the Imperial and Royal Tobacco Monopoly. These"—and here I pointed to the Romeo y Julietas—"are like new coals in the castle!"

The chauffeur continued chauffeuring. Outside the curtained windows, the scene that sped by might have come from the pages of Sir R. Burton's *Arabian Nights*. There were date palms and palms for coconuts, and an oasis—we were at that moment crossing the intersection of the Boulevard Santa Monica and the Boulevard Wilshire—of gaily splashing fountains. The vault of the sky, filled up with sunshine, had been turned into a golden bowl, like the dome on a Musselman mosque. This glowing light! This buttery air! Was I, who only a fortnight before had been a penniless refugee, awake? Or was I still shivering on the banks of the Seine, with thoughts of hurling myself into its dark, swift current.

Just then I saw, in the basket's corner, beneath a pile of greenish grapes, the edge of an envelope. I plucked it forth and ran a thumb under the flap. Inside was a photograph—how my heart leaped when I saw it: the curled hair, like a pile of pirate's doubloons; the thin upper lip and the knob of a chin; and, in the cheek flaps, the dear darling dimples. Also her neckline in a plunge. Madam Henie! My own true love! Handwritten upon her body, with large swooping ink lines, resembling school figures on a sheet of ice, was the following inscription:

> Dear Maestro: I have such gratitude you are coming so far
> to work on Everything Happens at Night. Your music will give
> to my feet wings. Yours always, Sonja.

"Driver! Driver!" I cried, while rapping once more upon the glass. "Madam Henie. The Ice Princess. Where is she?"

The shoulders of the chauffeur rose in a shrug. "Maybe," he responded, through the speaking tube, "Malibu."

W HAT AN ELONGATION! I can see now, rosy from its rub down, the tip top of the glans. *So, was ist los mit der Gans?* This motto we younglings shouted to the astonished Professor Pergam when he provided the lesson on Leda, daughter of Thespius, who experienced conjugals with a swan. Such a myth was no more shocking than case 51 in our well-worn Krafft-Ebing: a technologist whose mistress locked him in the WC and who later underwent lustful emotions, with paroxysm, upon the gymnastic rope. We could not help but note with sorrow that this gentleman was thereafter forced to fight the urge to swallow young ladies' urine. Other favorites? Number 17, the famed Jack the Ripper. Number 5, the stutterer. Number 2, the octogenarian and the gardener boy. Also of interest: the cases of the cobbler whose activities brought on a chancre, the governess and the spaniel, and the gentleman who claimed that he violated his sister at Bonaparte's request.

Hurry, Leib Goldkorn. Seize now the moment! Onward, Winnie Winkle!

Singing a song!

The limousine arrived at the villa early in the afternoon. The driver carried my gladstone-type bag into the foyer; then, without acknowledgment of the buffalo nickel I dropped in his palm, he departed. For a moment I stood, mouth agape, like the well-known idiot of Iglau. Everything about me was adazzle. There was glass in the ceiling, glass in the walls, and even glass bricks scattered here and there in the hardwood floors. On all sides, below, above, the blue Pacific, the equal blue of the sky. In the midst of this splendor, like an enormous shined shoe, stood a black Bechstein grand. This was, in the vernacular, a sore-eyed sight. Hardly able to control my excitement, I approached the keyboard and took my place on the stool. Out thundered the first bars of the overture to *Esther*. What a tremendous crescendo! As if an entire symphonic orchestra were playing the notes. Once again I felt myself in a dream state, overcome by the sensation that this noble instrument was not responding to my own ten fingers but to those of some invisible spirit, like one of those old-fashioned pianos that occupy the bistros in wild western films. I switched to the ending, the triumphant chorus in which the Hebrews celebrate their victory over both wicked Persians and the evil forces of the Third Reich:

Drink wine, eat sweets, and roast marshmallows
All Haman's sons will be hanged on the gallows.

What a melody! Worthy of Meyerbeer! This was the music that would save the world's Jews!

Suddenly the harmonies halted. The fallboard crashed down. The last chord—those Oriental half-notes, d-sharp, f-flat, b-flat, c-sharp—hung in the air. There was a woman in the room. Was she a mere trick of the light? A being manufactured from the baubles and bangles, the sapphire facets, that danced on the walls? Or was this blond beauty composed of sheer sound? Had I conjured her out of my chords?

"Esther!" I ejaculated. "Queen of Ahasuerus! Is it you?"

The young woman shook her golden curls.

"Ah! Madam Henie! We meet again!"

The little miss pouted, causing her lower lip to swell outward, as if stung by an adoring bee. Through the skipping sunlight, the sunbeams that glanced from the surface of the sea, I saw that the phantom female wore the costume—velveteen vest, fishnet-style stockings, open-toe pumps—of a French maid. "You got the wrong person," at length she said.

"Not Madam Henie?" But I had already heard that in her voice there was no hint of Norwegian nuance. Not only that, I could plainly see that this lass, in spite of a superficial resemblance—honey hair, cuddly chin, a tutu as frilly as that of a skater's—was not the Olympian.

"Heck, no. I'm a good friend of Mr. Zanuck's. He asked me to spend a little time with you. You know. To make sure you're comfortable."

Two buttons of her doublet, I noted, had come undone. "That is thoughtful of the great one," I said.

"Yeah, you bet it is."

There was a brief pause, while the young lady looked about, seeking perhaps some surface on which she could begin her task of shooing away the motes of dust.

"Fig?" I inquired, with a hand gesture toward the basket that sat upon the floor.

"Afterward," she responded.

It was interesting to see how, upon each respiration, both bosoms surged upward from her loosened bodice, like two of the balls that at that very moment sportsmen were batting over the tautly strung nets of the Malibu Beach.

"Might I make an inquiry? You are not Esther. You are not Madam Henie. When, then, is your name?"

There was, for the nonce, no reply. Instead, the housemaid seized my hand, raised it upward, and then—was this a California custom? A form of greeting?—introduced the whole of my index finger, you know, the pointer, into the depths of her mouth. What followed? A one-minute massage.

"Candace," she uttered at last, displaying, on her tongue tip, a circular mint. "Candace Kane. But call me Candy."

AH! AHA! NOW I have the answer to the riddle posed by the artwork upon the cover of my *Hustler Review*. What is a *Pfefferminzstück*? The sweet that Christians at holidays hang upon trees? A cane of candy! Will I soon approach a culmination? Time to think now of bawdery from the past. On, on with the onanistics! Naughty, naughty Onanette!

Oftimes did young Hans Maltz—yes, the same Gauleiter who later sent the family Goldkorn to its doom—lead the innocent Akademie students in search of pleasure, for instance to the balcony of the k.k. Hof-Operntheater, from which spot we would drop our eyes to the breast points—those snowy plump mice with perky pink noses—of the ladies below. But I wish to recall now one such excursion that I have never been able to forget.

Month: August. Year: 1915. Time: dead of night. Led by the mastermind, Maltz, we woodwinders crept in an Indian row toward the garden of Rennwig 30. We were followed by the percussionists and even a player or two on the strings. Crouching low, the adolescent Academicians stole through the gate and hop-hopped over the limestones embedded in the lawn to the rear of—why be coy?—the Goldkorn family abode. Not a word was spoken. No leaf rustled; not a twig went snap. Like shadows the invaders lay about the base of the mighty linden and cast their eyes up to the rectangular window, all pearly and glowing, at the middle of the second floor. Was this a game of childhood, in which the Indianer, we pale Viennese redskins, wait in ambush for Old Shatterhand upon his horse? A minute went by. A moment more.

"Pssst," said Pepi Pechler, pointing upward. "There! There! Do you see?"

A gasp went up from the student musicians. Pepi himself puffed up his round red cheeks, as if blowing upon a French-style horn. For there, on the far side of the windowpane, shadows, shades, silhouettes had suddenly appeared; the round wet shapes seemed to stick to the frosted glass like thrown pats of butter.

"Ah! Ah!" This exclamation came from Willi Wimpfeling, viola novice. "This is prima! This is wunderbar!"

At that a series of sounds—pops from the armpits, clucks from the tongue, even a fulmination from the zone of the buttocks— broke out from the percussion section. The woodwinders merely whistled.

The next speaker had thick lips and ears that, even in youth, were outstanding. Also telltale glimpses of scalp that showed through his pomaded hair. "Ho, ho, fellows! Isn't this enough? Shouldn't we be going? Come. Come, *Kameraden*. My treat at Demel's!"

"No! Stop! We are not finished here." That was Hans Maltz, my rival for honors on the flute. He made no attempt to disguise the hairs on his lip which, though sparse on that occasion, would in time grow into a moustache in the style of Thomas E. Dewey and which, along with the gap in his teeth, were a sure sign of a libidinous nature. Up he stood, beneath that linden, and raised his instrument to his bristly lip. Out came a cuckoo's trill, a repeated double note in the minor key, so clear, so vibrant, so song-filled that—and here we give due to the devil—one would have thought this was the very bird that served as the model for L. van Beethoven in his Symphony number Six.

At once the frosty fogged window shot up with a crack, and a voice of the female gender cried out, "Hansi! Is it you?"

I threw my hands over my eyes; but nothing stopped up my ears. Thus I heard the repeated call:

"Hansi, *Liebchen. Wo bist du?*"

No reply came from mischievous Maltz. Instead he filled the nighttime air with the silvery notes of the cuckoo, bird of ill repute, well known for stealing its rival's eggs and substituting its own in their place.

"*Gott im Himmel!*" groaned Pepi Pechler. "I can't believe what I am seeing!"

How, with such urgings, could one resist a small peek? Through my interlaced fingers I saw—in truth I saw at first nothing: only coiled clouds of steam as they poured through the open window and flew off wisping into the dark of night. Then, emerging from these mists, came Minkche, my beauteous and bountiful younger sibling. How ruddy her skin was from the heated spurts of the douche bath. Her hair hung like tendrils to her cheeks, neck, and shoulders. Her bosom bulged like a pneumatic tire as she leaned upon the window's ledge. At that sight the percussionists made, with teeth, tongue, and cheek, a sound resembling that of castanets.

Coo-coo, coo-coo: once again the song of the faithless egg stealer hung over the garden. Coo-coo: call of the cuckold! "Hansi! Where are you hiding? Won't you speak to your little honeycake?"

Now Minkche, the minx, leaned so far forward that her appendages hurled themselves from the window, like two pale babes escaping a burning building. "Ah-h-h," went the students from the Akademie für Musik, Philosophie, und darstellende Kunst. Even the linden, in torment, sighed.

At long last the future degenerate deigned to speak. "*Minkche, meine-Hebräischer. Minkche, mein Honigkuchen.*" At those murmured words the mistress of Maltz raised one hand to a spot behind her head and placed the other at her hip zone. She was like the Venus of Milo, before the amputation of limbs.

Oh, the debasement! The shame! Do not mistake me: the disgrace does not belong to Fräulein Goldkorn, who had surely become overwarm. No, it is I who belong in what in this country is called the doghouse. Not because I allowed my classmates into this garden—ah, evil Eden!—for what I thought would be a pleasant shadow show behind non-transparent glass. And not because I did not at that instant spring up and seize the lothario by the throat. If only I had! The deceiver! Dissembler! Twenty-three years later it would be he who sent his *Honigkuchen* to her death at Dachau. No, no, no: my sin was that even then, after the public display, I remained. Not just remained. I looked! I spied! I gazed! Nor was this the end of the horror. I soon felt, under my tongue, a syrup secretion. Simultaneously the muscles of my loins began to expand like taffy, specialty of Atlantic City, while those in my nates suffered a contraction like India rubber. In short, for the first time in my life I experienced the sensation of peppercorns.

And with my very own sister! This was worse than a play by Schnitzler! Worse, even, than Oedipus, who, according to Professor Pergam, took out for his sinfulness the balls from his eyes. Mine remained open, as Minkche, standing upright now, like that other Venus, the one of the Temple of Samos who was violated—this is yet one more case from the pages of Herr Doktor Krafft-Ebing—by a man, C, who placed a meat filet on a certain part. C? C? It is I, G! G!, who should be written about in text-books of pathology! It is I, the Tom Peeper, who should be shot!

CHILDHOOD! BOYHOOD! YOUTH! If only, once lost, innocence could be regained. What would I not give to be the lad who gaily skipped along the banks of the Iglawa, who lay amidst meadow flowers as the clouds above formed and re-formed the busts—Mendelssohn, Halévy, Meyerbeer—of great men. If it had not been for that serpent, Maltz, with his gift of forbidden knowledge, I might now be enjoying my annual purgation. Alas! At such memories there has been, in the zone of propagation, a definite retraction. Not even the thought of Miss Michiko, my hellion from Helsinki, can restore the mood of coquettishness. Nor can Miss Crystal, with her whip, her winks, her red-painted shoe, bring back to this spermary the feeling of spring.

And what of this demimondaine herself—at one time as pure, as full of sparkle, as her name? What trials she must have undergone to become transformed from the saucy muffin formerly disporting in the pages of the *Hustler Review* into this jaded Jezebel? Could it be that she, too, has been depraved by a man like Herr Maltz? Heavens! Could it be the heinous Hans himself? Might he not hold her in his power, just as he held the martyred Minkche in his thrall? After all, as is known by the clever Kakutani, as well as any other readers of my non-best-seller, the ex-Gauleiter was last seen in this same city of New York.

Oh, Crystal Knight! Have you run afoul of the sleek Svengali? Has he thrown you into a dungeon? Perhaps he has tied your wrists and your ankles to the rings in those moss-covered walls. I can see how you writhe, as the sweat balls fly from your bosom. The rats! Rats! Beware! Their claws! Their teeth! Miss Crystal! If only I could be your knight! To smash down the door! Cut through your bonds! Seize the villain by his throat! Then you could be the jailer and I could be the prisoner. You could lock me, like the technologist, in the WC. Tie me up! Feed me bread and water! Or even urine. What's this? *Was ist das?* Ah, ah! Greetings, red robin! Welcome back, little songbird. Thus we see what the power of imagination, and old-fashioned elbow grease, can accomplish. Two fingers, two fingers and thumb!

Live, love, laugh and be happy!

Let me describe now the life of L. Goldkorn and his French-style maid. Each morn she would rise at the dawning and dash to the seashore, where she would perform, with arm twists and knee bends, vigorous physical jerks. Next, she would leap through the tissue paper of foam and dive through the waves like a tuna. Within the villa, eyeballs pressed to the window glass, I would watch as this Aphrodite emerged from the foam, her corset oft askew, thus exposing the contrast between the skin that was tanned and that of the creamery below.

What of the rest of the livelong day? After ablutions we would share *un petit-déjeuner en tête à tête*. Boiled egg and healthful citrus, plus one half an apple. Then, into the ceramic bowl— remember I was but a youth of thirty-seven—a sturdy *Nummer zwei*. And so to work! I settled upon the bench of the Bechstein. Miss Kane, in her velveteen vest, her fishnet stockings, sat alongside. Thoughtfully, one after the other—this much resembles the custom the great Peary describes among the Esquimaux—she would place each of my fingers into her mouth. Thus with nimbleness would I attack the keys: the Haman theme, Mordecai's melody, Ahasuerus's love-struck lament—all the discords and harmonies that would transform *Everything Happens at Night* into *The Jewish Girl at the Persian Court.*

So carried away would we become that we oft worked through the luncheon hour—a dish of sprats, perhaps, if we remembered—and into the early afternoon. But never beyond fifteen minutes past two, which was when Madam Kane in haste departed in her open-topped coupe. *Where to, Candy, my little Kansan?* Thus did I silently wonder. *Why have you abandoned your lonesome Leib?*

Alone in the villa I would peck at the sharps and flats and then, abandoned, forlorn, lie down on the coverlet for a cat-type nap. Some two hours later my housekeeper, returning, would wake me with a gay toot of her horn button or, should that fail to rouse me, a stream of warm air that she blew in the spirit of friendship into my ear. Then hand in hand we would dash through the lengthening shadows down to the beach.

This was my favorite time of day. Miss Candy would shake the canister for cocktails while I, in my May Co. swimwear—boxer style, blue, with a red sea horse on the hip—drew a stave in the sand, along with the b-flats and   c-sharps with which Esther utters her cry of triumph.

"What's that, Shorty?" asked my companion, humming a tune of her own. " 'You Must Have Been a Beautiful Baby'?"

I laughed, and quickly traced the three jaunty f-sharps that accompanied the chorus of hi-jinxing Jews.

"Say!" declared the great Zanuck's personal assistant. "I bet I know that one: it's 'A Tisket, a Tasket'!"

"*Tsk, tsk.* Do you not recognize the Purim theme?"

"Poor who? Darryl? Believe me, that's one guy you don't have to worry about."

I pointed next to our refreshments—rather, to their silvery shaker. "No, no. Pour *him*. Ha! Ha! This is a word jest."

Which she got. Thus did we sit, sip-sipping, while Miss Candy kneaded the hirsute humps of my shoulders. Yes, martinis and massage, while the days grew shorter and shorter, and the sun, like the pate of a drowning man, sank into the surface of the sea.

Next? Next came dinner, always in a wee bistro at the Santa Monica Pier. Cloth of gingham. Wine bottle. A candle. The frozen tears of the wax.

And when the long day was done? Back to the cheery fireside which on those crisp December nights Madam Kane, with pine boughs and tinder, filled up with fire. Then we would while away the hours in chats, I about such topics as whether or not the sounds of nature, the twitter of birds, for example, or the sharp percussion of the beaver's tail—*watch out! Take care! The wily fox!*—are the building blocks of all human music, from the tom-toms of the jungle to the interludes and arias of Meyerbeer, the father of modern composition; and she about her girlhood in the state of Kansas, known because of its natural resources as the Breadbasket of the World. It was then that I learned of how, while leading her team huzzas—she demonstrated the way, beneath her pleated posterior, one might glimpse a bit of the sir-loins—she was approached by an employee of the Hollywood studio who, even before she had received her Gymnasium diploma, delivered her to the Fox King. *Give me a Z! Give me an A! Give me a N! And a U, a C, a K: Zanuck!*

And so to bed. Sweet dreams? Perhaps for Miss Kane. She would lie curled on her side of the mattress with her thumb like a babe's in her mouth; on occasion, from deep within her dream-adventure, she would express another high school cheer: *Dare-all! Dare-all!* Of course there is no need to explain that her innocence, like the sword of Tristan, lay between us. Not only that: I had my own dreams—of Miss Sonja Henie: her dimples, her dancing, her décolletage. Stealthily, in the dark, I would reach for the message that, as I had Yakhne's medallion once, I wore in a pouch round my neck:

STAR INSISTS NO BUT YOU

Then, in the light from the dying embers I would read another, more dire declaration:

NEED COMPLETE SCORE END YEAR

Every day, every hour brought that dread date nearer. Would I be able to finish my task of Hercules by that deadline? *Deadline*: the word, for my co-religionists, was all too apt. What had happened to those who were unable or unwilling to leave Vienna? Fools! Poor fools! They had clung to their furniture, their Biedermeier bedposts, the way shipwrecked sailors cling to a spar in a storm. And what of the Jews in the Sudetenland, which had been invaded such a short time ago? For that matter, what of the Jews of Paris, Warsaw, Budapest—yes, and when the tide should rise, sending its tidal waves before it, what of the Jews of London, New York, and even this City of Angels? How could I fail my obligations to Twentieth Century-Fox when the twentieth century itself was about to be submerged in the deluge? Thus it was that I slipped from under the sheets and trod in the wee hours to the bench of my Bechstein. Quietly, *pianissimo*, so as not to wake the teen from Topeka, I worked out the theme, in f-sharp minor, of my heroine's challenge to her people:

The ills of the Jews will continue to fester
Trust me to end them, or my name isn't Esther

And then one day, at lunchtime, the telephone sounded. My helpmeet picked up the instrument on the second ring. "Oh, goodness," she exclaimed, her suntanned face going as pale as a scraped piece of toast. "It's for you."

Quickly I gulped down a sprat and rose from the table. Madam Kane handed me the receiver. "Hello!" I declared, into the mouthpiece. "Here is speaking Akademie Graduate Goldkorn."

A female voice said, "Please hold for Mr. Zanuck."

Zanuck! The impresario! Founder of Twentieth Century-Fox! Also the creator of Rin Tin Tin. Instantly the palms of both hands produced a slick secretion. The same discharge appeared on my brow.

"Hello? Hello?" That was the voice of the living legend. "Maestro! Are you there? Hello?"

"I am here, your Highness."

"It's a lousy connection. How are you enjoying yourself out in Malibu?"

"I am enjoying myself very well, Majesty."

"Good. Glad to hear it. How about that Candy? Isn't she a peach?"

"A peach? Do you mean, Sire, a fruit?"

"Ha, ha. Say, how's that score coming along?"

"Score? As occurs in the football? *Ichywax-crakiwax-tackiphrax: Topeka!*"

"Ha! Ha! Ha! Say, that's great stuff. If the whole picture weren't set in Switzerland, maybe we could use it."

"Here is another encouragement: *Hold that line!*"

"Ha-ha-ha! Terrific. Listen, Maestro, we've got the whole picture in the can. But we don't have a note of music. Sonja's up in arms. I can't say I blame her. When she did her dance routine on the ice, we just threw in the 'Blue Danube' and a bunch of South American rhumbas. Rhumbas! In the Alps! We need you, Maestro. Are you ready to go to work?"

"Work, your Worship? Work on what?"

"On this piece of shit we're doing with Henie! Listen, we're having a screening at two-thirty this afternoon. Two-thirty sharp. I want you to see it. I'm sending the limousine. Sonja's convinced you can fix everything. She's your number one fan. We're counting on you, Maestro. Anything you want, just whistle. We'll have an orchestra waiting. Dancers. New sets, new lighting, the works. We've got all the stars ready in case we need principal photography. Bring your score with you. We'll go through the night if we have to. We've got to finish recording in twenty-four hours."

"Twenty-four hours? One day? But, my Lord, even Rome was not built in such a time."

"We're not asking you to build Rome, Maestro. Just take out the 'Blue Danube' and put in some stirring stuff, like in *Robin Hood*. Everyone says that score's going to win the Academy Award."

"But Excellency, I have already won from the Akademie this honor. From the hands of Franz Joseph, His *apostolische Majestät*."

"What is this? A stall? What have you two been up to out there? You probably haven't written a single fucking note!"

"No, no, your Eminence! Do not even think it. We are in fact making excellent progress. *Prima!* This morning I have written the scene of Haman on the gallows. In this aria he will sing the bass notes, b-flat, g-flat, with the rope around his neck."

"What the hell are you talking about? Haman? Rope? Aria—? There's not one song in the picture."

"Ha, ha! Here is a well-known *Lied*: *Cheer, cheer for old Notre Dame*—"

There was in my ear only a distant hum. Then the head of production said, "Who is this, exactly?"

"Here is speaking a woodwinder Graduate. *Glockenspieler* for der Wiener Staatsoper, formerly das kaiserliche und königliche Hof-Operntheater. This is in the city of Vienna, where, on the Kärntnerstrasse, at the Kruger Kino, I viewed *The Clash of the Wolves* and *Jaws of Steel* and, a personal favorite, *A Dog of the Regiment*. If you will permit me, Holiness, I wish to thank you not only for the excellent Bulova timepiece but for the many hours of pleasure you gave this lonely youth. *Danke schön!* And greetings to our four-footed friend!"

"Yeah. Okay. Vienna. I recognize the accent. Put Candy on, will you?"

In truth, my *femme de chambre* was already reaching for the receiver. She spoke into the mouthpiece. "Don't worry, Darryl. He's just a little, you know, eccentric. Like all those longhairs. A perfect gentleman, you know what I mean? What? Yeah, I'll tell him. Two-thirty? We'll be there. Okay. You bet. Not right now, sweetie. Just wait. Okay. You too."

One hour later the limousine arrived. It was the same black vehicle, with the same laconic liveryman, that had whisked me from the Union Station one month before. Clutching the score of *Esther* under my arm, I got into the rear, with Miss Candace Kane beside me. Off we went, down the Boulevard Pico della Mirandola, hung everywhere with snow icicles and snow stars in honor of the Christmas season. After a short ride we turned through the gateway of Twentieth Century-Fox. The phantasmagoria about us was more varied than the side tents of the Roumanian Circus: cowpokes and Comanches, pirates and plowmen, a sailor, a lumberjack, a chap dressed as Moses, not to mention a starlet in swimwear and a gentleman wearing a fez. As our car swept past, this human material smiled and waved and called out cheerful greetings: "Maestro! Maestro! Welcome to Fox!"

Our vehicle halted. My handmaiden and I entered a large building of lemon hue and climbed the stairway to the private kino on the second floor. At the front of this hall, surrounded by curtains, was a screen; at the rear were a number of windows, undoubtedly for the projectionist's beams. The room itself was filled with rows of chairs, upholstered in morocco, on the backs of which brass studs gleamed. Here, there, the head of an occupant lolled against the leather. The smoke of cigars curled and cued in the air. Madam Kane directed me toward a seat at the rear, put one finger to her lips, and then placed that damp digit endearingly upon the tip of my nose. I patted in eagerness the seat beside me, but she shook her head, sighed, and quickly ran down the aisle toward the door. "Miss Candy!" I cried. "Will you abandon your longhair?" At that instant I heard, as if from hidden gramophones, a burst of vulgar music. Above me there appeared a light shaft and, simultaneously, as if it had been splashed by a bucket of milk, the screen turned a gleaming white:

EVERYTHING HAPPENS AT NIGHT

There is no need to describe to the many aficionados of the cinematograph the story of the delightful photodrama that has, along with the pleasant *Goodbye Herr Chips*, also a film of 1939, captured the hearts of millions. But what of the younger generation? Lovers of music in the twelve-tone scale? What, too, of Madam Kakutani, my faithful Finn? For her, undoubtedly a devotee of Sibelius, a synopsis:

First we meet Mr. Ray Milland and Mr. "Bob" Cummings. These well-known actors play the parts of newspaper reporters who journey to Switzerland in order to seek the whereabouts of Dr. Hugo Norden, a Nobel Peace winner in hiding from his Nazi foes. Naturally both gazetteers become rivals for Madam Henie's affections—the clever photoplay artists have created an innuendo by naming her Miss Favor—when she bumps into them in a literal manner while on her Nordic-type skis.

Now begins the theme of romance as Mr. Ray Milland and Mr. "Bob" strive to, as Americans say, pitch to their Swiss Miss the woo. The climax of this courtship occurs when Mr. "Bob" Cummings trails his dimpled darling to a skating contest and then, under a comical misapprehension, attempts to give her instruction in the figure eight. Much amusement here as he slips and slides and does the bum fall. Finally, she takes pity upon him and—La-da-da-dee-da, E-sharp, E-sharp: *Der blaue Donauwalzer!*—begins to dance herself. What leaps and lutzes! The glides and glissades! Look! Look, friends! Upon one foot the sequined Scandinavian is spinning, spinning, dizzily spinning, all the while holding the other foot straight over her head. Even a Roumanian could not perform such a contortion. I confess to a pang of lickerishness as, beneath the folds of her tutu, there comes into full view her Norwegian fjord. Look again! She comes swooping toward us, arms aflutter, the torso zone bending so low that it is possible to glimpse, upon her mams, her paps. Here was the pinnacle of the *Liebesleitmotiv.* Mr. "Bob" Cummings, no less than the voyeur from Vienna, sits entranced, tormented by spiciness, until at last he gazes upon Miss Favor's heart-shaped face and utters with passion this excellent line:

A girl like you ought to be set to music—
you're a symphony for the eyes.

Now is introduced the deeper, more philosophical element. Our heroine, Henie, works for an ailing oldster who, in an astounding plot twist, turns out to be not only the acclaimed Dr. Hugo Norden *but Miss Favor's father!* This discovery is made simultaneously by the two reporters and by the agents of the Gestapo who arrive in a sled to arrest him. Next comes the thrilling escape. Mr. "Bob" and Mr. Ray—could these be the same humorists I later came to enjoy on my Philco-brand radio?—flee with Madam Henie and her father in the Germans' own sled. Quick as lighting grease the Nazis follow in a commandeered sleigh. Here we see the model for the exciting automobile regattas so popular with cinéastes of the present era. Gunshots, caroms, and, as Professor Pergam would call it, swift Aristotelian action.

At one point, when Mr. "Bob" turns his sled about and races at breakneck speed directly toward the sleigh of his foes, I felt my hair stumps rise atop my unhatted head. My heart seemed to split into a hundred small heartlets, each of them beating in agitation. On come the horses, along the narrow track. Closer and closer to each other draw the antagonists. Hooves thunder. Bridle bells jingle. The foam in the close view flies. I will not describe—why ruin this moment for those who have yet to see this cinema classic?—what happens next. It is enough to say there is a hair-breadth avoidance. After which, our magic carpet takes us to dockside. There, like so many great German speakers—Einstein, for instance, and Herr Thomas Mann—our own Dr. Hugo Norden, the great peace advocate, makes his escape to America. For the two reporters, a happy ending too. Mr. Ray Milland gets the story and Mr. "Bob" Cummings gets the girl. *Fin. Finis. Das Ende.*

"Bravo! Bravo! A capital production! My warmest congratulations to all!"

I was on my feet. I beat together my hands. Tears, why deny them, spilled from both eyes. Yes, ladies and gentlemen: in spite of widespread cynicism, love conquers all. And good, no matter how dark grows the day, triumphs in the end. "*Prima! Prima! Wunderbar!*"

A sudden silence fell upon the room. The empty beam flitted across the rectangle of the screen. The machinery for projection went faintly click and clack. Then, through the doorway at the front, two shadowy figures entered the room. The first of them started to speak:

"All right, Maestro. Spare us the sarcasm, okay? We're well aware we've got a dog here."

A dog? Could this be a reference to the featured player in *The Frozen River*? If so, the speaker must be none other than—

Before I could complete this thought the silhouette began to wave about him some sort of club. "What a picture! It's colossal! It's great! It's stupendous! The trouble is, it isn't any good. We can't open this crap. We'll lose our shirts."

From every part of the theater voices rang out:

"You are absolutely right, D.F."

"A brilliant analysis!"

"D.F., you hit the nail on the head!"

The dim figure spoke once again: "A million bucks! We're going to have to write every penny off to the IRS."

"Hey, I thought it was a swell picture." That was the second shadow. "Ha, ha, ha! Remember when she crashes into those two lover boys on her skis?"

No doubt about it: that voice belonged to my housekeeper, my helpmeet, my *Hausfrau*. Is this where she went on all those afternoons she disappeared from our villa? To stand by the Lord and Master? Yet her next words were not those of a traitress. "All you need is better music. You ought to listen to what Shorty wrote. It's better than 'Beautiful Baby.' "

The Fox King seemed to stare up upward, into the gloom. "What about it, Maestro? The sound stage is ready. The actors are ready. Everything depends on you. Do you have the score?"

At the back of the room I held up the opera pages. "Your wish, Sire, has been my command. None of this would have been possible without your genius. *Danke schön! Yes, a tausend Dank* to you!"

"What the hell are you talking about? All I did was borrow you from Warner's."

I raised then my hands into the indigo air. "O modest one! O sage! You cannot hide from me that you were aware all along that the story of *Everything Happens at Night* is nothing more than an ingenious retelling of the Book of Esther. No need to explain to you, O subtle one, the many features the two works hold in common. Dr. Hugo Norden, with his intelligence and keen moral views, not to mention the Mosaic style of his chin beard, is quite obviously a symbol of the Jewish people. No wonder Herr Hitler and the Gestapo seek to kill him, just as Haman and the enemies of the Jews sought to kill them, *both young and old, little children and women*, end quotation, upon the thirteenth day of the thirteenth month—"

"Thirteenth month?" cried the perplexed head of production. "Morrie Moscovitch a symbol? Are you nuts?"

"O Caesar! Clever one! To cast in this role an actor of the Hebrew persuasion. It is, to the wise, eh?, a word. Let us move on to Madam Henie. Surely it is evident to all that this daughter of Dr. Norden is none other than Esther, daughter of Israel, the nurse to and savior of her people. But what of our reporters? Here we must don our cap of cogitation. Mr. "Bob" Cummings is definitely the more ardent of our two amorists. *You are so alive*— such are the words he addresses to the honey-haired Henie. *So full of grace, rhythm, music*, end admirable quotation. Who can this be but Ahasuerus, who loved Esther, as it is written, more than all the virgins of the land?"

"*Ahasuerus!*" cried the Fox King.

"Gesundheit, D.F.!" murmured a minion.

"And Mister Milland? Here we have Mordecai. This becomes certain at the end of the entertainment. For it is he who, by inheriting the doctor's memoirs, will spread his message throughout the world—just as Mordecai, at the close of *his* drama, *wrote these things, and sent letters unto all the Jews that were in the provinces of the King Ahasuerus, both nigh and far.* Chapter nine, verse twenty. End quotation."

Then Zanuck, with zest: "Call the guards! The gatemen! Lights! Turn on the lights!"

"Wait! But a moment more!" I pleaded. "For now we come to the slyest touch. Yes, O Solomon, as sly as a twentieth-century fox. Note well, fellow filmists, how, in the Book of Esther, *Everything*—the king's selection of Esther, the hatching of Haman's plot, Esther's request to the king, and even the dancing and feasting of Purim: all of this *Happens at Night!* Exclamation."

"Where the hell are those lights? This is some kind of charade. Who is this guy?"

"Who am I? Only a humble tunester, Bwana. It is you who were the great guiding star. Together we shall create a masterpiece. Millions and millions will discover in a seeming lighthearted romance the message that will save *the young, the old, the little children and women* from the clutches of the modern Haman. Ladies! Gentlemen! We must work! Work with hammer and tong! The tooth and the nail! Let us go cracking! For the Jews!"

"In a pig's eye!" shouted the Fox King. "Lights, goddammit! Lights!"

Somewhere some person flicked then a switch. Fluorescence flooded the scene. At the front of the room a man in a moustache was shielding his eyes against the sudden glare. Padding in shoulders. Stripes on pants. Zanuck in zoot suit. With one hand he swung a mallet, as if riding on a lathered pony toward the open goal. His other hand, I saw, my heart sinking, was inside of Miss Candy's oral orifice. Up the aisles, faster than the gendarmes of France, came the officialdom of Fox.

"Grab him!" ordered their commander in chief. "This isn't the composer of *Captain Blood!*"

There was a scream, a cry, and many ejaculations. Then, over the hullabaloo, there rose a sweet, accented voice. "No! No! Let him be! This idea! It has deepness! It has the appeal! I luf it! Yes, luf it! Hoop-la!"

A little doll of a figure stood up on the cushion of her chair. I would know anywhere that hive of hair, the delectable dimples, the points of the pixie ears. "Ho-la!" I cried in return. "Madam Henie!"

Now Zanuck spoke with zeal. "Okay! All right! Whatever Sonja wants! Get that score! Prepare the ice! I want a hundred extras! In costume! I want the orchestra on the set! Sonja, sweetheart: get into costume. We'll start to shoot in an hour!"

I did not take my eyes from the face of the star. It was aglitter from the crystals in her ears and the diamonds at her throat. "Ah, Maestro!" she cried, even as, with her beringed hand, she blew in my direction a palm kiss. "We are to make now your picture. Ja! Jo! You betcher! I see it! I hear it! A world sensation! *Esther! Esther on Ice!*"

3

"Yoo-hoo! Yoo-hoo!" The cry, in a contralto, comes awarbling down the hallway. "Mr. Goldkorns? Is you?"

Madam Schnabel! And drawing closer, too! Frozen, in a trance, I wait. Louder and louder thud the footsteps, until—horrible sight!—the knob on the WC door twists right, twists left, twists right. Next the hook begins to gyrate like one of those needles that indicate to eager scientists a disturbance in the surface of the earth: in India, or Java, or the former land of Ceylon. Death to millions!

"Wait, Madam, I beg you. Here I am only reading."

"Is maybe a library for lending, Mr. Goldkorns? Or is a place for making business?"

"Business? Ha-ha! Business? Do you mean *Pu oder Pischee?*"

"And why is taking all day? What about other peoples?"

"Only five minutes, my good woman."

At this, a tremendous crash, as if the earthquake were occurring on Amsterdam Avenue and not far-off Assam. The little door of the cabinetto trembles, like a membrane stretched upon a beating heart. Again the concatenation. Madam Schnabel, like a ram for battering, is hurling herself against this puny portal. And what if she should break in? What if she should seize me by a leg bone? Or, with her avoirdupois, sit upon me? Salty thoughts. "Yoo-hoo-hoo!" calls once more the busty Brünnehilde, like a yodel expert, as in defeat she moves away. It is only natural to suppose that, under such an assault, I might lose my hard-won ribaldry. *Au*, as the Frenchman says, *contraire!* Even Mr. Ripley might not believe, in such circumstances, this swelling of hedonism. I cast my eyes down. What I see, rising in an eager manner, is a mirror image, in miniature, of myself: a bald head and two hairy shoulders. Thus did, in the fable of Professor Pergam, the youth Narcissus gaze upon his own likeness in the limpid stream. Congratulations, L. Goldkorn. You have achieved what in the world of sport endeavors Americans call a personal best. Almost five fingers!

"Yoo-hoo! Maestro! Hoop-la!"

A familiar voice. Where was it coming from? For a moment I stood, in confusion. The sky was—what else could it be in California?—blue. With the white wisps and whiskers of ponytail clouds. But behind this vault stretched another, of course cerulean; but the clouds in it, layers of them, long and lumpy, in the manner of intestines, were whizzing along in the December breeze, while these first clouds, feather tufts and starlet's eyelashes, were glued to the spot. In short, I was gazing up at a painted sky, hundreds of feet in width and height, property of Twentieth Century-Fox; while the real sky, property not of Zanuck but Zeus, rose to the heavens behind it.

"Maestro! Are you deaf, my dear? Like what-was-his-name? The composer. Also from Vienna. *Beethoven!*"

I turned. There, at the window of her mobilized dressing chamber, was Madam Henie—or so it appeared. Perhaps, like the very sky, this was not the World Champion but a dimpled double. How, in this land of illusions, could one tell the true from the false? For example, Candace the chaste, so girlish and pure— that was at one moment; and the next she had the producer's thumb, and forefinger too, inside her mouth. "Greetings, honored Henie. Have you by chance seen my *femme de ménage*, Madam Kane? Formerly the leader of cheers for Topeka?"

"Oh, she is with D.F. Do not please to worry. She will not be long. You understand my meaning, *jo?* This Zanuck, he's—what you say? Zippy. In and out. Like giraffes."

Giraffes? Was this a thing she had read in Krafft-Ebing?

"Come, Maestro. Come here. You will wait with me."

As in a trance I climbed the steps to her wheeled wagon, a variety of bedouin boudoir that could be transported to this spot or that one depending upon the demands of the cinéaste. Inside, all was homey: a zone for dressing; a zone for alimentation, with electrical Tappan-type range; also a zone for slumbers upon a Murphy-style bed. Curtains on windows. Doilies on chairs. Toward one of these the Olympian now pointed.

"Please, Maestro, to have a seat. And your hat give me."

The first of these suggestions I obeyed, sitting with crossed legs upon a chair with a design of gay chintz; but I kept my homburg upon my head—thus maintaining, in the Hollywood spirit, the illusion of either slick hair, shiny as a count's, or a full frizz, in the manner of Francis X. Bushman. More deception: on the outside the portrait of a man of the world, composed, legs crossed, debonair; but on the inside my heart was rattling to and fro like a leather bag struck by a boxer. And how could it not? The seductive Sonja was now dressed in the very tutu and bodice in which I had recently seen her aswirl on the ice.

"Cigarette?" asked the Scandinavian, holding out a silver container.

I was, of course, a non-smoker, the result of puffs upon a Trabucco D.D., biggest seller of our Imperial and Royal Tobacco Monopoly, when but a boy in Iglau. But I took the chic Chesterfield from its bin. *"Mais certainement."*

"Light?"

The cube in her hand, also silver, burst into a blaze. In that steady glow I watched her face draw near to mine: the apple cheeks and knob of a chin; the nose more pug than pointed; the curlets like bubbling butter; in each cheek a dimple, reminiscent of the dent in my homburg's crown; and the unblinking gaze of her Aryan eyes. Closer, too, came the burning wick, like the flame of a hypnotist. I sucked it into the open end of my cigarette and, so it felt, into the depths of my bowels.

"Himmel og Hav!" Sonja exclaimed. "Are you all right?"

"Top," I gasped, as the billows curled up past my hatbrim and the sparks tumbled down onto my herringbone pants, "notch."

"I am making a drink. Aperitif?"

Through the coils of smoke I gave a nod. Madam Henie hied herself to the bar and stretched upward on what I saw were bare tippy toes to the cabinet for glasses. I also noted that in the hastiness of the moment the rear of her bodice had been left azip. The bumps of the backbone, and more—two extra dimples, in the saddle zone—were thus exposed. Into clear glasses she poured something dark, clouded, cordovan-colored.

"To making the music together!" she declared.

"To our opera on ice! Salut!" I drank the liquid down. What was, on my tongue, in my throat, this delicious debouchment? Dubonnet!

My comely colleague settled just opposite, in a cloud of her own *eau de toilette*. "Maestro, I wish I could say how to you I am grateful that you answered my call."

"How could I not, Madam Henie? Did you not say"—here I pulled from below my clavicle the leather locket and drew from it the Western Union text—"INSISTS NO ONE BUT YOU? Quotation."

The eyes of the film star grew wide. "My Maestro! You saved the telegram! Around your neck!"

"These words," I said, "are to me the greatest compliment I have received since the prize of a Rudall & Rose—this is a wood-wind, of English manufacture—upon graduation day at the Akademie für Musik, Philosophie, und darstellende Kunst."

Now the little doll of a woman, a figurine of a figure skater, drew her chair even closer so that the caps of her knees touched mine. "Maestro, what you have said to me—oh, I am not finding the words to speak." Actions, as Americans say, are more laud-able than words: the great star lifted one of her legs and placed it within the angles of my lap. Only then did she resume. "What you have said, this is also a great compliment. Yes, for me, also, the second highest honor of my life."

Now it was my turn to feel amazement. This was a ten-time World Champion! A triple Olympic gold! My eyes smarted, though whether from nicotine or the force of my feeling I could not determine. "Ha-ha, Miss Sonja. I am only number two? The runner-up?"

"Oh, Maestro, if I told to you who was first I would have to reveal the deepest secret of my heart."

My own heart was now hurling itself against my rib cage, like a prisoner desperate to make his escape. Why this excitation? Because the heel of Madam Henie was pressing against the zone of my crotch, and her toes, each one red-painted, were waving about like five tiny flags. I managed to speak around the end of my hot cigarette:

"But have I not told you of my trophy? My genuine Rudall & Rose? Be fair: you must now tell of your greatest prize. What? Mum, Madam? Does this mean it was, ha-ha-ha, a loving cup?"

"No, no! Do not from me force this favor! Ask please anything else! Do you understand? *Anything!*" With this beseechment, she leaned so far forward that the vista of brisket I had so recently seen upon the screen became beholdable once again. But those had been mammaries in monochrome. In the colors of real life these pink paps stared up at me like two bloodshot eyes.

"You forgive me? You do not, my dear Maestro, insist? Oh, if we were in some other place—in Paris, in Roma, in your own wonderful Wien—then I could to you reveal everything, dear friend! But here! In this Hollywood! This golden ghetto! Do you know how many of *them* are about us? These fine gentlemen! Everywhere you look! In front of the camera, *Ja! Jo!* Also in the back. Think! They have written the words in my mouth! They tell me to move this way and that! Moscovitch! They have made him my father! Like lice, these peoples! I feel them! Under my nails! In my hair!"

That hair she now gave a vigorous shake, as if she meant to dislodge a nest of the parasites; and her mouth was turned down in a scowl. But to my eyes there was nothing to see but the highlights of Halo shampoo and the gay flash of toes, like the smile of lipstick-stained teeth. The happy truth had dawned upon me: Leib Goldkorn was having a rendezvous.

"Miss Sonja, you are not alone in having a secret in your heart. Now I shall reveal what is locked in mine. This is not the first time I have beheld your charms. The truth is, we have met before."

"Yes! Yes! Dear Maestro! I have possessed exactly the same feeling—since the day I heard first the notes of your music. That is why I called you to me, because of your idealism, your spiritual nature. Do you not agree that we know the true being of another through his art?"

"Madam, there is a misunderstanding. I do not mean that we have met through art. I do not speak of the Kruger Kino, where I received titillations from your roles in *One in a Million* and the excellent *Thin Ice*. No, Madam: we have met, if you will excuse the expression, in the flesh."

"What? Can such a thing be true?"

"1936. February. High in Bavaria. The twin hamlets of Garmisch-Partenkirchen. Yes, my dear Madam Henie: I was an Olympian, too!"

"Ah! Then you know my secret."

"*Nein!* But you now know mine. Ever since a certain night—surely you must remember: the lights, the snowy Alp peaks, the trumpet blare, and the shouts of the crowd—I have been a man who is in my modest way in love with you."

There was a brief pause. Silence reigned round us. Then the mistress of ice—believe it or not, Mr. Ripley, the Norwegian Champion from the age of nine—leaned forward even farther, like the dying swan of Pavlova; now a keen observer could note the great curve of pale skin, smooth and white as a ski jump, upon her dorsal parts. "You must to help me," she declared. "I beg you to help me."

I was, at this beguilement, completely under the spell of the star. "Whatever you say, Henie honey."

Then she raised her torso, still in its tutu, and displayed the bootie that she grasped in her hand. "Assist me please to put on."

At this sight a tide of zestiness surged through my piping. The shoe was made from white leather, with two rows of eyelets and laces in a state of abandon. But what made me gasp with delight, yes, and shiver with qualms, was the blade that stretched from toe to heel on the sole. It gleamed in the light from the incandescent bulbs. It was sharp as a knife or a razor. This was the life of adventure!

"Oh, hurry!" said Henie. In my lap, her toes tossed and twinkled, like the hot little flames on a menorah. The ankle bone ground with impatience against my groin. With one hand I seized the soft leather; with the other I touched the cold steel. My tongue, like that of the boot, hung outwards. Then, as a great ocean liner maneuvers with untold power toward its berth; as the snout of a hog burrows with eagerness into the earth for a truffle; or as with deftness the hand of a surgeon enters a new-made incision, so this foot at last came to rest in its shoe.

"KAMERADEN! WAS IST *das leichteste Objekt auf Gottes gute Erde?*" Thus did the fun-loving Pepi Pechler set his fellow woodwinders a conundrum: "Friends, what is the lightest object on God's good earth?" This was, for those of us in the Akademie class, a puzzler.

"*Ein Stück Papier?*" asked the pale-faced Willi Wimpfeling. "A piece of paper?"

"*Dummkopf!*" exclaimed the gap-toothed and downy-lipped Maltz. "*Das ist eine Feder.*" He thought it was a feather.

At the front of the room Professor Lajpunger looked up from where he was scribbling names in the attendance book. When he looked down, the oboists and clarinetists, chimed in:

"A pin!"

"A dust mote!"

"I know! A bacterium! A germ!"

Here was the contribution of our favorite flautist: "*Ein Schmetterling.*" A butterfly.

But Pechler held up both of his short-fingered hands. "*Nein! Nein! Nein! Idioten! Die Antwort ist ein Schlong.*" The male member.

"*Was?*"

"*Was ist das?*"

"*Ein Schlong? Ein Schwanz? Warum Schlongfleisch?*"

Pepi broke into a triumphant grin. "Why? Why? Because even a thought can lift it!"

Now, a full eighty years later, I have before me the proof of this theorem. Mere meditations upon Madam Henie have resulted in a complete regeneration. This is no hip-hopping robin but a fiery phoenix sprung from lust ashes. Rebirth! Renewal! Hello, Mr. Johnson! And how was this resurrection accomplished? From thoughts of that boot. That blade. Look! What have we here? A gumboil? Ha, ha! A war wound! From what Americans call two-fisted action. Yet, in spite of fatigue to forearms and wrist, I must continue. Already the noontime hour approaches. Clara, for her injection of medicaments, calls. Is there to this task no terminus? Incessant Sisyphus? Is that my fate? Perhaps it would help if we returned to that fateful February of 1936. It was then that for the first time we shall find *Leib verliebt*. Yes, Leib in love.

From the front of the autobus came a whoop of laughter. It woke me from my nap. I looked about. There were, aboard our climbing, lurching, gear-groaning vehicle, some ninety-odd people, a figure that included the trainers and coaches and government officials who, in the aggregate, outnumbered our fearless athletes. All wore the yellow and black stripes of the Austrian national team. Those who had not already done so were dashing left, across the aisle, to peer out the frosted windows toward the side of the twisting mountain road. Another laugh and yet another and now a great guffaw as the long-distance racers and then the slalom experts and finally the hockeyists each in turn saw the amusement.

What, I wondered, was the jolly joke? On the right, I knew there was nothing: a sheer drop, half a kilometer to the spearpoints of the firs and evergreen pines in the chasm below. And there? On the left? With the sleeve of my coat, a colorless gabardine, I rubbed a porthole in the rearmost pane. Also nothing: only the granite's blank face, with snow for a beard, an icicle moustache, and a muffler of mist. Yet the laughter continued, and even grew, until the whole team was pressed against the window glass like a swarm of festive honeybees. Even the driver, bent over his wheel, had the giggles. Then one of the contingent, it was a Military Ski Patrol racer, pulled away from the others. This soldier, flat-chested beneath his two-tone stripes, with a tight leather helmet, caught my eye. Here was Schütze-Grenadier Schmidt; he gave me a sad, surreptitious head nod. There was a pause, and then a shrill squeal from the gears—almost as if our autobus, in brand a merry Mercedes, were joining in the laughter. Onward we went, upward, until even Leib Goldkorn, sitting above the left rear pneumatic tire, could see the sign that had already given thousands of visitors to Garmisch-Partenkirchen so much delight:

ACHTUNG!
WARNING!
Dangerous Curve
35 Kilometers
Jews 150!

Amongst those on our vehicle were two dozen ladies, including Hedy Stenuf and Liselotte Landbeck, crack Austrian figure skaters, as well as the teenager Ilse Pausin, who with her brother hoped to take a gold in the pairs. Not present: Fräulein Yakhne Goldkorn. That is to say, she was indeed on board our Mercedes and a full-fledged member of the Military Ski Patrol racing quartet—but not under her own name, which would have disqualified her as a Jewess; and not as a member of the weaker sex, which, while not technically against the rules, was even worse: unthinkable.

Had anyone, in fact, thought it? Unlikely. In my sibling's chin, a masculine cleft; in her throat, the apple named for Adam. Hair thinning in clumps from the days of her youth. Shoulders broad, hips narrow, calves like those of a mountaineer. Perfume? Ha-ha! The smell, rather, of her ever-present Trabucco cigar. More? A walk like a highway trooper as he approaches his unfortunate victim. A voice like Ezio Pinza. To conclude, here we have not what Americans call a peach. Still, there was in her eyes, a melting milk chocolate, and in her surprisingly thin wrists and lady-like ankles—yes, and in the ballast of her bum zone, especially when enclosed in elasticized racing tights—something of the eternal feminine. If anyone within the *österreichischer olympischer Verband* had noticed, he did not say a word. How could he? Yakhne was not only the fastest skier on the military patrol, she was by far the best shot—able to load, aim, and fire in less than two seconds and hit the target, a pink balloon the size of a grown person's head, at 85 meters and more.

These feats may have caused a sensation in Austrian circles of sport but were no surprise at Rennweg 30. The family Goldkorn had known of Yakhne's obsession from the earliest days of 1933—indeed, from the very first day that Herr Hitler took over the government in far-off Berlin. For three years our markswoman had continued her practice—daytimes in the far reaches of the Wienerwald, and ofttimes at night in the gallery, filled with gourds and glass vessels, that she had set up in our cellar. When Yakhne was not shooting she was out on the slopes, slaloming, snowshoeing, schloss-schlossing; even in the heat of summer she would, with strapped knees and ankles, make circles around our mighty linden, going faster and ever faster, like *der kleine Neger Sambo*, who in the folkish tale is chased by the tiger.

My sister, in short, was in the grip of fanaticism. For month after month she would eat nothing but unbuttered rye, a diet first advocated by a compatriot of Miss Michiko, the famed Paavo Nurmi, known to the world as the Flying Finn. Yes, rye husks, a compote of lingonberry, and on weekends a fish paste in order to settle the sharpshooter's nerves. An officer, an underofficer, and two enlisted men: that was the composition of the Military Patrol. Of all those who arrived that day at Garmisch-Partenkirchen, for that matter of all those anywhere on *Gottes gute Erde*, only I knew the secret identity of Schütze-Grenadier Johannes Schmidt, who had made such a sensation at our national trials, and who now was the first of our athletes to disembark from the autobus, trailing behind the blue smoke plume of a he-man's cigar.

Question: would Yakhne succeed, through the whole of the IVth Olympiad, in maintaining the masquerade? At first, it seemed she would be exposed before the games had even opened. Snow fell in fitful spurts through the whole of February 6, the day of our arrival. The crowds, pouring off the trains from München, trampled the streets of the town into a swamplike slush. Brass bands marched through these paddies. The red and black banners of the Reich waved from every housefront, obscuring the painted scenes of peasant life. Each minute loudspeakers barked, *Achtung! Achtung!*, while the horns of autos, stuck fast in the slurry, created a cacophonous blare. In the great stadium, nestled beneath the slopes of the Gudiberg, an urn burned with a continual *olympisches Feuer*. Into that open-air arena marched in strict formation the many fellowships of the host nation:

Strength Through Joy leagues, Hitler Youth regiments, and the many Labor Battalions. At last like Lippizaners came the thousand athletes from all twenty-eight national teams. Herr Hitler stood on the reviewing stand, hatless in the downfall of snow. The first to march by were the Greeks, sons and daughters of those heroes of old. As they passed beneath the Führer's gaze they threw out their right arms. In response the crowd, a hundred thousand strong, thundered with delight: was this the Olympic, or the Nazi, salute?

With dismay I saw that the nation of Austria was next. What, you may ask, was an Akademie Graduate, thirty-four years of age, doing high in the Alps, within a brand-new coliseum, and only fifteen paces from the leader of the Thousand Year Reich? Was Leib a luger? A bobsledder? A twirler on ice? Ho, ho! Laughter of amusement. Recall, please that I was at that time for the Wiener Staatsoper a *Glockenspieler* and it was upon that instrument—or, more precisely, upon the steel harmonica—that I had been chosen by lot to play within the ranks of the olympisches internationales Orchester.

A-flat, b-sharp, c-sharp, a-flat: the opening notes, by Haydn, of "Ach, du mein Österreich." With my hammer I struck them, even as I peered through the slats of my lyre-shaped instrument at the yellow-and-black-clad members of our national contingent. A tremendous bravo from the Bavarians! A roar of fellow feeling. For there could be no doubt about this salute: the stiff arm, the stiff hand, chest out, eyes right. Greetings to the Führer! Behind my stainless steel octave I held my breath. My mallet stood frozen in air. Where was Schütze-Grenadier Schmidt? There! With the rest of the Ski Patrol. All four soldiers took the turn around the frozen surface of the skating rink and approached the reviewing stand. Eight eyes snapped to the right, including the two that belonged to my sister. All four arms shot up and forward. The horizontal bars of my instrument might just as well have been the vertical ones of a prison; trapped behind them, I was unable to speak, unable to move, unable to play a single note. For at the end of Yakhne's outstretched hand there protruded, like an outsized middle finger, all twenty centimeters of a Trabucco *Doppeldezimeter*.

So thick were the snowflakes, so dense the flurry of hats the

Münchners hurled into the air, that no one took note of my sister's insouciance. On went the procession, nation after nation, from Brazil to France and on to Japan. As each country marched beneath the reviewing stand and offered its salute, Herr Hitler responded with a womanly gesture of acceptance: beneath his iced-over moustache, a girlish giggle; and the right arm and hand bent backward, in the posture of a Grecian maiden who carries an invisible urn. Suddenly, midway through the parade, his arm shot upright and he cried out, "*Halt!*" Once more my mallet stood suspended, at the very crescendo of "*Ja, vi elsker dette landet,*" which as everyone knows is the Norwegian national anthem. Directly below, the team from that ice-bound land had come to a halt. Here were the great gold medalists to be: Ruud, the tiny ski jumper; Ballangrud, triple winner at 500, 5000, and 10,000 meters; and the famed Oddbjörn Hagen, cross-countryist nonpareil. But it was not these true Nordic types that the Munich masses craned forward to see. There, at the center of the delegation, in a tiny tutu and with feathers like wings on her soft leather shoes, stood a pink-cheeked and blond-headed damsel, with a nose like a button and a chin like a knob.

Sonja Henie!

The instant I saw her, with those dimple clefts and the little points on her ears, I experienced what must frankly be called an upsurge of *Sensationslust*. My breath turned to fire inside my lung sacs. My eyes bulged in their sockets as I leered without shame behind my lyre. An instant later this outpouring of rut turned into rage: the leader of the master race had left his platform and, holding a snowball, was now striding through the ranks of skiers and skaters, straight for the near-naked Norwegian. There, bowing, bending, knocking his shoe heels, he seized her hand and to my horror placed upon it his moustachioed lips. An outrage! An insult, in my opinion, to humanity! Worse was to come: he raised the *Schneeball*—no, it was clearly a chrysanthemum blossom, as large and white and feathery as the hat upon Henie's head—and pressed it to her bosom zone. Yes, before the eyes of one hundred thousand souls, he was performing a twiddle! What, under such scrutiny, could the skater do? She gave a laugh, or an approximation of such, and put her arm around the dictator's neck. She raised a foot backward—for those with eyes to see, a parody of the Reichschancellor's salute—and kissed the cheek flesh of the Führer. A furor! An animal bellow! A wild haloo! Thus responded the masses, while I continued to play the anthem, music by Rikard Nordraak, lyrics by Bjørnstjerne Bjørnson, "Yes, we love this land"; but my eyes were blind with salt-filled tears, and my heart was an open wound into which more salt had been poured.

The ten days of the festival sped quickly by. It soon became apparent to everyone that the real star of the IVth Winter Olympiad was not any of the athletes, not even the dashing downhill Deutschländers F. Pfnür and C. Cranz, nor the keeper of goal, J. Foster, who secured for the underdog Brits the hockey gold: no, the true hero was Herr Hitler himself. He appeared at each venue, his hair slicked across his forehead and his body wrapped in a black battle coat of full-length leather. Larger than life, his portrait waved from the flagpoles. His voice crackled upon the radio beams and rose and fell from the loudspeaker cones. This was the god, almighty Zeus, before whom all men must kneel.

And who was his consort? Hera? Henie. She was here and there and everywhere floating at his side. She wore a gown as white as his clothing was dark, goddess of Day upon the arm of Night. Her bodice blossom, that same pale chrysanthemum, was always fresh, always blooming, as if by some trick or magic or gift from Olympus it had been bestowed with everlasting life. About this couple the glow of a thousand bursting flash lamps created a heavenly aura. But Leib Goldkorn was not blinded by such radiance. I knew that this hypnotist, Hitler, intended to secure Madam Henie's favors the instant he draped round her neck the first-place medallion.

That event, the figure skating for ladies, took place on the final day of the festival. The stadium was filled and so were the grandstands above it. Total spectators: an unbelievable two hundred thousand. By midafternoon, it was clear to the members of the olympisches internationales Orchester that we need keep only two national anthems on our music stands: that for Great

Britain, whose Cecilia Colledge, a lass in her teens, was mounting a surprising challenge to the reigning champion; and of course that of Norway, whose great star, already ahead after the compulsory figures, would be the last skater to enter the rink. Meanwhile the sky above us, so close and so blue, hung lower and lower, like a canopy supported by the bedposts of the Alps. Night approached. Great searchlight beams rose into the sky like toppling Greek columns, and splashed like molten metal upon the ice. There Miss Colledge, aged fifteen, was flying into the air, spinning round and round yet again. All eyes were upon her, save mine. I was peering toward the open end of the stadium, through which the skiers from the Military Patrol must make, after a march of twenty-five kilometers, their entrance. After all, the other musicians in our band would have to retain one more sheet of music; the Akademie Graduate, however, knew that Austrian anthem by heart.

A shout went up from the galleries, the grandstand. The English skater had followed her double axel with an unheard-of triple. The applause came thundering down. We were, it seemed, upon the verge of a revolution. This Colledge, so calm, so serene, had already made up the three-point deficit in the school figures. All about me my fellow percussionists were beating the rhythm of the "Sugarplum Fairy," which she had chosen to accompany her last series of jumps. Yet even as I struck my parallel bars, the heart in my breast was hurting for Henie: was the great Queen about to lose her throne?

Then something caught my eye. Across the ice, the first team of Military Patrollers was coming into the stadium. From my throat there flew a gasp of dismay. Where was the yellow and black? What I saw were green tops and red trousers. Heavens! Italians! The Italian team! Was I going to have to play the 'Giovinezza?' Up went their time on the scoreboard: 2 hours, 28 minutes, 35 seconds. Where were the Austrians? Why had the bees not come back to the hive? What had happened to Schütze-Grenadier Schmidt?

Ahhh, that was the exclamation from the crowd; then Ooooh, like an echo. Miss Colledge had just emerged from a triple lutz-double toe combination, her sequins and rhinestones all adazzle in the crisscrossed beams of light. Nothing, it seemed, could stop this usurper from seizing the crown.

Aha! Here were the Austrians! 2 hours, 36 minutes, 24 seconds! This was not by my lightning calculation a total disaster. Less than eight minutes separated the top two teams. Since each missed balloon in the snapshooting contest added a penalty of three minutes to the total score, my own country could win if its opponents should fail to deflate just three of the twelve pink-hued orbs. Already the first of the *Fascisti* was taking aim, at 110 meters. I heard next a series of pops, no louder at this distance, and over the music of Tchaikovsky, than the rude noise that Pepi Pechler made by stretching his cheek with his thumb. Into the air rose three smoke puffs: simultaneously the trio of spheres disappeared. The second Italian achieved no less. My heart, like a stone, was sinking. From my lips there issued a groan. Were we to be defeated before Yakhne had even a chance? No! There was hope! The third of the marksmen had left one of his globes untouched. There it was, blushing like the face of a maiden who has just heard a non-couth remark. I shut my eyes, unable to watch shooter number four. But my ears could not block out his rifle's faint percussion, like popping kernels of corn. I forced open an eyelid. He had missed! There was the first sphere, still intact. Alas, the second had passed into the realm of non-existence. And the third? Unable to look directly, I cast my eyes back to the Italian, above whose weapon there curled a puff of white smoke, like that which marked, in his own country, the selection of a pope. *Sì! Il Papa! Viva!* A portrait in pink! A head of helium! *Il pallone!* The balloon!

There was, from the crowd, a tremendous ovation. The teenager, whirling like a Turkoman Dervish, was concluding her performance. Now the mob from München, and all those in the grandstand too, were on their feet. They made even the giant search beams wink and waver with their shouts and applause. Score: 418.1. To win, Miss Sonja Henie must skate as she had never before in her life.

The Military Ski Patrol from my own beloved country was in the same predicament: they must shoot with absolute perfection. France, which had arrived at the stadium with a score of 2 hours,

40 minutes, 56 seconds, had been mathematically eliminated from a first-place finish, as were the teams of each nation that followed. Everything was up to Schütze-Grenadier Schmidt and his, or her, Austrian brothers-in-arms.

The age of miracles, perhaps, had not ended. Could it be that on Olympus the gods had decided for their amusement to intervene? No sooner had Madam Henie started her program than, tutu twirling, bodice agleam, she whirled so high off the ice that each and every spectator instinctively searched for the undetected partner who had hurled her into the air. A cry, a roar, went up from the grandstands. Then, as the champion vaulted upward again, rising higher and still higher, over the horns of the one-quarter moon, the fickle crowd flew into a frenzy. Pavlova? This was also Nijinsky, and the illusionist Houdini, too.

Nor was the miracle limited to free figure skating. Across the stadium the Austrian marksmen were actually hitting their targets. The first set of balloons disappeared in three rapid bursts. To my delight, to my amazement, so did the next group of diminutive dirigibles. The greatest pressure was on the third sharpshooter, since the fourth, Schütze-Grenadier Schmidt, had never been known to miss. Poof! Pang! Pow! Just like that, orb, globe, and sphere utterly vanished. And next came Yakhne! The victory was, as Americans say, inside the bag!

So was Madam Henie's. Her program, to the dances of Delibes, was coming to an end. The skater executed a brilliant Axel Paulson jump and then fell into a graceful layaway, her back bent, her arms extended. From this she rose into a tremendous spin, a breathtaking merry-go-round, which to the human eye seemed to consist of multiple faces and as many arms and legs as a Hindoo goddess or god's. Sonja! Shiva! Points: 424.5. Madam Henie had taken the gold!

At that very moment an auto car, an open-topped Daimler, entered the stadium grounds. A man in gleaming black leather stood upright next to the driver. One hand gripped the windscreen; the other was raised in a feminine manner to receive the salute of the crowd. Herr Hitler! He had come to present the medal to his mistress. Slowly the topless vehicle circled the floor of the stadium. Then, at the reviewing stand, it came to a halt. To the cheers of hundreds of thousands the Führer stepped out. Up the flagstaff went the blue and red cross of the Norwegian banner. And up onto the rostrum, with a brave smile on her lips, stepped Miss Sonja Henie to receive the laurels from her would-be lover.

Ja, vi elsker dette landet, Som det stiger frem! So played the motley musicians. Not I: I was transfixed at the sight of my dear sister Yakhne as, in her disguise of a lowly private, she raised her rifle high. She pressed her cheek to the wooden stock. She lined up the sight and the target. Double detonation: bullet and balloon. Again the Jewess placed the stock to her jaw and pulled the trigger. *Bang!* went the powder and *poof!* the rubber globe. Now the score stood as follows: Italy—2 hours, 37 minutes, 35 seconds; Austria—2 hours, 36 minutes, 24 seconds. We had taken the lead! Huzzah! And with only one more balloon to go! Poor pink globule. Already Schütze-Grenadier Schmidt was taking aim. The Austrians were about to seize the prize.

Meanwhile Madam Henie was preparing to receive her own reward. The trumpets hit and held a high C. The drummers played a drumroll. The skater bowed her head; standing above her, Herr Hitler lowered the ribbon about her neck. Then to my horror the Norwegian maiden stretched upward in order to bestow—not on the cheek flesh but on that moustachioed mouth—a kiss. To the *Glockenspieler* the scene was grotesque. Would the gods of the Greeks allow this travesty to reach a culmination? How could one of their champions become a darling to a dictator? Ladies and gentlemen, what happened next was not an action of the gods. A certain steel-tipped mallet flew end over end through the air and, as if thrown by Old Shatterhand himself, struck the leader of the master race between the blades of his shoulders. Down he ducked. At that precise instant the gong of the olympisches internationales Orchester loudly resounded. Everyone turned round, to where the great gold disk, like an enormous first-place medallion, continued to pulsate and throb.

Was I the only one who realized there was no part for that instrument in the Norwegian National Anthem? I raised my eyes and gazed far afield. There, clear across the rink, a balloon hung in the air, as rosy as a salmon in the act of leaping the falls. Missed! Yakhne had missed! One hundred and ten meters away she stood, still aiming her army-issue gun. But the smoking muzzle was not pointed at the Military Ski Patrol target but at the precise spot where the Führer's head had been. The bullet had whizzed through the space in which he had been standing and embedded itself in the bronze of the gong. What had I done? Oh, Leib Goldkorn! Buffoon and meddler! You saved with your mallet the life of this Haman! This Herr Hitler! This Hun!

COULD IT BE that sixty years later I am enduring such torture in payment for that crime? I do not refer to the fact that on the underside of my manly part I have sprung a definite corn. Let such afflictions strike! Boils and blisters, carbuncles and cankers! They are as nothing compared to the plague, made all the more bitter by its ironical nature, that befalls me at this moment. For if I have struggled through this long winter morning to achieve in my privates a perpendicularity, now, as we approach the noontime hour, I cannot induce this unruly member to go down. All too much does this resemble a curse of the gods. He who asks for their favor must abide the cruelty of their jests: perpetual life but not perpetual youth; infinite knowledge in a body that must decay and die. So did my efforts at libido provoke this laughter. I am not unlike one of those figures that were revealed when Pepi Pechler removed the silvery stars from our illustrated texts: a satyr forced to persist in his vigorishness for over two thousand years. Thus was I condemned to suffer, perhaps for eternity, the very fate—this magnification of the unmentionables—I had so eagerly desired. Has Dr. Goloshes for such a calamity a cure?

Yakhne! Forgive me! My people! Do not accuse me from the grave. Is there no way to atone? Perhaps if I could rescue Miss Crystal Knight from the clutches of her Teutonic oppressor—or if there were yet some way I could redeem the Jewish nation through my art, as I came within a whisker of a cat of doing at the studios of Twentieth Century-Fox. Where were we? Ah, with Madam Henie! Her skate boot upon my lap. With its oh-so-sharp blade. I was, from spiciness, in a semiswoon. As if from a great distance I heard Sonja's voice: *Now you will please to help me with the other.*

Down dropped the second bare foot, with its ankle, its arch, and its toes like a tulip bouquet. Here was the boot and here the blade. I pulled; she pushed. We achieved an insertion. With fumbling fingers I knotted the laces.

"Now," said Madam Henie. "Please to zip me." So saying she stood and turned upon me the snowy slopes of her lumbars. A hint of fanny; a hint, topside, of mams. I stood also and, as commanded, closed tight the fastener. Next, an amazement: the film star executed a hop and leaped into my arms. She was not, in truthfulness, the proverbial feather: my knees buckled and the brim of my homburg slipped over my eyes.

"Come, my luf! We make work! Hoop-la! We make the art!"

I turned. I staggered toward the doorframe. Then, as a husband transports his bride over the threshold—though in this case we were not going in but going out—I carried Madam Henie down the wooden steps of her portable paradise to where a cart and driver were already waiting. In this jitney we drove off to where the dream of *Esther: A Jewish Girl at the Persian Court* was about to come true.

The building we approached, a stage for sound, was as big as an aerodrome hangar. The great Zeppelin IV could have fit with comfort inside. From behind the huge sliding doors came notes of a Meyerbeer-style melody. Wait! This was *my* music, from Act One of *Esther*: the Dance of the Damsels. Strings, two clarinets, oboe and flute; also french horns, percussion, celesta.

"Madam Henie, do you hear? My music! My rhapsody! The dance before Ahasuerus. How could such a thing be?"

Just then the doors swung open and no sooner had my companion and I stepped inside than I received to my question the answer. The Fox Symphony Orchestra sat in a half circle facing the left-hand wall. Against that surface, in my own hand notations, were projected the sharps and flats, whole notes, half notes, yes and all the lyrical words, of the *Esther* score. There was no conductor. The musicians—and to my astonishment I recognized at once two or three hideaway Hebrews from the Wiener Staatsoper Orchester—were fiddling on their own. Hard to hear these arpeggios, with the Oriental grace notes, the quivers and

quavers—not so much because the FSO lacked depth of dynam-
ics but because of the competing cacophony of sound. Everywhere carpenters were hammering nails and sawing pieces of
wood. Welders in welding helmets caused their flames to snap
and sizzle as they made fast their metallic joints. Chug-chug went
quite loudly a machine for cooling the hundreds of square meters
of ice that took up most of the studio floor. On that same flat floe
one hundred skates went swish and then swoosh, as the Virgins
practiced their enticing turns. Above all this din men and women
ran this way and that way, shouting queries and commands.

"Quiet! Quiet on the set!" That voice, thundering close by, was
the loudest of all. Immediately everyone—the musicians, the
hammerers, even the skaters—fell silent. "Lights! Light test!
Lights!" boomed the voice, from practically by my side. I turned
toward the speaker, but he and everything else inside the vast
building were lost in the sudden burst of illumination. Bulbs
blazed from the rafters overhead. They glowed from the walls
and shot up from reflecting devices upon the floor. The great
oval of ice was transformed into a mercurized mirror, as bright
as the noontime sun. "Okay, okay," came the decree, in the
same deafening tones. "Kill 'em!" As suddenly as the lights had
come on, they now switched off, leaving a smell of vapors. For a
moment I stood, blinking and blind.

"So this," came the voice, speaking now at a normal volume,
"is the famous Maestro."

The spangles fled from my eyes. I looked leftward and down.
There, sitting upon a round black cushion, was a gentleman
holding the sort of speaking tube through which Candace Kane
had in youth uttered her exhortations: *Give me a T, give me a O,
give me a P,* and so forth: *TOPEKA!* He was dressed in tweed cloth
and had, on his head, a soft felt hat with a turned-down brim.
He continued to speak, around the stem of a smoking pipe: "The
great composer. A real longhair, huh?"

"Ho! Ho!" I laughed, tapping my homburg. "Under this hat
there is not the coiffure of Herr Beethoven."

Now Madam Henie seized my arm and drew me to the side.
She hissed her words into my oversized ear. "This man is director.
Mr. Irving Cummings. No, no—not related to our handsome

Bob. It is trick, that name. It is disguise. In truth he is one of *them!* Israelite! Look at nose. Like *Elg.* Our Norwegian Elk. We shall fix this Cummings! We shall fix this Moscovitch! We shall fix them all! This was told me by my friend. My friend, the Führer. At Garmisch-Partenkirchen. It was our big secret. He is going to seize all this tribe. He is going to put them into park. *Ja-jo,* a game park! With the *Elgen* and anteaters and all other bent-nosed creatures. Ha! Ha! Ha!"

"Ha, ha," I laughed. "What do you mean? A game park?"

Instead of replying she snapped her fingers at Katz-Cummings. "Give to Maestro the tube for speaking. You will not give me commands. I only act for my luf-boy."

"Whatever Sonja says," answered the hidden Hebrew. He rose from his seat and handed me the cone. "D.F.'s orders. I'll be your assistant. Just tell me when you want lights, camera, action."

With that Madam Henie cried, "Ah! Now you are director! You are my Maestro, you betcher! How I will obey you! I am the slave girl to art!"

The next thing I knew she had turned and put on my two lips both of her own, allowing to slip between us what I am to this day convinced was the tip of her peppy tongue. Such smoothness, ladies and gentlemen! Such creaminess! Like a saltimbocca. My head from these erotics went into a reel. Miss Sonja hip-hopped on her skate shoes to the rink and swooped off across the frozen water. For another moment I stood—and who does not after his first human kiss remain for a time lost in wonder?—clutching to my breast the megaphone that amplified every beat of my overfull heart. Then, weak-kneed, I sank down upon the round black cushion of the director's chair.

What happened next filled me with the emotions of amazement and dismay. For no sooner had my buttock zone made contact with the leatherette surface than, as if the whole seat had springs inside it, or else a fuse for explosives, the Graduate of the Akademie für Musik, Philosophie, und darstellende Kunst found himself flying at a breathtaking speed through the air. Up, up, I rose, faster than a steam locomotive, higher than even a trained athlete could hurl a stone. Off went my homburg, tumbling like an autumn leaf torn from a treetop. Still higher I rose, sweeping outward, over the ice, like a lone petrel lost in the winter storms. Far below I saw the foreshortened figures of the film folk as they stared upward with the same open-mouthed awe with which, thirty years earlier, we citizens of Iglau had watched the Archduke Ferdinand and the Emperor of Abyssinia sail over our heads in the lighter-than-air zeppelin.

At this glimpse of my receding colleagues I began with apprehension to wave my arms. No sooner did I do so, however, than the Fox Symphony Orchestra, no doubt confusing my gestures with those of a conductor, broke out into the overture to *Esther: A Jewish Girl in the Persian Court.* Desperate now, I leaned out over the distant crowd and, expelling the words into the wrong end of the speaking tube, cried out in my native tongue, *"Hilfe! Hilfe!* Help! Oh, people! People! *Leute, Leute!"*

From the faraway earth I heard a familiar voice—it was that of my assistant, the so-called Cummings—echo my own: *"LIGHTS!"*

Immediately all of the incandescent lamps blazed forth again, shimmering and glimmering off the great slab of ice, as if I had flown all the way to the Arctic Circle and seen a display of the Northern Lights. "Friends, good friends!" I called out once more in my muffled voice. *"Kameraden!"*

And from Katz-Cummings: *"CAMERA!"*

"Nein! Nein!" I screamed, swooping and swerving through the invisible ether. "Here! Up here! Attention! *Achtung!"*

"ACTION!"

Many events now happened at once. The FSO launched into the plaintive lament in which Ahasuerus sings of his abandonment by Queen Vashti and his wish for a new bride. Oboe, piccolo, tambourine, strings. At the same time a great jeweled throne was pushed out onto the ice and the man who had been seated upon it rose to his full height. He wore a golden crown and loose pantaloons, also gold-covered; his chest in its hairlessness was bare. "Bob" Cummings! The former international reporter! He opened his arms and opened his mouth. These were the words that came out:

I am a monarch who owns all the world's wealth
Emeralds and opals and the roe of fine sturgeons

But the love of my life has departed by stealth
Hegai, my Chamberlain: bring forth the virgins!

Now the full orchestra took up the Dance of the Damsels, even as, their skins oiled with myrrh, and with flowers adorning their hair in the style of the famed Madam Lamour, fifty hot-blooded maidens twirled onto the ice.

High in the air I strained forward, the better to discern décolletage; strangely, as I did so my cushion tipped, too. Next I leaned sideways, in order to pick out the pretty profiles. What was this? My chair zipped to the side as well. Could such a thing be? Was my position in space dependent solely upon my will? Another experiment: I pitched forward and remained in that position. Down and down I plunged, to no more than a foot above the ice. The dancers whizzed and whirled about me, their gossamer gowns flying high enough to permit a view of the sirloin section.

Leib Goldkorn, my fine fellow, you are having a dream. Such was my notion. I threw back my head with delight and, sure enough, my magical carpet sent me soaring once more into the yonder. What do Americans, at the fulfillment of all wishes, say? That they have died and departed to heaven? But I was alive! Every blood vessel was brimming with blood. My nerves were sending one to another electrical sparks. In my body the bones were like an All Hollow's Eve skeleton doing a jig. My thoughts flew even faster than I did, back to the days when the evil Maltz led his companions to the loges of the k.k. Hof-Operntheater in order to spy upon the heaving of the mams below. But this was better! A winged balcony that would quick as J. Robinson transport me above bounding bosoms or beside the sportive hip thrusts, or all the way down to the calf tendons and ankle tendons and the slice and slash of the quicksilver blades. Such a thing had not been dreamed of even in the forward-looking writings of Mr. H. G. Wells.

To view all these concubines has become a bore
Each is the same, I cannot keep the score

It was Ahasuerus who sang those words I knew so well. I crouched forward, allowing my obedient genie to whisk me to where I could observe the king's face from merely a few feet away.

What do I see? Has my luck some
How changed? That lass is buxom!

I twisted about to view what had caught the king's eye. There, amidst the thin-shanked members of the corps de ballet, from whose flat chests the breasts hung like handkerchiefs from a pocket, one Miss alone possessed top-drawer mammilation. Indeed, beneath her filmy filigree two bosoms the size of human heads seemed to be in lively concourse each with the other. Again I zoomed closer, until the air about the whirling woman was filled with her zest. In the pits of her arms, moist mats of hair. In the flesh roll at the midriff, a dusky navel. On the chin, in the Swanson style, a dark mark of beauty. Red hair, red lips, pinkish gums. No wonder there now spread across the face of "Bob" Cummings a broad beaming smile. Even I, at the sight of her rump fruit, felt a detectable surge of the salty.

Cease, Musicians! You virgins, go hide
The great Ahasuerus has chosen his bride!

But hold! There now strode onto the ice a forceful figure. Mr. Ray Milland! This was the mighty Mordecai, who led by the hand a dainty darling, wrapped head to toe in flowing veils.

Stop, Sire! That woman is comely, of that there's no doubt
But I have brought you a maiden who I swear will best her;
She has beauty sans blemish—no hump, limp, or gout
Here is the daughter of Abihail, my cousin Esther!

On every side the chorines fell backward, leaving the veiled virgin alone on the ice. From my own flying throne I pointed a finger toward the woodwind section of the FSO. Immediately a solo flute began its rapid slide through a series of consecutive tones, up the scale, down and up once more, a glissando in the manner of Korsakov. With my left hand I pointed to the string section, where a violin took up the melody, *con tremolando*: an arabesque for these arabs. Now I nodded to the daughter of Israel, the first of whose veils at once fell away. Closer I came, and still closer. It was like looking at a fine lady through the other side of her dressing mirror: overcast eyes, elfin ears, and, yes, the nose shaped from cookery dough. Smile, please. Please, a little wider. *Danke schön*. So we begin the *Leitmotif*, the *Leibmotif*: Dance of the Seven Veils.

Here is a puzzle. The dance in conception was entirely chaste; this virgin was as cool and pure as the ice upon which she glided. All was modesty: she dared not even glance at the manly nipple points of the man who ruled *from India even unto Ethiopia*, end quotation. Nor did she invite, with split kicks and can-cans, attention to the infernal parts. Then why, this is the conundrum, were my own privateers in a state of carousal? The answer lay in my fingers. I had need only to wave one of these digits and an entire brass section filled with its tantaras all of the air. The percussion pounded at a sign from my pinkie. With but a slight crook—there! you see?—an entire harem, half a hundred human souls, spun into rapid motion, darting this way and that way, like fish in a school or molecules suspended within a vapor. Light, yes, and darkness I controlled with a finger snap. With my pointer I caused this one to speak, that one to be struck into muteness. Thumbs up, approval. Thumbs down, my wrath. All the world was to me as a puppet to a puppet master, or as a subject to a hypnotist, or the condemned man to the executioner with an axe. But I, a simple Jewish woodwinder, already well on his way to a state of baldness, needed no strings, no weapon, no swinging watch. Power! Power, friends! That is a stimulant stronger than the potions of Aphrodite. I had both the muscles of Hercules and—we dash up, we dip down, we loop the loop— Mercury's wings. No wonder that the gods, as even Professor Pergam had to confess, were filled with lustiness, spreading their seed not only to the other dwellers upon Olympus, but to mere mortals, and even birds, bulls, and beasts.

Sogar die Griechen hatten ihre Schweinereien. Yes, good professor: even the Greeks had their swinishness. What, then, prudish Pergam, of your former pupil? What of the naughtiness inside his pants? Up rose the bone in his herringbone. Up Donner, on Blitzen, as the folkish verse has it: and up I sailed, high as the steeple of St. Stephen's, from which vantage I could in safety watch the scene below.

Madam Henie had by then for a future world audience repeated almost the whole of her Olympic program, with all of its leaps, axels, and lutzes. Her veils lay behind her, billowing over the ice like a trail of exhaust. Bashful yet bold, the virgin tiptoed in her tutu toward where the king opened his arms to embrace her. Ray Milland, all asmile, waited to join them hand in hand. The crowd of contestants, excellent sports, took the flower petals from their hairdos and tossed them skyward—that is all contestants but one, Porasta, the aforementioned redhead: in real life played by the starlet Virginia Field, whom I had seen, along with Mr. Moscovitch, at the Kruger Kino in *Lancer Spy*. She stood to one side, plotting with that actor now. In short, we had reached the first act finale, also known as the Great Quintet.

Down I dropped, as fast as the express lift at the former S. Klein's, with the megaphone placed so as to conceal my mortification. I pointed first to "Bob" Cummings.

Ahasuerus:
>   *Could this be the queen who will share my throne*
>   *As pure, as frail as a dove?*
>   *Beside her my Vashti looks like a crone*
>   *Love! It is love!*

Next, Mr. Milland.

Mordecai:
>   *Sing praise to the Lord and kill lambs by the dozen*
>   *Now that the king for a queen has chosen my cousin*

Now the nod went to Madam Henie herself.

Esther:

> Am I worthy, one maid out of so many virgins
> To rule over the land of ten million Persians?

And on to Miss Virginia Field.

Porasta:

> Could it be? Is it so? Have I been bested
> By this stripling, blond-headed, and completely
>   flat-chested?

Fifth, Mr. Moscovitch, in his toothbrush moustache.

Haman (bass pizzicato):

> He wants someone new
>   O what a disaster
> He's chosen the Jew
>   Not my daughter, Porasta
>
> He can't defy me
>   I'll cause a disaster
> I'll get revenge
>   From our lord, Zoroaster
>
> The Jews will be killed
>   O what a disaster
> And I'll be fulfilled
>   The world's lord and master
>
> Ho! Ho! Ha! Ha! Ho! Ho!

Now the unsullied Sonja, standing directly before the king, fell back into her Olympic layaway. Suddenly the megaphone in my lap did a little jump, all on its own. What Moscovitch, his hair slicked over his forehead in Führer fashion, had predicted was already true. This was a disaster—and one that I, with my foolish, fumbling fingers had brought on myself. The zipper! The zipper, friends! The very one that, only a short time before, I had carefully closed was now, slowly, steadily, at the pace that a man will climb down a ladder, coming undone. The further Madam Henie leaned back the more exposed became her brisket. Yet no one said a word. The orchestra played. The dancers danced. The soloist continued her fateful twirl. But in my trousers the peppercorns were at the boil. Before anything could happen, we had, à la Donizetti, the reprise:

Ahasuerus: *Could this be the Queen who will share my*
     throne?
Mordecai: *Sing praise to the Lord and kill lambs by the*
     dozen
Esther: *Am I worthy, one maid out of so many virgins?*
Porasta: *Could it be? Is it so? Have I been bested?*
Haman: *It's a disaster, a disaster*
                         Etc., etc.: roundelay

Now Madam Henie went into her fabled Spin of Shiva. Heavens! With an audible rip the whole of her bodice from centrifugal force tore away. What could the poor actress do but spin even faster? There was, before our eyes, a blur of boobies, with more teats than were possessed by a Holstein. Here was, as Americans say, a sight for eyesores! A definite enticement! Off I sailed, higher and higher, pulling like an aviator upon what is known as the joystick. In my spermary I felt a disturbance of Vesuvian proportions. What was this heat? This shuddering? These pinpricks and needles? At that precise moment there came to my ears the one word a member of the alienist guild would say I most dreaded to hear: *Cut!* And it was repeated, *Cut! Cut, goddammit!* until at last it was echoed by Katz-Cummings:

"Cut!"

Through the open doors of our hanger Zanuck and his followers were coming at the trot. Once more the Fox King gave cry: "The lights! Kill those lights!"

"Lights off," ordered the incognito Cummings, and the bright bulbs, with a series of popping sounds, like a man stomping upon Dixie-brand cups, went out. The great room was now illuminated at a normal level.

"You!" shouted Zanuck, thrusting his mallet for polo in my

direction. "What the hell are you doing on that boom?"

I looked about me. The dream, it seemed, was over: the magic carpet was in fact a kind of crane, at the end of which both the camera and I were seated. "I, Excellency?"

"Yes, you! Who the hell are you?"

"Ha, ha! This is a royal jest. You know me well, Sire."

Sonja's voice rang out plaintively from the center of the ice. "This is the Maestro—is it not?"

"*Maestro?*" This was a different speaker, standing to the Fox King's right. "Schmaestro!"

Where had I seen this man before? With his padded suit and pencil moustache? Suddenly I knew. Paris! The Théâtre Égyptien! The box of honor! Jacques L. Warner! He turned to his fellow mogul. "That's not him, Darryl. I never saw this guy in my life."

"But I have a telegram! Visible proof! Look! Look, here. You had but to command, Highness, and I obeyed."

Zanuck: "Let me see that thing."

"With pleasure, O exalted one." So saying, I removed the precious paper from its leather pouch and sent it slipping and sliding over the heated currents of air, down to the floor of the sound stage. A minion plucked it up and brought it to the head of production. Pulling on his moustache, he perused it.

"It's true. I remember. I sent the telegram."

Now M. Warner turned upon me. "How did you get your hands on this?"

"Don't you remember? At the *Pasteur* premiere? It was delivered by Western Union."

"Yes, but not to you! Not you! It was meant for me!"

The person who shouted these words was not either of the movie monarchs but a third gentleman, short, hair-shy, and also familiar. Who was he? Where, from when, did I know him? He pointed to the wrinkled parchment in Zanuck's hands. "There. Look. It's there in black and white."

But the pharaoh of film was still staring upward to where I was perched. "All right, Mister. What's your name?"

"Goldkorn, Leib, Graduate of—"

Zanuck: "Goldkorn! Goldkorn! You idiot! We wanted *Korngold!* Are you blind? This telegram is addressed to Erich Korngold!"

What? The ten-year-old composer of *Der Schneemann,* the ballet-pantomime I had seen in my youth? Not to mention the Sinfonietta, which the prodigy had conducted at the Philharmonic as a mere teen. "Korngold?" I weakly replied.

"Yes, Korngold, you schmuck." That was Jacques Warner. "He did *Captain Blood* for us. He did *Green Pastures.* For *Anthony Adverse* he got the Academy Award!"

"Ah!" cried the hundred good folk gathered around us, like a chorus from Verdi. "Impostor!"

"But my name was called! '*Télégramme pour M. Goldkorn.*' I can still hear the words."

"One million dollars," screamed Zanuck, trembling with zealotry. "One million dollars because of a cross-eyed French Telegraph boy!"

"Get down from there," cried the composer of the Piano Trio in D, a work he had presented at the age of twelve.

Zanuck: "Lower that boom!"

Now the genie, no longer in my employ, took me rapidly down to the earth. "Ha, ha," I declared, rising from my leather cushion. "It's a misunderstanding."

Jacques Warner stepped forward. "Give me that!" Rudely he snatched away my megaphone.

Suddenly the air was rent by a horrible shriek. Madam Kane, my own *femme de chambre,* stood with her hands over her mouth. With wide, frightened eyes she stared over her fingertips to a spot—let us say it was below my belted waist but above my knocking knees.

"Ah!" cried once more the Verdi chorus: "Monster!"

There, with a will of its own, stood what in olden days had been hidden behind the silver stars. There was no concealment now. In all its peskiness it remained: my shame, my pride, my abomination.

4

AND HERE IT stands still, as raw and red as the face of an apoplexy victim. Thus shall it persist until the day of my demise, or until, like a ski patrol target, it bursts asunder. Ha! Ha! Bitter laughter.

Bulova watch time: *Mein Gott!* Fifteen minutes before the hour of one, *post meridiem!* Long past the appointment for Clara's injection. Up, up with my gabardines. Who would have thought it? Even the triple-sized trousers of V. V. Stutchkoff cannot in current conditions be brought to the waist. What to do? The precious moments of spousal life are afleeting. A last glance at Miss Crystal Knight. It was not, it seems, to be. From the pages of her gravure I make a kind of cradle, with which to conceal my wantonness; and then, with thoughts not of the past but the future, let us bid the frozen waters of my cabinetto *Auf Wiedersehen!* Good-bye! *Adieu!*

Not so fast. Bowser, the boxer type, has lurked beyond the door. With what buried memories—of bratwurst, perhaps, inside the doughy bun—does the brute leap for my manliness. Advanced years have brought on this judgment error. I laugh at his toothless gums, the feet with blunted claws. But the howls, the growls, are a different matter. Surely they will bring the family Fingerhut with threats of eviction. Think of it: to be thrown onto the Avenue Columbus, with only our Posturepedic, our Flamingo tumblers, and two thousand unopened books.

"Yoo-hoo! Mr. Goldkorns? Is you? You have finally finished your business?"

Madam Schnabel! And I, with my Stutchkoffs—and not just my Stutchkoffs, also S. Kleins—like horse hobbles at my ankles! Between me and the misdemeanor of nudity is only the tube of a magazine. With a shuffle, like a man walking through snowdrifts, I reach the stairway to the roof. Bowser makes a last leap upward, only to collapse in a saliva spray upon the bottommost step. Upward I ascend, dragging my garments behind.

130 W. 80th Street is not, between the Avenues Columbus and Amsterdam, the loftiest building. Far from it, friends. *Hausfrauen,* plumbing workers, bedridden patients, even children home from *Schule* for a repast of bread and bologna: any of these or a thousand other curious neighbors could through blinds or curtains gaze down upon the black tar paper with its white-skinned satyr. Even passengers hurtling high in the heavens might glance from their airships and think, *This is not, surely, the season for naturism.* Could it be

that at this very moment some person is with his finger dialing the digit Nine, the digit One and then One once more? What if, upon perusal of her morning paper, Miss Michiko should read that her favorite author—how she had praised his artistry, his ambition, his exuberance, too! Yes, what if she should read that her own Leib Goldkorn had been apprehended for attempting an exhibition? Better, at once, to hurl myself to the pavement. Yes! Perfection! To end the life of this sufferer upon the very date he was born. Happy Birthday to you!

But no. Here is the ladder, with its daggers of ice. Impossible even to think of a descent without double hand holds. Thus even this minimal modesty—I have seen similar pouches, upon Papuans, in the *National Geographic* pages—is cast to the November winds. A step down. Another. My pantaloons drag about me, now blowing upward, now dragging down, like an airman's collapsed parachute.

Arrival: the window of my humble home. It is a simple matter to push aside the iron gate and raise the glassy pane. *Voilà!* Here am I in the gloomy cave, with the stalactites—this is the word for mineral growths moving upward—of my autobiographical volumes meeting the stalagmites of these same memoirs drooping down. Even at midday, all is in shadows. Real life, thus spoke Plato, is in the sunlit world outside. Such is the murkiness in which Leib Goldkorn must spend his days: the Frigidaire's rattle; the blank Admiral's eye; the sink, whose drip I can no longer accompany with my paltry stream. Aha: the Posturepedic, upon which Clara has in near certitude breathed her last. *Was ist das?* The squeak-squeak of the bed springs? My wife is upsitting! Could it be that she has seen me? Not possible: her eyes are filled with cataracts, the way a salt cellar is filled with crystals of salt. Then why this welcome? With arms outspread, wig hair askew, and both zeppelins down to the waist zone. A big smile and—could it be? A wink, such as certain women will give to visiting sailors.

"Frankie! *Mein* Frankie! You are back from Miami! What have you brought your sweetheart? Coconut candy? A grapefruit basket? Oh, Frank: *Kom putzen inter mein kleiner knisher zein grosser gland putz!*"

Two phenomena of medical interest now occur at one and the same instant: Clara falls backward, makes in her throat the sound of a Listerine cleansing, and gives up, or so it seems to her yokemate, the ghost; and the entire length of my male member suddenly vanishes. So complete is this disappearance that for a moment of madness I actually search for it upon the floor. I grope, too, with my hands at the spot where it had last been seen: nothing, neither the stick nor the stones. It is as if Hegai, the keeper of King Ahasuerus's harem, had struck off my privates with a single blow of his scimitar.

What next for the eunuch? Inside the crisper of the Frigidaire is the needle for inoculation. Should I, after all, give the medicaments? Or call the MD., Goloshes? Or perhaps sit like Satan until the kidneys of Clara, if they have not done so already, flag, fizzle, fail? From her throat, there is now not the least suspiration. Is there a mirror? A looking glass? No, only one of the mismatched flamingos. On the surface of this vessel there is no breath cloud. *E morta!*, as they say at the end of Puccini. Could the insulin cocktail stimulate revival? Or could a call to the boys of the emergency service bring her back with breast thumps to life? Alas, our instrument because of default to the Bell Company has long since been disconnected. Should I breathe into her mouth and with such a kiss restore her to life? Like the Beauty who sleeps and the Prince who is charming? Ha! Ha! More bitter laughter. Thus, as the grains of sand run from the top of the hourglass to the hourglass's bottom, do I stand debating. Leib Goldkorn is not at all times a pleasant man.

Now, into the coils of this brain, there enters a wicked thought: our policy of insurance! With Metropolitan Life! One thousand American dollars, all premiums paid. I am rich! Rich, friends! There is enough to pay arrears to Fingerhut, *fils*; enough for a plate of Roumanian broilings; enough for the vacuum tubes of the Philco; yes, and perhaps even a pair of sharkskin trousers of my own. Above all, above everything, my Rudall & Rose! At last! Long last! I shall be able to claim it from the shelves of the brothers Glickman! Dear Randy! Trustworthy Ernest! Let there be music! Columbus and Amsterdam shall be filled with silver tones!

But where is that ticket for prawns? This was my clever plan: to secret it inside the pages of Miss Michiko's—*celebrates the redemptive powers of the imagination*—favorite memoir. But what pages? In which volume? The books lay in profusion about me, up to the ceiling, against all four of the walls. Did I put it at the top of a pile? No, that would be, to a bungling burglar, too obvious. In the middle, then. But of which of these towers? This one? That one? The one over there? Here, to hand, is a copy of the first, also the last, edition: nothing inside. Here is another: not a scrap. A third, fourth, and fifth. Emptiness, even after a thorough flipping and a vigorous shake. I stand on a chair and reach high overhead: paper aplenty, page after page, but no sign of the yellow-tinged slip from the Glickmans. Too clever, as the Englishman says, by a half. Leib Goldkorn! You have outsmarted yourself!

"Hello? Liebchen? Is you?"

Clara! The spouse! A breather! Yes: with red roses in her cheeks! How to explain it? No, not the miracle of the resuscitation—how to explain this joyous leaping inside my heart?

"Yes, honey, here is the birthday boy."

On the lips, a smile; in the eye, a definite twinkling. "Maybe you have for me a Campbell's chowder?"

A small thing to do: open a can, add to it water, bring to a simmer over the blue flame of the Magic Chef stove. Hold the spoon. Hold the napkin. Afterward, plump the pillow. Welcome, Madam Goldkorn, to the land of the living.

Return, now, to my more difficult task. On the floor, underfoot, are the scattered volumes of *Goldkorn Tales*. Here's one, upside down, like a little fairy house: *Good evening, my name is L. Goldkorn and my specialty is woodwind instruments, with emphasis on the flute.* Excellent prose. And a snappy beginning. Let us read on. First we have adventures at the Steinway Restaurant, including the death of V. V. Stutchkoff. Next, danger to the Jews. Then emotions toward the Widow Stutchkoff, Christian name, so to speak, Hildegard. A blond beauty when in her chipper years. Concert by the Steinway Quintet of the "Indian Love Call." This was music making such as could not be heard on WQXR.

The light fades from our windowpane. But this is not a book that a reader can put down. Soon I lose myself in my own adventures— saving Madam Stutchkoff, in the drama *Othello*, from the grasp of the dusky Moor; saving her once again from the clutches of my old adversary, Hans Maltz, when he attempted to take over the Steinway Restaurant. Difficult, as dusk befalls us, to make out on the pages the printed words. But I need no book to recall how this same Hildegard welcomed me at her own private apartment. What was her greeting? *Door's open, dear!* Oh, the candlelight upon the curls of her hair! The removal of her sleeping gown. Ach! Ach! At these thoughts my Jewish-style member makes, from its abdominal refuge, an appearance. Hello, traveler: long time no see! How happily I cantered among the widow's flesh folds. With, upon her Sealy-brand mattress, many teeth nips and finger pinches. I am able with honesty to say that on that occasion there was achieved a near penetration.

Let us turn to the final page of *Goldkorn Tales.* On the banks of the Hudson I played with my flute, my Rudall & Rose, sweet instrument of youth restored. The magic melodies. Would that I could play now for Miss Michiko, as she sits reading and typing, typing and reading, a Finnish rhapsody. And what of a tune for the sleeping Clara? And for Madam Schnabel as she exercises her contralto chords. Yes, and for Miss Crystal Knight, so that, in the depths of her dungeon, she might have a moment of hope. And Madam Henie? The Pavlova of Ice? Too late! She died in the same year as many other outstanding leaders: D. D. Eisenhower, liberator of Europe; J. L. Lewis, hero of the workingman; also B. Karloff, J. Garland, R. Taylor, her colleagues in the world of cinema. But we must not in our sadness forget that in that same 1969 human beings landed upon the moon. Perhaps Miss Sonja, with all the other great artists, such as the composers Mendelssohn and Meyerbeer and also Herr Korngold, *e morto* in his prime: perhaps she sits now on that satellite, whose surface some say, surely in jest, is made from cheese—or perhaps on Mars, half-covered with ice. There she can dance, blades flashing, and look out through the vast reaches of space to where we, her faithful fans, endure year after year upon the green and blue ball of the earth.

Fire

Cast of Characters

In addition to many of those in ICE,

IN NEW YORK CITY
Michiko Kakutani, book critic, *New York Times*
R. Bernstein, her assistant
Clara Goldkorn (see cast of ICE)
Pepi Pechler (see cast of ICE), also L. Goldkorn's best man
A Hindoo, vendor of newspapers and sweets
General de Gaulle, French patriot
MP, a young member of the Military Polizei
Anon., a large gentleman in telephone booth

ON THE BELL TELEPHONE
Miss Trixie, loves Ravel's *Bolero*
Miss Corky, enjoys taking baths
Miss Bitch, teaches lessons
Miss Crystal Knight (see cast of ICE), also a hater of men

ABOARD THE *AMAZONAS*
Miss Carmen Miranda, Brazilian Bombshell
The Rhythm Boys of Brazil: Tono, Bernardo, Felipe, the bearded one
A. Toscanini, Italian conductor
R. Shaw, chorus master
J. Bjoerling, tenor (Radames)
Z. Milanov, soprano (Aïda)
Hans Maltz (see cast of ICE), also German secret agent
Herr Schwartz (see Hans Maltz)
G. Vargas, *Presidente* of Brazil

Others: Court of Palms staff, Lloyd Brasileiro personnel, Vargas entourage,
musicians, singers, elephants, etc.

1

Leib Goldkorn
180 W. 80th Street 5-D
New York, NY 10024
August 15, 1997

Miss Michiko Kakutani
The *New York Times*
Times Square
New York, N.Y.

My dear Madam Kakutani,
Greetings from L. Goldkorn, Graduate, Akademie für Musik, Philosophie, und darstellende Kunst. It has been now twelve long years since your insightful critique of *Goldkorn Tales*, my memorial volume, in the *New York Times*. *Artistry*, end quotation. *Ambition*, end quotation. *Commodious talent* and *humanity*, these are quotations, too. Thank you, once again, for these generous words. The unfortunate truth is that, in spite of such praises, and a spicy portrait upon the cover, this work was a non-starter. Yet I have not for this time span been able to forget the person who saw with such clear-sightedness into the author's heart. Thus I shall come at once to business: may I invite for a second time (perhaps you did not receive from the postal service my letter of 1985) my Laplandic lass for a lunch?

Fear not! Do not misapprehend. It is my pleasure to inform you that I have been for fifty-five years a happily married man. Ha! Ha! Did you think I intended a proposition? An adventure? *Pas du tout!* A tea, yes, also a crustless sandwich, followed by a depth-discussion of music and literature, such as the thematics in the excellent O. Henry and G. D. Maupassant. A meeting of souls, *ja*? As described in the texts of Plato.

A happily married man. This is relative. Sometimes, in carefree moments, for example during a Riverside Drive promenade, I have slipped my hand about the flesh folds of Frau Goldkorn's waist. Once—this was in the years of D. D. Eisenhower, liberator of Europe; to be exact, April 1958—my lifetime companion requested that I blow upon the crimson polish she had applied to her toes. On my knees, like a Musselman, I did it. Then off, off ran my helpmeet, to discuss with Mr. Frank Fingerhut, the *père* not the *fils*, the non-payment of our monthly rent. On another occasion some force, a breeze or breezlet perhaps, caused me to wake: there, in the moonlit window, sat my yokemate, applying a hand massage to her breast fruits and pressing, between her sirloins, the Ivory soap dish. Like ivory the bulge of her throat, the slope of her shoulder, the swell of the abdominal zone. I had, at the gleam of a garter trolley, a paroxysm. And now? Clara now? Even though it is three-fifteen, Bulova watch time, on this summer afternoon, there she lies asnoring. Sans hair, as the poet says, sans teeth, sans sense: sans all! Oh, Miss Michiko! Loneliness!

And how, Madam, are you? In good health? Eating the calcium-rich sardines? Are you in amazement that I can remember each word of your excellent review? Harken, Kakutani, to this: The capital of Alabama is Montgomery. Highest point: Cheaha Mountain, 2,407 American feet. State flower: Camellia. Cotton, livestock, peanuts, hogs. The capital of Arizona is Phoenix. Highest point: Humphreys Peak, 12,633 feet. State flower: Cactus Blossom. Fruit, alfalfas, beef cattle. These are the memory gymnastics with which I keep myself in fettle. To ward off the disease that Dr. Goloshes calls "Uncle Al." And the capital, Miss Michiko, of Finland? Is it not Helsinki? Do we not find in the frozen northland rye oats, peat products, and excellent herring? I have always had a spot of softness for what Americans call platinum blondes. Gentlemen prefer them, too!

Where, then, shall we have our tête-à-tête? I am proposing the Court of Palms, the Hotel Plaza. This is at the corner of 59th Street and the famed Fifth Avenue, opposite the statue of Napoleon upon his horse. A pleasant tropical oasis in the heart of the busy city. Cooling drinks. Atmosphere suave. It was at this establishment that Mr. and Mrs. Goldkorn consumed at their wedding feast the Grand Carousel of confections. That was a mere sixteen days after our meeting and sudden ecstatics at the Tivoli Jewish Art Theater. Romance in a whirlwind. Conception of our still-born Martha. Love, Madam, at first sight.

The Plaza: our arrival by taxi. A white gown, with white gloves: this was the former Miss Litwack's attire. The groom wore what is called a suit for monkeys. Best man: Pepi Pechler, also an Akademie Graduate, and owner of the T.J.A. Theater. Those were the dark days of the Second World War. Literally dark: over the glass panes of the hotel stretched black linens, lest the least chink reveal to the lurking U-boats the blaze of happiness that burned in Leib Goldkorn's heart. Then away! Away to the ritual breaking of the hymen at the snow and ski lodge in Syracuse, New York. Honeymoon. Alas, there was not at that season any snow. Also, poor Clara here began the series of head pains that were the first signs of the dropsy to come. Still—*ach*, Miss Michiko, I have for some reason snapped here my Scripto pencil: still, we enjoyed the calm company each of the other and the sight of the squirrels and chipmunks busily hiding away their winter nuts.

Let us meet on the last day of August, the 31st, at 3, *post meridiem*. This is the time at the Court of Palms for cuplets of tea. Once more, like a gypsy, I read your thoughts: *How will I recognize this prize-winning Graduate?* Answer: by the photograph which with this clip for paper I now attach. True, true: it is not recent. In fact, it was taken aboard a mighty steamship in the fateful year 1941. That is L. Goldkorn, dressed in herringbones. A five footer five. Woodwinder's lips. Ears—ha! ha! ha!—that resemble those of the young elephant just then a hit on the screen. *Dumbo!* Do you recognize the lady with whom I am "arm in arm"? Who coyly kisses my cheek? Your task will be easier if you note, upon her head, the tangerines and seedless grapes. Another clue: those dark-skinned gentleman who cavort to either side. The famed Rhythm Boys of Brazil. Miss Michiko, meet Madam

Miranda! Confession: I am not near our century's end any taller. Thick lips, still. Definitely hairless. And the style of my haberdashery now consists of large-sized gabardines. To prevent any possible error I shall sport, in the buttonhole of my lumberman-type jacket, a sprig of—what is your favorite? Gardenia? Carnation? Forget-me-not!

Will we establish, at our rendezvous, a rapport? Will we become intimate chums? Only time, as they say, will tell. As summer turns to autumn with its falling leaves, and then winter comes with its mackinaws and ginger snaps, our friendship may ripen. There is no need to restrict our intercourse to dry and dusty books. What young man, bursting with vigor, reads these days Washington Irving or Anatole France? My expertise is on woodwinds. The day may come when, reaching about the torso, I might instruct you upon the fingering of the flute. Is it not the case that in the Finnish sauna cold water is thrown upon the red hot rocks? And that the saunaists are beaten on the back and the loin sector with twigs of thorns? Perhaps you can make upon my own shoulders—these are hirsute, like the woolly ancestors of friend Dumbo that are sometimes discovered beneath the Finlandic ice—a demonstration. Yes, you can beat me! Beat me! I will not cry out. I will not beg for mercy. Like the lusty Lemminkäinen, hero of the *Kalevala*, folkish epic of your people, the devoted Leib will bear with stiff lip his fate.

Sixteen days! Sixteen days, Miss! Thus must wait, turning the calendar pages, the *triste* Leib for his tryst.

Sincerely yours,
L. Goldkorn, Graduate
A.f.M.P.u.d.K.

*T*EA FOR TWO, *two for the tea*
A fine summer day. Too torrid, perhaps, for my red and black plaid. One hundred percent sheep's wool. But the high standards of the Court of Palms demand of its patrons jacket, Arrow-brand shirt, and tie. The latter finery, souvenir of Miami, I obtained in the same manner as my panama hat. Both were left oblivious by Father Fingerhut as he performed acrobatics upon our Posturepedic.
A me for you, a you for me

On the outside of my Thom McAns, a shoeshine; heel lifts within. Nose nicks and chin nicks from the Gillette brand. Look sharp, haha! Feel sharp! Under each armpit, a bay rum sponge. Final perusal: Finnish phrase book. Check. Senior citizen underground pass, with transfer. Check. One cylinder, Life Saver-brand pastilles, multiflavors. Check. Foil-wrapped sanitary, watchdog against disease. Check. This Trojan type was found by the wronged party when prying open by force Frank Fingerhut's tightened fist. After his seizure of heart. Long odds, undeniably, not even the chance of a Chinaman; but is not the motto of the scouting movement, Sir R. Baden-Powell founder, *be prepared?*

No personage near us to see or to hear us

"Mr. Goldkorns! Why are you whistling? Why cheerful and chipper?"

Can this be? It is less than one hour since I administered the noontime injection, after which it is this *Hausfrau*'s habit to fall deep in the arms of Morpheus, awakening only at the evening prospect of mushroom cream. Clairvoyant Clara! To sense my guilty secret!

"Whistlings? What whistlings? Perhaps, you know, a few bars of 'Hatikvah.' "

"What are you doing with the Admiral? Help! He's taking the television to the brothers Glickman!"

"No, no. Calm yourself, Madam Goldkorn. I would never remove this appliance to the shop for prawns."

What an amazement! Shadows, wisps, illusions—that is all, with her cataract-clouded eyes, that Clara can see. Still, she notes my presence at the back of the Admiral, an instrument that has been blank from the moment that N. Armstrong, a non-Jew, walked in haziness upon the surface of the moon. 20 July. *Anno domini*, 1969. Exhaustion of the vacuums. Still, like drowning victims who cry out from within the wreckage of their sunken vessel, or tap-tap-tap upon its iron hull, voices emerge yet from the wood-style veneer. To these ghosts—one can barely discern whether they lisp in English or some foreign tongue—the comatose Clara likes to cock an ear. To while away interminable hours! Interminable years!

"Mr. Goldkorns, I am not hearing Merv Griffin."

"Wait. We have now warm-ups." Indeed, I have turned on the instrument, but not before first leaning behind it to extract the remains of this year's savings—nine fives, with the image of A. Lincoln, who set free the slaves, and two George Washington ones. Forty-seven dollars. Not counting the expense of florals, which I now remove from the Frigidaire.

No friendly relations to make us vacations

"Flowers? Why flowers? And why in such hot weather a lumber jacket?"

We won't have it known, honey—

"Stop, sir, this singing! And what is that odor? Bay rums! I am smelling bay rums!"

That we own a Bell telephone

"What is this funny business?"

Day will break and you will wake in order to bake da-dee-dum-dee *ein Honigkuchen!*

"Help! Police! Is hanky-pankies!"

For me to take for all the goys to see!

"Where are you going? Out windows? Forsaking! *Der mann far-lost zayn weib!*"

We will raise a family, a boy for you, a girl—Ah, Martha! Little Martha!—*for me*

"*Der shmutziker mamser!* Frankie! Pepi! Milton! *Vey ist mein emes liebchens!*"

I'm going to have tea for two, dee dindle dum, dum dindle dee, *and two are arriving for tea!*

From the circle of Columbus to the Monument of Napoleon we have but a brief perambulation—a stroll among, upon the right hand, the toot-tooting taxis, the eager Knickerbockers all helter and skelter; and, upon the left, the ladies with borzois, the lasses and lads with their wooden hoops. And here, all golden, is the statue of Bonaparte, a gift of the children of France. With awe I stare up at the conqueror not only of continents, Italy and Egypt and the Holy Roman Empire, but of Josephine and Marie Louise, heir to a mighty throne. With his outstretched hand he points me, a fellow five-fiver, across the crowded thoroughfare to the entrance of the Hotel Plaza. There smart liverymen stand at attention. Sunshine gleams in the window glass. Atop the green-stained turrets wave the stars and stripes—fifty of the former; do you know how many of the latter? Thirteen! One for each of the original colonies, of which the first to ratify the Constitution was wee Delaware: one of only four states whose capital begins with the identical alphabetical letter. Chemicals, petroleum, broiling chickens. Dover. So, even in this moment of doubt, of qualms, all mental functions remain intact. No sign of Uncle Al.

Doubt? Qualms? Can Leib Goldkorn be suffering, in the vernacular, cold toes? As if he were some youngling who has never eaten wild oats? Or experienced a fertilization? Think of the motto of the Artilleryman of Austerlitz. Was it not *l'attaque! L'attaque! Toujours l'attaque!*? I must copy the Corsican: forward! Across the boulevard, you *boulevardier!* Yet much as I try to lift them, these McAns remain stuck to the heated pavement. Beware, Leib Goldkorn! You are heading toward a Waterloo. Imagine what Madam Kakutani will see, as she gazes across the Court of Palms table. A Bonaparte? A Beau Brummel? Not precisely. A hairless old Jew, one who must make water eight times in the night. Size of gabardines: 44. It is not too late. Retreat! Sound the retreat! I might still return to hearth, home, and *Hausfrau.*

No! Never! No, no! There now arises in the eye of the mind the Late City Final Edition. 3 April. 1985. Ah, the smell of the newsprint. The rustle of crisp pages. And what do I see? Section C, page 24, column 3. Here, all afresh, are the words that Miss Michiko used to describe the present speaker: *A person of some culture and sensitivity.* End quotation. Ah! Wise woman! She knows I have been a *Glockenspieler* for both das kaiserliche und königliche Hof-Operntheater and the Orchester der Wiener Staatsoper, as well as a former subscriber, *New York Herald Tribune. Hyvää päivää, rouva.* This is "Good afternoon, Madame," in the Finnish tongue. A heel click, a hand kiss, a bow. *Hauska tutustua.* "A pleasure to make your acquaintance." Away, abdominal butterflies! Bulova watch time: 3:07. Our imp is becoming impatient.

Everything at the Court of Palms is as it was upon my nuptial night. The tables with tablecloths and the chairs with wicker woven into the backs. The band platform with piano and double bass. Here are the smoothly gliding waiters with napkins over their arms. And at the center, just as during the dark days of war, is the display of éclairs, petit-fours, and the fingers of ladies. I can see those same candy-coated almonds, pale pink, Easter yellow, a grassy green, which—there, at that corner table, where three dames now eat their fritters—the best man, Pepi Pechler, and my bountiful bride would exchange from lip to lip, and from mouth to waiting mouth.

"May I help you?"

The speaker: a woman of heft, dark-haired, in my judgment a cup number C.

"I am wearing a tie from Miami. Also a surcoat. You see before you a citizen since the year 1943. I request, therefore, a table: a table, you know; you know the kind I mean—"

"I'm sorry. What kind of table?"

Across my cheekbones spreads the strawberry flush, up and over my brow. This awkward moment is reminiscent of the time that, suffering a stoppage, I was examined by a Goloshes, M.D., assistant. A woman of gender. Shirtless before her. Also undershirtless. With pantswaist at the ankles. My voice drops to a whisper: "For two."

I am led to a spot at the back of the Court, next to the wall of mirrors. I place my lumberman, with the souvenir photo inside the pocket, on the back of my chair, and sit down. To one side, the musical bandstand, at the moment absent of musicians. To the other, one of the palms-in-pots that have given this room its name. A *prima* location. The Court itself is perhaps one-half full, with a yield of some thirty or thirty-five women and perhaps one dozen men. More guests walk the hallways on the far side of the transparent partition. But where is Miss Michiko? Spread before me are coiffeurs in profusion: redheads and brunettoes, locks in gray and curls in black. There is the twin who has the Toni and there a peruke in pink. Yes, I can see the false goldilocks, which have from a bottle been bleached. But nowhere, in this sea of tresses, is there a Baltic Sea blonde.

Now comes forth a waiter, a sophisticate with a waxed-type moustache. "Would the gentleman care to order?"

I hand wave the menu away. "Grand Carousel," I say. "Tutti-fruttis for two."

Impossible to disguise, in that attendant's eyes, the look of amazement. For this Pechler favorite costs, if I am remembering correctly, three twenty-five.

Three twenty-five! Little hand on three! Big hand on five! Almost a half-hour late! An unthinkable thought: what if the coquette has already arrived and, not seeing the dawdler, departed? Could such a thing be? No, no: for would I not have seen her going out as I, but a brief moment tardy, came in? Then where is she? In this cosmopolitan Court there are all manners and races of people: Jews and non-Jews, an *Afrikaner*, Malayan traders, whispering Arabians, and even, with short black hair and her face pressed to the partition glass, a tea-colored Nipponese. But nowhere, in all this motley, is my far-flung Finn.

Saanko suudella kättäsi, rouva? This, on page nine of my phrasebook, means, "May I kiss your hand, Madame?" An excellent way to break apart the ice. Ah, here comes the Carousel of confitures. Also a pipkin of Lipton-brand tea. Should I have, whiling the time, a jelly? Perhaps a frozen pudding? What's that: a pandowdy? Leib Goldkorn, what are you thinking? If I partake now, and the Kakutani should spy a missing maraschino or half-eaten ingesta, might she not take offense?

What is that sound? Piano chords? Yes, and a pianist. His bent back, and his hair pony, are toward me; the reflection of his face and hand knuckles may be seen on the waxed surface of this Bösendorfer-brand grand. Accompaniment? A near-hairless bassist. Trills. Tremolants. Tremolos. Then music hall tunes. F-sharp, f-flat, c-sharp. "Some Enchanted Evening."

Have I the daring to seek out once more the time on the Bulova? Gift from D. F. Zanuck. Souvenir of a half-century past. Princely salary. Dinner upon the Santa Monica Pier. A French maid in stockings. Three forty-one, and the seconds hand circling, endlessly circling, 3:42, 3:43, like a prisoner in a prison yard. It must be admitted that something has gone amiss. Is it possible that my admirer is not going to come? Have I mistaken the time of the assignation? The agreed-upon date? Horrors! Is August a month in which one may not eat oysters? *Thirty days hath September*— With fumbling fingers I fish forth the folio of Finnish phrases. Alas! The vellum I seek is no longer inside. Ah, there it is, atop the caramel clusters. On the instant I unfold the creases of the sweet billet-doux:

August 22, 1997

From the desk of Michiko Kakutani
The *New York Times*

Mr. Leib Goldkorn
130 W. 80th Street Apt 5-D
New York, NY 10024

Dear Mr. Goldkorn:
Ms. Kakutani has asked me to inform you that she
will meet you at the Palm Court of the Plaza Hotel
at 3 PM on August 31st.

Yours truly,
R. Bernstein
Assistant to Ms. Kakutani

Speak for yourself, Miles Standish ha, ha, ha! Thus said the Indian
maiden to John Smith when he attempted to propose on behalf of
his friend. Surely it is significant that Miss Michiko similarly uses an
amanuensis when enscribing this note of romance. Too bashful to
reveal your heart, my little Pocahontas? Must you speak through a
lackey? *Yours truly,* note you that? Can that be the emotion of a
stranger? An anonymous pusher of pen? Never! No, never! *Ach!*
Each time I see these words, *Yours truly, truly yours,* I record degrees
of warming within my S. Kleins. *3 PM.* Thus writes the Pilgrim of my
heart. *August 31st.* There has been no error. Ah, coquette! Why such
coyness? Do not hide behind others. Play not peek-a-boo in back of
a palm pot. Show yourself!

Missä rautatieasema on? "Where is the train station, please?" No,
no: mistaken page.

Onniteluni, rouva, charmikkaasta ja ilahduttavasta hatustasi.
"My compliments, Madame, upon your charming and delightful
hat." With such urbanity one thaws the cool Nordic heart. Even the
strictest rabbi, surely, would permit the sampling of a small goose-
berry tart. *Voilà!* Excellent crusts. But thirst-provoking. This tea is
now like the cucumber. "Waiter! If you please! A schnapps!"

"Of what sort, sir?"

"Plum. You know, plum brandy. And will you have the kindness to—this will be our little secret, ha-ha—leave the bottle."

"But of course. It will just take a moment to cross to the Oak Room Bar."

And no sooner has my servant departed than there—there, *Across a crowded room,* ha-ha-ha!—I see her, precisely as, for these many long years, I have imagined her: tall, firm of flesh, twin-bosomed, with golden curls falling like coin stacks to her shoulders. Ah, if that Lapp would come to my lap! I glance at my Bulova. Exactly four, *post meridiem.* Of course! *Spring back! Fall forward!* I have failed to adjust for summer savings! It was now, by her watch, and all the millions of clocks in our eastern zone, exactly 3:00 P.M.! Mystery solved! Oh, my eager Aryan! A Joannie on the spot! With joyfulness I jump to my feet.

"Miss! Oh, Miss!"

That cry fills the whole of the Court and causes even the electrified candles to flicker. The Nordic stands in her tracks. In a daze of delight, with, in my nether parts, a definite peppercorn feeling, I dart between the tables to her side. Then she turns and casts her pale eyes and the dark pinpricks of her pupils upon me.

"Kakutani!" I cry. "Let us have a coition!"

I shall make a tall story shorter. Mistaken identity. Mild indiscretion. Understandable error. Why, then, especially after hearing my explanation that I have taken the wrong pig by the tail, does she create such a stigma? Or strike with one's weighty purse, and on the noggin, a nonagenarian? Or send flying, for a *faux pas,* his Panama hat? This is an overreaction, in my opinion. Luckily, the pianist, and the bassist too, break into a lively melody, "Oklahoma"—Sooner State, mining interests, natural gas—in order to distract the teatime guests from the hullabaloo. At my table slivovitz awaits. Thoughtfully uncorked. Chin-chin! And still, in the parts of propagation, the bonfire burns. Skoal! To my Norse nymph! On and on the seconds hand goes tick-ticking by. Is it my imagination, or is the boulevard without falling into shade, into shadow? Cheers, friends! Down to the hatch! What is that rustling? Over my head, a ventilation is passing through the leaves of the palm. Such a soft sound. A sighing. What is called, in onomatopoeiatics, a susurration. Mud in your eye!

The palm: prince of the vegetable kingdom. Many a day I would stare upward at the mighty trunks and leafy fronds that towered high above the Muscle and Malibu beaches, just as I used to do as a boy, in expectation of a glimpse of Madam Lamour. That was at the Kruger Kino, city of Vienna, where the sight of that female Tarzan, in teasing sarong, would ofttimes in the viewer produce a stiffy.

In California, in the winter of '38–'39, there were no such thoughts of romance. I was hungry, I was homeless, I was heartbroken and Henie-less, too. No studio would employ a man whom Zanuck, the Fox King, had made a blackball. Even worse, none would consider making my *Esther: A Jewish Girl at the Persian Court* into a motion picture. Remember: Herr Hitler had invaded the Sudetenland. He had seized Bohemia, Moravia, Slovakia, Memel. Next, the arch-Aryan renounced his peace pact with Poland and, with Merry England, his naval agreement. A child could read the hand script upon the wall. And what did Mr. Cohn, Mr. Zukor, Mr. Mayer, Jacques Warner et Frères produce for the heedless masses? A film in which a man stuffed with straw dances with a man made of metal. "Beer Barrel Polka," so sang the millions, instead of Mordecai's c-sharp lament. Carefree! Oblivious! Wearing the nylon stockings! Fools! Fools! Applauding M. Rooney when L. Goldkorn, penniless, without even his panpipe, was forced to lead the vagabond life.

In brief, I tramped the seashore in search of the bounty of the deep. Astounding the items that are washed up on the Malibu sands, from A for Armadillo, shell of, to Z for Zeppelin, twelve-inch model, a trinket for a child. These, of course, were non-utilities; other parts of this alpha-beta, however, played a more important part in my story. I speak of *B* for *Boater*, a type of straw hat; *G* for *Grunions*, the little silver-sided darlings that one may eat, head, tail, digestives, and all; *H* for *Hairpiece*, see under *T* for *Toupee*; *R* for *Revolver*; even *X* for *Xavier Cugat*, photo portrait of, with inscription: *"por Carmen, mia compañera."* Nor must I omit the *P* for *Perambulator*, in which I mobilized the whole of my treasure.

Thus day after day, season after season, yes, year after year, I wheeled this hoard along the sandy shore. If only my fellow Academicians, schoolmates of yore, could have seen the hardy outdoorsman. Skin: tanned to the color of a bean for coffee. Scalp fringe: ringlets in the style of Victor Mature. Arms, legs, the zone of the torso: abulge with biceps. Upon the Muscle Beach I would sometimes astound the enthusiasts by lifting—*Hoop-la!*—the whole of my Perambulator, with all its heaping contents, including a Goodrich-brand tire, into the air. In short, the one-hundred-pound weakling, into whose face the whole world had so oft kicked the sand, had become an All-American Boy.

Alas, it was only upon the surface that I appeared the C. Atlas. Inside, Leib Goldkorn had no more bones than the jellied fish that washed upon the shore. I had not, in my peregrinations, ignored world events. Each day the sunbathers would leave behind portions of their *Times*, their *Examiners*. Through the open windows of seaside villas I heard the broadcasts upon Stromberg-Carlsons. Woe! Suffering! Sorrow! In September 1939 came the invasion of Poland. 1940 was darker still. Herr Hitler had one success after another. Norway and Denmark invaded. Luxembourg defeated and brave Belgium, too. The Dutch? Another domino. Then, in the month of May, at Dunkirk, the British were driven from the Continent.

June was the darkest of all. The beachcomber had been strolling along, listening to "You Are My Sunshine," Andrews Sisters rendition, upon some invisible Philco, when there came of a sudden the following announcement:

The War Department has just announced that the German Army has marched into Paris. The French armed forces have ceased all opposition. The Cabinet has made a formal offer of surrender. Meanwhile tens of thousands of civilians continue to flee from the capital to the south. We now switch you to London, where dawn is just breaking. The next voice you hear will be that of the leader of the Free French, General Charles de Gaulle.

"Mesdames et Messieurs! Citoyens de la France! Les amis de la nation française dans tout le monde entier! Tout les hommes qui respirent l'air libre. Ecoutez à mon appel."

In a daze, stricken, I wandered oblivious until I fell in exhaustion upon the Malibu Beach. Midnight the hour. Overhead, the moon, upon whose surface those in Iglau claimed to see the face of Franz Joseph. Also a thousand twinkling stars. Not, in brief, a wisp of cloud. But to the trained eye, the practiced ear, it was obvious that somewhere in the Zone of the Tropics a storm had recently raged. With what thunder did the waves throw themselves upon the beach. Half in exhaustion, half in a fury that their long journey was done. High flew the sea spray! Almost to the circles of caw-cawing gulls. Onward, upward crept the tide, until the breaking waves gnawed, with their flashing, foaming teeth, at the lone figure of the Graduate upon the sand.

What did it matter? Let the devourers come! France had fallen! Fair France, my second homeland, my refuge, the hope of all mankind for 150 years. It was from that great nation that Napoleon had set forth to free all of Europe's Jews. Now that same land was under the heel of their oppressor. The horrible Hun! Only one man, the brave General de Gaulle, dared fight on. How could such a thing happen? How could it be borne? Thus sat I, staring at the angry ocean, just as, in a similar moment of despair, I had felt myself drawn to the swirling Seine. Only this time my task was easier. I was not required by an effort of will to plunge into the dark, deep waters; now those waters were rising to overtake me.

It was at just that moment that a twinkling, a winkling, no more than a firefly's flash, caught my eye. There! Again! Something was aglimmer within the green and black tumult of the waves. Up, up, Leib Goldkorn: now down in your Wellingtons to the edge of the non-Pacific. Yes, there was indeed something atumble there, something shining, something silver. I watched with weather eye. Left, right, now on the rise, now hurled to the depths, this mysterious object was twirling and whirling like one of Miss Candy Kane's cheerful batons. Madam Kane! No sooner had I conjured her name than, like a honeymoon husband, I began to yank off my boots, rip asunder my shirt sleeves, and remove both lower limbs from my herringbone pants. Then, with forefinger and thumb forming a nose clasp, the non-swimmer dashed into the hubbub of the sea.

What a tempest! With a surf slap my legs went from under me. My head was beneath my heels. I tossed every which way among the white caps, like a sock that is agitated amidst a front-loader's suds. No sooner had I opened my mouth to cry for assistance than the seawater went foaming and frothing like a bock-type beer to the very depths of my gullet. The paw of a bear, such was the sensation, struck me a blow on the ear. Down I went. The weeds of the sea wrapped like winding clothes about me. Then, at that desperate moment, through the stinging salt and blinding billows, I saw the glint of metal, the spark of silver, like the blink and reblink of a friendly lighthouse lamp. Up I rose. "*Gott! Gott!*" I shouted, before a fresh breaker fell upon me like a Niagara and sent me sinking again. Now the tide had me, dragging me downward, as if the eight arms of an octopus were pulling me to its lair. Once more I glimpsed the winking light, spinning on the surface like a rescue ship's propeller. Up I soared, with water shooting from every orifice, in the manner of the fountains of urination at the Schönbrunn gardens.

The third time down, I knew, was the last time. Yet down I went. No hope in struggle. Why thrash one's limbs? An odd peaceability overcame me. Death? What was it? Only sleep. And into a sleep I descended—one filled with dreams of childhood walks along the Iglawa, the whistle of the *Leopold II*, the answering call of the tree-bound birds, concerto for steamboat and swallows, with sunshine accompaniment—until the sea surf cast me, like a piece of my own flotsam, upon the solid strand. C for Corpse? I opened my eyes. There, standing on end, was the thin shining reed. How, in the moonlight, it glowed. A bar of pure silver.

Joy, warm and sweet, like a syrup for waffles, filled my heart. I knew what this was. A flute! And not just a flute. No, no; no, no. Was this not the very instrument with which I had hoped to bribe the Second-Place Finisher to send my family to safety upon the Danube? Had that malicious Maltz not dropped it into the very waters upon which the Goldkorns had steamed to Dachau? Let us ponder. The Danube flows to the Black Sea; the Black Sea is, at the Bosporus, joined to the Aegean; the Aegean to the Mediterranean; that ocean, by the Suez Canal, the Frenchman de Lesseps founder, is connected to the Red Sea; the Red Sea debouches to the Gulf of Aden; the latter is a component of the Indian Ocean; the Indian Ocean merges with Timor, Coral, and Tasmanian seas to become the great Pacific, which, after crossing the International Date Line, thus causing a Thursday, let us say, to become a Wednesday, at last expires here—here upon the Malibu shore. What a long journey! Filled with adventures! Thus was restored to me my Rudall & Rose.

I seized the shining shaft. I glanced at my watertight Bulova. Five minutes past two, *ante meridiem*. Then, just as I was, clad only in my wet May Co. drawers, I dashed up the beach to the nearest villa. It loomed, on its stilts, above me. The lights were out. Inhabitants in the land of nod. Now, as Professor Lajpunger had often instructed, I expanded the diaphragm and filled with air the sacs of the lungs. Then, with lips pursed like those of little Leib, the dream-whistler, I poured over the mouthpiece the warm breath of life. Seawater came out, along with a guppy. And then the sound of music:

TWACK! TWARP! TWIRREEP!

Overhead, a door flew open. Footsteps resounded upon the deck. Then a voice rang out. "Who the hell is making that racket?"

"Racket? *Qu'est-ce que c'est* racket?

Allons enfants de la Patrie,
Le jour de gloire est arrivé!

It is with this *chant de guerre* that all French folk will defeat their foes. My instrument has circled the globe to find me. It has saved me. It has called me to duty with General de Gaulle."

"Oh! Oh! It's Shorty!"

"Him! I'll kill him! I'll strangle the son of a bitch!"

The first speaker was Miss Candace Kane. In negligible negligee. Brisket exposure. Also the flank. Her companion wore not even a stitch. This was Zanuck, the Fox King. I recognized him not by his facial moustache nor by his manner but by the mallet for polo that waved before him.

Aux armes citoyens,
Formez vos bataillons

"Do you hear, friends! Do you see? My abecedary is now complete! F is for Flute! Ha! Ha! Ha! Yes, and for Freedom! For Fighting! And for Farewell. Good-bye, my dears! *Au revoir!* Leib Goldkorn is off to the battle! F! F is for France!"

I T   H A S   G R O W N dark in the Court of Palms. No sunlight shines through the outer windows. The electric candles have lost their current. The Court itself is almost deserted. Here and there a waiter is removing, from a table, the tablecloth. Both the pianist and the bald-headed bassist have vanished. A lady with a costume of a hospital nurse, including starched headdress, is running over the carpets a Hoover. *Ehkä voimme viettää tunnin poreammeessa. Saunassa. Ehkä voimme hakata toisiamme piikeillä?* These words, the invitation to the steambath, to the pleasing blows of the thorns, will not by Miss Michiko be uttered in proximity to L. Goldkorn's ear. But oh in the depths of these gabardines the fire still burns.

"*Garçon!* If you please!"

The waiter, wax on his moustache tips, and a goiter from a surfeit of sweets, steps to my table. I hold up a fiver.

Waiter: "What is that?"

"For you, my good fellow. For the condiment Carousel. For the schnapps. When you bring change, make a deduction of fifteen cents. Excellent service."

"Sir, the bill is one hundred and twenty dollars, tax not included. I have it here."

"What? Am I in your opinion a country pumpkin? I have purchased these sweetmeats before. The cost was three American dollars and one American quarter."

The waiter, instead of responding, places before me first the menu and then the bill. Imagine the depths of my horror to discover that the charge for the schnapps alone equals sixty dollars, the tea ten, and the Carousel twenty-five. I can, through the cords in my throat, barely utter objections. "Mistake. Definite error. Sixty and ten and twenty-five, this is not even one hundred dollars. It is only: wait, I am making lightning calculations—"

"But, sir, the Carousel is twenty-five dollars *per person.* You ordered for two."

"*Wasser! Ein bisschen Wasser!*"

Something in my manner must alarm him, for, with tea towel flapping, he turns on his heel and makes for the kitchen. Now what must occur with the speed of lightning is not a mental calculation but a physical act. I jump to my feet. I pluck up my Panama. Then, pausing only for a quick bite of crumbcake, I dash for the exit of the Court of Palms. Has anyone seen me? Will I be called before *die Polizei?* But no one seems to notice. The Hooverer continues hoovering. The waiters clear off their tables. The doorman, with finger and cap brim, gives the salute. Only one person, the black-haired Oriental, remains with her face pressed still to the glass. What's this? A shy smile? A wee winsome wave? But I have no time to engage, with this Nipponese cleansing lady, in banter. Out I dash, into the lamp-lit air. Run, Leib Goldkorn! Run like a thief in the night. Hopeless endeavor: for no matter with what speed I hurl down the boulevard I cannot escape, in my infernals, the still-raging fire, or the knowledge that I have been by Miss Michiko, in the vernacular, left standing up.

2

THE HINDOO! THE *Hindoo!* The face of that newsman, round, with small poxes and Boston Blackie moustache, hangs before my eyes. Also a turban, like a sugar meringue. Onward lopes Leib, retracing the path along South Central Park to the Circle of Columbus. There, on his pedestal, stands the great Jew. Now down, down, into the pandemonium of the underground and through the labyrinth of shaftways and alleys—here those who have suffered eviction from the family Fingerhut must make urinations against the walls—to the station of the now-defunct IRT. I, too, feel the urge to release the pressure that has, moment by moment, mounted within my S. Klein skivvies. I do not speak of number 1, nor of number 2, but of number 3—the birds, you know, and the bees.

Where in the name of Heaven is the Broadway Local? Futile to walk to the edge of the platform and lean, as is the custom of Knickerbockers, over the abyss. Of equal fruitlessness: peering pointedly at the face of one's Gruen or Bulova or Benrus-brand watch. I thrust my hands into my pockets. How hot, in these gabardines, the gonadium! How hard! On guard, Leib Goldkorn: in this netherland, with its sparks, its smell of sulfur, the screechings of what sounds like human victims, even a gentleman in a Panama hat can become through temptation a bounder. Deft digits desist. What's this? A rumble, a reverberation. From the depths of the tunnel a warm, sour breeze. Now a light, an illumination: VAN CORTLANDT PARK. Here is our conveyance. All aboard!

My destination is but three stops distant: 66th Street, 72nd, 79th. Exit from train car. Beware the closing doors. And here, in his stall, is the Hindoo, surrounded on every side by his wares.

"Good evening, sir!" Thus does he address me. "Milk Duds? Delicious Black Crows?"

In the past I have been overcome by bashfulness when making my annual request. Now my tongue is not tied. "Greetings, my good fellow. One issue of the *Hustler, s'il vous plaît.*"

The price? $5.99. I hand over two Lincolns. The Indian hands over the rotogravure, whose plastic wrapping I rip apart with my incisors. Cover, in tasteful pink and quiet gray: a Fräulein, fingering with one hand the filigree of her—this is also a word that displays for us onomatopoetics—panties; while her other hand rests upon the bosom zone, from which the lingerie and lace is atumble. Navel, hips, torso; and of the paps, a peek.

"This is a pretty gal, sir." So babbles the Brahmin. "A frank gaze. She wants to get down at once to business."

In the past I have been forced to turn each of these pages, from front to back, and, like a Yeshivist, back to front, before encountering, in her studded straps, Miss Crystal Knight. Now the gazette falls open of its own accord to page 161. And there, next to a display entitled "Bottoms Up," subtitled *No Ifs, Ands, Just Butts About Us*, is none other than my inamorata. How different she is from the lassie whose acquaintance I first made so many years in the past. Here is hip heftiness and breasts like Volkswagens. Still, I recognize her red boot, a signature item, and, in her hand, the cat-o'-nine. Around her neck, like the choker on a bull terrier, is a collar with spikes. Worse, a chain runs from a ring in the wall to a manacle about her ankle. Inhuman! Tied up like a beast! Yes, she is beaten. There on her torso, and on her calf, are the bumps and bruises. One eye is swollen shut. Yet in the other glints an innocent iris, the color of bluebonnets, state flower of Texas. If only she could speak! The pity is that her thoughts must be spelled out in capital letters that seem to pour from her red-painted lips:

I HATE MEN

Also we see the familiar numerals that are printed just beneath the razor-sharp heel of her boot:

1-800 525-POON

"By all means, sir. You must dial this number. Then you will have a pleasant chat. Look here. Here is your sterling." Swami speaking. In his hands he holds, from my two five-dollar bills, the change.

At the idea of such colloquy, the heated coal lumps of my spheres blaze even higher. Everyone recalls how the maiden Pocahontas taught Mr. Standish to create a fire by rubbing together two sticks. Now my own mistress had kindled in me such a conflagration that I actually look down at my gabardines to see if they are in flames. Next I look up. There, at the end of the IRT platform, stands the Bell Telephone kiosk. Quick as J. Robinson, Negro-American sportsman, I dash to the spot, only to find that the receiver hangs downward, like the neck of a strangled goose.

Out of order? A non-functioner? With hands atremble, I lift the instrument and return it to its hook. For a brief time man and machine in muteness regard one another. In that hiatus I explore my pockets for the proper jeton. No, no, this is a lemon lozenge. Life Savers brand. Ah, here is the coin with the profile of G. Washington, who, upon being confronted with the evidence of the felled tree of cherries, replied, "Father, I did it with my hatchet." End quotation. Brave boy. So. Remove receiver. Insert jeton. Slight pause—oh, the beating of this heart!—and then: There! Like the drone of a honeybee, or a ritornel upon an oboe, a buzz. A buzz, friends! A definite buzz!

Of all the plethora of the Pacific I retained hardly anything for myself: *F* for *Flute*, of course, and a few selected items from the category of the *B*, *H*, and *R*. Everything else, including a working *Unicycle*, was sold at auction for a sum that enabled me, in that fall of 1940, to purchase a non-sleeper accommodation, Los An-geles–Chicago, on the Super Chief, and a similar ticket on the Twentieth Century Limited to New York, New York.

This is not the occasion to relate the multifarious adventures of that journey, though it might be mentioned that in its course I traveled through one dozen states, with much variation in tem-perature and rainfall, topographical features, and types of vege-tation—sugar beets, soybeans, and sorghums. Immediately upon my arrival in the great city I went from the Station of Pennsylva-nia, Harrisburg and the mountain laurel, to the consulate of la Belle France.

Hélas! It was closed until further notice. A sign in the window begged to inform all interested men and women that the head-quarters of General de Gaulle's government, the Council of Defense for the French Empire, could be found at—the address was high on the western side of the city, in a section inhabited by Harlemites. Thither I directed my steps and, after a lengthy jour-ney, climbed the stoop steps to the door. There I received, from the *jeune fille* at the receptionist's desk, a hero's welcome: a bosom clasp and a miniature flag for the lapel. Yes, and on both of my cheeks she placed, with lip paint, a tiny tricolor as well. I was now a soldier in the Free French Forces, but sad to say with no battle to fight. The general was mobilizing his army in Angleterre; to that far-off land I would have to find the way by myself.

B-FLAT. F-SHARP. C-natural, C-natural. These tone touches are a thing not dreamed of even by Mr. Wells, not to speak of the Scots-man A. G. Bell. D-flat. D-sharp. D-flat. Here is a charming rhapsody uncannily close to the opening bars of "How Are Things in Glocca Morra?" Let us complete this digital ditty. So: a click, a breath, the voice of a female:

Hello, there! Welcome to the House of Pain and Pleasure.
Where boys become men and men are reduced to whimpering
boys.

What need for a panpipe? Did I not possess a genuine Rudall &
Rose? Unfortunately there were, for a flautist, no open positions—not at the Metropolitan Opera, not at the Philharmonic of
New York, not at the Rheingold Orchester upon the Jones Beach.
The winter months were coming on. Fortunately, for a five-cent
coin one could enter the system for rapid transit and sleep
through the night in a warmed and rocking carriage. During the
day I sat with crossed legs on the platform and played selections
from Meyerbeer: *L'Africaine* and *L'Étoile du Nord*. The pennies
rained down to my beribboned boater. With these I could make
a regalia at the Horn & Hardart. In the jeton, out the creamed
spinach and the pie of lemon meringue. Coffee poured at the
boil from a dolphin's silver mouth. A warm spot to sleep, a filling
fricassee, a life making music—why was Leib Goldkorn not content? Because with each new day there arrived, in the discarded
Journal-American, dire informations: night raids on London, the
advance of Herr Rommel on Tobruk, the Italian attack upon Hun-
gary and Roumania. The season of spring brought, instead of
sunshine, storm clouds more menacing still: Greece, the land
that had first practiced democracy, was humbled by the Huns;
now, in 1941, just one year after the fall of France, the master
race invaded the Soviet Union and marched toward Moscow,
toward Leningrad. And during that year, in which the world had
been turned upside down, what had I accomplished? Twiddling,
twiddling, twiddling of thumbs.

Marchons! Marchons! To the fight! It was not a secret that,
while America was not itself engaged, it was each day and each
night sending supplies by ship to the foes of der Führer. Would it
be possible, this was my inspiration, to smuggle myself aboard?
Lend Leib, ha-ha-ha! And had I a choice? If I did not go forth
from the city of New York to meet the monster, the monster
would soon be in the city of New York. Only I knew what fate

would be in store for her millions of citizens, no matter their race, color, or credo. Did I not possess, inside my shirt, next to my torso, Haman's most terrible words?

Arabs and Esquimeaux, whomever I choose
The whole world—Oh, hear me!—will be turned into Jews

No, no. General de Gaulle awaited. The time had come for Leib Goldkorn to go to war.

I CAN'T WAIT TO *hear your voice, Stud. Are you ready for me? Because I'm hot and wet and ready for you. If you aren't man enough for me, or not eighteen, hang up right now.*

"Yes, Madam! I am hanging! Up hanging at once!"

At each of the piers along the Hudson were tied the Liberty ships. Even at two o'clock, *ante meridiem*, all was abustle. Beams of light rose into the fog-filled night; machinery clanked; cargo by the ton rose into the air. High above me, on the decks of the ships, sailors and stevedores moved about their many tasks. Naturally the entire area was *verboten*. A wire fence, sharply spiked, stretched across city blocks. The only entrance was watched by a sentry with a rifle on his back and, on his armband, an MP. *Member of Parliament? Mezzo Piano? Ah! Military Polizei!* How was a volunteer for Free French Forces to make his ingress? As follows: I walked with smart steps to the sentinel and, disguising with slang speech my enemy accent, said, "Top of the morning, Bud. Have you perhaps for my Pall Mall cigarette a phosphorous match?"

The MP, a mere youngling, a non-shaver, took from his pocket a book of such lucifers and produced most kindly a flame. "Here's your light," he declared. "Where's your cigarette?"

"Do you know, Pal, for what stands the letter *R*?"

"Huh?" was the lad's response upon hearing my non-sequitur. Then he fell speechless as I removed from my gladstone-type bag an example of flotsam that had washed up with the tide at the Malibu Beach.

"R, you see, is for Revolver, right, Mack?"

He nodded a whiskerless chin.

"Attention: you are in, as we Americans say, the alphabet soup. Now I am offering a proposition. I will not with this weapon make a fulmination and you, Buster, will not utter a word for one complete moment. Do we have, on this, the gentleman's agreement?"

Ha! Ha! Ha! If only the youth had known that in this wolf's clothing there dwelled a sheep. I had no knowledge whether this pistol had in its cylinder any munitions, or, if it had, whether because of immersion in the salt-filled deep such bullets were bootless. But the MP had gone pale at the whiff of these grapes. "All right, Bub. Turn now to the fence. *Prima!* Commence counting: one-Mississippi, two-Mississippi, up to the number sixty. *Ach!* I have almost forgotten introductions. My name is *J. Smith.* A non-German speaker."

With those words I hoisted my gladstone and quickly ran off to where, on either side of the dock, two great ships loomed up out of the fog and mist. At that moment, however, the sound of a klaxon filled the air. Betrayed! At only the count of ten! Out of the gloom there came racing toward me an Alsatian-type animal, cousin to the Führer's fanged fiend, the bitch Blondi, and the Zanuck discovery, Rin Tin Tin. Saliva, I saw, flew from its canines, and its eyes, in its fury, had turned the color of blood. Upon the instant I opened my portmanteau and removed four non-kosher cheese and hams. What had been provisions for a journey were now, in a peace offering, devoured by these powerful jaws.

Once more I made my way down the wharf, until it became possible to read the names that were painted on the ships' twin bows. To the left, the A. *Glazunov;* home port, Murmansk. To the right—

But before I could make out the fog-shrouded letters a cry— *There he is! That's him!*—rang forth, and a patrol of stout soldiers trotted toward me with lowered bayonets. From this dilemma I could not extricate myself with either a Revolver or a tune on the Rudall & Rose. Ham sandwich? Hopeless. Instead I ran down the dock between the two vessels and—this is a stratagem one sometimes sees in films of the old West—hid myself between two huge, foul-smelling wooden crates. The posse galloped by. The next thing I knew I, and both boxes—I could see the long gray gun muzzles of a "tank" protruding from each container, and smell the crank oil, too—were rising skyward. Higher we flew, and still higher, twisting, dizzily turning, until we swung over the side of the A. *Glazunov*, non-Jewish composer, and began to descend toward what I saw was the cargo hold.

From the fire, as the fellow said, into the pan for frying. For there, in the bowels of the freighter, I could make out the waiting arms and waiting faces of the Russian crew. How they hated the Germans! Intruders upon their soil! Defilers of their women! They would tear this *J. Smith* limb from limb. At the last possible moment I gathered my strength and leaped from the sinking platform onto the whitewashed planks of the deck. Bending low, I raced in what I believe is called the aft direction and then, throwing upward my gladstone, I hurtled into the first of a series of lifeboats and pulled the stiff canvas cover over my head.

W ITH A PLEASANT ringing sound my investment drops to the return slot, thus allowing me to dial, or, to speak strictly, percuss the same numbers once again.

Hello, there! Welcome to the House of—

"Greetings, Madam. I wish to speak to Miss Crys—

Where boys become men and—

And so she continued, saying, because of what may have been early signs of Uncle Al, the very words she had before. On this occasion, however, there was a difference. I did not obey her. How could I? If a meat thermometer were to be thrust into my manly parts, the cook would discover that the roast was done. With both hands I clutched the receiver. There was a click, followed by the sound of symphonic music, of the sort that I used to hear in the Otis-brand elevators at S. Klein. Then a different voice, definitely female, said, "Hi, my name is Trixie. What's yours?"

"Here is speaking Leib Goldkorn, Graduate of the Akademie für Musik, Philosophie, und darstellende Kunst."

"*Kunst?* You're my type of guy, Leib. I get hot with a man who knows what he wants."

"Ha! Ha! Not beating the bush!"

"Oh, Leib, you're on fire! I bet you've got a big one."

"Pardon?"

"Are you ready to whip it out?"

"A whip? Have you psychic powers, Miss Trixie? I have just at this moment been admiring the cat-o'-nine."

"Whoa, there, Stud! You're going too fast even for me. What I want you to whip out is that Amex or MasterCard or Visa."

"I did not perhaps hear you correctly. Because of the rhythmical music. Reminiscent of the *Bolero* of Ravel. Famous Jewish composer."

"Amex, Master, or Visa—"

"Ha, ha! This is a misunderstanding. I have passed, in the year 1943, my naturalization examinations. Judge Solomon Gitlitz presiding. Franklin Pierce? Fourteenth president, your honor. Famed for the Gadsden Purchase. In short, Miss Trixie, I am a first-class citizen. I have no need of visa."

"But if you don't have plastic, how are you going to pay for this call?"

"Pay? But I have inserted the jeton—"

"Call the 900 number. This is a business, you dumb prick."

"900? What means 900? Ah-ha! Here is an additional Bell telephone number: 1-900 588-HOTS."

From Miss Trixie, no response. Silence absolute. End of the bolero.

At ten in the morning, Bulova watch time, with a horn blast more mighty than any such toot of the *Leopold II,* the A. *Glazunov* pulled out of the harbor and set off for Murmansk upon the open sea. A day and a night and a day passed by, which caused the canvas above me to turn an eerie orange, a solid black, and orange once more, like the lid of a sunstruck eye. Not once did I stir from my redoubt, but remained as silent and still as a cockle inside a cockleshell. All too soon I devoured both of my remaining cheese and hams and consumed the entire contents of a Mission Bell. Chardonnay. Vintage unknown. By the second night I had no choice but to abandon my hideaway in order to make, over the rearmost rail, my ejectamentas. It was what old salts call three bells. The ship, save for the vibrato in its tautly strung wires and the bass notes of its turning screws, was soundless. Ash pieces like moths whirled about me. Above, uncountable stars. Below, the sea in its phosphorescence stretched out behind us, as if we were steaming not in a convoy to an uncertain destiny but were upon what had once been the gay Champs Élysées. This pattern—huddling like a hermit by day, performing at the stern numbers 1 and 2 in the dead of night—lasted for another forty-eight hours, surely time enough for our vessel to have crossed the thirtieth meridian, which would place us just south of Iceland at the approach to the Norwegian Sea. Then why with each passing hour was the climate growing hotter? One would have thought we were nearing the equator instead of the Arctic Circle. Inside my cocoon the air was so stifling, so torrid, that I could feel the flesh of my body being slowly transformed into a coquille St. Jacques. How much longer could the stowaway, Goldkorn with gladstone, hold out in his lifeboat? Deathboat, rather! At least the Soviet seaman would have no need to cobble together a coffin. I had crawled into mine of my own accord. By the fifth day my mouth felt as if it had been stuffed with surgical cotton, and in my throat was the sensation of soda-type crackers. Soon I fell into a delirium. I thought I heard, over the sound of my own breath rasps, snatches of music: Verdi. A mezzo cries out to her tenor, "Ritorna vincitor!" This was not surprising. Upon his expiration an ordinary man, a non-Graduate, will see before his eyes a lifetime's phantasmagoria, back to his earliest memories—Papa's meerschaum, even, or Mama's paps. But for a First-Place Finisher such sights would of course become sounds: Return Victorious! That is just what I, with the assistance of Monsieur de Gaulle, had hoped to do. Alas, to the strains of the umlauted Aïda, I sank now into what I feared would be my final rest.

Only to wake again at the strike of the third A.M. bell. Creature of habit, Leib Goldkorn! With a painful effort I hauled myself over what nautical chaps call the gunwale and dropped to the deck. Sole possession on this occasion, the silver baton of the Rudall & Rose. Do not think I meant to accompany movement of bowels with a movement of Brahms—the way, outside the WC at Demel's, 24 Kärntnerstrasse, a string trio played Lehar transcriptions. This was not a stool trip. No, no: I was intent upon flinging myself into the locker of D. Jones. And why not be accompanied, as were the ancient Egyptians, by favorite knickknacks? Was this flute not as faithful as the family cat? Had it not come to me like Venus out of the waves? So to the waves it would now be returned.

Thus did I arrive at the stern of the smokestacked steamer. What a sight: water, water everywhere, as the famed mariner declared, but not a potable drop. There was one last instant of regret—had I truly, at such a young age, not yet quite forty, fingered my last fandango?—and then I climbed, I clawed, I clambered onto the tossing taffrail. Directly below, the whirling propellers had churned the sea into a froth. Clutching the flute at either end, I held it at arm's length and bent both legs, like a man about to launch himself upon a silver trapeze. Count of three, good fellow. Count of three. *Eins, zwei, drei—!*

What was this? Delusion? Fantasy? Trick of the light? It seemed that someone—one of the crewmen perhaps, or an officer, or else a worker from the kitchen—had left on the nearby deck boards what looked to be a basket of mouth-watering fruits. Ah, magnanimous Marxist! To each according to his needs! But what if this vision—look, a banana, an apple, grapes in a bunch, and was that purple oblong not a plum? What if this bounty were only a mirage, as the poor Arab, crawling across the sand-strewn desert, believes that he sees palm trees and cool pools of water and females in flimsy gauze? Could these figs be such a figment? But with what precision did the half-moon shine down upon this pineapple and those cherries. With what clarity did it illuminate the nectar on the nectarines. Could such a cornucopia be a chimera?

As a leopard leaps from its limb, Leib fell upon the compote. Real! It was real! I stuffed an orange, a pear, and a tangelo all at once, peels included, into my mouth. Ripping, tearing, grinding seeds and meat and skins between my jaws, I was just about to consume a kumquat when the entire bouquet began to vibrate and then, as if it were a strange alien spaceship, rise five full feet into the air.

"*Caramba!*" That was a woman's scream—the very same woman

who, pale of skin, with black eyelashes and full painted lips—balanced these edibles on top of her head. *"Idiota! Cretino!"* she cried, with undeniable justification. I had devoured the better part of her hat.

"Pardon! Pardon!" I cried, spitting out a pasteboard peach. "This was a fata morgana."

At that instant four swarthy chaps, each with a thin, pencil-style moustache, rushed forward out of the shadows and seized the present speaker—two at my wrists, two at my ankles—and lifted me skyward.

"Rápido, levele ao mar!"

"Silenciosamente! Silenciosamente!"

What was this language? A Latin derivation. Spanish? Roumanian? The men themselves were olive-skinned, with dark, brilliantined hair. They wore shiny silk blouses and balloon-type pants. Somewhere, I knew, I had seen these costumes, and the rude gentlemen inside them, before. But when? Where? One of my attackers now grinned with a flash of white dentines and made a gesture—the pointer finger drawn across the throat zone—that needed no translation.

"Say a prayer, gringo. You got one moment to live."

At that the quartet carried me to the railing and suspended me by the heels over the side. Headfirst I hung, as does the deep-sea fish whose captor wishes to share the moment in a photograph. Was I disheartened? Filled with terror? *Pas du tout!* Ha! Ha! Thus did I laugh in the face of my tormentors. Poor fools: how could they know that they were doing for me the very thing I had hoped to accomplish myself? Indeed, just as I had counted to the fatal *drei*, these four fellows—what were they, in their puffy pantaloons, gigolos? Gypsies?—began a similar tally:

Um—

And here, as I swung salami-style backward and forward, I caught with my eye the upside-down visage of the frightened female. Her eyes were wide and her lips, in helpless beseechment, formed a ring like a cherry Life Saver. Ah! I knew her! Cugat's *compañera!* Carmen! Madam Miranda! And that meant that my oppressors were none other than—

Dois—

The Rhythm Boys of Brazil! Percussionists in each of her films! Now two of these conga experts leaned far over the railing, so that I dangled against the iron hull.

Três!

"Gott im Himmel! Was ist diese Schweinerei?"

It was none other than I who had in his native tongue made this exclamation—not from fearfulness but because of what I had seen, in plain white letters, painted on the rusted metal.

AMAZONAS

And, beneath it, the home port:

RIO DE JANEIRO

No sooner had I uttered those words than I felt, instead of the sensation of falling, a lifting motion. Up I went until I stood once more upon my own two feet at the stern. Dizzily I blinked—and blinked again. The Boys were standing at attention and giving me, with their outstretched right hands, a kind of salute.

"Mein Kommandant!"

"Wilkommen auf den Amazonas!*"*

"Entschuldigen Sie our mistake, mein Herr.*"*

"I do not understand. Why are you speaking *auf Deutsch?*"

"Ha! Ha!" laughed the tallest of the Rhythm Boys, displaying thereby a golden incisor. *"Macht er einen Witz?* A joke?"

"Silêncio, Tono!" This came from a broad-shouldered Brazilian wearing, about his neck, a foulard in red and white polkas. "The *senhor* is correct. What if we were heard speaking the tongue of the Germans?"

"Agreed," said the shortest and darkest-hued of the percussionists. "In English, then: welcome aboard, Senhor Comandante. We are prepared to follow your orders to the death."

"Comandante? Orders? There has been, gentlemen, a boner. Mistaken identity, perhaps."

"Ha, ha, ha!" laughed the Boys in chorus. "No need to pretend any longer, Senhor."

"You don't have to be afraid of us."

"We have been expecting you all along. A German speaker, of course. And look, there, in your hand: how could we be so blind—yes, blind pigs, *porcos*—that we did not see it?"

"This, fellows? You mean my Rudall & Rose?"

"*Sim, a flauta!*" That exclamation came from the fourth of the Rhythm Boys, a thin chap with, in addition to his pencil moustache, a billy goatee on his chin. "Were we not told that the *Sturmbannführer* would be disguised as a musician? A player in the woodwind section?"

A chill, a breeze of forebodement, passed over my hairless head. *Sturmbannführer*? That was a major in the dread SS. *Caramba!* "No, no, friends. We have here coincidence. This flute, ha-ha-ha! A fluke. Now I will say, *Good night, good night, gents, and bon voyage!*"

"Wait! Wait, Senhor! *Por favor!* Will you desert me?"

It was Madam Miranda. In her eyes, black-lashed and lined with mascaras, I saw the tears tremble. Her red lips, with a tongue between them, made a prayerful moue. She wore, beside the tatters of her headdress, a two-part blouse that crisscrossed tightly against each papilla. And where were the white bunnies inside? There! There! Stirring snowily with each of her pitiable sighs. "I need you," she breathed in a whisper, leaning close to the lobe of my ear. "Help me, o *meu caro senhor.*"

What I did next was by reflex. I reached into my pocket and set my *H* for *Hairpiece* in place. Now, with curls falling to either side, I turned toward the vocalist. "Leib Goldkorn makes your acquaintance, Senorita. Please note how my hair parts in the middle."

But it was the raucous Rhythmaires who responded. "*Uma peruca! E viva!* This is the perfect disguise."

And, from the short one, who was practically, in color, an *Afrikaner.* "Goldkorns! *Um pseudônimo! Maravilhoso!* The name of a Jew!"

To these remarks I made no objection. I stared instead at Madam Miranda. Now all was clear crystal. This damsel—how thin her waist was, a man could put his two hands around it; and look at her ankle, the way the little bones slipped into the sole of her shoe: this *Carmencita* was in the proverbial pickle. These

Axis agents had her in their power. Clearly they meant to use her in their evil schemes. Desert her? Never! Here was a reason for living!

"Herr Sturmbannführer," said the Boy with the whisk broom beard. "I introduce to you now the troops at your command. Here is Tono"—that was the tall one, with the tooth—"Bernardo"—a bow from the chap in the polka neckwear—"and Felipe, who also is playing a *flauta*." The dark-skinned native grinned and held up not a flute but a fipple recorder. "So. You will come please to our cabin? We have much that we must now discuss."

"*Jawohl!*" I replied. "But first perhaps we might have a lamb chop? And a wee glass of schnapps?"

All four of the Boys from Brazil stood upright and raised their arms toward the dimming stars. As one they cried out, "*Heil Hitler!*"

"Hello? Hello? Is the speaker Miss Crystal Knight?"

Please deposit three dollars and fifteen cents for the first three minutes.

"Moment. Moment, please."

I hastened to the Hindoo, fiver in hand. What, from his array of riches, to purchase? Mars Bar? Wrigley-brand gum? Would it not be prudent, when speaking to ladies, even upon the Bell telephone, to freshen the breath? "Sen-Sen, *s'il vous plaît.*"

"No Sen-Sen. Certs."

"*Certainement*, ha-ha! But *vite! Vite!* No, no change in dollars. Only silver coins."

Now, in quick hops, back to my private booth. "Madam, here is the proper amount. A Roosevelt dime, another such dime, this makes twenty cents; a quarter, a Jefferson nickel, now we are at fifty, *Verstehen?* Two more quarters, one dollar; three dimes, a nickel, *mit* portrait of Monticello—this is in Virginia, also known as Old Dominion—and quarter, we have now a sum of one dollar and sixty cents. Ergo, one dollar and fifty-five cents yet to go. This is an excellent form of mental gymnastics. Quarter, quarter, quarter, quarter. Nickel, nickel, dime and nickel, plus a final quarter, one last nickel.

Voilà! As requested, three dollars and fifteen cents!"

Welcome to the House of Pleasure. If you want to talk with
a real college girl, press one. If you want a professional
woman, press two. Dominance, press three. Boys will be
boys, press four. Group sex, press five. Anal, press six. For
breathtaking eavesdropping, press seven. Fetish hot line,
press eight. Shemales, press nine.

"Hello? I am wishing as advertised Miss Crystal Knight. Is she
what is called a co-ed? Perhaps at NYU?"

Please make your selection.

"Two! Two! Professional woman!"

"Hello, big boy. I'm so glad you called. I haven't been with a hunk
like you in such a long time! I really need what you've got. I'm starting to get hot just thinking about it. What about you? Are you hard
and horny?"

"*Pardon?* Do you mean Horn and Hardart? This is a non-existent
firm."

"Not so firm, hon? Wait till you feel Corky's magic fingers. You
won't be able to resist Corky's luscious lips."

"*Corky.* This is a pleasant moniker."

"Fair is fair. You know my name. What's yours?"

"Speaking Leib Goldkorn, Graduate of the Akademie für Philosophie, Musik, und darstellende Kunst."

"Are you feeling a little lonely, Leibie? Haven't got a girl?"

"*Au contraire.* I had today with a golden-haired Finn an assignation. Perhaps you, too, are an advocate of the sauna?"

"Huh?"

"The steam bath. The water. The heated rocks. As Dumas said, in·
defense of Dreyfus, *Jacuzzi!* Ha-ha. This is a word jest."

"Oh, sure, a Jacuzzi. Well, this is truly amazing. I really think you
must have mental powers. Because not only am I a true blonde, I
was just drawing my bubble bath when you called. All I've got to do
is take my panties off and get into the water. Shall I do it?"

"Removal of undergarment?"

"Right. I've got my thumbs hooked into the elastic. What do you
say? Shall I pull them down?"

"Yes, please."

"Okay, here we go. I just have to give my butt a little wiggle. They're pink, these panties. With a border in black. They feel so silky when they slip off my ass and go down my thighs. There! Okay, Leibie. They're in a little pink bunch around my ankles."

"These words have created in me, Miss, a titillation."

"What next? I think I'll bend down and test the water with my elbow. Here we go. I just have to lean over. One of my tits is hanging right over the edge of the tub. My ass is way up in the air. Yes, this water, it's just right. The steam is rising all around me. It's making me wet with perspiration. Shall I climb in? First one leg? Is that what you'd like? Then the other?"

"*Ja.*"

"But you'll come in after? You won't leave me all alone? I want you, Leib Goldfarb. I need you with me. Let's take this bath together."

"Miss Corky, it is time for magic fingers."

"Oh, just one second, hon. Being with you, it's driven me crazy. Just out of my mind. Otherwise I wouldn't have forgotten. I know it's silly. But of course it's the law. Just tell me and then we're going to have our steam bath. Okay? I'm already in the water. You can see how my breasts are floating. Now, then: how old are you, sweetie? Oooh, look my hair is all spread out. It's floating, too. Okay, over eighteen?"

"I am, Miss Corky, ninety-six years young. Ha! Ha! Ha! In three months, ninety-seven! Hello? Do you hear me? I am feeling hot chilies. Hello? Are you there?"

Please deposit three dollars and fifteen cents for an additional three minutes.

Carmen Miranda! Cugat Confidant! A bashful native lass, she had fallen—like Miss Candace Kane before her and Miss S. Henie, too—under the spell of Zanuck. Undoubtedly his agents had traveled to Rio, just as they once had to Topeka, and dazzled with false glitter this simple singer of folkish tunes. Now she was by contract bound to the Fox King. In her first filmic endeavor, entitled *Down Argentine Way*, by coincidence directed by the Jew

Katz-Cummings, she had played a chanteuse of Latin-style madrigals. This kino I had seen at the Mr. Roxy Theater shortly after my arrival in New York, New York. The upper billing, above even that of D. Ameche, belonged to Miss Betty Grable. Two blue eyes. Two excellent legs. Two healthy mams. Also, alas, two chins. But the true attraction was Madam Miranda. The garmenture! The forearms! The ankles! And what a smile! The redness of lips! The firmness of gums! The glare of teeth, like a mint display. Yes, this was the persona we had lined up along the Sixth Avenue to see: Bombshell from Brazil!

Now I had seen her again, the very person. Or had I? Once back in my lifeboat, I slept through the night's remainder, the morning hours, and into the next afternoon. All that I had experienced: had it been real or the phantasmagoria of a dream? Had I truly eaten a cardboard cantaloupe? A mango of papier-mâché? Could the Rhythm Boys actually have mistaken me, Leib Goldkorn, for an officer of the SS? Had they then regaled me with a feast of Ritz-style biscuits, covered with liver pâté? And had I in fact agreed to meet with them the next night at our secret spot in the stern? Above all, when I clicked together my McCans and with gallantry kissed in farewell the epidermis of Madam Miranda's hand, did she in real life murmur, "Must you go, *meu machão?*"

With delight I shivered. Then I shivered again. The temperature, inside this lifeboat, was falling. It was true, then! All true! We had crossed the equator. All was topsy-turvy. Summer was winter. January existed in July. And Goldkorn was now a secret agent of the Reich! Worse: Madam Miranda was a prisoner of her marimbists! There was not a moment for Leib—let us admit that he, too, was upside down, his heels atop his head in love: not a moment to lose!

But what was I to do? And how to do it? The light of the day still lingered. On this same deck passengers sat wrapped in blankets, sipping their bouillon tea. Only a few yards away sportive youths were exclaiming in the throes of wind badmitten. Their elders, more calmly, propelled disks into numbered squares. All of this—not to mention the physical jerks, the Scottish dancing, and the shooting of skeeters from the stern—should have alerted me that this was no ship of the merchant marine and that what I had taken to be "tanks" bound for Murmansk must have been machinery, for instance, a tractor or thresher, for the great rancheros of the pampas. But a stowaway would be treated no less harshly on a passenger liner than on a ship for lend-lease. And if I were caught, what would become of Madam Miranda? Just then, in the midst of procrastinations, I heard the far-off strains of violins. Verdi! Again *Aïda*. Act II. Scene one. The dance of the Moorish slave boys. Now I knew this orchestra was a real one. Even more: hidden among its woodwinds, like an Ethiope among the Egyptians, was a *Sturmbannführer*, the real German spy. Clutching my own reedless instrument, I threw back the canvas cover and sprang to the deck.

The music was coming from the forward part of the ship. Off I went in that direction, down one metal staircase, down another, only to come up against a door on which was written in plain Portuguese, SOMENTE PASSAGEIROS DE 1ᵃ CLASSE, First-Class Passengers Only. Nonetheless, the *senhor* from steerage marched boldly through.

Now, nearby, chords swelled in stentorian fashion: the trumpets of the victorious Egyptian army. With haste I moved the length of the hallway and trotted down three curving steps into a gleaming lobby that was filled with ladies and gentlemen of the type that K. Marx in his *Kapital* calls *swells*. They were having their highballs and late-afternoon schnapps. Amidst this crowd I looked, in my herringbones, like a hobo: with BO whiffs and a non-shaven beard. So thought the two blue-coated employees of Lloyd Brasileiro, who drew themselves up to guard the doors on the far side of this mezzanine. Yet it was from behind those portals that I could hear Radames, the tenor, being greeted by Pharaoh, a deep-throated bass.

"Ha, ha!" I laughed with casual air as I approached the crewmen. "I am not a *schnorrer*."

"*Entrada prohibida*," said one of the husky Brazilians.

"The Maestro," said another. "He is making rehearsals."

Open, Sesame! It was as if, with the simple gesture of raising my Rudall & Rose, I had uttered those mystic words. The sentries, saluting, pushed wide the entrance, and, to the wails of an Ethiopian chorus, I stepped into the room.

And what a room it was—a large salon filled with ebony tables and chairs, crystal chandeliers, a great gilded mirror, and a carpet in beige and rose. At the front sat almost one hundred musicians. It was they who were providing the melody to which the Egyptian priests gave thanks for their victory to the bird-headed gods. Instantly the *senhor* knew, by these sonorities, that this was neither the Orchester of Philadelphia nor that of the cities of Boston or Chicago; nor was it the Philharmonic of New York. No. This could only be world-famed National Biscuit Company Symphonia.

"Ah, Madonna! Ah, Dio! You must-a sing-a the music. Sing-a!"

Yes, and that white-haired chap, though lacking his frock coat, could only be A. Toscanini himself. Now I understood: The Maestro was returning to Rio, where a half century before, with this same opera, he had made his debut. Up and down, went his baton, round and round, never varying, as if it were being wielded by a human metronome. *Ach!* For a dizzying moment I found myself so deep in a trance—look, in the mirror, at those eyes! See how a flame burns in each black, deep-set pupil!— that I feared I would paw at the ground three times, like a hypnosis victim convinced he was a horse. The Maestro was a mesmerist!

Who can say how long I might have remained under this spell had not Aïda—the world-famed Milanov, a minimum two-hundred-pounder—suddenly spied, among the downtrodden Ethiopes, her very own father?

Che veggo! Egli? Mio padre!

And I? Goldkorn, Leib? I, too, could hardly believe my eyes. For there, in the woodwind section, sat none but my nemesis. *Ja!* It was he! Herr Hans Maltz! Number Two Finisher. He had not even bothered, this party member, to don a disguise. Two black hair curls on his forehead. Demi-moustache. A gap, as wide as that which separated the fangs of a viper, between his incisors.

Chin dimple, too. This was the man who had sent the family
Goldkorn to their deaths at Dachau. This was the ravisher of
Minkche, dear younger sister. What? Was Leib living? Taking
breath after breath while that guilty Gauleiter still walked the
earth? In my waistband was the Revolver. Now I knew why fate
and tide had washed it to the Malibu shore: so that I might at
this instant revenge myself upon my ancient antagonist.

At once I dropped to my knees and began to crawl among the
chair legs and tables toward where, in response to the urgent
oblongs of the Maestro's baton, all the soloists and the double
chorus were simultaneously singing. Hidden, so to speak, by this
hullabaloo, I made my way between the seated musicians, past
the sawing strings, the tap-tapping toes of the trombones, and
into the section for winds. There, just ahead, were the piccolos;
one minute later I found myself at the feet of the flutes—in particular at the bluchers of SS Major Herr H. Maltz.

"Greetings, sir! Surprised to see me? Did you not think that I,
too, had like a dog died in Dachau?"

No response. The Second Placer was playing solo accompaniment—and, I noted with disconcernment, that he did so upon a
definite Rudall & Rose—for the massive Milanov.

"What? Can it be you do not recognize me?"

Silence, still.

"Well, sir, I have not forgotten you. Maltz! The guileful
Gauleiter. What are you doing, may I inquire, in this hemisphere? On a goodwill voyage, eh? Ha! Ha! Ha! *Hans across the
sea?*"

The flute, of English manufacture, fell from the flautist's lips a
fraction of a second, no more than an eighth note, too soon. The
Maestro might be myopic, but he could hear, in an entire aviary
of cheerful chirping, a single sour lark. "Signore Schwartz-o! You
want-a to kill me? To put-a the knife into *mio core? Imbecille!
Cretino! Disgraziato!"*

"Schwartz?" said I, *mezzo voce.*

"*Ja!* This is mine name. What is yours?"

The moment of truth. "Goldkorn. Graduate, Akademie für
Musik, Philosophie, und darstellende Kunst. Class, sir, of 1916."

Schwartz/Maltz stared down to where I squatted, but in his

round, gentile-style eyes there was no spark of recognition. The three-measure rest for the woodwinds was already at an end. Maltz again raised the flute to his moustachioed lip. But before blowing into the mouthpiece, he airily said, "You have a mistake made. I have in my life never seen you."

Then out came the staccato one-quarter notes as Pharaoh and his people pronounced yet again the glories of Egypt, and Radames, portrayed by J. Bjoerling, sang about how all of his nation's treasures could not be valued more than *d'Aïda il cor*, the fair maiden's foot, in the L. Goldkorn translation. What an explosion of sound! Toscanini, brows abristle, whipped the finale into a fury. Difficult to imagine that every passenger aboard the *Amazonas* did not hear the deafening *crescendi*. Why, even the fish in the sea must have felt our *forte*, our *fortissimo*, and the circling albatross our *appasionato! Abbandono! Agitazione!* So carried away was I by the performance that, as if I too were a Biscuiteer, I placed my own Rudall & Rose to my thick puckered lips and blew three lilting notes over the embouchure.

TOOT! TWEAT! TWANK!

On the instant all ninety-four members of the Symphonia fell into utter silence. I looked at the Maestro. His hands, balled into fists, were beating the two sides of his crimson cranium, and the double rows of his teeth were grinding against each other with more throbbing vibrations than the *Amazonas*'s twin screws.

"*Mein Gott!* It is you!"

I whirled around. If Toscanini had turned red, Maltz had no blood in his veins at all. His whole head looked, in its squareness and paleness, like a bar of non-sinking soap.

Leib Goldkorn: "So, sir: you have recognized my musical style."

Major Maltz: "I was only following orders!" The man's hands were shaking. Sweat poured over his brow. "I am just a little sausage!"

Before my eyes—for the hundredth, the thousandth time—rose a Viennese scene: the not-so-blue Danube, the barge, the *Kalliope*, and the family Goldkorn, *Mutter, Vater*, big sister Yahkne, little sister Minkche, as they steamed not downriver to the safety of Budapest, but upstream to Dachau.

I fought down the rage that, with this memory, surged through my plexus. "I am not here for revenge, Mr. Maltz. The past we will settle later. I now know your secret: you are a German spy. I know, too, that you have a mission on board this ship. Tell me: what is your wicked plot?"

"An agent? A plot? You have too many novels been reading. I am like you: a refugee. I a new name have, a new life—as a simple musician."

Here I pointed the barrel of the Revolver at my antagonist's chest. "Do not take me for a fool, Herr Sturmbannführer. You have captured Miss Carmen. I know all about the Brazilian Boys. They are spies, too. What scheme are you up to? Why have you involved Madam Miranda?"

The Second-Place Finisher, with aplomb, crossed his arms and his legs. "Such nonsense! Perhaps the sufferings of your people, of your poor family, have a little your mind affected."

"I am not a madman. Do you see? This is a working weapon. Tell me! Your plans! Your plots! Confess, or I will put a bullet into your heart zone!"

To my astonishment this Schwartz, or Maltz, smiled even more broadly. "You want to shoot me? Excellent! Shoot, please. It is an honor to die for der Führer!"

Yes, I believe I would have done the deed—and how, at a distance of two American feet, could I have missed?—had not, at that instant, the Maestro not given a sharp rap with his baton and said, with terrifying sweetness, "Signore Schwartz-o. Would-a you be such a gentle-a-man-a to please, per favore, join us once again?"

All ninety-five members of the NBC Symphonia seized their instruments. Yes, all ninety-five. Leib Goldkorn was no less under the spell of the Maestro's will than any of the musicians around him. Yet for inexplicable reasons Maltz, who had, in the face of death displayed such insouciance, now began to cower in his chair. With trembling hand he pointed at me—rather, at the Rudall & Rose which hovered at my lips. "No, no, nein!" he gasped. "Not that! Please! Bitte! Bitte! I beg you! Anything but that!"

Came the downbeat. Enter the strings. Toscanini gave a nod.

On our left the trumpets, with mutes, picked up the theme. Now the Maestro turned toward the woodwinds. I placed my fingers on the fingerholes. The oboes sighed. The clarinets uttered a moan. I puckered my lips, awaiting my cue.

"No! No!" cried Hans Maltz. "White flag! Surrender! I am the Gestapo agent. A major in the SS. It is true, we have a plan. This Toscanini! He is a Roosevelt ally. A Good Neighbor provocateur. *Ja,* and our bitter foe. Everywhere he goes, in each spot he plays, the people turn against the Reich. This cannot in Brazil be allowed. Here we draw the line. If necessary, he will be removed. We know how to give special treatment. *Bitte!* Do not play a note. I will tell more. We are going this Vargas to kidnap. *Ja!* Getúlio Vargas! Ruler of Brazil! Wait! No flute! I can't bear such a sound! It will be during the *Aïda!* The *Aïda* without the Jew lover, Toscanini. This Vargas, he all women loves. How he loves this Miranda! She will him seduce. Drive from him the senses. Then, as her love slave, *ja?,* his *Liebesgefangener,* he will to *Deutschland* the allegiance of his nation pledge. One hundred sixty millions in population! Control of all shipping lanes! And the iron mills! The coffee! The potash! All of this will belong to the Reich!"

But my eyes were on the crook of the Maestro's finger; I saw his eyebrow arch. Excellent: this was my entrance.

TWEET! TWITTER-TWEET! TWITTLE-TWAT!

"*Madonna!* I'm a gonna kill-a that Schwartz-o! To make-a such noise! To do such-a thing to Verdi! He play like-a pig, now he die like-a dog!" All the NBCers sat stunned while their leader pulled first at the band of his collar, which he hurled toward the woodwinds, and then at the band of his watch, which came flying after. "*A morte! A morte a quest' animale!*" Now the entire score of *Aïda* whirled end over end, trailing loose pages like a comet. From this action, perhaps, we derive the expression *to throw the book at him.* It knocked over a piccolo player, two seats to our right. The real damage, however, came from the podium, both stalk and stand, that the Maestro ripped from its base and, with a shot-putting motion, sent into a near-perfect parabola. One end hit Maltz square on the forehead, and, as he fell backward, into the kettledrum, the other end swung round and smote him in the center of his sternum. He lay flat out, blood pouring from his ear; his breath, what little remained of it, rattled ominously in his throat.

"*Bello*," exclaimed Toscanini. "Now I'm-a happy. The storm, she's-a passed. Sunny the sky, no? Smooth-a the sea. Are you ready? Miss-a Milanov-a? Signore Bjoerling? *Bene!* So, Signore Schwartz-o, now we gonna give you a beautiful solo. Ready? *Cantare!*"

Of course Signore Schwartz was not ready for anything, unless it was a tent for oxygen. Once more the Maestro peered near-sightedly in the direction of the winds. "So? Is a problem-o? Why you no play-a? Why you no sing-a? Schwartz-o? *Dov'e quest' uomo?*"

"Signore Schwartz"—the speaker was none other than myself—"is *indisposto.*" I stood upright. Then I climbed onto the ex-musician's chair. "Have no fear, your Excellency. Speaking is Goldkorn. Goldkorn, L. I am prepared for the first flute position. Akademie Graduate. Class of '16. So: *Eins, zwei, drei!*" Thus it was that I blew over one end of my silver instrument and the no less silvery notes emerged from the other.

"H A ! H A ! H A ! "

"Ho! Ho! Ho!"

"Don't! Don't! You're splashing me! Ha! Ha! You watch out! I'm going to splash you back!"

"*Was ist das? In dem Wasser?* A foot! *Mit* toes! I shall now recite a folkish expression. *This here little piggy went to market, this here little piggy—*"

"Hey, that tickles!"

"*He stayed home. Und this here little piggy had a Schnitzel,—*"

"That's it! Squeeze them! Lick them!"

"*But this here little piggy is sad because he had none.* Now we come to the last of these fellows. Do you know what he did, Fraülein Corky?"

"Oh, Leib! Oh, Leibie! No one has ever made me feel like this before."

"*Wee, wee, wee! This is his Geschrei. All the way home.*"

"Oh, Leibie, look what I found! Floating in the water!"

"An Ivory-brand?"

"No, no. There. Between your knees. Oh, it's so sweet and pink. What a darling! A dear!"

"Do you mean perhaps a duckie?"

"Yes, your rubber duckie. I want to touch it. There. Oooh! It's so hard. Now I'm going to give it a kiss. Poor little rubber duckie. Yum. Do you feel that? Yum, yum, yum."

"Miss, I must ask you please for a stoppage."

"What? Stop?"

"Please do not kiss the duckie."

"You don't want me to suck your cock?"

"We have for pleasantries no more time. Less than one minute by Bulova. Soon we shall hear the voice of the Bell operator. Each second is now precious. Please, will you do it?"

"Do what, for Christ's sake?"

"Wield now with sharpness the twigs."

"Twigs?"

"*Ja!* The twigs of flagellation."

"Flagellation? But I thought you didn't want—"

"Upon my back zone. Upon the shoulders. Beat me! Whip me! Make blood! Make boils!"

"Hey, listen. I'm sorry. You got the wrong number. Press three. I'm not into dominance. Jesus! It makes me sick!"

"Hello? Hello? Operator? Miss Corky? Hello?"

Three bells. Time for my secret appointment. Slowly, then, to the stern. The light came from the stars and the moon, which in America is thought to be made from Limburger. An absurdity. Limburger is made from cheese. Cheese is made from milk. There are, on this lifeless satellite, no cows—except for the one that jumped over it. Ha! Ha! And the dish ran away with utensils! This popular jingle brought to my lips a smile, which caused such a jolt of pain that I made an ejaculation: "Ouch!"

"Senhor Goldkorns! We are here. At the rail."

Yes, there were the Rhythm Boys, in their silky blouses and harem-style pantaloons. I took a step forward, into a light shaft. At once the quartet, as if they were a single person, uttered a gasp. They rushed ahead to where I was dizzily attempting to stand. "Senhor Comandante!"

"*O que aconteceu?*"

"*Olhe todos esses calos!*"

"Such lumps! Such *caroços!*"

The bongoist, Bernardo, bent down and touched one of the dozen or so bumps that protruded from my scalp zone like grade A eggs from a carton. "Comandante, can you tell us who has done this thing to you?"

To this question I, with truthfulness, nodded. My attacker had been none other than Arturo Toscanini. How to explain this? No sooner had I produced from my Rudall & Rose two half notes in d-flat and a b-natural eighth than the Maestro, with a bull-like bellow, plunged from the podium and, scattering violas to one side, violoncellos to the other, made straight toward where I stood on my unfolded chair.

"For Verdi!" he'd screamed, beating with his fists upon my physiognomy. "For Beethoven! For Brahms!"

Felipe, the fipple flautist, importuned me. "Tell us, Senhor. His name!"

"Schwartz," I softly replied.

There was a sudden burst of crepitation, and at once I saw, agleam in the heavenly light, four unsheathed knives.

Also gleaming was Tono's golden tooth. "You don't worry, Senhor Comandante. We are going to take care of him."

"No, no, wait!" I managed, in spite of my swollen tongue, to exclaim. "Halt, *Kameraden!* There is no need for these violent measures."

"*Por que não?*" demanded the Boy with the billy goat beard. "This agent has discovered our plans. If we do not act he will reveal them to Roosevelt, to the Jews!"

"No, he will not," I replied through cracked lips. "Mr. Schwartz will interfere no more. He has been dealt with."

"What?"

"*É verdade?*"

"Dealt with? By who?"

Here I lowered in bashfulness my puffed-up eyelids. "Goldkorn of the Gestapo."

"*Maravilhoso!*" exclaimed Felipe. "Did you use your Luger, eh? Or—*oi!* Into the belly with a knife?"

"These were my weapons, friends." I held up both my fists. "With these I have beaten our enemy into a coma. I do not believe he will leave the—what do the mariners call it? The bay of sickness?—alive."

"Ooooh, *meu herói!*"

I whirled about. It seemed, in the dim light, that a pile of tangelos had started to talk. There, beneath a heaped-up fruit cup, was Carmen Miranda. At the sight of her—the wet, lipsticked mouth, a tip of a tongue, the tooth flash—the blood surged through each one of my head bumps, like air through organ pipes. Playfully she crooked her arm and, this too was an enticement, made a bulge of her biceps. "*Que homem!*"

"Ha! Ha! It was nothing. You should have seen me on the Muscle Beach."

Now the billy beard spurred his fellow Rhythmaires into action. "Tono! Felipe! Quick. To the *hospital.* Take that Jew where no one can find him."

Both men, the tall one and the short, held up their arms in a stiff salute. "*Heil Hitler!*"

But the Brazilian Boy was not done. "Bernardo, we shall search the spy's cabin. We must discover if he has an accomplice. Carmen! To your stateroom. If there are more of these Jews you are at risk. Lock your door, *você entende?*"

"*Sim, sim.* But I want to take Senhor Goldkorns with me. Look at his poor head. I'm going to cure all those *protuberâncias.*"

"No, no. It is I, Madam Miranda, who will take care of you. You are in danger, *ja?* I will be the guardian of your body. So. Now we have each his tasks. Let us do our duty." *Mach schnell!*

"C ERTS, SIR?"
"Tic-Tacs. Thanks."

The star's cabin had three sections: a bedroom, a dressing room, a living room, near the wall of which was a sofa of zebra stripes, into whose cushions I now softly sank.

"*Só um momentinho!*" cried out Miss Carmen as she ran to the bar zone for some cubicles of ice.

"Please, I am begging you: do not concern yourself with me. I have big informations but small time in which to speak."

"But, Senhor Goldkorns," said the singer with a glistening gum smile, "do we not have together all of the night?"

With that she walked, ice bucket in arms, back to the couch and sat in abutment beside me. Flank, in frankness, to flank. "*Pobrezinho*," she declared, gazing at my wounded head. "What have they done to you?"

"It is nothing, Madam. *De nada*, ha! ha!"

"But look at those *batidas*, those *volume*. How they must pain you!"

"These wounds, my *Weltschmerz*, to make a small jest—they do not matter. I am only one man. My pain is a small potato. We have in our hands the fate of millions."

Now the Bombshell took from the bucket a single ice piece and, reaching upward, placed it upon my scalp. "Does that make better?" she asked, as she maneuvered the cube among my protuberances like a toboggan between the Alps.

"Attend, please. There is afoot a plot that might change the course of all history. If it succeeds, what a catastrophe! The Third Reich will receive tons of potash. It is up to us, you, Miss, and I, Leib Goldkorn, to prevent this crime."

"*Sim, é realmente machão. I know what I must do. Nossa Senhora! Esses calos!*" Here my companion placed both her hands on my padded shoulders and thrust herself up to her knees. Then she began to lower her lips toward my half-frozen cranium—in popular parlance, a numbskull.

"Madam Miranda, pay me now attentions. I am about to reveal to you my true identity. I am not the person you think I am."

"Mmmmm, mmmmm," murmured Miss Carmen as, one after the other, she began to suck upon my lumps, the way a child might upon a Popsicle array.

Through the length of my spine went sensations of both heat and cold. Think, for comparison, of chilled soured cream in steaming borsht or, contrarywise, fudge upon an American sundae. "It is true, I am a musician. And I am a woodwinder, that is true as well. But here, my dear, is the surprise—"

I have already described, have I not, the style of Carmen Miranda's dickey? A swath of silk behind the neck that descended from either shoulder, made a cross at the breadbasket, and then a bow tie at the dorsal. Thus was each bosom separately supported, like a wounded arm in a sling. At that moment my corneas were from this cleavage directly opposed, my pupils a mere inch from her paps. A smell rose from her body, like the chocolate aroma that comes from an overheated radio. As if that were not enough, the breath from her mouth passed over my skull as, in tango time, she started to hum:

Ay-ay-ay-ay-ay, I like you very much—

It was undoubtedly because of these provocations that I began to feel, in the depths of the infernal regions, a gamboling.

Ay-ay-ay-ay-ay, I think you're grand—

"I am not for the Nazis a spy. *Au contraire.* I was in my youth a Yiddish speaker and even enjoyed nothing so much as a slice of pitchai. In short, Goldkorn is no *nom de plume* but the name with which I was born."

"*Meu Deus!*" Carmen cried, shrinking into the couch's far corner. "*Um Judeo!*"

"Ha! Ha! Expertly circumcised."

At this revelation the film star gave a joyful start. Both halves of her brisket heaved with delight and her eyes—the kohl made the lashes stick together, like the legs of an insect—opened wide. "*Isso é possível? É que isso pode ser verdade?*"

"Not only possible, Senorita, but a provable fact. Further informations: you, too, are not the person you seem to be. Aha! Did you think I did not know? From the first moment I saw you I comprehended you were not an agent of the Reich. Here, these were the words I said to myself, is an innocent flower that has been rudely plucked. Pardon poetics. In plain English: I know that you are the prisoner of the Rhythm Boys. Have no fear. I will not abandon you—not to Herr Hitler and not to Darryl F. Zanuck."

At last the comely Carmen knew she had nothing to fear. From

gratitude, yes, and I believe from affection, she threw herself
once more upon me and gave my scalp lumps a thorough massage. "Lumps? Bumps? *Calos? Caroços?* No, no, stupid Carmenzinha! *São chifres? Chifres!* The whole world knows this! Horns!
The sign of *O Diabo! O Satã! Chifres!* The horns of a Jew!"

In the old days, at Demel's, the waiters would apply a match
to a hollow brandy apple. Now, at the vigor of this chafing, my
own heart, like one of these fruits, burst into sudden flame. Thus
burning, I reached in abandonment toward Miss Carmen and
seized a hip. Here was the moment for a roughhouse.

With a pleasure cry my partner leaped completely off the
couch. If she had been a palmist, able to read my most hidden
wish, she could not have performed an act more convivial than
the following deed: she unstrapped her shoe, a leather pump;
placed it in her hand; and, like the goddess Minerva, or perhaps
Diana, hurled it aloft. It struck at my chestbone, creating such a
wave of epicureanism that in spite of a thorough knowledge of
all of Moses's Commandments, I produced such a stiffy that the
front of my herringbones rose upward, as if a member of the
scouting movement, see aforementioned Baden-Powell, had set
upright a pole to support his tent for pups. Madam Miranda,
upon seeing the phenomenon, staggered backward and in
speechless wonder gazed.

"Ha! Ha!" I laughed. "This is the work of Rabbi Goldiamond."

What happened next made me think I had entered the Hindoo
nirvana. She bent, this goddess, and unstrapped her second
shoe. "*Bastardo! Filho da puta!*" she exclaimed, a non-translat-
able Portuguese endearment, and drew back her arm. "*Judeu
sujo!*"

In a daze of anticipation I drew back first the lapels of my herringbone and next, with buttons flying, the front of my shirt.
"Here, honey! I am making for you a bull's-eye!"

Alas, just then, when the harpoonist was about to loose her
harpoon, there was a knock upon the door. End of erotics.

"*Quem está aí?*" asked Carmen.

"The Brazilian Boys!" I said, with a groan.

Indeed, from the fury of the fusillade that ensued—a banging,
a thumping, a rattling of hinges—it sounded as if all four of the

Rhythmaires were simultaneously pounding on the portal.

"Quick! Senhor Goldkorns! Hide!"

There are occasions when an Akademie Graduate does not need a second admonition. I dove for the back of the couch, but at once discovered that there was insufficient space between the rear of the furniture and the stateroom wall.

"*Momento!*" sang out the barefoot Bombshell, even as she gestured frantically toward her dressing chamber.

There was a tremendous thud at the door, a brief silence, and then another such concatenation, accompanied by a splintering sound. Just as the cabin door cracked and gave way, I took two hops into the bedroom and rolled beneath the four-poster. Madam Miranda gave a squeal of surprise. From my hideaway I with surreption lifted the taffeta-type fringe. There, in the center of the living room, stood Arturo Toscanini. He was dressed in what I believe is called a Long Johnny and a nightcap with, upon the apex, a ball of wool.

"*Dov'e l'uomo?*" he demanded. "Where is he?"

"Who, *caro?*"

"*Il uomo! Il traduttore!* I heard-a his voice!"

"But, *meu Arturo*, you can see for yourself. There is no one here."

Poor Maestro! Even a non-physician could see that the great conductor was a victim of somnambulism who, in the course of his dream, had wondered all the way from his first-class cabin.

"Not-a here? Not-a here? I'm-a going to show you who's-a here!" With that the Maestro did a brisk sleepwalk, first to the couch, then to the bar, then to the open closet door.

"*Ah, giustizia!*" he exclaimed and began to hurl not only the songbird's hats but her clothing—the coats and capes, the gowns and dresses, her vary-colored unmentionables—into the air. "*Dov'e il criminale! l'animale!*" What a moving spectacle: the man who had mesmerized thousands and hundreds of thousands had at last hypnotized himself. I would have been tempted to leave my sanctuary and relieve him of his obsession, had I not known that to wake a noctambule in the course of his excursions will bring on a fatal cramp. Luckily, Madam Miranda came forward and seized his hand.

"*Pobrezinho!* Look at your *manos.* Were you so eager to see your Carmenzinha? Did you hurt yourself on my door?"

The Maestro blinked, then stared down at his torn knuckles. "*Questa? No!* Not-a from door-a. From head of *l'assassino!* He was a-killing Verdi! He was a-choking him inside-a the grave!"

"Oh, let me make it better. Yes? No? Does this feel good?" With those words she took the Maestro's middle finger inside her mouth and performed a vibration.

"Ah, *mia Carmencita!* What-a you do to me?"

"*Arturo, caro.* Be my *herói.* I ask one more time: let me sing in this opera the part of Aïda."

"No, no, *non è possibile.* Ask-a me something else! Ask-a me to cut off-a my arm! *Sì!* Both my arm-as. I'm-a gonna conduct-a the orchest with-a my feet! Go! Go! *Via!* Get-a a knife! Get-a a saw! I do it! Both arms-as! Both legs! You make-a me a *quadripeligio!* But you can no sing-a the Aïda!"

"But your Carmenzinha does not want you to lose an arm. *Por que não?* Because then you would lose this little finger."

Now she took his pointer and placed it in her mouth, and next his ringer, his pinkie, his thumb.

"Oh, what you do to the Papa? You give-a him such-a big *passione!*"

"Yes? You say yes?"

"Oh! My Miranda! My Carmencita!"

"Ah, Papa! *Meu namorado!*"

How old was Toscanini? A septuagenarian, surely. No matter. With the strength of an Olympian he swept the singer into his arms and carried her to the bed, from beneath which I had been peeping. Naturally I could no longer see what was occurring between somnambulist and songbird. But from the giggles and grunts, the gay exclamations, together with the sharp slapping retorts and the manner in which the mattress rocked above me, it was clear that the couple were engaged in a game of knock hockey.

On and on this contest continued, with cries of victory and groans of defeat. How the frame shook and shuddered! How the feather bed's feathers flew through the air! Yes, the whole mattress had burst asunder. The downy contents, fluttering by me, tickled my nose parts. "Ah! Ah!" This was a non-voluntary ejaculation. "CHOO!"

Instantly the agitations above me ceased. Silence complete. Then the air was filled with a shriek and, in Italian, imprecations. The next thing I knew all four posts of the poster, together with mattress and bedding, were turned asunder. There stood Arturo Toscanini in his birthday suiting and, just behind him, Carmen Miranda, wearing only her trademark chapeau.

"*A morte!*" bellowed the conductor. "*Lo soffoco con queste mani!*" Then, as if he were indeed determined to choke me with his bare hands, he lunged past Miss Carmen, who—it was not, alas, the occasion to note her sportive physique—started to wail.

Toscanini: "I'm-a murder this-a Gold-a-korn!"

The Graduate: "Ha! Ha! I can, your Grace, make explanations."

Toscanini: "Then, Carmencita, I'm-a kill-a you."

Miranda: "No, no, Arturo. Who is this man? I have never seen him before. Kill him, yes, kill him; but do not kill me."

The Graduate: "Et tu, Brazilian?"

By then the conductor—how strong, how cold, his hands were, like icy manacles—had me about the neck and was shaking me the way, in an opera production, a man will make a sound effect with a piece of tin. But all the thunder came from Toscanini. "Who's-a this man? This Gold-a-korn? A tormentor! He destroy the music! Make-a the noise like-a pig. Now he spy under the bed-a. *Pervertito! Degenerato! Pederasta!*"

I tried with indignation to tell my attacker that I was a Graduate, but the two thumbs on my windpipe prevented anything but a gurgling sound from coming out. From above me, from what in the Wiener Staatsoper would be high above the proscenium, a dark curtain started to fall. Back and forth went my head on my neck. My body hung limp from the noose of the Maestro's hands. The lights were dimming. Was this the final chord?

"*E questo cos'è?*" exclaimed Toscanini. "What is-a this?"

Madam Miranda uttered a cry and pointed to where, for a horrible moment, it seemed to both her and the Maestro that my intestines, all white and slithering, had been shaken out.

"*Esther,*" I managed to gasp.

"*Questo?*"

"*A Jewish Girl in the Persian Court.*"

Toscanini removed his hands from about my throat and snatched up one of the music sheets that had torn loose from my torso. "Why you have-a this music? Is an op-er-a, no?"

Here was my chance. I had to seize it. "Your Lordship, I am not only a flautist, First-Place Finisher. I am also a composer. You hold in your hands my life's work. You must give it a premiere. Thus the world will see how Hitler, the modern Haman, has decreed the death of every Jew."

"This Hitler! How I hate-a him! Also Mussolini. Oh, if I could kill-a one man, just-a one man, I kill this Duce!"

"Yes, yes: we will expose him, too! Is he not already a character in the *Aïda*? Did he not invade Abyssinia? Did he not, like Pharaoh, make those folk his slaves? Just as Hitler now does with the Jews! Maestro! You will be the new Moses! You will set my people free!"

"Yes, Gold-a-korn. I like-a this. *Va bene.* But in my head is a confusion. In the *Aïda* I'm-a show the suffering of the Ab-a-assynian peoples. This *Esther*: here I'm-a show Hitler, no? Hitler and the Jews. *Ma,* how I'm-a gonna to do both? Is not *possibile.*"

"It is, your honor! A definite possibility. Miss Carmen is the key. She must play the Aïda. She will sing Verdi's notes and Verdi's words. But I shall add, from the *Esther*, a brief interlude of my own."

Now Carmen burst forth with an exclamation. "Hola! This is the idea of a genius. *Um gênio!* Goldkorns!" And holding the flat of her hand at chin height, she blew me the likeness of a kiss.

"What? *Maledetto!* What-a you are saying? To change-a the note-as of Verdi? To change-a the words? *Un' abominazione!* I have devote-ed my life to make-a *restora, uno restaurazione,* of each note-a—not just-a how Verdi wrote but how he hear-a in his-a head! His brain, it's-a my brain. His ear, it's-a my ear, same-a with eye. All exact-a! Ah, Carmencita! You think-a I no see how you give-a this Gold-a-korn the kiss! I see! I see! Is a plot! *I due conspiratori!* Carmencita! Carmencita! I'm-a love-a you. *Sì,* love-a you. *Ma* I'm-a love-a Verdi more. Change-a the note-as? Eh, Gold-a-korns? I'm a change-a you! I'm-a make you the dead man. I'm-a make-a you the *Giovanni* ghost!"

Here a strange thing happened. As the Maestro spoke, he began to change color. At first his feet, then his calves, then the thighs—up and up, zone by zone the blood rose in his body like mercury in a thermometer, turning it from fleshy pink to crimson. At last it filled his throat, his face, and the very whites of his eyes. For a moment it appeared that even the ball of his nightcap would through the force of his feeling turn into a candy-style apple.

"Arturo! *Arturo, meu!*" cried Madam Miranda. "What is happening? Speak to me!"

But the Maestro did not utter a word. He stood petrified, with one fist clenched above him and his lips, beneath his moustache, twisted into an expression of both rage and surprise. It was as if he, himself, had been transformed into the Stone Guest of Mozart or had become, after all, Moses, about to hurl down the tablets instead of the baton. Brain seizure. The great Toscanini had suffered a stroke.

At that instant there was a rattling sound, like that made by snakes about to strike. Congas! Bongos! Castanets! Then, just as Miss Carmen wrapped herself in a bedsheet, all four of the Brazilian Rhythm Boys burst into the room.

Felipe looked from the statue of Toscanini to Madam Miranda to me. "*Quem é?*" he inquired.

Bernardo: "It is the Maestro."

The billy beard: "Who did this? How did it happen?"

This was, for Leib Goldkorn, a crisis. Into my mind, concerning Miss Carmen, there had entered a wee doubt. Of which side—that of the Axis? That of the Allies?—was she the advocate? Was she a Good Neighbor, this songstress? Or a Nazi? With a single word she could expose me or save me. What would that word be?

"*Oi, meninos!*" Thus did she start to speak. "The Maestro is now our prisoner. He can no longer hurt our cause. I did not do this alone. Once again we must thank Goldkorns of the Gestapo. It is he who has made it possible for me to star in *Aïda*. Hail to our leader!"

A shout went up from the *Kameraden*. They gave me, first, a series of genial backslaps, and then the stiff-armed salute. Eagerly they awaited their orders.

"*Achtung,* gentlemen. We have only three days until we reach Rio. There is much we must do. To work! *Ja,* to work. Everything will depend upon our premiere!"

3

QUARTER, QUARTER, QUARTER, quarter. Quarter, quarter, quarter, quarter. Quarter, quarter, quarter, quarter. One dime. One nickel. *How are things in Glocca Morra?* No, no: incorrect. 1-900, 588-HOTS. *Voilà!*

> *Welcome to the House of Pleasure. If you want to talk with a real college girl, press one. If you—*

Three! Three! *Gott im Himmel,* three!

> *Hello, you sniveling worm. You called the right place. We're going to hurt you and then we're going to make you pay for it. You will be our slave. Do you think you can handle that? Are you eighteen? If not, hang up now.*

"Eighteen, *Ja!* Eighteen!"

"Hello, this is Bitch Adder, and I think men suck. Who is this?"

"Here is Leib Goldkorn, Graduate of the Akademie. I wish, please, to speak with Miss Crystal Knight."

"Crystal? She's not available. But I can be the schoolmaster of that academy. Have you been naughty-naughty? Have you spilled your ink?"

"*Was ist das?*"

"I think you need to learn a lesson. It's time you got a good paddling."

"Madam, I am not allowed by the Bell Company such tomfoolery. I am making an insistence. Put please Miss Crystal upon the mouthpiece of the telephone."

"Wrong answer! Bend over! Pants down! I'm going to give you bad marks."

"Miss Bitch, you are speaking to a First-Place Finisher. Also, I must warn you: Goldkorn is no greenhorn. Do you think, with such favors, to make a distraction? I know the conditions in which you hold Madam Knight. Yes, with her wrists in irons. With nutrition of bread and water. In a dungeon with rats."

"Hey, my mistake. I figured you for a bottom, not a top. Okay, I'm spread-eagled."

"This is not tolerable! You must fetch Miss Crystal at once. You must unchain her. I will inform authorities! I have seen what you have done to her. She was once a smiling lass. At the sight of that youthful creamery one cried, 'Excelsior!' Now Leib Goldkorn puts down his foot. I will not accept substitutions. Do you wish me to call the mounted police?"

"Hold on, okay? Hold on."

"I am holding."

The pause that occurs is marked by the arrival of the Number 1 Local. What hordes of peoples pellmell depart. From all four boroughs the natives of Gotham descend to savor the broilings at Williams Bar-B-Que chicken. Also sturgeon of Greengrass.

"Hello."

There is no need for identifications. On rare occasions voice and visage cannot one from the other endure separation. The leap of my heart, like a springbok, tells me that at last this is Miss Crystal Knight. Breathlessness.

"Hello? Are you there? Is it my master?"

In those tones, those syllables, there was a rawness, a roughness, that sometimes attends the words of a lifetime smoker. But hidden in that huskiness there was a sound—what comes to mind? A lamb on the frisk, with about its neck a silver bell. Yes, a pure and innocent chime.

"Greetings, Miss. Here is Leib Goldkorn, sometime *Glockenspieler*. May I ask, how is your health?"

"Fine, Master."

"I understand. You must guard your words. Are you at this moment within the confines of your dungeon?"

"Yes. Is it too dark for you to see? They don't allow electric light. Only candles."

"But this is a disgrace! It is medieval. These people—have they not heard of Voltaire?"

"Candles and—way at the top, a window with bars."

"*Ach*, Miss. Such pain I feel at the thought of you forsaken. With rats, *ja?* With water drips. With the green mold slime upon the stones."

"Look, Master! There goes a rat now! Oh, it's terrible. The beady eyes! The teeth! The whiskers on him! Oh, Larry—is that right? Larry? I'm completely helpless. It's coming closer! It's crawling over my shoe."

"The red one?"

"If only I could shake it off. But I am tied to the rock. Oh! It's climbing my leg."

"Heavens! Does this mean you are now in irons?"

"Yes, around my ankles, around my wrists. My legs are spread wide. My arms are too. There is a collar around my throat."

"*Mein Gott!* The fiends! But how are you in such conditions able to speak on the Bell telephone?"

"I'm cold. So cold. I'm not wearing anything, you know. Just the red shoe. It's got a five-inch spike. And leather straps. They go around my thighs. Between my buttock cheeks. Circling my breasts. Double Ds. Oh, this water drips like ice! The shadows! What's in the shadows? Is it *them?* Are they coming? To beat me? With canes. With whips."

"I know who this is, your tormentor. He was once an agent of the SS. My nemesis! The Nazi!"

"Oooh, Nazis!"

"We must now trick him."

"But how? They come every hour. They'll see if I'm gone."

"I am having an inspiration! Attend, please. I must take your place. It is already dark. By snuffing more of the candles, we shall make it even darker. In the remaining lumens my body, in the irons, in the strap works, will, in spite of shoulder hairs, be taken for yours."

"But they will beat you. You want to switch back from dom to sub?"

"I now will come closer. Is there a—in my tongue we say *ein Burggraben*. A *Wasser* moat. Perhaps with alligators. These reptiles are native to Florida, capital Tallahassee. Peanuts, tourism, and citrus. Yes, I am now arriving. Do you see me? Do you hear me? Apply please the manacles! Hello? Are you present? Where is the candlelight? Where the bread and water?"

Please deposit three dollars and fifteen cents for an additional three minutes.

On we sailed, ever southward, a day and a night and yet another day. Then, at midafternoon, the entire ocean turned from blue to brown, as if, in a mirror image, a gigantic dust storm had suddenly obscured the whole of the sky. Here was the Amazon! The earth of the continent, the mud of its swamps, the rich soil of its pampas—all this churned now hundreds of miles out to sea. Food for thought. Does not the river of our lives carry in its currents the detritus of long-forgotten deeds? What if, on the Iglawa, I had not heard as a youngling the whistle of the *Leopold II* and the answering call of the nuthatch and finch? Would the Graduate, who thus learned from birdsongs the secret of instrumentals, be floating off the primitive land of Brazil? Once more we see how the waterways of the world—from the mighty Amazon to the tiny tributary of my youth—flow each with inevitability into each.

From that moment forth, steaming now eastward, we never lost sight of the land. São Luís, Fortaleza, Natal; then, resuming our southward path, Recife, Maceió, Salvador: each of these cities and settlements hove into view—was that a faint fado? A smell of spices?—and then disappeared in a cloud of our own swirling smoke. On one such afternoon, leaning with leisure against what navies call the starboard, Miss Carmen linked with suggestiveness her arm into mine and—this candid moment was caught in the lens of Bernardo's Brownie—placed on my cheek a definite lip kiss. Ah, Mistress Miranda!

"Tic-Tacs?"
"Kit Kats! Quick!"

Do not think that the last days of our cruise were spent in such carefree carousals. Hour after hour we of the fifth column locked ourselves in Carmen's cabin, making preparations for our premiere. I sat in one corner laboring upon both the score and libretto of my beloved opera. *A Jewish Girl in the Persian Court?*

No Longer! It was *Esther in Egypt* now. All this new material was to be inserted into *Aïda's* second act. But how to make such a transformation and at the same time create—this was a bow to our hosts and to Vargas, our victim—a certain Latin flavor? I could not, of course, ask either Ramfis or Radames to perform a rhumba; yet with a subtle shift of tonalities, and the introduction of *Afrikaner*-American motifs, mixed with a sprinkling of Gershwinonics, I managed to produce for the Moors and the Slaves a definite South American dance. Ha! Ha! A little black samba!

Nor were my confederates idle. The Boys had not only to guard our two prisoners—the gagged and roped Maltz, who had been smuggled from the infirmary; and Toscanini, whose frozen muscles bound him more securely than any number of knots—but to practice their parts in the rhythm section, copy out the new pages of *Esther* for the entire NBC Symphonia, and coordinate their actions for the opening night. And what of poor Madam Miranda? She had the most difficult assignment of all. Unable to practice with the orchestra, she was forced to sing her new lines—

I am a servant, a slave, as low as an amoeba
I! I! Daughter of Solomon and the Queen of Sheba—

a cappella, save for the primitive accompaniment—bongo, gourd, castanet, and Felipe's fipple flute—of the Rhythmaires, poor substitute for a cast, chorus, and orchestra in their hundreds.

My body does ache and my bones have no marrow
There's no rest when you serve the mighty Pharaoh.

Ilhéus, Alcobaça, Mucori, Vitória: closer and closer we drew to the home port of our steamship and the site of Leib Goldkorn's operatic debut. As the sun began to set on our last night at sea, I decided to take one last stroll aftward—to where, at the sound of three bells, I had once thought to extinguish the very life that now had such import for all of the world. Imagine my astonishment upon discovering that the shuttlecockers and

skeeters, the promenaders and sippers of bouillon had all vanished from the rearmost decks; and that in their place the crew
of the *Amazonas* were frantically attempting to duplicate both
the Palace at Memphis and the Gate of Thebes. Indeed, the
whole of the stern had been transformed into a replica of the
Kingdom of Egypt. Huge murals of the banks of the Nile—here
were palm trees, swift-sailing feluccas, the Pyramids in per-
spective—hung suspended in the air by the same cranes that
had hoisted me aboard at the Hudson piers. Out of the very
hatch into which I had nearly descended, a great plaster cast of
the Sphinx, wearing in modesty double brassiere cups, stood
poised to ascend. Lamps and lanterns had been strung everywhere, from—here I employ once more the language of
Limeys—the fantail to the poop. On that deck a group of stew-
ards were assembling a semicircle of music stands, while
beneath it, in its protective shade, more of these white-coated
fellows were arranging row upon row of folding-type chairs.
Only then did the tardy truth dawn upon me. The world premiere of *Esther in Egypt* was to take place not in the Imperial
Teatro of Rio but here, where I stood, on the deck of the *Amazonas* itself.

"Can you move, Slave?"

"Ha! Ha! Not even a pinkie."

"Excellent. What do you see?"

"Nothing."

"*Nothing, Herr Obersturmführer!*"

"Nothing, Herr Obersturmführer. Ha! Ha! This is excellent
preparation for when I shall meet your cruel employer."

"No speaking, swine! No thoughts! You cannot see because I
have put your filthy head into a hood."

"Perfect! This is a technique to be found in the works of L. von
Sacher-Masoch."

"Silence! Speak when spoken to! Are you cold? Are you shivering?"

"Oh, yes. All ashiver."

"*Yes, Obersturmführer!*"

"*Ja, mein kleine Obersturmführer.* Ha, ha, ha."

"Perhaps you would like some heat, eh?"

"You mean a steam bath? Hot rocks? This is a healthful recreation."

"*Hund! Schweinehund! This* is what I mean! How do you like that? And that? Hot wax from the candle! There! Upon your throat! Now do you laugh? Upon your breast! Why no laughter now? There! Upon the fat of your belly!"

"Oooh! Ah! Aha! Ow!"

"You pig! You dog! You dare lie to me? *Scheisskopf!* Did you not tell your Master you were cold? That you could not move? More wax! Upon your shoulders!"

"Ah! Ah! Ha! Ha! No. *Nein!* I swear! I did not make prevarications."

"Swine! You are lying again! You said you were unable to lift a finger! But what do I see? One part of the pig is moving. One part is hot. Yes, hot as this candle."

"You mean my Jewish-style member? How did you know this? It is in truth making an occupation of the Stutchkoff forty-fours. Ha! Ha! It thinks it is still a boy!"

"*Arschloch! Schwein!* Are you not ashamed?"

"No, no: I am minding both Ps and Qs. I am in the Bell Telephone booth. Private. Like a cabinetto."

"Listen! A miracle! A pig can talk. Just like a human! It feels shame. It wants to make excuses. *Excuse me for my detestable behavior! Excuse me for my public display. I am only a pig. Oink! Oink! Excuse my* Schweinischkeit! Say it! Say it!"

"Oink?"

"*Excuse me, Herr Obersturmbannführer! Excuse me, Master!*"

"Excuse me, Herr Obersturmbannführer."

"What? He dares address an officer? An officer of the SS?"

"But you said—"

"Can I believe my ears? Now he actually talks back? He must be taught a lesson!"

Crack!

"Did you hear that?"

"Yes, Master."

Crack! Crack!

"Do you know what that is?"

"A cat-o'-nine?"

"Yes! Now we shall turn you around. We no longer wish to see this detestable thing. Face the wall! Hands out! Feet wide!"

"Is it a flagellation?"

Crack! Crack! Crack!

"Ow! It stings! Ha! Ha! Ha! It burns!"

"Beg! Beg for forgiveness!"

"Do you think, Miss Crystal, that we might use the shoe?"

"On your back!"

Crack!

"On your calves!"

Crack!

"On your thighs!"

Crack!

"Ow! Oh! It hurts! It hurts!"

"Will you not beg? *Forgive me, Master!*"

"Forgive me, Master. Don't forget the nates."

"Beg! Beg!"

Crack! Crack!

"Beg, Jew! *Excuse my* Schweinischkeit!"

"Ah! Oooh! Oh, Miss Crystal! Excuse, please! Ow! Ow! A thousand pardons!"

"Pig! Dog! Grovel like a dog! Beg, *Hund!*"

"Yes! Oink! I am a pig! Forgive me! Bow-wow! I deserve to be beaten! Beat me! Like a dog! Bow-wow-wow! Look! I am a Jew! I confess it! A living Jew! Yes! Up my back! Now down!"

Crack! Crack! Crack! Crack!

"Why am I living? That is what is detestable. That is the disgrace. Bow-wow-wow! Oink! Oink! Oink! All the rest have been destroyed. All the others. Minkche! My little darling! Bow-wow-wow! With the beauty mark! Yahkne! The champion skier! Her Trabucco cheroot! The manly one. And here am I! Not a man. An animal. A swine! Mama! Papa! Where are you? Do you see me? Do you wish to beat me too? You sailed away! I stayed on the bank! Take the whip! Beat your bad boy! Bad boy! All the lovely musicians! Gone! Gone! Those dear people! The music they made!"

Crack! Crack! Crack! Crack!

"I am a not even an animal! I am an insect! A louse! What noise does a louse make? Yew-yewie-yew! I suck people's blood! That's what I do! How could I go on living? I? I, alone! Of all Europe's Jews! Beat me! Harder! I deserve it! The cat-o'-nine! Ah, my professors! The learned men! Pergam! Lapunjer! Oh, oh, Rabbi Goldiamond! Beat me! Beat me with the whip! Again! Yes, again! Bow-wow-wow! The cur! The doggie! This Bowser! Bad boy! Bad boy! Beat him! Beat him! He should not be alive!"

"Larry? Hello? Are you all right? Larry? Oh, Jesus!"

Please deposit three dollars and fifteen cents for an additional three minutes.

There was no sleep that night for Leib Goldkorn. Useless to count the wool-bearing sheep. I went out in my herringbones to greet the dawn. The sun, *natürlich*, rose in the east. To my fearful eye it looked raw, like uncooked meat, from which the juices ran upon the swollen sea. I shivered—not because, at latitude 22 degrees south, the last days of summer were still within winter's grip, but from foreboding. *Nonsense, my fine Graduate*, thus did I reproach myself. *Chin ups!* But now the fiery orb—chariot, according to Professor Pergam, of the god Apollo—climbed limpingly into the nearby clouds, which wrapped themselves about it like soiled bandages around a wound. Clouds? Why clouds? These were the first we had seen in either the tropic or temperate zones. A breeze sprang up, raising my leftward lapel. The ocean liner tipped on a sudden swell. From within, something fell, making a sound of broken glass. We hove about, so that the sun, in its reddened rags, was now behind us. West! We were heading west! Rio lay just ahead.

"HELLO? HELLO? MISS Crystal? Look! I am weeping salt-filled tears! Tears from gratitude! Do not fear abandonment. Wait. Wait, please. I am coming back. Yes, coming back to save you! Moment!"

Just after noontime we sailed into the Baia de Guanabara. There lay the metropolis, spread out before us, ringed by mountains and hills. On the port side rose the famed Sugar Bush, at four hundred meters; and towering yet higher, soaring over everything, was the Morro da Corcovado, atop which with arms spread was the figure of Jesus, of course a Jew. Slowly now, puffing black smoke from both smokestacks, we made our way northward, past the gleaming Praia do Flamengo—even on a day without sunshine the bathers bobbed on the wavelets and lay stretched on the sand—the Naval Academy, and toward the docks at Ilha das Cobras.

All along this route steamships and sailboats, tugs and schooners followed in our wake or kept pace alongside. There was a boom, a second boom, and a dozen white wreaths of smoke, like rings from cigars, floated above the guns of the Brazilian Navy. It was a salute. And so were the fountains and sprays, the leaping geysers, sent skyward from the ships of the Municipàl Departamento de Fuera. Now, as we slowed even further, tiny motorcraft crisscrossed beneath our bow; from every direction—from the beaches and wharves, and from across the bay at Niterói—a thousand self-propelled vessels, rowboats, paddlers, dugouts, and dinghies swarmed about us like iron filings about the great magnet of our hull.

Then, to my astonishment, both anchors dropped from either side of our bow. We were not going to dock. I peered out at the waterfront. Every pier was packed with the Brazilian natives, as were the great avenues that ran parallel to the shore. More people had crowded onto the rooftops of the nearest buildings—the Ministério da Marinha, the Museu de Caça e Pesca, and even the Banco do Brasil.

"Listen! Do you hear?" That was Bernardo, who had come up beside me from the decks below.

"Yes. Música!" Indeed there was music, tangos, sambas, roulettas, along with the regular beat of a military band. Was it a parade? A fiesta? I could see flags set out all along the seashore. Children, darting through the crowds, waved pennants cut from paper. "It must be," I said to my companion, "a national holiday."

"No! No! Listen!" He was pointing over the railing, at all the upturned faces within the vast flotilla. They were grinning. They were nodding. From between cupped hands they shouted and yelled. "Carmen!" That's what half of them cried. "Carmenzinha!" And the other half? "Toscanini! *È viva! Viva Toscanini!*" For a moment I stood, stunned, as unmoving as the Maestro himself.

"*Rápido! Para a cabina!*" Bernardo exclaimed.

H<small>INDOO</small>: "*HUSTLER?*"

"Hershey! Hurry! *Mit* nuts!"

Inside our stateroom all was confusion. Tono raced frantically from one side of the living space to the other, attempting to organize our new score into piles for the brass, the woodwinds, the strings. Felipe was cutting cloth patches he would apply to the chorus, and Madam Miranda was in the dressing area, alternately singing a difficult aria

O patria mia, mai più ti rivedrò. . .
O fresche valli, O queto asil beato
(Oh, my native land, with its rivers so broad
Oh, fresh valley, where this pretty foot so oft has trod)
                        L. Goldkorn translation—

and atomizing her throat with a bottle. In the bedroom the billy beard was wrestling with Herr Maltz, who, though ropes zigged and zagged over his torso, nonetheless had sufficient strength to hop about on the four legs of his chair. Only the Maestro stood calm, like a rock amidst this chaos of crashing waves.

"*Oi,* Boys!" cried Bernardo, as we burst into the cabin. "The people! They are calling for Carmen! They are making a *rebelião!*" Without breaking stride he crossed to the parlor porthole and jerked it wide. Immediately the shouts and cries assaulted us, along with a more ominous sound: clanks, clunks, the ring of reverberations. The makeshift mariners were hurling objects against the metal plates of the hull.

"*Puxa!*" cried the Bombshell. "These are my fans, *meus fãs.* They love their Carmen!"

Before anyone could think to restrain her she dashed forward and thrust her head, heaped with paw-paws and avocados, through the circular window. A roar went up, and grew louder and louder as, first with one hand, then the other, Madam Miranda blew to the multitude her many moues. But the shouting did not cease. Now the crowd was calling for Toscanini. I glanced back toward the Maestro. Would this tribute wake him from his trance? Surely he could hear how, even after more than fifty years, the people had not forgotten him. Alas, the Stone Guest stood unmoving. His eyes did not blink, nor did his breath stir the least hair of his gray moustache. Would it, I thought with sudden horror, cloud the surface of a mirror?

Once again it was the broad-shouldered Bernardo who acted first. He flung wide a second porthole, this one in the bedroom. Tono and Felipe, seeing his intention, sprang forward and seized the comatose conductor. Together they hauled him, as butchers might a side of frozen beef, to the open window. With Bernardo's assistance they pushed his head, with its white wisps of hair and its ghostly complexion, all the way through. Once more the populace let out a roar. The next thing I knew, the goateed Rhythm Boy was propelling me to the spot.

"Senhor Comandante," he implored me. "O braço! Levante o braço!"

I am a non-Portuguese speaker. Yet I knew all too clearly what was required. I crept up behind the Maestro and thrust my arm, still in herringbone, through the gap. While Tono manipulated the head upward and downward, I waved the ersatz limb in the air. The lovers of music sent up a thunderous ovation. The population was applauding the puppeteer.

W H A T I S E E upon returning to the Bell Telephone booth takes from my pulmonaries the last gasp. The door, which I had left open, is now closed tight. Through the tint of the glass I am able to make out a barrel-chester, six-foot-two, cheeks all astubble, with low brow and lantern-type chin. In short, a non-Jew. He is just—oh, misery!—inserting his store of jetons. How I am mocked by the sound of that merry *ting* and *ling* and *ling*! Time now for the non-believer to offer fervent prayers. *Grosser Gott:* Let the line be busy. Stretch forth your hand, Almighty, and cause the Betty or the Beverly at the other end to be not at this time at home.

Mein Gott! Is this gentleman to speak all night? Wait! Wait! Hurrah, friends! The answer to fervent prayers! *La voiture est arrivée!* Another Number 1 Local. On its way to the Borough of the Bronx. Ha! Ha! Ha! Now the conversation—*Well, good-bye, Thomas or Timothy or Chris or Mary Ann. Christ be with you*—must at last have a conclusion. What? *Was ist das?* Is he so bewitched by the chatterbox that he has not noticed that his conveyance has already opened its rubberized doors?

"Pardon, my good fellow. Excuse, please! Ha! Ha! But you in your heart-to-heart are about to, as they say, miss the boat."

No response. Rather, the monopolist turns upon me his back, the instrument like a leech to his ear.

What to do? I rap with the rim of a quarter dollar upon the glass. I finger point to the face of my Bulova, where the hand for seconds is hurrying by. I make, hand palm to hand palm, the international symbol of supplication. Now occurs the straw that makes the camel turn back: the insertion of—*Ting! Ting! A-ling!*—three more jetons! I make the fateful decision.

A booth of Bell manufacture is hinged in the center with a handle on the leftmost side. This I seize with resolution, causing the portal to slide in accordion fashion wide enough to allow Leib Goldkorn within. "Sir, I am to the city of New York, New York, P. Minuit founder, a payer of tax. I have a right to facilities. I am speaking of an emergency call. Life, ha-ha, or death!"

At last! A reaction. The gentleman, his neck is as thick as a sequoia, inquires of me why I do not engage in an act of self-propagation.

"Sir, there is no need to speak here with such salt."

Now I find myself clutched by my shirtfront and lifted into the air.

"Please! Do not mistake me! I am making an offer. All of my monies. I shall make lightning calculations. Original sum: forty-seven dollars, legal tender. Less Abraham Lincoln five, this was for, at the Court of Palms, tariff and tip; less fifteen, condiments from yon concessionaire; less six, *Hustler Review*, acquired from the identical source. This leaves a sum of twenty-one dollars. But hold: from the hand of the Hindoo I received change in silver, only a portion of which was expended on telephonics. Twenty-five dollars! Here! Do you see? Twenty-five dollars! This is more than Minuit spent for all of Manhattan! Can we achieve consummation? Put her there, partner! We make the deal!"

One hour after sundown Felipe and I sat with our instruments in the woodwind section of the National Biscuit Company Symphonia. My companion wore his Gypsy silks, the air-filled blouse and pantaloons, while I was dressed in the frock coat of yet another five-fiver, A. Toscanini. Black shoes, stiff shirt, striped pants, and a tiny winged collar: in short, the tux fit yours truly to a T. Beneath the poop, the last of the crowd were filing into their seats. All afternoon ferries had shuttled *Amazonas* passengers to the shore and, toward dusk and after, guests, dignitaries, and ticket holders back to the decks of the steamer. These decks were now tilted. Indeed, the entire ship was in the rising sea tipping constantly leftward and right, like an enormous metronome. To the west, inland, beyond the circle of hills, the sky flashed with light and the tom-toms of thunder steadily beat. I glanced down, to where the scenery was lit by the strings of colorful bulbs. In the background, behind the pillars of the palace, the Arabian desert stretched off as far as the eye could see. Had it rained in these sands, even once, since the storm that had lasted forty days and forty nights?

Eight o'clock, BWT. Also time for the onset of *Aïda*. R. Shaw, the chorus master—it was he who had rehearsed us in the opera, while the Maestro recovered from what all believed was a *mal de mer*—paced about at the rail of the poop. The NBCers repeatedly sounded their As. Mr. Bjoerling, inside the palace, cracked with audibleness his knuckles. Madam Milanov, trying with non-success to secret herself behind an obelisk, cleared from her throat a frog. Eight-ten. At the front of the stage the prompter—it was the billy beard, I could see his reddish goatee—leaned round his box, a furrow of anxiousness upon his brow. Where at this moment were the rest of the Rhythm Boys? Felipe, with fipple flute, a kind of alto recorder, was by my side. Tono was standing guard outside our stateroom door. Directly below me sat Bernardo, balancing his bongo, in the audience's second row. Now the rearmost sections of that throng began, in rhythmic manner, to clap their hands. They wanted the opera to begin. But how could that occur when the two people most indispensable to that performance—Vargas, the dictator, and the conductor Toscanini—had not yet made their appearance? More minutes went slowly by. The wind picked up. The thunder grew louder. Finally, at half past the hour, the trumpet section rose for a fanfare—not that flourish that begins the *Celeste Aïda* ("instep *divina*")—but the triple high Fs of the Brazilian National Anthem. Gétulio Vargas was coming on board. Beneath the poop deck all in the audience stood. R. Shaw motioned for the rest of the Symphonia to get to their feet as well. In their blue uniforms the crew of the *Amazonas* saluted. Then Senhor Vargas appeared and, with his entourage, walked to the front of the crowd. *O Presidente* was a man of middle age and middle height, with a belly that bulged through what looked like an admiral's outfit of cream and gold. He wore thick eyeglasses in heavy black frames. No moustache. He and his aides, mostly militarists, took up the whole of the foremost row. Only the chair on the ruler's left remained empty. When he sat, so did the crowd, along with the Symphonia.

It was then that the leader of the Boys craned round the box of prompts and, with an eyebrow arch, delivered a glance of significance to his partner on the poop. At once I rose and walked to the front of the orchestra. In a clear, non-shaking voice I announced that A. Toscanini was still underneath the weather. A gasp rose from all ninety-four throats.

"What are you saying?" asked Shaw. "That the Maestro will not conduct? My God! We'll have to cancel."

"Not necessary. What is the expression? On goes the show!"

"Are you mad? Do you expect me to do it? I've got a chorus to lead. They're onstage. I can't be in two places at once."

"Go, sir. Go to the choristers."

"But who will conduct?"

I gave a slight smile and with deftness turned my Rudall & Rose on its end. A second gasp, louder than the first, rose from the members of the Symphonia. There had slid into my hand the very baton that had so often hypnotized them and that even now, as I raised it, continued its mesmerization, as if it were the Maestro and not his messenger who was attached. Time for the down-beat? I looked over my shoulder and, as protocol demanded, awaited the approval of the real *comandante*. But Vargas, clearly, was in a vexation. He looked this way and that. He crossed and uncrossed his lower limbs. On his face was an angry scowl.

Oooh, went the assemblage, as a wave lifted the stern of the *Amazonas* into the ink of the night and then dropped it downward with such force that it seemed that even the painted Nile must spill its banks. Clearly the performance could not be delayed any longer.

Luckily, at that very moment the dictator and all his minions jumped upright. Vargas was suddenly asmile. Now I saw the reason. A woman, wrapped in a dark silken gown, swept onto the stern and approached the head of state. On her head was a sort of sombrero whose crown was a tall mound of dates. Madam Miranda! The militarists stepped aside. For a moment the world's two most famous Brazilians stood facing each other. Then Vargas spoke:

"Our bird, she was a true bird of paradise, flew away. Away! Her song could be heard only in the cold land of the North. The nation that was left behind mourned her with sighs. Our hearts turned to stone. How it warms me to say, on behalf of all the people of Brazil, including our Indian and Negro minorities, *Welcome back, beautiful bird, to your native land. Here you reign as Queen.*"

With those words he bowed, took the singer's hand, and kissed it. After that he turned it over and buried his face in the palm. Nor was that all: he nibbled her wrist and then, right through the soft silk of her gown, mouthed the crook of her arm. Here was Latin charm! For a moment I lost myself in admiration. But only for a moment. The next thing I knew the Don Juan had stood once again upright and, with outstretched arm, was issuing a command to the poop. "*Alô, músicos! Començem! Començem a música!*"

At those words a surge of voltage went through every part of my body and made even my hair fringe stand upon end. I rapped with the baton upon the top of the music stand. I rapped again. Then I lifted the wand into the air. "Ready, gentlemen? *Eine eins, eine zwei, eine drei!*"

Ho! Ho! Ho! These gullible goyim! So easy to fool. All the time I held in my unopened fist the change from the five-dollar bill. Ha! Ha! The barrel chester never thought to ask. I fooled him! But who, in a retrospective, is the joke upon? My treasure is spent. This—*quarter, quarter, quarter, quarter*—will be my very last call.

Strings, just a few of them, and in the highest register: the peacefulness of the Valley of the Nile. Then a nod to the violas, the deeper waters that run beneath the great river's moonlit surface. Next the violoncellos, with their suggestion of the rumors of war. How easy it was! The baton in my hand weighed less than a pick for a tooth, less than a hair, less than a feather. It seemed to move through the air all on its own, dipping, soaring, pointing, but always circling, as if the hundreds of rehearsals and performances of *Aïda* had somehow become ingrained in the wood. Imagine a man who, hoping to teach his dog to perform a retrieval, ends up by miraculously training the stick.

At the end of the overture, Ramfis and Radames stepped from the palace and began to talk of war and peace. Then the priest retreated and the young warrior began his great aria that combined the twin themes of the tragedy: how he would secure for his nation a great victory, *e la vittoria*; and how with those spoils he would build for his beloved Aïda a throne where she might rest the sole of her feet, *trono vicino al sol*. The conclusion: a high note, C over C. Ah! Bjoerling held it for three seconds, for five, for an astounding ten: Ah-h-h-h! The baton, all on its own dipped downward, as if, like a dowser, it had found water. Pause. Applause. Indeed, a rousing ovation.

Then this rod, without waiting for silence, roused itself in a no-nonsense manner and struck the downbeat for the duet. Here Amneris, the daughter of Pharaoh, asked the handsome tenor if he were perhaps smitten by someone with a finer turned ankle than hers. He denied it, but she wondered to herself if his heart had not found *un altro amore*. Round and round went the baton, churning the air into music the way a paddle makes butter from cream.

Enter Aïda.

I glanced over my shoulder. Yes, the mammoth Milanov had stepped out of hiding and was in full view of her lover and her rival. The wand in my hand began from excitement a kind of vibration. The violins shivered, too. Amneris, with false concern, asked the slave girl why, *Piangi?*, she wept. At that instant, behind me and before me, I could hear two separate whooshes of rushing air. The first came from the influx of oxygen as the soprano expanded her mammary to take in a breath. The second was like the sound a trumpet will make when the trumpeter wishes to blow from his mouthpiece an excess of saliva.

Ohimè! cried Aïda, just as Verdi had written.

Suddenly the baton stopped in midair, almost wrenching my arm from its socket, like a recalcitrant crank on an old Model T.

Ohimè! cried the slave girl once again, a repeat not in the score. I whirled around. The Ethiope, in all of her avoirdupois, was staggering, her arms clutching her flank zone. Then with a thud that must have been felt all the way to the steam room, she dropped to both knees and keeled onto her side.

Pandemonium. In the audience the ladies were screaming. The gentlemen, on their feet, were making exclamations. Bjoerling stood immobilized, wringing his pudgy hands. The aides to O *Presidente* had instinctively reached for their hidden weapons, while the dictator himself removed his tongue from Madam Miranda's inner ear.

"Back! Back! Stand back!" Thus shouted the goateed prompter who, leaping from his box, was the first to reach the stricken singer. He bent over her, covering with his own body her sirloin and saddle. Then he looked up. "*Um médico. Ha um médico aí?*"

On the poop deck all the musicians were on their feet, peering over the rail with concern. All but one. Felipe sat in his chair, his wide lips spread in a grin. Then it struck me. This native, black-skinned, squat, his hair in a nap style, was in fact only a step removed from his jungle home. That instrument he held in his lap: that was no fipple flute. It was a blowgun. He had struck Zinka Milanov with a poisoned dart!

"Hello? Hello? To which young lady am I speaking? Miss Bitch? Miss Corky? Miss Trixie, the devotee of Ravel? Hurry!

Every second is precious! I must speak once again to Miss Crystal Knight."

In those moments of confusion the Brazilian Rhythm Boys put into effect the rest of our plan. Tono had come up from our cabin with the new score for Act II, scene two. While the orchestra members remained at the rail, he and Felipe slipped the words and music onto their stands. Down below, Bernardo and the whisk beard were no less busy. The former slipped in and out of the chorus, while the latter directed the efforts to revive the downed diva. This proved not possible. The singer lay on her side, mouth agape, brisket heaving, like some great sea beast that has beached itself upon the shore. It took four men to lift Madam Milanov, that manatee, to their shoulders and carry her off to the decks below.

Just then there was a sudden bright flash that lit up the whole city of Rio, from the Copacabana to the Corcovado. A few seconds later the thunder rolled over us, as if one of the batteries of the Brazilian Navy had fired a broadside. In the crowd, umbrellas, like tropical flora, began to pop open. Already people were starting to move away. They were stopped by a sound of rattling: the leader of the Rhythmaires was clacking his castanets.

"Stop! We shall continue. Not a single note will be missed."

"But how can that be?" This was R. Shaw. "We have no understudy."

"Aha!" cried the prompter. "But we do!" Smiling broadly, the billy beard pointed to the first row of the audience. There Madam Miranda was standing upon her chair. She gave, with her shoulders, the slightest shrug. The gown she'd been wearing fell into folds at her feet. What a sight was now revealed! Bare breasts, save for, at each pap, a pasty. Within the omphalos, a red ruby glowed. Over the infernal region was a black piece of cotton, hardly larger than an eye patch, held in place by what I believe is called a string in the key of G.

A cheer went up from the employees of Lloyd Brasileiro. At the sight of her footwear, a sort of sabot, through which one could see all five red-painted toes, the substitute conductor also wished to utter a huzzah. But the near-naked Nile Maiden held up her hands and, with the first words of her song—

Ohimè! di guerra fremere
L'atroce grido io sento.
Per l'infelice patria,
per me, per voi pavento—
(Oy veh! These war cries in my ears
Each one nastier and meaner;
They fill my eyes with tears,
I tremble to the root of my femur)
L.G., translator—

all fell silent. When her aria was done, everyone in the crowd dashed hurriedly back to his seat. *O comandante supremo,* on his knees now, attempted to stuff cruzeiros into the singer's elasticized strap. In my hand the magic baton sprang fully erect. It trembled and tingled. It glowed with fire. I could not restrain it. Headlong it leaped, into the rest of *Aïda.*

"Miss Crystal? Honey, I am once again here."

"Too late, Larry."

"But what can this mean? Is he coming? The torturer? The jailor?"

"Shhh! Yes. Don't you hear him?"

"His name! Give it to me! Is it Maltz? The villain!"

"We can't speak his name. We'll be punished."

"Let me then describe him. Two curls on the forehead. The hair in a central part. Chin cleft. Gap in the forward incisors. Picture, please, Thomas E. Dewey. *Ja? Ja?* Am I correct?"

"Oh, that laugh! The clanking chains! His boots on the stones! He's coming!"

"Miss! Do not despair. I will confront him. It will not be the first time that he finishes, to Leib Goldkorn, in second place."

"No, you can't fight him. No one can. It's the end. Goodbye, Larry. If only you had come sooner."

"*Goodbye?* But the three minutes are not up."

"I am going to throw myself into the—what do you call it?"

"*Ein Wasser* moat?"

"Yes! Into the moat!"

"But the alligators! They are definite meat eaters!""

"Better to be eaten alive than to face *him* one more time."

"Wait! If we cannot fight we can flee! Come with me to the Avenue Columbus. Miss, I am making a heartfelt proposal."

"How can we flee? There are guards. There are ramparts. No man can leap them."

"Is it true? Are we doomed?"

"Oh, Larry! I have an idea. But would you be willing? Would you trust me? Would you do what I say?"

"Your wish, Miss, is my command performance."

"All right. It's our only chance. Do you see what I have in my hand?"

"A whip, ha-ha-ha? A cane?"

"No! I mean, *yes!* It is a whip *and* a cane."

"Can such a thing be?"

"A riding crop! Slave, onto your knees."

"Yes. I am dropping. Question: will the Bell telephone cord make the needed extension? *Ja!* No problem."

"Now—onto your elbows. Quick! All the way down."

"I am making with difficulty the maneuver. We have in this cubicle cramped spatials. This is reminiscent of the American craze: as many as ten youthful collegians would in such a booth swallow goldfish."

"Are you down? On all fours?"

"Wait. *Moment.* Ouch! I should apply to the Roumanian Circus. Ah, *voilà!* I have succeeded. Am I once more a canine? Woof! Woof! Or perhaps a pig?"

"No! Fool! A horse!"

"A horse! Ha! Ha! Are you, you know, going to mount my back?"

"Yes! We'll leap both the moat and the ramparts. They won't be able to catch us."

"An excellent idea! All aboard! Are you putting your foot in the stirrup?"

"Oh, I'm riding bareback. Can you feel me? The weight of my ass? I'm squeezing you with my calves, with my thighs."

"You are as light, Miss, as a wee jockey boy. To win the race you must now apply the whip."

"There! Do you feel that? On your neck? On your shoulders?"

"Ouch! Ouch! It hurts!"

"Trot! Trot! Do you feel that? We have to go faster."

"We are now at the trot! Ha! Ha! I am a horsie! Your little horsie! Nei-gh-gh-gh!"

"Faster! A canter! A gallop! A run!"

"For velocity, Miss, the jockey must apply a hand slap to the rump."

"There! You nag! There! You have to go faster! They are after us! Faster! They will turn you into glue!"

"Ah, do you see what is happening? I am feeling oats. Look at this! I am developing the shlong of a stallion! You have done this for me, Miss Crystal. Ah! I feel the peppercorns!"

"Move! Move! They're gaining on us!"

"Ouch! Ouch! I am in my stride striking alternately my head and buttock against the walls. What speed! If I were not hairless my mane would be flying!"

"Look! It's the moat. Can we leap it?"

"To stimulate the jump the jockey must use the heel. The heel and the spur. Kick! Kick me, honey! Nei-gh-gh-gh!"

"I am! There! In the ribs! It's a five-inch heel! How do you like that? And that?"

"Oh! Ah! Such a *Sensationslust!* Look at the size of this Johnson! Kick! Kick! It is on fire! It is sprouting wings! Ah, ah! Over the moat!"

"Oh, no! Look! The ramparts! They are eight feet tall! Can we do it? There! There! The whip! The flat of my hand! And there! There! The spike of my heel!"

"Ah, we are flying! Pergam! My professor! Pegasus! I am Pegasus! A paroxysm! It is approaching! Just what the doctor has ordered!"

"Here it is! The wall! Jump! Jump, you bag of bones! Fly! Fly over it! Fly into the air!"

"Oh! Oh! Miss Litwack! Clara! My true love! Show me? Where does it go? Into which orifice? There? Are you certain? All right! Very well!"

Please deposit three dollars and fifteen cents for an additional three minutes.

"No! Oh, no! Operator! Sweetheart! I have no such sums! I am on my knees to you. Will you have mercy? I will send an order of Western Union. To the Company of Bell Telephone. Hello? Operator? Hello?"

"Goodbye, Larry. It's been a gas."

"Miss Crystal! Oh, Miss Crystal! Don't leave me!"

"Gotta go!"

"Tell me! One thing! Where are you? Where is the dungeon? Tell me that!"

"Riv—No, we are not allowed to give that information."

"What? What? I am hearing a buzz."

"Bye, bye."

"Ah. Ah. Oh. Oh."

The rest of Act I was performed just as Verdi had composed it. Madam Miranda, Bjoerling, and the Amneris completed the trio: Aïda torn between love of her warrior and love of her country; Radames filled with anxiousness, lest his passion for the slave girl be discovered; and Amneris, also a woman of heft—might we speak of a mezzomorph?—continuing to voice her suspicions and pain. After that Pharoah appoints Radames as *il condottiero supremo*, the Commander in chief, and all cry out for death and destruction—*Guerra e morte, morte allo stranier!*—to the foreign foe.

It was not to Pharaoh, however, that Aïda expressed her feelings, nor to Radames, and not even, as is the custom, to herself. Instead, Madam Miranda directed her words to *O Presidente*. At one point she leaned from the edge of the stage, so that her mams dangled before the dictator like breadfruits from a tree. *Qual poter m'avvince a lui!* she sang: His power binds me to him; and then, vamping at Vargas:

Deggio amarlo, ed è costui
(I am doomed to love him)
L.G., trans.

Now the crowd gasped at the sight of the chorus. The lightning bolts that flashed overhead were mirrored in the insignia that had been in haste slapped upon the singers: the zigzag emblem of the SS. *Guerra! Guerra!* chanted the choristers. And who among us could hear without a chill of horror their final words: *Sterminio! Sterminio!* Exterminate them! Nor was that the only feat accomplished by the Brazilian Boys. When in scene two the High Priest and his men pray to the pagan gods for the success of their armies, each of the clergy bore the cosmic symbol of Good Fortune, the swastika, and Ramfis himself wore on his lip—this inspired titters in some, terror in others—a toothbrush moustache.

Fearing impending barometrics, we allowed no intermission before the start of Act II. The stage was cleared, Amneris appeared on her sofa, and the Dance of the Moorish Slaves began. How the baton swooped and soared through that *accelerando!* It slashed and sliced through the air like one of the broomsticks in *The Sorceror's Apprentice*—except that this was not animation but animism: a wand with a mind of its own, a stick with a soul. With both hands I grasped it, breathless and panting, until at last the dancers departed and Aïda joined Amneris upon the stage.

Miss Carmen, I noted, had added to her scant apparel. Around her neck was a six-pointed star. How could the audience mistake what nation and what people she sighed for when she sang that it had been long since she had seen her brothers, *e dei fratelli,* or, *dal suol natio,* set the soul of her foot in her native land? Thus did the daughter of Israel confront the *figlia dei Faraoni,* daughter of the Pharaohs, over who loved Radames the best. Suddenly the baton in my hand started, like a swagger stick, a martial motion. What was that sound in the distance? The return of the victorious soldiers! It was the end of Act II, scene one. Scene two, my very own *Esther in Egypt,* was about to begin.

Even as I raised my hand for the downbeat, I could not help but recall how this same work of Verdi's had once been performed in this very city. The whole world knows the date: 30th June, 1886. A Wednesday. The hour: eight, *post meridiem.* It was at that moment that, from the string section, an unknown violoncellist arose to take the place of the stricken conductor. Who was this? Dark curly hair. Dark moustaches. Height, sixty-five inches. Arturo Toscanini! He had seized the baton. Who knows? It might be the very one that now had me, and not vice versa, by the hand. Had I been chosen to carry on the tradition? Would this performance of *Esther* not prove, in similar fashion, a world-shattering debut?

In came the procession of the triumphant army. Warriors and charioteers, the priests and the populace, marched before Pharaoh. Then Radames, the conquering hero, appeared. He asked that the prisoners be brought forward. And on they came, poor wretched Ethiopes, each one of whom bore upon his breast a yellow star. We had reached the decisive moment. *Tua pietà, tua clemenza imploriamo,* the war victims begged, holding their chained hands to heaven. But the priests, hard-hearted Hit-lerites, showed no mercy:

A morte! A morte! A morte!
(You must kill them!)

Now the remnants of Jewry, tears streaming, fell on their knees:

Pietà! Pietà! Pietà!
(Take pity upon us.)

Back and forth the argument raged, like the battle between the wind and clouds, the thunder and lightning, above the *Amazonas.* Again and again the Israelites implored the fickle Pharaoh, only to be answered by implacable *Fascisti:*

Morte ai nemici della patria!
(Death to the enemies of the Reich!)

Suddenly the baton in my hand began to shake. With all my strength I clung to it, as a pilot will his vibrating stick in a storm. Simultaneously the NBC Symphonia broke into a lively samba.

Ay! Ay! Ay! Ay! Ay!

Aïda! She made an abdominal dance between the two competing choruses, until she stood directly before the great Vargas of Brazil. Then, while the Rhythm Boys provided percussion, she broke into a Leib Goldkorn *Lied*:

My name isn't Carmen, nor Aïda, not Hester
My father was Abihail, and I am called Esther

The real *condottiero supremo* half rose from his chair. His eyes, glazed and glassy, were fixed on the dancer's brisket.

Oh, Presidente! Oh, Sire
Hear Esther's plea—
She'll fulfill every desire
Shall she sit on your knee?

The dictator nodded. She leaped to his lap, draping her long, sun-browned legs over his crease-free trousers.

Don't touch! Don't touch! If you want a favor
Don't touch! You can't continue to waver

Vargas: "Ah, Bird of Paradise, you make my limbs quaver."

The Allies and Axis are making a din.
If you don't take sides it will be a great sin.

Vargas: "I know this. Come closer. Which side will win?"

Are you joking? Do you play the jester?
Do I have to tell you, a poor slave called Esther?

Lightning. Thunder.

Oh! This storm! It's like a nor'easter!

Vargas: "I see, my Songbird, that you're on a quest here."

In your hands you hold millions of fates—

Will it be Germany or the United States?

Vargas: "May I take off your hat, Dear? It's covered with dates."

Decide! Decide! Will you wait for the dawn?
I shall no longer beg! I will no longer fawn—

Vargas: "But, Bluebird, tell me: which side are you on?"

Must you ask? Or must I continue to pester—?
The answer resides in my name, which is—

"Esther!" That word was shouted by the bearded Brazilian Boy, who had jumped from the prompter's box. "That's not her name! Something is wrong here! We've been betrayed! O Comandante! Listen to me! She's no Jewess. That's just a part. What the real Carmen wants is for you to make a treaty with the Thousand-Year Reich."

"*Jawohl!*" shouted Bernardo.

Tino and Felipe also leaped to their feet. "*Deutschland! Deutschland!*" they shouted. "Ask her! She'll tell you to make the pact with Herr Hitler!"

The dictator stood, too. He nodded toward Madam Miranda. "She is the most popular figure in our land. I cannot disappoint her. I hereby declare that the allegiance of the great nation of Brazil shall belong to—"

"Wait!" There was another thunderclap. A figure in white appeared on the poop deck. "Wait a moment-a!" Toscanini! Inside a bedsheet! Alive! Like a statue of earlier Romans, he stretched his arm forth from within his toga. Instantly the baton flew from my hand to his. He raised it in wrath, his eyes shooting sparks. His tongue, when he spoke, was a flame of fire. "Signore Vargas-o! You no listen-a! It's a plot-a! They are *male! Male! Fascisti!* Evil a-mens-a! I play for you Americana! Sousa, *sì?* 'Star-a Spangled-a Banner!' 'Old Black Joe'!"

At these words the chorus of prisoners and slaves broke into song:

Oh, say can you see—

Immediately the priests, the chorus of pagans, attempted to thwart them:

Deutschland, Deutschland, über Alles—

But the Jews were winning! Were these tears that blinded my eyes? Only in part. The heavens had opened. Freshwater streamed with the salt. Still the song of freedom soared through the storm:

By the dawn's early light—

Vargas put on his admiral-style cap. "Maestro! You are the Honorary Citizen of the nation. I cannot deny you. Brazil must be a Good Neighbor."

A thunderclap, louder than all the rest, struck just behind me. I whirled. Not thunder! Maltz! Hans Maltz! Holding my own six-shooting Revolver!

"*Achtung!* I demand from each person silence! I demand to move no one! You will with America not this pact make. You will make it with the Reich! This man, this Goldkorn, is not what you think. He is a spy! *I* am the *Sturmbannführer*. Hear me, Fräulein Miranda! He has fooled you. You have a Jew for a lover taken! A member of the international conspiracy. Kamerade Karmen! You are a member of the *Volk*. Speak to O *Presidente*! He will to you only listen!"

Vargas: "That is true, my little Lark. You are the true spirit of our nation. Our Florence Nightingale. Our Joan of Arc. Yes, a Helen of Troy! To which side shall I declare allegiance? Tell me once and for all."

All eyes turned to the Bombshell from Brazil. Slowly she raised her hands and—can you imagine the depths of Leib Goldkorn's disappointment? The depths of his betrayal?—removed the six-pointed star. Then, as the lightning flashed about her, she turned toward the prisoners and cried out in a-flat minor:

Sterminio! Sterminio!

Morte ai nemici della Brasil!

What an uproar on the *Amazonas!* The two choruses dueled and Toscanini mouthed maledictions. The Rhythmaires shook their gourds and rattled their castanets. Vargas, supported by his aides, cried out, "So be it. I hereby declare that as of this moment the nation of Brazil shall be the faithful ally of—"

TWAT!

That note could only have come from a Rudall & Rose. It was answered by a chorus of trumpets and a roll of thunder. I looked at Toscanini. Pale-faced, he held out his hands before me. "No! No! Goldkorns! I'm-a beg you! No!"

TWANK!

Down on the deck, all—the singers and soloists, those in the crew and the crowd—were holding their ears. Again the note I had sounded was answered not only by the trumpet section but by the beating of the bass and the kettledrums. Behind me Maltz raised the Revolver—but toward his own temple, as if he meant to shoot himself in the head.

TWIRRUP!

Heavens! These were not trumpets! It was not thunder! Nor had there been drums! Elephants! Elephants from *Aïda!* They were amok! They were stampeding! They were bearing down on the stern!

TA-ROO! TA-ROO!

People were screaming. People were running. The aides of the *comandante* were shooting their weapons into the air. No use. On came the beasts, crushing everything before them. *This* is what I had seen—not "tanks," not threshers—in the huge crates for packing. Pachyderms!

TOO-RAA! TOO-RAA!

Down went the palaces. Down the obelisk, the pyramids, the replica of the Sphinx. The maddened herd swept all before them. Off the port side, off the starboard, men and women jumped for their lives. The Rhythm Boys grabbed Carmen and ran for the lifeboats. Maltz, my rival from boyhood, aimed his weapon at Leib Goldkorn. "*Heil Hitler!*" he cried, and pulled the trigger. The bullet struck me square in the chest, directly over my heart. I fell backward, eyes open, hitting the back of my head upon the poop's iron floor. I looked up. There, far off, was the figure of my fellow Jew, Jesus, holding out his arms in a vain attempt to calm this world of mad beasts and men.

With the last of my strength I turned my head. Toscanini, too, had his arms outstretched, as he led the NBC Symphonia in a medley designed to pacify the pachyderms. Alas! It was like the orchestra that had played upon the sinking deck of the *Titanic*. The poor crazed mammoths trampled everything in their paths— the stage, the sets, the abandoned chairs—before the force of their stampede took them right through the taffrail and into the Bay of Guanabara, where they floated off like the tops of the icebergs that had brought the great steamship down.

My sight grew dimmer. My breath grew slack. What were these harmonies that now I heard? Could it be? Was it the dying man's final wish? The Maestro was playing my own composition! The score on the music stands! How sweetly it played, the Symphonia. How lovely such Goldkorniana. I took one last breath and closed my eyes, oblivious to everything, including the fact that the lead-covered missile had burrowed its way through the entire last act of *Esther*, coming to rest between the hanging of Haman and the dance of the joyous Jews.

4

*K*NOCK, KNOCK.

What's that? Some person is striking the booth of the Bell Telephone.

"Sorry," I cry, from where I lie cramped and curled upon the floor. "*Ocupado.*"

Rap. Rap-rap-rap. An insistent concatenation.

I perform a torso twist and stare upward. Someone, a woman, is pressing her face to the glass. Dark hair. Short stature. Tea complexion. Deep almond eyes. Where have I, in the past, seen these features?

Rap-rap-rap.

I look more closely. This person is holding an object, with red and black squares. Board for checkers? No! Ah! *Mein Gott!* It is my lumberman's coat! Now I recognize her: the Nipponese! The cleansing lady! I had left this apparel at the Court of Palms.

"Mr. Goldkorn? Leib Goldkorn? The writer?"

Here is poignance. She has seen my name on the label. She has followed me all the way to the B. Greengrass and Williams Bar-B-Que chicken. I gather beneath me my legs. I thrust forth my arms. "*Moment!*" I declare. "I am attempting to rise." Pulling upon the Bell extension, with leverage against the walls, I clamber upward and push open the doors.

"Miss, a thousand thanks! You have retrieved for me my jacket. One hundred percent wool."

"Absent-minded author!" she said, with a shy smile. "You left it on the back of your chair."

She holds it, as a valet service, outward. I turn my back and slip it on. When I turn round again, the Asiatic is present still.

"Once more, kind lady, my thanks. And now, ha-ha, goodbye!"

She does not move. Her narrow eyes seem to glisten. "But, but," she begins. "I do not understand."

"Ah! I am a fool! *Dummkopf!* Please, you must forgive me!" And into her little hand, whose fingers I gently open, I place—hang the extravagance! The poor woman had gone to great lengths—all my remaining money: sixty American cents.

Home! Home, friends. No place like a home. Thus I trudge up 80th Street, past the Avenue Amsterdam to number 130 West. Up one flight. Another. Another. Exhaustion overwhelms. The staircase towers. The fourth floor. The fifth. Greetings, Bowser. No reason to summon the tunes from *Tannhäuser.* I am too weary; my old foe is

too deaf to hear. Auxiliary stairs, tar paper roof, and then the final
aerobics to my window.

Chick-chick-a-boom, a-boom chick-a-chick

What is this sound that comes through the half-open pane?

Chick-chick-chick, chick-a-boom!

With caution I step into my own abode. All is in order. Madam
Goldkorn in a doze from dropsy. The pillars of books stretch floor
to ceiling. The drip of water from the porcelain sink.

*That's all you've got to say
To chase the blues away—
    Chick-a-boom!*

These sounds, like voices from space, or from the dead under
ground, come from the Admiral TV. The picture? Dancing dots. I
reach into the pocket of my gabardines. "Awake, Madam! Clara,
awake! I have for you a special treat."

On the face of my helpmeet one eye lifts open. The other follows.
Each is clouded and tinged, as is Formica, with a yellow rheum.
"Slim Jims, Mr. Goldkorn?"

"Better! Better than that!"" I hold forth the treasure. "Can you
see? Can you read the verbiage? A Kit Kat. For my kitten, ha-ha!"

From the covers a hand emerges, and a stream of clear liquid
spills from the corners of her mouth. "Give me!" she demands.

"Wait. First the wrapping. You see? Now the faux silver foil." I
give her the wafers, coated in finest milk chocolate. In three bites,
without aid of dentures, the confectionary goes down.

*The song of love begins
    The night they met, down in Rio
In a cafe by the bay they romanced
    To a midnight serenade*

"Guess what? Honey, I have more."

"More?"

I plunge once more into my trousers. "Look. A Hershey. Note: with nuts!"

"Mr. Goldkorns, are we having a Valentine's Day? Why this bonanza?"

"Does a man in America need a special day to show his feelings for his lifelong companion? Here. It's crumpled. Eat."

She told him to forget
  The night they met down in Rio
And there were tears in their eyes
  As they danced to a midnight serenade

Naturally the sweets will kill her. Even if I should retrieve from the crisper the syringe I could not undo this act of mercy. Two bars! One square, a tiny taste in her condition would do. I believe that she, now reaching with a bosom display for a glass of water, knows this too.

All that remained of their love were
  The stories of a midnight serenade

What broadcast is this upon the Admiral? Is it a film? Or the Amateur Hour of Mr. Mack? I remove my lumberman's jacket and drape it upon the back of the windsor. Then I drop with fatigue upon that chair. Nothing to do but listen to a few more of the top ten tunes.

Buona notte, moonlit sky
  Say goodnight but not goodbye

What's this? Aflutter to the ground? Something has fallen from the pocket of my red and black plaid. I snatch it. *Mein Gott!* Could it be? The photo! The photo from the Brownie! Miss Carmen, apucker at my cheek! With Felipe, Tono, the billy beard! Behind us the vast expanse of the sea. This could only mean one thing. She had come! Miss Michiko! The Kakutani! She had arrived late at the Court of Palms and slipped the memento into my pocket. A love token! The tardy darling! My dear friend! My Finn!

"Clara? Miss Litwack? Awake, honey? Listening to the hit parade?"

Eyes closed, mouth closed, stains from chocolate upon doily and chin. Breathing? Is she breathing? I hold my own breath. The zeppelins, motionless, have at last gone into the hangar. One foot, with toes, hangs limp from the blanket. Asleep then. Or in a coma.

Suddenly a wave of weariness overcomes me, as if I too had eaten a fatal potion. From my hand drops the faded photo; onto the kitchen table I lay my head. Shutters fall over my eyes. In the dream that comes I hear more songs, more music, and confused talk of a baron, a baroness, mix-ups with airline stocks, and how one man takes another man's wife.

Then, at about midnight, I feel all about me a rise in temperature, as if, at a tiptop restaurant, a waiter has provided me with warm towels. I open an eye. Heavens! My hands are covered with blood! So is the tabletop! So are the walls and the floor. Wait! Not real blood. A red light. Could it be? A light from the Admiral.

Ay-ay-ay-ay-ay!
I like you very much!

Carmen! Carmen Miranda! Her hat, magenta, her lips, in ruby, have made the whole room crimson. Green beads. A nude midriff. Look, there are the Rhythm Boys. And there, the lights of the Copacabana, Sugar Bush in silhouette. A miracle! A definite miracle! Here is the picture as well as the sound!

Ay-ay-ay-ay-ay!
I think you're grand!

Rio! Could this be Rio? Was my inamorata, Madam Miranda, singing once more a love song to me?

Why, why, why, why, why when I feel your touch
My heart it starts to beat to beat the band?

I am, at bottom, a materialist. Miracles do not in truth exist.

What I see now upon the screen of the Admiral is but an illusion. Here are no vacuum tubes. Here is an instrument equipped only for black and white. It is more likely that I have entered the land of the dead. Heart spasm. Lobe convulsion. Yes, this is the explanation for the presence of Mr. Don Ameche and Miss Alice Faye. All we ghosts must wander forever through this tropical scene. Now there is revealed the greatest of secrets. Heaven is but the replication of the happiest night of one's life.

"Clara! Leib calling! Are you hiding?"

Of course she must, upon this distant planet, be a resident too. I must search for what in America is called the better half. Thus does eternity for me begin. With female choir. With dancing palms. With musical accompaniment.

See, see, see, see, see the moon above

"Clara! My sweetheart! You are the one I love!"

Way, way, way, way, way up in the blue

"Where are you? Miss Litwack! Yoo-hoo!"

Water

Cast of Characters

In addition to many of those in ICE and FIRE,

IN NEW YORK CITY
Clara Goldkorn (see cast above), a dropsy victim
Martha Goldkorn (see cast above)
Ernie Glickman, a plump broker of prawns
Randy Glickman, his thin brother
Goloshes, M.D., a physician

ABOARD THE *AMAZONAS*
Three Japanese cosmeticians
Hans Maltz (see Herr Schwartz, in cast above), also manager, Steinway Restaurant

ON THE ISLE OF HAWAII
Esther, a bathing beauty
Rick, possibly her brother (V. Mature)
Elderly gentleman, her father (W. Pidgeon)
Vahitai, a witch doctor
Aitutaki, a savage god
Ru-hamabu, heavy-set prince
X. Cugat, Latin conductor
D. F. Zanuck (see cast above)
Irving Cummings (Katz-Cummings, see cast above)

AT THE STEINWAY RESTAURANT
Former waiters
Mosk (now majordomo), Ellenbogen, Margolics
Former musicians
Salpeter (first violin), Murmelstein (second violin), Dr. Julius Dick (bass)

H. H. Levine, former hired gun, now bouncer
Mlle. La Tour, cigarette girl
Miss Beverly Bibelnieks, former victim of near rape
Miss Corky (see cast above)
Jesús, a Puerto Rican, former near rapist
Chino, Puerto Rican, his partner
Martinez, former master of broilings, now a chef
Rabbi Rhymer, former rabbi, now rap artist
Hildegard Stutchkoff, former L. Goldkorn inamorata, owner Steinway Restaurant
Harry Schwartz (see Hans Maltz)
Miss Crystal Knight (see cast above)

Shelly and Joy, Steinway Restaurant employees
Rudy Giuliani, mayor of New York City
Sammy, his driver
Celebrities
T. Brown, H. Evans, T. Cruise, G. Stephanopoulos, and G. Steinbrenner, D. King,
S. Lee, P. Daddy

Others: subway passengers, Japanese aviators, ambulance drivers, policemen,
South Sea Islanders, Fone Fancies

1

Rain! Forty days of the deluge. Forty nights. On this flood our ancestor Noah sailed forth on an ark loaded with giraffes, tree sloths, and every other sort of animal, including domestics. Here is the source of the American expression *raining both cats and dogs*. Also insects. The non-koshers. And turtles, whose descendants one can purchase in F. W. Woolworth's, oft bearing upon their backs a portrayal of the Statue of Liberty or the Stars and Stripes. From this sea ship I am likewise a descendant and so, ladies and gentlemen, are you. For did these creatures not embark, as it is written, "two by two"? Leib Goldkorn translation: male and female, boy and girl, the ram, ha-ha, and the woolly ewe. Imagine the flirtations! Above deck and below. Also shellfish.

Ach! I am stepping with my McAns, non–mink-waxed, into a water puddle. The size of beautiful Lake George. And in my hand, instead of a sturdy bumpershoot, I possess only this paltry parapluie. In the city of New York the rain never ends. Oh, these swollen rivers! How they lock us in their embrace. To the east, no visible bridges, no borough of Brooklyn or the leafy Queens; to the west, no hint of Palisades, Meadowlands, or the great continent beyond. Only mists, drizzles, a curtain of gray. It is as if the Isle of Manhattan and all its inhabitants are floating off in the downpour like that mythical ship of the animals, upon what was doubtless a fairy tale sea.

It isn't raining rain, you know, I quote the Jew Jolson, *it's raining violets.* Tell that, sir, to the marines! The water, here upon Central Park West, is now to shins. The crowd of Gothamites, eager to cross to the Museum of Nature—question: were the dinosaurs, whose bones one may in that building inspect, on board Noah's seagoing vessel? And what of the Sperm-type whale, likewise on display? Ha, ha! A child could see through such fables: the crowd, to continue, cannot cross to the safety of *that* haven for mammals. I, too, wish to make a crossing—not to enter the museum but to the underground B train, terminus Coney Island. Alas, we non-swimmers stand in vexation upon the shore.

What else does A. Jolson declare? Not clouds: daffodils. Daffiness! Yet there is some truth to this lining of silver. In the dankness, the dampness, the drip-drip of inundation, the female half of the population has begun to express its animal nature. Think of my own little Ark, I mean of course 130 W. 80th Street, which floats upon the floodplain between the Avenues Amsterdam and Columbus. The ladies, in this weather, have grown wanton. At night, Madam Fingerhut: one hears, through wallboards, her hedonistics. And in my own bed? There the former C. Litwack has of late crossed the midline of the Posturepedic, where she performs unprintables behind my back. And more! All fifth-floor tenants are aware that Tuesday at the dusk hour is when Leib Goldkorn strives for a defecation. Yet when, to lightning flashes, I opened the door to the cabinetto, there sat Madam Schnabel: legs asunder, elbow points upon kneecaps, her bosoms swaying each against the other like straphangers on the defunct BMT.

Where in this hothouse of hormonals, can one escape provocations? A prisoner in my bedroom, a fugitive on my floor, I cannot enter even the lobby zone since that is where the cleansing lady from the Court of Palms now lurks to summon me for orgiastics. Hence I am unable to visit my letter box, into which each day the postman deposits, from my favorite Finn, a feuilleton:

> Why do you treat me with such coldness? Every afternoon I await you at the Plaza but you do not appear. When I seek you out you turn your back upon me. Have I offended you, my Leib? If only you would spare me a moment, I would tell you—it is a mystery: I cannot explain it, I cannot fight it—how full my heart is at the thought of you.

Thus do we note how even Miss Michiko, in this monsoon, has become a bit of a chippy.

Watch out! Attention, ladies! Too late. The number 10 autobus has made a manifestation, thereby creating in our little lagoon a tsunami. Ha, ha: douche bath for all. Yet in its wake there is an opportunity to wade at mere ankle depth to the 81st Street station.

Where, in such a typhoon, is Leib Goldkorn traveling? Cocktails with Kakutani? There are obstacles to such a dalliance. I do not refer to the fact that the Coney line debauches at the Circle of Columbus, leaving me to walk through the swamp of South Central Park. I would gladly risk a rheum to have, with my lovelorn Laplander, a heart-to-heart. The difficulty is that I owe the Hotel Plaza a sum of one hundred and twenty dollars, plus taxables and gratuity: a total of let us round off to one twenty-five. Surely I would be apprehended the moment I appeared at the entrance to the Court of Palms and led off, before the eyes of Miss Michiko, in manacles. No, no, better to let her remember the sophisticate, the *person of some culture and sensitivity,* this is a quotation, and not the wretched beggar, without even a Gillette shave, who would greet her in the debtor's gaol.

One hundred twenty dollars, plus honorarium. Ransom for a king. Yet Madam Kakutani is not the only one who has a claim upon that sum. It is by coincidence the exact amount required to redeem my Rudall & Rose–model flute from the Glickman Brothers. All winter long I have with fruitlessness searched, in the pages of my memorial volumes, for the ticket from the shop of prawns. And what of Fingerhut, the *fils?* Here is the equivalent of three months of rent-controlled arrears. Not to mention that other woman in my life, Miss Crystal Knight. What are the discomforts of a prison for the penniless compared to the torments she must suffer—the rack and the rodents, a diet of bread crusts and water—in her underground dungeon? With one hundred dollars I might bribe her captors, leaving an extra twenty-five to arrange a week's concealment at the luxurious Johnson Lodge, choice of cereals and sanitary facilities *tout compris.* Ah, a liaison for Leib! No more candids in the gazette, no more telephone pleasantries. Away with self-fondlings and auto-emissions, as prescribed by Goloshes, M.D. I shall have Madam Knight, to quote the words of Professor Pergam, *in propria persona.* Hello? H. Johnson Lodge? A King Coil, queen-sized, *s'il vous plaît!*

Friends! Loyal readers! To understand why we have embarked on this journey we must go back to the wee hours of the morning, when I lay asleeping. Through my head there passes the usual childhood dream of the family Goldkorn. The scene: our summer garden. The personae: Mutter and Vater within the linden shade; Yakhne, in sunshine, performing her calisthenics; and Minkche, approaching with pitcher, through whose transparent sides I view the half lemons that tumble amidst the ice blocks. These last, striking against each other and against the beaded glass, make a soft tinkling, a reminder to the sleeper to rise and empty his urinary in the kitchen sink. Action: Minkche fills the glass of each perspiring parent; then Yakhne seizes the pitcher and drinks from the lip; last, Minkche, mincing, approaches little Leib. The boy in short pants and the nonagenarian in nightie each grind a fist into the groin, as if intending to squeeze the bursting bladder the way his sister had the juice-filled lemons. She comes closer. She leans toward Leib, so that her breasts hang before him, each one as plump, as pink, as a *Pampelmuse*. The next thing the dreamer knows she has poured the contents of her pitcher not into his glass for highballs but into his lap. *Ha-ha!* laughs the family Goldkorn, parents and siblings, pointing to the puddle of lemony liquid in which he sits. Even then, I slept on, until from the tiptop of the linden, an old-world *Spechtvogel*, a new-world woodpecker, flies downward and begins, with its beak point, to beat on the side of my skull. "*Ha-ha-ha!*" the Goldkorns gleefully exclaim. "*Er hat seinen Hosen gepisst!*" No translation required.

I woke, with a feeling of dread. Indeed I *had* wet myself—and not just myself. Both my helpmeet and I were awash with excretions. To add to my horror I saw that other items—the McAns and the gabardines and a shade of a lamp—were also bobbing in the brine. What a nightmare! All unknowing, I had filled the whole flat with pee pee.

Of course it *was* a nightmare, a frightful *Alptraum*; if I had any doubt of that, the sharp-billed bird now resumed its battering: there, and there, and there once again, as if my head were some dainty—a snail's shell, an acorn—it was determined to shatter. Once more I opened my eyes: this was no woodpecker. Instead, a steady stream of water was pattering onto my pate, as if a Chinese torturer had been assigned to obtain a confession. Up I sat, looking about me. The roof was leaking! Not just in one spot but in five, ten, a score. The rainwater poured into our fifth-floor flat like the ocean into the hold of a floundering freighter. Moreover, the tide was rising. Already it covered the seat of the Windsor-type chair. Look! My books! *Goldkorn Tales!* The pages of this lifework would soon be a pulp.

What was that smell? Like the yolk of deviled-style eggs? Consolidated Edison natural gas! The perpetual pilot of the oven had been extinguished by the flood. Invisible fumes were filling the air. And was this not fitting? The working out of a preordained fate? Leib Goldkorn was now being given a rare second chance. Here was a way to join all the lost Goldkorns. Not to mention my schoolmates, my teachers, and all the musicians of Vienna, Warsaw, Budapest, Berlin—indeed all the Jews of Europe who had in their millions stood at the Magic Chef door. I rose from the bed and, holding high the hem of my nightdress, waded across the kitchen. The gas was bubbling up from the broiler like percolations from a non-gentleman in a tub. I pulled open the oven. The stench overwhelmed me. I placed my head like a roast inside.

But wait: what was that yellowish scrap deep in the corner? A leftover from a fricandel? Impossible. The oven had not been used in decades. Slowly, dizzily, I stretched forth a hand. I had it. Heavens! The ticket for prawns! Lethean Leib! I had not placed it in the memoirs, after all.

What I wanted now was not the door of the Magic Chef but that of the half-submerged Frigidaire. I rose and struggled through the waist-high currents to that high-ticket item. It took all of my strength to pull it open. Inside, the twenty-watt bulb was fitfully blinking. I reached upward, groping between the two trays for ice. There! I seized the prize: a wallet, flat and frozen as a fillet of flounder. How much was within? One hundred and twenty-five dollars? Everything, my life, my death, depended upon it. Alas! The parts were clamped together like the two halves of a clam. Once more into the deluge. This time I crossed to the silvery Sunbeam, into which I dropped the billfold like a Pillsbury waffle or a piece of toast. There was a flash, a sparkle, and, in both ankles and elbows, I felt a kind of tingle. But the coils of the appliance had begun their cheery glow. Meantime, I gathered together my apparel items, shoes, trousers, lumberman's jacket, and with haste pulled them on.

"What is this? Have we won the Lotto, Mr. Goldkorn?" The speaker was the former Clara Litwack. She had partly risen, so that her leftmost breast floated clear of her bodice, like one of the Sperm types that had surfaced from the deep. "I smell a definite rump steak."

The leather! It was burning! I snatched forth the wallet and, by the Frigidaire light, started to count. There were tens. There were twenties. When I reached one hundred I started to laugh. A hundred and five, a hundred and eight, all together one hundred eleven. Close enough! Ha! Ha! I was within reach of the goal.

"Leib Goldkorn, has there been an accidental? What has dampened the sheets?"

I did not answer. I made my way to the Admiral and carried it to the window. I unplugged the Sunbeam and balanced it on top of the set. Then I started to climb out, into the light of the rain-filled dawn.

"Why do you laugh, sir? Will you not allow your wife into the joke?"

"Ha! Ha! Ha! I will tell you. Do you see this? Do you know what it is? Ha! Ha! Ha! A pocket wallet! I have been saving it! Year after year, Madam! And for what? Ha! Ha! Ha! A rainy day!"

Have you seen the salmon who hurl themselves gasping up cataracts to the still waters where the females lay eggs and the males oblige with a pollution? With no less hardiness do these Knickerbockers fight their way up the torrents that cascade down the steps of the transit. With both hands on the railing I make the descent. The spray above flies about me. The maelstrom below threatens to suck me in. But lovers will brave any danger, as seen by newlyweds who in their aphrodisia go over the Niagara Falls.

An Admiral, *mit* sound, *mit* picture; a Sunbeam; a Philco, lacking only vacuums: would you care to make an evaluation of worth in American dollars? Fifty? Thirty? Surely fourteen!

"Two bucks," those were the words of Ernie, the plumpish Glickman.

Said Randy, the thin one, "And that's a gift."

"But we'll give you twelve for that wristwatch," added Ernie, pointing with forefinger toward my Bulova.

L.G.: "What? For a watertight? You are surely making a Joe Miller."

Randy: "It's no joke. With the two for that other crap, you'll have the fourteen you wanted."

L.G.: "Observe, gentlemen. Do you see, on this heirloom, the motto? *In time with your music.* Look once more. *D? F? Z?* This was a gift from the Zanuck. We are speaking of seventeen jewels."

Ernie: "We'll throw in a umbrella. You can't go out like that. It's coming down in buckets."

The thoughts of Leib Goldkorn: *In truth there was, for Madam Goldklorn, submerged now in rising waters, no longer the need to time either her lifesaving injections or the three-minute boil for her chowder. Begone good Bulova! And those waters: was it not the landlord's task to make timely repairs? Let the* fils *fix the rooftop. Let him provide for private time in the WC. Also: no loitering in lobby. Then we might speak of payment for arrears. Let us turn next to Madam Kakutani. Could we not meet in the nearby Sturgeon King or the Williams Bar-B-Que chicken? One does not need a palm tree motif, with piano solos, to discuss the work of Anatole France. That leaves the Rudall & Rose and Miss Crystal Knight. But do they in truth make conflicting claims? Would it not be possible to charm the guardians of the latter with the former's tones? Yes! Yes! Ja!*

Randy: "Cat got your tongue or something? What do you say?"

L.G.: "In the corner, gentlemen. The green bumpershoot. Is that recommended for sturdiness?"

Ernie: "Naw, take that one. Genuine bamboo."

L.G.: "Here is the Bulova, *mit* expansion-style band. No need for further dickers."

Ernie: "Here you go: two ones and two fives."

Randy: "How come, if you don't mind me asking, you had to have exactly fourteen dollars?"

L.G.: "Not fourteen, Mr. Randy. [Taking out defrosted wallet] One hundred and twenty-five. Aha! Ha! Ha! Ha! Does that sum not ring the bell?"

Ernie: "Not for me. Say, that's a nice wallet—"

L.G.: "No? No memory function? What about this? Eh? [Takes ticket from wallet, with flourishes] The ticket! The ticket, good Ernest. The ticket for prawns!"

Randy: "I can see that. What's it for?"

L.G.: "You are making a pretense, no? It is a ploy for business? This is the prawn for my Rudall & Rose!"

Ernie: "Your what?"

L.G.: "My flute, sirs. A gift from the Fox King? By no means! From the Emperor. His *kaiserliche und königliche apostolische Majestät*. From Franz Joseph himself!"

Randy: "Wait a second. You mean that tin whistle you left here— when was it, Ernie? Back in the eighties? Sometime like that?"

Ernie: "Oh, yeah. I thought we'd never get rid of it."

L.G.: "Let us end discussions. Here are the Lincolns, the Hamiltons, the G. Washingtons, too. Exactly one hundred and twenty-five dollars. Bring me at once my flute."

Randy: "But we can't do that—"

L.G.: "Pardon?"

Ernie: "We sold it. A year ago. A year and a half."

L.G. (stunned): "Sold it? But this is not a possibility."

Randy: "What'd we get? One-eighty, if I recall."

L.G.: "No, no. Error. You are speaking of another instrument. How could you sell mine? That would not be constitutional. [Hands money, wallet, and ticket to Randy] Look. Look for yourself. I have the original prawn."

Ernie: "Read it. The option runs out in six months. After that, it goes to the highest bidder."

L.G. (pale, staggering): "It's a robbery! *Gonifs!* I will call the Attorney of the District. Help! Help! Herr Morgenthau!"

Randy: "This wallet sure looks familiar. Ern, you ever see it before?"

Ernie (examining wallet): "Yeah, there's something about it. Look at that monogram. F.F. [To Leib Goldkorn] What's that stand for?"

L.G.: "What? F.F.? This is nothing. We have here a pocket wallet. To carry American money. On each bill is a portrait of a president. You know, a *Founding Father*. I have seen this hand-sewn on many such purses."

Randy: "Wait a minute. You know who had a wallet like this? Frank Fingerhut. Remember? Used to come in all the time, back in the sixties."

Ernie: "Your landlord, right, Mr. G.? Friend of the missus?"

L.G.: "Ha, ha: what is known as a friendship of Plato. No touching."

Randy: "Didn't he die in a strange way? Wasn't there something suspicious? A scandal?"

Ernie: "Sure. His wallet was missing."

Randy: "Right. Right. And so was his hat and his tie."

L.G.: "This is an outrage! Instead of the guilty party, the adulterer, the exploiter, we blame the victim!"

Ernie: "The cops haven't closed the books on that one. They still come around asking questions."

"Ah!"

(With that exclamation the former Bulova owner staggers backward, a stain spreading across his trousers.)

Randy: "What's this? Hello? Mr. G.?"

Ernie: "Quick! A chair! A glass of water!"

Randy: "Uh-oh. Looks like he had an accident. Ain't that number one?"

(The Brothers surround their customer, chafing his hands, slapping his cheeks, sprinkling his face with water. Eventually Leib Goldkorn opens his eyes.)

L.G. (in a weak voice): "Mr. Ernie. Mr. Randy. Tell me: this man, the one who purchased the Rudall & Rose—did he have a moustache?"

Randy: "Come to think of it, he did."

L.G.: "What else? Be so kind. What facials?"

Ernie: "Hair like this. Two curls on the forehead."

Randy: "And a gap in his teeth. Like, like—what's his name?"

L.G.: "Thomas E. Dewey?"

The Brothers (together): "Right!"

L.G. (sitting upright): "Question: do you still possess the weapon I brought you? The year was 1946. Alas, I am not able to present the prawn."

Ernie: "I'll check. [Goes to locked shelves, peers inside] Yeah. It's here."

L.G.: "I will give you in exchange fifty American dollars. Asking no questions. Is this a compact?"

Randy: "Why not? It's three times what we paid you."

(Ernie retrieves the weapon and hands it to Leib Goldkorn, along with his wallet, from which he extracts the agreed-upon sum.)

(Leib Goldkorn rises from the chair, seizes the umbrella, and heads for the door. He turns for a final word.)

L.G.: "So, Herr Morgenthau, you are in pursuit, eh? The bloodhounds draw closer? So: lay on, Macduff! But I have now my

Revolver. Before my capture I have some business with a certain SS agent, the ravisher of Crystal Knight, Second-Place Finisher Maltz."

72nd Street/West Central Park. 59th Street/Circle of Columbus. Farewell, Kakutani! 7th Avenue/53rd Street. 47–50 Streets/Center of Rockefeller, non-Jewish tycoon. 42nd Street. 34th Street, "Remember me to Herald Square!" My fellow travelers are also suffering the damp. Puddles between knees. Water dripping from hat brims. The same raindrops fall from the tunnel cracks and make mud pools between the electric rails. Broadway/Lafayette, we are here! Change to F train. 2nd Avenue/Houston. But one station now to go. Then I shall see her. With studs and red-painted toes. Fingerhut, Father in Heaven! His pink back! The shlong on him! *Gott! Mein Gott!* Like a boa constrictor! Temporary insanity! Before my eyes, a curtain of blood! In Argentina: innocent, your honor! Also in Arabia, in Italy, and all Latin nations! A crime of passion! A husband's rights. Lord, stop the rain. Five days is enough. Extenuating circumstances. I never spent the money! Never counted it even. I put it, ha-ha, on ice. Yes, yes, the world is wicked. *Man's heart is evil from his youth.* Biblical quotation. But spare us! I think they were in congress. I saw their skylarks with my eyes! Relent, Lord! Oh, mercy! Statute of limitations. His heart stopped of its own accord! Ah, here is the Street of Delancey and Essex. Final destination. Imagine: people believe in such prayers. Rose glasses! In the sky, pies! I possess the *Revolver*. Miss Crystal! Leib comes!

2

Fifty-six years in the past, it was also the rain season in Rio. The storm that struck us in the harbor was followed by others, equally fierce. Of course the passengers had long since departed. The Maestro, the members of the NBC Symphonia, and the Shaw choristers performed for a week at the Imperial Teatro and then moved on to São Paolo and Buenos Aires, before sailing back to New York from Montevideo. Madam Miranda made three separate tours of the city—a miracle of meteorology: each time she did so the clouds withdrew from the Sugar Bush and out came the beaming sun—after which she took off in the four-engined clipper for the lair of the Fox King, who arranged for her to appear in the tragidrama *Weekend in Havana*. Featuring the Rhythm Boys, too. Vargas, O *Comandante*, retreated to the Presidential Palace; if his nation's potash was not destined for America, neither—and here we see how one individual may intervene in the flow of history—was it delivered to the Third Reich. Thanks, Leib Goldkorn! As for the deserted *Amazonas*, she was towed back to the Niterói wharf for reparations to the poop, the taffrail, the stern. I, too, needed time to recover from wounds. Naturally, while in the bay for sickness I was asked how I had boarded and by what means I intended to pay my fare. "Ha, ha! Penniless!" This was my plea to the purser. "I can offer only apologetics." Luckily that gentleman was a music lover; thus, in a blue jacket of the Lloyd Brasileiro, with two lines of brass buttons attached, I was engaged to stand at the top of the "gangway" and play a tarantella—*TWEE-HEET! TWEE-HOO!*—whenever the captain or some other dignitary came aboard. In this manner I would not only pay off past debts but secure my passage for the long journey home.

And what a voyage it was to be—sailing westward, ever westward, until, like the Jew Magellan, we had made a circumlocution of the globe. Patagonia and Japan, Ceylon and Cape Town, Casablanca and Lisbon—these were the lands where Leib Goldkorn would have to, as the expression goes, sing for a supper, before disembarking in the port of New York. Shipshape at last, we steamed forth from the Baia de Guanabara in the month of November, 1941.

There were, on this occasion, no fireboats and no fountains, no pleasure craft about us, and no naval salutes. Silently we made our way down the coast of the continent, past the Falklands, and through the storm-filled passage named for Sir Francis Drake. Next we were upon the vast Pacific. No event occurred to mark one day there from another. Each was as smooth and as unvaried as the dark, banknote-green sea.

Of course I no longer slept in my lifeboat, but shared a cabin with three other navies whose task it was to bring first-class passengers their blankets and biscuits and bouillon-flavored tea. From habit, mixed also with nostalgics, I would rise each night at three bells and make my way toward the stern—that is, to the very spot where only the encounter with Madam Miranda—*meu caro senhor*, thus her ear whisper—had saved me from an act of despair.

It was upon one such night, shortly after we had steamed northward over the equator, that I first noticed the group of what I supposed to be amateur uranologists. This was composed of three Nipponese gentlemen who stood at the taffrail and, with spyglass and sextant, seemed to be checking our course against what the poet R. Browning called the pale population of Heaven. Translation: stars. With my own unaided eye I could distinguish many of the figures that Professor Pergam had taught us: Boötes the Herdsman, for example, and Musca the Fly; and there were the wings of Pegasus, who was born—this was a tall tale of the Professor's—from the blood of the beheaded Medusa. Such were the wonders that, as we continued westward and north, the little band of cosmetologists met to study. Every twenty-four hours they would transfer our position—5 degrees latitude, 8, then 13, by 140, then 147 degrees longitude west—from the zodiac above to the rolls of their oilskin charts.

I could not help but notice that on the fifth night the Asiatics were in a state of unusual excitement. Their talk was filled with high-pitched exclamatories and the starlight winked upon the spectacle lenses that they turned with eagerness to the sky. Suddenly, to my astonishment, they lifted a copperish cylinder over the stern and began to pour its wine-colored contents, and then the container itself, over the side. Then, without a further word, the Orientals departed, leaving the barrel abob in our wake.

"Wait! One moment, sirs!" I shouted, for in their haste the astronomers had forgotten their nautical charts. Alas, they were already too far off to hear my cry. I stepped from the shadows and, grasping the oilskins, leaned over the vacated rail: there, into the phosphor of the sea, the barrel continued to pour forth its purple ink.

My cabinmates had long since told me that the three Asiatics shared, upon the boat deck, a deluxe-type suite. It took some time for me to negotiate the ladders and passageways to their door. I was just about to knock upon it when I heard, through the partly opened window, the sound of voices:

First Japanese: "We have marked the spot."

Second Japanese: "Admirar Yamamoto must arrive there two days' time."

Third Japanese: "Thus his aircraft attack from east, out of rising sun."

Second Japanese: "Amelicans can't see! Brinded!"

First Japanese: "We predict total destruction Amelican freet."

Third Japanese: "Two year minimum, maybe three, to restore. Meantime, we drive imperiarists from Pacific."

Second Japanese: "They must protect own cities, Ros Angeles, San Francisco, Seattle, from our pranes. You have free hand everywhere—Europe, Aflica."

First Japanese: "Let us dlink to our friendship."

Sounds, then, of glasses clinking one against the other. Had I heard correctly this pidgeonese? In the dim light that spilled through the window I spread out the nautical chart. Here was our latest position, marked on the map with an X, just as it had been on the sea's surface by a spreading purple stain: latitude 22 degrees, longitude 158.

Third Japanese: "Pardon, please. One smarr probrem."

First Japanese: "Plime Minister Tojo cannot authorize surprise attack without definite assurance Reichschanceror make immediate decraration of war on Amelica."

The Reichschanceror! That meant A. Hitler! Who else was in that stateroom? I drew closer, in an attempt to peer through the closed slates of the blinds.

"But my *heilige Freunde*: you know that the Führer has already such a treaty solemnly signed. Such doubts you need not entertain."

That voice! The intonations! I knew it! Yes! I had known it almost all of my life!

"Ah," said the third Japanese, "so. That is why Admirar Yamamoto sail toward this secret spot. But he cannot raunch aircraft without definite assurance from honorable Herr Hitrer."

First Japanese: "Just as Reichschanceror wish Amelican to be distracted on west, so honorable Tojo wish him occupied in east. Treaty not enough."

"I understand. *Meine Freunde*, will you also to me a guarantee make? That immediately upon receiving the assurance of my government the attack will begin?"

Second Japanese: "We have many spy on island. Many seclet agent. Yamamoto will see from fragship our signal. In sky, giant frare."

First Japanese: "Ha! Ha! One hour later: no more Pear Harbor."

Third Japanese: "No more Amelican freet!"

Horror upon horror! These were not cosmeticians! They were Nipponese agents! Their government was planning a secret attack. Yes, and Germany would then make a declaration. This was World War! Without the least forethought—such was my determination to prevent that cataclysm—I whirled about and began to pound with both fists upon the door. When one of the plotters opened it I stepped with boldness inside.

"Tea, gentlemen? Cube of bouillon? Has no one made such an order? Nor for coconut-type macaroons? Ah, my error! Well, *gute Nacht*. Bon voyage!"

"Yes, yes. You go now!"

"Wait! How foolish I am. I almost forgot. Did someone misplace this interesting document? A map of sea and stars? It was left unattended at the stern. I too am a student of the heavens. I see, my friends, that you have marked here not only our position, but—look, do you see? The exact moment of a solar eclipse. In just thirty-eight hours. *Post meridiem*. Ah: here is my own constellation. Have we here fellow Scorpions? *Exercise caution: this is a poor time to undertake new ventures. You will meet a beautiful woman, but do not dabble in world affairs*—"

"Seize this man! He is an enemy of the Reich!"

The speaker was no Nipponese but my nemesis, Herr H. Maltz.

"*Banzai!*" cried the others in concert and dashed toward me from every part of the room.

But my Rudall & Rose reached my lips before the Asiatics

arrived. TWAARP! TWIRRUP! This was the highest point of that instrument's register. The Japanese, jolted, froze in their tracks. Maltz, at these sonics, threw his hands over his eardrums. This was my chance. I leaped upon him and pulled from its holstery the very same Revolver he had so recently discharged at me.

"Ah-ha!" That was my exclamation. "Now the tables are turvy!"

"No shoot! No shoot! Sullender!" The Japanese, who only moments before had bragged of driving every American from the shores of the Pacific, now bowed down before this would-be Yank. Maltz, however, put his hands on his hips instead of in the air.

"*Freunde!* You need no fear to have. This Herr Goldkorn is from long ago to me well known. He will not dare to shoot. Seize him!"

The Orientals—their almond eyes as round now as filberts—looked up from their prostrate positions. For a moment they hesitated.

"Maltz!" I declared. "Do not move please further one American inch. I will be forced to commit here a terrible act."

But the Gauleiter, laughing, took a step closer. "Shoot, *mein* little Leib! Kill me before I kill you."

I raised then the Revolver until my childhood rival appeared between its sights. My finger tightened upon the trigger. Who could blame me if I set off the detonation? Here were three witnesses to testify that my own life had been threatened. Self-defense, your honor! Even the Talmud says that in such conditions a man might commit torts. Was this not, moreover, the ravisher of Minkche, my own flesh and blood? Had he not sent off the entire family Goldkorn to death in Dachau? I closed one eye, taking aim with the other.

"Rook! He shoot!"

"Purr trigger!"

Maltz merely showed his teeth in a grin. "*Nein.* I do not think it." He moved boldly forward, so that the barrel of the weapon pressed against his chest plate. I raised my second hand in order to steady the first. A discharge now could not miss the heart.

Then through the ether there came to me a voice from another hemisphere and another era in time. Here was Rabbi Goldiamond speaking in a tongue I did not know I remembered. English-language translation: *If a starving man in a forest should come across a sparrow's nest with an egg inside, before eating he must throw a stone into the nearby brush, so that the mother bird, thus distracted, need not witness the loss of her young.* Now my heart beat as if it, and not that of my antagonist, were about to be pierced by the bullet. Had this Maltz not a mother? And was I truly in danger of starving? Did not the possibility exist of averting world war through a discussion with my old school chum?

"Gut. I knew it. A Jew will not a gun fire."

Instantly the Nipponese leaped upright, pinning my arms to my sides. One of them now pulled forth a derringer-type weapon of his own. "I kirr him!"

"No! Too much noise. Rook: I have razor." He did indeed; the blade glittered in his hand.

"Wait. Make rots of brood. Maybe this just a silly fool. Not hear prans for attack."

"*Au contraire*, gentlemen. I heard of your evil scheme every word. Even though I am not yet a John Q. Citizen, I feel it is my duty to alert my countrymen."

"We must eriminate him! Quick. Get pirrow. Suffocate!"

"Even better, I stlangle him myself."

That was the largest of the Mongolians. He raised his hands to my throat, only to have the Second-Place Finisher knock them away. "This is *unmöglich*. A non-possibility. We must with care think. We do not want anyone this body to find."

At that the Asiatics all began to shout at once:

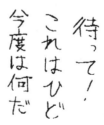

今度は何だ
これはひど
待って！

"Ha, ha, listen, fellows: do you know the one thing I fear the most? Water. I have been terrified of drowning since I was a tot. So shoot me, if you wish; or stab me with a knife; or choke me to death with your hands. You can even make me take poison. But please, please, I beg you: don't throw me in the ocean."

"Ah!"

"Ah-ha!"

"Ha! Ha! Ha! No more noise of frute."

"Fool! You have just your fate sealed." That was Hans Maltz. "Are you *ein Wahnsinniger?* Have you gone crazy?"

Before I could respond, the hirelings of Hirohito had whisked me through the cabin door and out to the boat deck rail. It was, I saw in a glance, a long way to the gray-green Pacific. Yes! *Crazy like the fox,* that is what I would have answered had I not found myself tumbling downward from what was the equivalent of a six-story building. Or if not the fox, then the clever Herr Rabbit, who in the folkish tales of Onkel Remus similarly employed depth psychology to trick his antagonists into hurling him into the patch of briars. There was, of course, one difference. Such thorns were to Herr Rabbit a familiar habitat; but Leib Goldkorn was—as I recalled the moment I struck bum foremost the sea's surface—a non-swimmer.

Down, down, down I went, a full fathom and more, until I thought I must touch the sandy bottom. Then, like the belly-type dancer in Frank Fingerhut's ball point pen—another souvenir of Miami—I started to rise, slowly at first and then with such tremendous velocity that I broke the surface in a geyser of foam. In triumph I raised both arms—the one holding my flute, the other my *Revolver*—and cried out like the boastful bunny: "Ha, ha! Ha-ha! I have won the contest! If you killed me, *ja?* Or if you kept me a prisoner—then I could not warn my government. Now I am free! Mrs. Roosevelt! Mr. Bernard Baruch! On guard! Ha! Ha! Ha! You see? America has its new P. Revere!" There was, of course, no reply. The great ship, with its light strings still beaming, slipped silently away into the blackness of night.

And now? I was all too clearly approaching what in the vernacular is called the last roundup. I thrashed for a time, first on my back, then on my belly; but soon I grew as still and silent as the stone I would resemble when dropping to the deepest depths of the sea. There was, however, no such descent. In fact I floated, with the waterline at my waist. Instantly I understood what had happened. It was the *Esther*, the score of my opera, *A Jewish Girl at the Persian Court*. The pages, upon contact with the ocean, had expanded, gripping the torso to which I had strapped them like a life preserver's ring. Tears, salty as the sea, filled my eyes. Art! It was art that had saved me, as in truth it must save us all. My arias, my melodies, the soulful laments and pep-filled Purim dances—these countless notes had gathered about their creator like millions of minnows, buoying body and spirit, just as, had we but ears to hear it, each of us is buoyed by a worldwide sea—the birdcalls in the air and the rondos of whales in the ocean, on land the hum of the Harlemites, a doorbell's chime, the pleasant do-re-mi of the lift doors as we reach our floor: yes, by a sea of song. With such blissful thoughts I watched as the sky underwent its morning ruddification and the sun bobbed upward, to the accompaniment of the music of the spheres.

Leib Goldkorn! How dare you while time in this idyll when the world is each moment drawing closer to war? Thus purposefully I paddled, making toward the west. Impossible not to note, however, that I was now lying lower, and that with each stroke I took, lower still. A predicament: the very opera that had saved me now threatened to drag me down. The pages, grown sodden, clung to me the way a vest of cement oft embraces an Italian. Did I dare cast it asunder? Never! Better to die with my creation than live without it. Higher and higher rose the Pacific about me. Deeper I sank in the trough of its waves. My shoulders, my throat, my chin—each went under. All too soon the ocean closed over my head. It is of interest to note that on this occasion there was no life review: no vision of walking along the Iglawa or lying amidst the Wienerwald fronds, no glimpse—here was the pinnacle of pleasure—of Madam Litwack's garter trolleys. Melancholic Dane: dismiss your doubts. Death is a sleep without dreams.

At that crucial moment, something struck me on the crown of my half-submerged head. Animal? A shark approaching for aperitifs? Vegetable? A giant sea pod about to entangle me in its roots? No! Mineral! Metal! It was the copper cask that the cosmeticians had thrown from the stern of the *Amazonas*! The dye inside had been replaced by air. I heaved myself upward and clasped the circumference. It bobbed like balsa. It careened like a cork. Saved! The very folk who hurled me overboard had provided my life raft. Do we not see here the hand of providence? Had I not been spared in order that, in turn, I might spare the world?

Now the sun came out in earnest. It lapped up the few wisps of cloud the way a cat might its morning milk. Everywhere, in every direction, the sea stretched forth with a flat, dull sheen, like a pan that has been seasoned with lard. No hint, on the horizon, of smoke; no sign, in the air, of a bird winging its way toward a perch on land. Already my arms had begun to ache, as if the vessel they held were an overweight partner in a dance. My legs, which dangled still in the water, had long since gone numb from the chill; but my dorsals, my neck, my unhatted head were approaching the boil. Worst was the thirst. Every drop of liquid had been sucked from my body, that's what it felt like, as though I were a portion of meat being koshered by the salt-filled sea. My tongue was swollen; my throat seemed stuffed with NBC crackers. If only some ink had remained in the barrel I would have drunk it with as much eagerness as plum-yellow schnapps.

How much longer could I survive? Time and again I felt my eyes drop shut and my arms begin to loosen their hold; but I knew that sleep was as dangerous for me as for the great R. E. Peary at the North Pole or poor R. F. Scott at the South. On and on I drifted, hour after hour, mile after mile. A last hope: with great difficulties I managed to remove my Lloyd Brasileiro trousers and, with the pant legs, attempted to lash myself to the metal drum. Non-success. The loose knot gave way and the navy worsteds sank at once out of sight.

I knew that I must soon follow. In despair, in desperation, I began to search through the pockets of my double-breasted and—*Thank you, Jesus!* I would have cried if I'd been a Christian—found a small stub of pencil. More luck: the outer layers of my score, those exposed most to the sunlight, were as dry as parchment. With my last strength I clutched the wee twig of wood between my aching fingers and slowly, taking a full minute to form every letter, started to write:

ACADEMY GRADUATE LOST AT SEA! LAT. 22. LONG. 158. DO NOT ATTEMPT SEARCH. HE IS NOW LIKE HIS ANCESTOR JONAH IN THE BELLY OF FISHES. HA! HA! TAKE PLEASE THIS NOTE AT ONCE TO MR. HOOVER. JAPANESE ARE PREPARING SURPRISE ATTACK. ON PEARL HARBOR AND SEATTLE. ADMIRAL YAMAMOTO TO GIVE COMMAND WHEN HERR HITLER GUARANTEES DECLARATION OF WAR. THIS IS DEFINITELY NOT A JEST. HERE SPEAKING IS AN AKADEMIE GRADUATE. FIRST-PLACE FINISHER. WOODWINDS. ENTIRE FAMILY VICTIMS AT DACHAU. FAREWELL, DEAR AMERICA! LAND OF PILGRIM'S PRIDE! GOD SAVE THE KING!

Off went the drum, with its message inside. And down went Leib Goldkorn, into what Americans call John Paul Jones locker.

How long, you ask, did I remain in the kingdom of the dead? It might have been but a single moment. It might have been a hundred years. All I knew, upon waking, is that the Messiah had in the meantime without doubt arrived.

"Here we go, Mister! I've got you!"

Was the speaker an Angel? One of the Seraphim or Cherubim which, according to Rabbi Goldiamond, would escort to the throne of Heaven all those who had never touched pork? Certainly this was no creature of planet Earth. The head, as hairless as my own, was without ears and not only shaped like a light bulb but was so white and bright it glowed like one too. Nor was the epidermis composed of human-type skin; this tight, rubbery substance was as blue as the sky from which the being had dropped. *Are you a Martian?* I opened my mouth to inquire, but a rivulet, not words, came out.

"Don't talk. Relax, okay? I'll get you in."

Odd, the organism could speak in non-accented English. Had it taken on, for this incarnation, the body of an actual person? One of its arms was under my chin; the other pulled us both in a powerful stroke through the surging sea. Behind me the alien's feet—could I believe my eyes? Was that crimson polish upon the toes?—were kicking up a froth. It was then that I felt, against the back of my neck, near the collar of my double-breasted, a certain pressure—as if, between my rescuer's body and my own, there were a pair of muskmelons. Could it be? The thought no sooner flashed through my mind than I dismissed it. Yet those feet—the excellent arch, the dainty ankle—were clearly feminine. The bald head, however, was that of a man, and so were the broad shoulders that now cleaved the waves. Was this lifeform an hermaphrodite, combining, as in plants and certain insects, both sexes into one? Curiosity soon got the best of me, as it did, in the fable, the cat. I twisted about in one quick motion and found myself staring down at two indisputable mams.

"Hey! Hold still! We'll be ashore in a jiffy!"

Instantly I turned back, closing my eyes. But I could not shut out the sensation, so firm and yet so soft, like Jell-O-brand fruit cups, of what I now knew to be a creamery. At the center of my frozen limbs, deep within the infernals, I now felt the first warm flush of peppercorns.

"Is it true? Am I dreaming!"

"It's no dream, Mister! These breakers are real! We're going in!"

And in we went, lifted high, thrust down low, turned head over heel by the tumultuous billows. Through it all I could only think of one thing: that my obvious shamefulness was covered now by nothing more than May Co. drawers.

A blue lagoon, the scent of flowers, a fringe of majestic palms: Leib Goldkorn, in spite of indiscretions, you have arrived in Paradise. Across from me, all asmile, sat my savior. A perceptible bosom. Legs with hams. And a neck with only a hint of Adam's apple. "Pardon, Miss," I said, addressing the bathing beauty. "Could you tell me, please, your name?"

She smiled even more widely. How white her teeth were, like Camay cakes, how round her cheeks, how pointed and pert her little nose. "Yes," replied the mermaid, reaching upward and removing her scalp—rather, the cap upon it, beneath which her auburn hair remained upswept like a meringue. "It is Esther."

Dusk upon Rivington Street. The bells of the First War-saw Congregation are now making a polka. Six o'clock, *post meridiem*. Rain! Rain! Come again another day. Why did I not demand, of the Glickmans, a pair of hip garters, or, for wetness, Wellingtons? My gabardines are soaked. My Panama is besotted. In this ghetto I have not set foot for many years. Yet all the familiar landmarks—the shop of Sheftelowitz, the dealer in saltwater fishes; that of the tobacconist, Prinzmettle, and of the merchant of bedding, Herbert Pipe; also the Premisher Butcherie—are still open for business. This is in spite of the fact that in the Jewish Quarter one cannot with ease discover, amidst the crowds of Ukrainians, Hispano-Americans, and Coloreds, even a one-quarter Jew. Ha! Ha! With a play of wit I dispel anxieties at the closeness of my paramour. Also unchanged: the facade of the Steinway Restaurant. A narrow door, curtained windows, and the world-famous sign, the work of the artist Feiner, which depicts a Greek-style maiden holding, beneath her breast-fruits, a high-heaped platter, along with the words HOME OF THE ROUMANIAN BROILING.

This queue is a non-mover. In almost one hour I have not advanced the length of a single block. Yet more folk have lined up behind me. They stretch to Allen Street and disappear around the bend. Each moment a new limousine draws near, joining the others that crouch with metronomes waving. Even during the broiling craze in the long-ago Ragstat era—this is when A. Einstein and Benjamin Leonard and Queen Wilhemina would drop in for a herring appetizer—one never saw such a crowd milling in rainstorms at the restaurant door. Readers of my memorial volume will forgive me a moment of nostalgics. For it was behind these walls that I saved Hildegard Stutchkoff from robbery and ravishment by two Puerto Ricans; there, too, that I rescued her from the lecherous grip of the Blackamoor; and there, at last, and by candlelight, that I was admitted trouserless to the surface of her Sealy.

It is not, however, the widow I seek this evening. Behind that facade, perhaps in the upper apartments, perhaps in the depths of the gentleman's WC, Miss Crystal Knight is at this very moment a prisoner. But how, this is the question on everyone's lips, can I know that fact? So profound was her fear that, when asked the location of her dungeon, my phone friend had answered, *Riv— No, we are not allowed to give that information*. One syllable! One little slip. But it was the only clue I required. *Rive Gauche*? Certainly not, and not the fun-filled Riviera. For that matter, it was not our own Riverdale section, Borough of the Bronx, or nearby Riverside Drive. No! This could only be Rivington Street, in the heart of the Jewry; for it was there, on the block between Eldridge and Allen, that H. Maltz had so beguiled the grief-stricken owner of the Steinway Restaurant that she had allowed it to become transformed from a *fleishidek* establishment famed for its pitchai slices and rollmop salads to a dairy emporium, entirely dependent upon soy products, and then, one shudders to say, to the dreaded "Jewish style," at which meat and milk are without a care mixed. Not only that: our beloved institution was altered from one that played the works of I. Berlin and S. Romberg, J. Rumshinsky and I. Dunayevsky, the composer of the catchy "Song of Stalin"—in other words, from the *crème de la crème* of Hebrew melodists, heirs to Meyerbeer himself, to one that permitted Victor Herbert medleys and then the overtures of R. Strauss and R. Wagner, whose motifs I can hardly bring myself to whistle to a dog. What next? Pisk, Mr. Webern, and the cacophony of the twelve-tone school? Cacaphoney! That is my opinion.

At last: arrival at the Steinway Restaurant door. Full night has fallen behind me. What storms, I wonder, lie ahead?

"*Bon soir, Monsieur.* Party of four? Have you a reservation?"

The Frenchman has not addressed the query to me but to the gentleman who preceded my entrance into—this is a new development—the small, leather-padded foyer. That chap, instead of replying, removes from his pompadour his tall silken hat.

"Ah, Monsieur Steinbrenner," says the maître d'. "*Excusez-moi.* I did not recognize you. Your table is ready."

It is indeed the Yankee Doodle, accompanied by sycophants and wives. There is a brief moment of confusion as they remove their minks and mufflers at the check-in counter. Next the door to the dining room opens, allowing in first a thunderous roar, a blaze of light, and then a round-faced maiden who wears nothing but a shiny tiara in her heap of hair and, over her right and left bosoms, a tray filled with mint creams. And below? One dares not look below, especially when experiencing, in one's own nether parts, a sensation akin to the warmth of a toddy.

"Mademoiselle La Tour," thus speaks our Continental, even as he accepts a bank note from the Doodle, "will show you to your seats."

She does so, though even after the door closes behind her, the lights, through a kind of psychological momentum, continue to flash against my retinal rods and the sounds—the thump of some giant's feet, a chorus of primitive tom-toms—still beat against the tympanums of my inner ears.

"Well, well," says, in an altered tone of voice, the majordomo. "Look what the cat dragged in."

I lean forward, blinking in disbelief. Could it be? Beneath the suave demi-moustache, the rouged cheeks, the pearl-stuck cravat, was this the Lithuanian waiter? "Mr. Mosk!"

"So? Don't make a federal case out of it."

"Don't you recognize me? Leib Goldkorn? A member of the Steinway Quintet? I played first the Rudall & Rose–model flute and then the Bechstein Grand. For more than twenty-five years!"

"What's the name again?"

"Goldkorn, Leib. Graduate of the Akademie. Don't you remember? I will hum for you a Yip Harburg selection. 'Happiness Is a Thing Called Joe.'"

"Wait! I remember. What d'ya want? Can't you see we're busy?"

"A table for one, s'il vous plaît."

"Are you nuts? We got a dress code here."

"But how can you refuse me? These are the pants of V. V. Stutchkoff. Yes, the founder's son. Size forty-four!"

"That don't cut no ice. You need a reservation. You gotta call a month ahead of time."

Was this not the very situation for which I had prepared myself at the shop of prawns? "Ha! Ha! I thought there might be some little difficulty. Here you are, my good man." So saying, I peel from my bankroll an Abraham Lincoln and thrust it toward the erstwhile waiter.

"Are you kidding? Here's what I got from the last guy. A C-note. This is a gold mine. The dough keeps rolling in."

"I understand, Mr. Mosk, that you are giving me a hint. I have not offered sufficient funds. Look: here is Old Hickory, the victor of

New Orleans. What? More than twenty dollars? This is extortion, sir. I insist that you permit me to step inside. Or there might be difficulties. I am not a man from Missouri. Woolens cannot be pulled over my eyes. I know for a fact that this is a Maltz establishment. He keeps here Fone Fancies. Somewhere in the House of Pleasure he has imprisoned Miss Crystal Knight."

"Any trouble?" Those words, addressed to Mosk, come from the counter of the haberdashery, from behind which there now steps a mighty six-footer. Impossible not to recognize in that lantern-type jaw, the bony ridge over the eyes, the ears like handles upon a jug, the former bouncer: H. H. Levine!

Mosk: "Naw, no trouble, Happy. Our friend is just leaving."

"Leaving? But I have only arrived. I am a close acquaintance of Madam Stutchkoff. I demand to be taken to Miss Crystal Knight."

Levine: "We got new management."

Mosk: "We got new rules."

"Yes, yes. Then lend me, please, a coat and a tie."

Levine, shrugging: "He doesn't get it."

Mosk: "Listen, Mister: you wouldn't have a good time in a place like this. Why not walk over to Ratner's?"

"Ratner's? But that is a dairy establishment. Without even solo piano."

Levine, while pushing me backwards: "Why don't you people stick to your own kind?"

"What? What can such words mean?"

Mosk: "I gotta paint you a picture? This ain't no beanery. We don't cater to kikes."

With one hand at my collar and the other at the seat of my gabardines, H. H. Levine ushers me to the Steinway Restaurant door. As I depart in one direction, a man and a woman—even a glance reveals that this couple were definite English swells—rush through in the other. Behind my back I hear Mosk's words of greeting:

"Ah, Lady Tina! And Lord Evans! *Enchanté!*"

Let us step forward in time one quarter of an hour. A chauffeur in uniform, the cuffs of his twill-type jacket as far over his wrist bones as those of his twill-type trousers are over his Thom McAns, stands at this same Steinway Restaurant door. Who is it? Hard to tell, since the brim of his cap is also well over his eyes. Clue: McAns. Yes, this is Leib in livery. I push my way into the foyer and am greeted, of course, by Monsieur Mosk.

"Hey, buddy, deliveries at the rear."

"Mistaken identity, sir. Here speaking is a coachman. I have an important message for the Doodle. Now if you will step aside. *Pardon. Pardon.*"

Of course this is not, as is required by barristers, nothing but the truth. Oh, I am, though a lifetime non-driver, a chauffeur. For have I not in the preceding moments paid the whole of my treasure, my hoard of seventy-five dollars, for the rental of the garments of the automobilist at the wheel of an Abraham Lincoln Continental? But which master I am now the servant of—whether it was Herr Steinbrenner or Lord Evans or one of the other anonymous owners of the score of limousines at the Rivington Street curb—I cannot say.

Mosk: "The Doodle? Okay, but make it snappy."

At once I move forward and push through the padded doorway into the dining zone.

How to describe the scene than now assaults my senses? Even a Dante, a Virgil, might be tempted to put down his pen. Darkness, yes, an abundance of darkness; but at the same time there is inexplicable light. Rays in primary colors stab about in every direction, like the beacons of searchlights that frantically hunt for enemy aircraft. Revolving globes hang from the ceiling like great mirrored eyes that cast sparkles and spangles throughout the room. Through it all, like clouds split by lightning, hangs the smoke of uncountable cigarettes. It is as if a hundred photographers stood about me, old-fashioned cameramen, whose every shot releases a cloud of sulfurous vapor and a flash of mercury strong enough to turn the black of midnight into the blaze of high noon.

For a moment I stand, stunned, the way a venison is said to halt when stricken by headlamps at the side of a country road. I am brought from this trance by the *thud, thud, thud* of percussion that, in wave after wave, breaks against the skin of my body and passes through the soles of my shoes. The very walls of the room seem to be reverberating, thumping inward and outward like the speaker of my Philco before expiration of the tubes. I step forward, a single seed in this great vibrating gourd, a solitary blood drop, that is what it feels like, in a huge convulsing heart.

In a moment I come to a cleared space where men and women are dancing together. Dancing? Together? They writhe, they twist, they collide with the force of catapult stones. On their faces, the lips are back, the teeth are bared, the eyes are wide and staring, as in a mask from the South Sea Isles. Above them, on a high platform, a near-naked female dances alone. Her blond hair sways back and forth behind her dorsals and, on her chest, her bare bosoms careen like balloons from which the air is escaping. Could this be, I wonder, a Fone Fancy? A modest glance at the sirloins confirms my suspicions: show-through silk in the skivvy, with opaque black trim. "Pardon!" I exclaim. "Are you Fraülein Corky?"

Before she can reply, two doors swing open at the back of the room and a procession of cooks and waiters enters from what I know to be the Steinway Restaurant kitchen. At the head is Ellenbogen, transformed by silk pants and silk-banded headwear from the waiter he used to be into a distinguished-looking person. Behind him, wearing a hat as tall and white and fluffy as a Yorkshire-style pudding, strides Martinez, the ex-master of broilings. Next come chefs and sous-chefs and—what's this? Can I believe my startled eyes? It is Chino! Chino! One of the Puerto Ricans! When last seen, a wispy-chinned lad. Now, three decades later, a mutton-chopped adult. And look! Right behind him: Jesús! Also a non-Sephardic. He, too, has aged, but it is not possible to mistake those two closely placed, liquid-filled eyes—which, when he attempted to force himself upon Miss Beverly Bibelnieks, yes, in the manner of a Hussar, had stared at me narrowed and squinting, like the yellow eyes of a wolf. Now he and his accomplice have escaped from jail. Why have they returned to the scene of the crime? For revenge? An Hispano-American vendetta? To murder us all?

On and on comes the parade, through the burning phosphor, in and out of the closely set tables. At the rear a half dozen scullions are lifting high into the air—higher even than their own stiff white hats—a great silver dome upon a silver platter. How it gleams and glows! It seems to capture every stray beam of light. Now, to my surprise Ellenbogen—only the small square of white cloth on his arm serves as a reminder of his former station—turns toward where I am

standing, next to a table of aristocrats. Amazingly, when he reaches
that spot the old waiter stops and bows, with one knee touching the
ground. Martinez follows, as does everyone else in the train, even
the busboys. But Chino glances up to where I remain on my feet.
"Goldkorns! Is you? ¿Cómo está usted?"

"Error, sir," I declare with insouciance. "I am a Lincoln limousine
driver."

Now Jesús addresses his old antagonist. "Ha! Ha! Señor Goldkorns! Hard time, we did hard time, but no hard feelings."

Only now do I notice, atop his head, and Chino's too, the high
headgear. Crooks? Cooks! Earners of an honest living. Relieved, I
bend toward the ex-prisoners.

"Psst. Tell me. Who are these grandees? Is that Prince Philip, perhaps?"

"You don't got eyes, gringo? That's Cruise. You know, the actor.
Look at that smile, man. A million-dollar smile, right? Look at that
chin."

"¡Loco hombre! I'm looking at his woman. You see her, Goldkorns?
You want some of that?"

"Would you be so kind? Who is the gentleman with the hair?
Resembling a pineapple?"

"That's El Greco, eh? Comes in all the time. What's his name,
Chino?"

"Stephanopoulos."

"And the Afrikaner? Also with hair? There: like a porcupine."

"What? Goldkorns! ¿Está en vivo en el planeto de Marte? Or
asleep twenty years? Man, that's Don King!"

"These names do not, as we say in the vernacular, ring the bell. I
am not, owing to the lapse of Herald Tribune home delivery, au
courant with affairs."

"Oh, man! You pulling my leg? Jesús! This Goldkorns, he don't
know Puff Daddy."

By now all the servants are rising. The sous-chefs struggle to lift
the platter into the thickened air. As they do so, the music ceases. All
about us the dancers come to a stop. Even the smoke seems to grow
sluggish, staying its movement in the atmosphere. Now Martinez,
standing on a chair seat, prepares to raise with flourishes the silvery
covering. The guests at the table stare upward without uttering a

single word. At adjoining tables the diners also pause, knives and forks motionless in their hands. Off comes—it is like a St. Peter's in pewter—the great dome. What a sight greets my eyes! For there, with a *pomme* in its mouth and a pom-pom on its tail, is the forbidden beast itself: the glazed, staring eyes; the round, hunched shoulders; the four folded hooves, as uncloven as the devil's. Pork! It is pork! A whole suckling pig!

Now the search beams swing round, one after the other, illuminating the metallic platter and making the animal glitter and gleam, as if one of the *sauciers* had doused it with brandy and another one had set it alight.

"Oooh!"

With that exclamation, rising from every quarter in the room, I cannot help but feel a chill in each of my extremities and a sensation of hollowness within my heart. I know what all those in the Steinway Restaurant are worshiping. It is the Golden Calf.

Now an aged gentleman—by this I mean someone more advanced in years than the present speaker—pushes through the crowd; rather, the pack of men and women fall back before this centurian, who, wielding his cleaver, approaches the beast for the ritual carving. On the head, a skullcap; on the nose, circular spectacle lenses; on the chin, a long white beard that spreads like the bib that gentiles wear when eating crabs. Margolies! It is Margolies! Dean of the Steinway Restaurant waiters! High in the air the priest raises the shining blade. Descending it snaps open the pigskin, releasing a fountain of juices. Once more the knife is raised, once more it drops. Now the pale flesh is exposed; and now the bone, ribcage and chestbone, and a hint of the inner organs, pearl-like and intact. On every side the gentiles strain forward, their mouths open, as if in anticipation of the blood-filled flesh. And the Jews? As in days of old, they are the slaves and servants, delivering to their masters the forbidden feast.

And now come three new Israelites. At the sight of these men, Salpeter, Murmelstein, Dr. Julius Dick, my heart soars within me. Here are the surviving members of the Steinway Quintet. Impossible to avoid the inevitable thought: could this trio become a foursome? Dr. Dick possesses still his double viol; it towers above him as he edges through the mute-mouthed crowd. But what of Salpeter, the first violinist, and young Murmelstein, the second? Neither man has with him his violin. Surely room might be found for a flautist without his flute? I am able to whistle, if called upon, cadenzas from *Call Me Madam*. Dreams. Hopeless dreams. Murmelstein hops like a youth of sixty onto the bandstand and bends over—it is not a Bechstein, nor is it a Bösendorfer; but it is a keyboard nonetheless. Dick follows, hauling his fiddle onto the platform, and Salpeter sits before his own instrument, which must, from its shining cylindrical surface, be some sort of drum.

Salpeter: "A one-ah; a two-ah; a one-two-three!"

How to describe the resulting din? Each plucked string of Dr. Dick's double bass resounds like a cannonade. Useless to clap my hands over my ringing ears. Murmelstein attacks his keys like a man who has made a pact with the devil: for hidden in that device is an entire trumpet section, invisible strings, klaxons and bells, and above it all the clarion call of what sounds like a steam calliophone. The crowd, in response, goes into a frenzy, twisting and jerking and hurling themselves against each other, knocking their partners to the floor. There is a sudden howl, a scrape, a high-pitched squawk, as if the poor porker, under a kind of anesthetization, has awakened with a squeal of terror. In fact this caterwaul is created by Salpeter, who stops the disk that spins before him and sends it screeching in the opposite direction.

Who is that man approaching the bandstand? Short, stout, with a nose that dives down into his moustache. Heavens! Rabbi Rymer! The man who made Leib Goldkorn and the former Clara Litwack man and wife! He climbs onto the platform, seizes the microphone, and, in the style of our fathers, begins to chant:

Rymer:
> *There was a man wit a tan in the lan of Uz*
> *Job had a Jag checkered flag play tag wit da fuzz*
> *Bossest hog in da catalog*
> *Cuz*
> *He was upright, recondite, every Sunday night*
> *Went to confession wif his Smif-n-Wessun*
> *Had faith in Jesus 'n' Joseph 'n' Mary Jane*

Speed, bleed, weed, 'n' cocaine
'N' Able
Drink any dude unda da table, wit Black Label

Chorus
(Salpeter, Murmelstein, Dick):
  Ballin' in da fast lane, chillin' on da block
  Golden chains, Einstein brains, sportin' a Glock

Rymer:
  Fifteen hos in Versace clothes covered head to toes wit
  Oil o Olay
  Gold-toof bitch don' wear a stitch got her ass onna pillow
  She give the alarm break her arm like da V da Milo
  A kilo
  To his valet
  A Benz for his friends, a 'Vette on a bet
  Nuffin he don' buy us

Chorus
(Salpeter, Murmelstein, Dick):
  Job be pious!

Rymer:
  Grand for tips 'n' on his lips a holy prayer

Chorus
(Salpeter, Murmelstein, Dick):
  Boss player! Boss Player!

Hard to believe that anyone could comprehend the meaning of these words. Is the language English? Hebrew, perhaps? Is it even human speech? At the table the guests are eating the suckling pig. Mr. Cruise gnaws on a bone. Mr. D. King tears the skin. How wet their fingers! Their chins! Nor does the crowd, swaying, faces aflicker, teeth agleam, seem to grasp what only I have deciphered: that these poor Jews were attempting to express their own sufferings through the tale of their unfortunate coreligionist. Now the aptly named rabbi resumes:

Rymer:
> *Up in heaven by a 7-Eleven with the angels singing chords*
> *by André Previn*
> *God sat at da feast*
> *"Don't wanna boast but he be the Man coast to coast*
> *At least in the East"*
> *Tha's his toast*

Chorus
(Salpeter, Murmelstein, Dick):
> *Ain't no mirage! Head nigga in charge!*

Rymer:
> *Then up stood a bro of high birth going to an fro on da earth*
> *"That muthafucka crowdin' my turf*
> *Put forth thine hand, smite him in his gland*
> *Give his hos to his foes, make him speak prose*
> *Rip off his contraband"*
> *God withheld his rod*
> *"You got a case of a-nomie? Talkin' bout my homie*
> *A boss ghetto styler, got hisself a Rotweiler 'n' a*
> *AK 47"*
>
> *But Satan wassn't done wit his hatin'*
> *"Deny his lays, snatch up his purses, not to mention his verses*
> *All his praise turn into curses"*

Chorus
(Salpeter, Murmelstein, Dick):
> *Whadaya know? Done seen this story on da video*
> *Gonna test the power of this dude's religion*
> *Look who's comin': a stool pigeon—*

Rymer:
> *"Wussup?" said Job. "How's tricks, 'fucka? Why the alarm?"*
> *"First thing, sucka, you bet da farm on the Knicks*

Lost all yo bread
J hit the trey couldn't cover the spread
You dead—
Them hos didn't knows da Xs and Os caught a disease
Ain't psychosomatic
A automatic between the knees"

Chorus
(Salpteter, Murmelstein, Dick):
    It's da rape from Hell, see?
    I's only excape to tell thee

Rymer:
    "You talk the talk, nappy head nigga, wit yo' PRAISE DA LORD
    Now walk da walk,
    I's happy pull da trigga, put you on a pine board
    Outline in chalk
    Forget abouts you family tree, going down on a APB
    All yo riches them yaller bitches you fake-ass schemer
    The King o' da Universe puts you inna hearse no top down
        Beemer
    Meet yo maker, faker, take dis fag inna body bag"

Chorus
(Salpeter, Murmelstein, Dick):
    Goin' crazy, bats in da belfry
    Rate this a X tape
    I's only excape to tell thee

Rymer:
    But Job ain't bout to jump from da Tappan Zee
    "You think this dampens me? Shit happens, see?
    Naked I came from da womb
    Naked I goes back to da tomb
    Take my hos 'n' my hoard but blessed be
    Da name of da Lord"

    Pigeon grows a tail two horns 'n' a fork
    "You wish you never borns in New York"

Gave Job boils on his balls, sores 'n' tsouris
Wrung his tongue couldn't rhyme worth a dime calls
"Cure us!"

Chorus
(Salpeter, Murmelstein, Dick):
Cure us!

Rymer:

Come the worst trick of Satan
Made him sick in da dick forget masturbatin'
The G jes stutter
"J-J-J-Jee-sus!" he's pleadin'
Up the devil stands takes his nuts in his hands 'n' cuts
No ifs ands and buts
Wit a box cutta
Job got the hex of Oedipus Rex whole box of Kotex
Won't stop the bleedin'
Cocksucka!

Chorus
(Salpeter, Murmelstein, Dick):
Doth thou retain thine integrity
O say can you see?

Rymer:

Blind on hands and knees tries to find his main squeeze
"Hey, baby! Yo, wha's goin' on—?
Look at that blond-headed witch, in her Guccis
Ho of Babylon—

Here, ladies and gentlemen, all heads turn to where the Fone Fancy continues her gymnastics upon the raised platform. Her golden locks fall as advertised to her buttocks. Her shoulders, her mammalia, her maidenly midriff—all shine with moisture as if she has just stepped from her bubbling bath.

Rymer:
She wiggle that ass full of sass hold aloof

That gold toof can't hide her uncloven hoof
Looks down at that chump sees only a stump
'N' toss her head high—

Suddenly the chant comes to a halt, the music ceases, and the illumination swings to where the dancer had brought to a close her undulations. Into the silence she hurls the words of Job's wife:

Curse God and die!

From the crowd, a low, animal roar. Mouths gaping, they surge toward where her greased body glistens in the light. There now occurs to Leib Goldkorn a thought so terrible that with a vigorous head shake I attempt to drive it from my brain. It remains. Will this young woman, so sportive in figure, be set upon by the hungry masses? Is this a sacrifice—a human one to match that of the animal only moments before? In short will—here we see the infectiousness of Rabbi Rymer's idiomatics—Corky be a Porky?

Before I can either speak or make a movement, the deafening music resumes, the crowd breaks into its dance, and someone pulls upon the sleeve of my chauffeuring jacket.

"Psst, Goldkorn. Look. Do you see? That chair."

It is Margolies. Cautiously he leans close, whispering by my ear. I look to where his spotted hand is pointing. A small, dark man, with goatee wisps and shaded glasses, sits with a superior smile.

"Do you mean, Mr. Margolies, the *Afrikaner*?"

"No, no. Not Spike Lee. I mean the chair. You do not remember? Who sat there? She had a cigarette in a holder. A habit, you know, a nervous tic, of picking the flake of tobacco from the tip of her tongue. I saw this! I changed the ashtrays. I brought the black coffee. Goldkorn, do you know of whom I am speaking?"

My voice has died within my voice box. I can only nod.

"Yes," cries Margolies. "Sarah Bernhardt! In that very chair!"

Then the waiter also falls silent. Does he feel in his breast the upward welling of shame that now fills mine? It is distress at what we have allowed our world to become.

3

Bulova watch time: eleven hours, twenty-two minutes. *Ante meridiem.* Evidently the silver chronometer had come to a stop. No match for the ocean's depths, its brine-brimmed waves. Then why was the hand for seconds, like a loyal ox at its task, still plodding around? And why was its little heartlet audibly beating, like that of *ein Summervogel* at the sight of an open flower? Could I really have slept through the afternoon hours, the whole of the night, and the following morn? Easier to believe that I had passed some strange form of International Date Line that caused my timepiece to run backwards, as crossing the equator will create a counterclockwise movement in a tub. I had, in my life's journey, just turned forty-one: in other words, I was a youth of the twentieth century, trained, like our modern pilots, to trust instruments and not the senses. Very well: eleven twenty-three. I had lost a day in my life.

I looked about me: the beach, white and blazing; the blue-tinted sea; the green palms overhead. Overhead? I sat up with a start. Someone had dragged me—yes, there was the trail across the sand—to the protection of these fronds. Who could it be but the darling Esther? My queen! Once more I felt myself overcome with gratitude at this blessing. The heroine of my oratorio had come, bronzed and bountiful, to vigorous life. Together, through my music, we would save the Jewish people from their implacable foes. But where was the Persian princess?

"Yoo-hoo! Esther! *Mein Wundermädchen. Wo sind Sie?*"

No reply, save for, in thick brush beyond, the chatter of a monkey; and, overhead, the rustle of a tricolored parrot taking flight. I scanned the shining sea. No question Miss Esther was a champion swimmer, as skilled in her element as Madam Henie had been on ice. Had she dared, in her Australian-type crawl, to make for another tropical island, or even the far-off California coast? No, no. Not even an Olympian could accomplish that feat. In my veins and arterials the hot blood seemed to freeze. Had I lost her, my human haddock, even before I had been able to reveal her very first lines—

Why have I, a mere maiden, daughter of Abihail
Been thrust with such rudeness into this women's jail?—

or clasp with manliness her soft, white hand? Gone! Drowned! A mermaid submerged in *la mer!*

It was only at that moment of anguish that I noticed the trail of footprints leading from my shaded retreat to the trees behind me. Of course! Esther, seeking assistance, had run off into the wild. Ah, the enchantress! But were the dangers she faced within the depths of the jungle any less menacing than those in the depths of the sea? What sharp-toothed tiger, what spotted leopard, lay in wait to pounce upon her? Over what distances could the hidden snakes spit their venom? And what of the poisoned darts of the Pygmies? I had, in order to save her, not a moment to lose. Snatching up my only belongings—the Rudall & Rose, of course, and my Revolver—I followed the impressions of heel, arch, and wee winsome toes into the primeval forest.

Immediately the world turned from noon to night. Only the odd ray of sunlight was able to penetrate the curtain of leaves that stretched above, and even these stray columns and odd patches were blackened by zigzagging insects and crawling bugs. Vines hung about me like man-made nooses. Roots rose up to trip me like the fingers of buried hands. So thick was the air that I felt I must be wading through a vat of heated liquid. At each turn pointed petals slashed at my skin, burying themselves in the cloth of my blue double-breasted.

Which way, this was the question, to go? To the left? The right? Straight ahead? And, having done so, how could I be certain I would be able to retrace my steps to the place where I had begun? If only, like the principals of the famed Humperdinck opera, I had been able with bread crumbs to mark my way. Alas, even if I had possessed such a loaf, I saw at once that any trail would be devoured completely by the disciplined armies of ants. And where was my soul sister? Similarly awander? *Esther! Esther!* With repetitions I called her name. But the syllables died before my face, as if swallowed by acoustical cotton. On I plunged—tripped, rather, stumbled and crawled, deeper and deeper into the gloom. At length I raised to my lips the London-made Rudall

& Rose and poured forth the melody that accompanied, not Hansel and Gretel but Tamino and Pamina, as they journeyed in Mozart's opera through the pitch-black cave of the night:

TRRR-WITY! TRRR-WATY!

Instantly there was a crashing sound, followed by that of cracking twigs, thrashing foliage, snapping vines. The beasts in their hundreds were fleeing—yes, even a python coiled out of sight. A honey bear ran off on its hind feet while its forelimbs, or such was the illusion, were pressed to its ears. A half moment later and I was left in deeper darkness and a stillness more profound. But wait! Within this utter silence I thought I heard a soft but steady percussion. My own heart? No, these sounds came from afar. Tom-toms! And if there were drums, there must be drummers! Human life! We were saved!

Now I had a surer path to follow than either bread crusts or the marks left by travelers on the trunks of trees. Each beat of a drum was like a knot in an invisible rope that I groped my way along. In time—the Bulova now registered one minute to one—the air about me began to grow lighter, brighter, and suddenly, without warning, I stumbled into a clearing.

What a welcome sight now met my eyes. Here was a native village, with a score of huts made from palm leaves and ribs of bamboo. Smoke rose from cooking fires. Dogs ran about, tails curled over hindquarters or dragging between their legs. The tiny town seemed to be inhabited only by women and children, some at their mothers' breasts, others clinging to their skirts of grass. Here was a paradox: they, the primitives, were unembarrassed by the exposure of either paps or mams, while I, who had lived many years in the Vienna of Schnitzler, automatically clasped my hands over my boxer-style drawers.

"Ha! Ha! *Guten Tag, meine Damen!*" I shouted. "I come in peace!"

The women, heavyweights all, whirled about. "*Komabalu! Komabalu!*" they cried, pointing first at me and then into the sky—no, not the sky, but toward the vast bulk of a giant volcano that reared upward behind the village. White jets of steam spurted from the jagged cone, and a tiny stream of orange-colored lava spilled down the side to where a group of males—they had bones around their necks and paint like bolts of lightning upon their bodies—danced in a circle about the pool of molten ash. Here were the tom-toms, a row of stretched skins, which other men were beating with polished sticks. To one side of the glowing pool was a tall statue, with a red-painted tongue protruding from its scowling mouth. At the feet of this figure—surely this was the god of the volcano—the priests of the tribe had thrown themselves down upon the earth.

A dark-skinned witch doctor—he also wore a necklace of bones, with, in addition, two horns that grew in the style of a Viking from the sides of his head: this witch doctor emerged now from behind the statue. With one hand he shook a shaft that was covered with feathers and had a blade at its tip; with the other he pointed to the far side of the bubbling pond of lava where I saw, with horror, a huge iron kettle—surely the boiler from some stranded steamer—beneath which a pile of tree twigs and tree branches had been piled, and out of which there peeped the bare heads and shoulders of two Caucasian gentlemen, one bearded and one whose cleft chin was shaved. Suddenly, like one of the white bolts of lightning that zigged and zagged across the black torsos, the truth struck me: these were headhunters! Cannibals! Eaters of human flesh!

"*Abab-ma-u-aliki!*" shouted the witch doctor, shaking his spear once again.

"*Aliki, Vahitai,*" answered the dancers and tom-tommers. Then they rushed forward, in order to dip their own spears into the sacred pool of lava. With these flaming torches they ran to a small reed house at the back of the clearing and set it afire.

"No, no!" groaned the old man inside the great tureen.

The young man, his black hair was slicked back and shining, also spoke English: "You foul devils!"

In less than ten seconds the flames engulfed the dwelling, bursting through the roof and consuming the Christian-style cross that hung over the door.

Amazingly, the savages seemed to have learned some English

as well. "We have obeyed your will, O Vahitai," they cried in unison, over the smoking ruins.

Vahitai, the witch doctor, responded: "Not my will, but the command of Aitutaki." At that word everyone prostrated himself once again before the statue of the god.

What next? No sooner had Leib Goldkorn set himself this question than the answer—in the form of a young man, fatter far than any of the females of the tribe—emerged from the doorway of the largest hut.

"Ah, Ru-hamabu," murmured the crowd. "Our prince!"

The waddling adolescent threw a leopard skin over his shoulder and moved slowly across the clearing, until he joined Vahitai in front of the carved figure of the god. The high priest seized the boy by the loose flesh of his arm.

"*Biku-biwa!*" he commanded the people. "Stand aside!"

They did so. Then an amazing thing happened. The witch doctor placed a hat of what must have been peacock plumes on the perfectly round head of the prince and under the protection of those magical feathers the youth not only walked to the glowing pond, he waded right through it and emerged, the liquid lava lapping at his ankles, unscathed on the other side.

From the onlookers, there came an aboriginal huzzah: "*Aitu-taki! Amabulu, Bula-bu Aitutaki!* Our god is a mighty god!"

But the display of that deity's power was not done. The plump prince continued walking. He stepped untroubled over the burning embers of the charred church and, with a mere head shake, seemed to will the lingering smoke clouds away.

"Ah-h-h," sighed the natives at what was now revealed to their eyes.

I, too, made a similar exhalation. Up to that moment I had been able to tell myself that there was some chance that I was still asleep beneath my roof of palm fronds and that everything I had witnessed was either a dream or a fragment of a South Sea adventure, featuring Miss D. Lamour, that I had viewed at the Kruger Kino, upon the Kärntnerstrasse. Alas! It was not Lady Lamour whom I now saw unveiled through the last wisps of smoke; it was, with her hands tied behind her to the rough bark of a tree, Fraülein Esther!

Now my heart beat with such violence that both rows of buttons upon my double-breasted shook like acorns dangling from a wind-tossed oak. What was going to happen? Were the carnivores going to throw the swimmeuse into the pot with the doomed men? Were they saving her as some sort of unspeakable dessert? All too soon did I learn that she—how glossy her lips were, how kempt her crown of hair—was to endure a fate far worse than such a horrible death. The doughy dauphin came at last to a halt only inches from where Esther strained against her hempen bonds. Her one-piecer had disappeared. Her hip bones were now draped by a carmine-colored sarong, while a garland of orchids tactfully covered her teats. Toward this bathing beauty the corpulent child now lowered his head, his lips protruding, as if to steal a kiss.

"Please! I beg you! Let her be!" That was the elderly gentleman.

His companion, clearly bound hand and foot, hurled himself against the sloping sides of the vat. "You black fiend!" he cried.

"No, no, Father," Esther spoke sweetly. *Her father!* Then who was the handsome chap with the dimpled chin? A brother, perhaps? But what was Esther saying now?

"Do not lose faith. Have you not always taught us that God will protect us?"

"Ha! Ha! Ha!" That cruel laughter came from the head priest, who had joined the blubbery boy. "You say your god protects you. He is a weak god! Aitutaki much stronger! His fire burns down your god's house!"

"You may burn down His house," replied Esther, taking such a deep breath that it rustled the petals on her well-located lei. "You may even torture and burn His people. But there is only one King of Heaven and His spirit can never die."

How my heart swelled at the words of this Jewish girl! It was as if her ancient namesake had stood before the evil Haman and declared her faith:

You can rob us and beat us and crush us with your power
But this only deepens our faith: three cheers for Yahweh!

"Matu! Silence!" Old Vahitai stamped the earth in his rage. He raised his spear so that its tip approached the adorable button of her belly.

"Leave her alone! Do you hear me?" cried the dimple-chinned young chap.

"It's all right, Rick darling." Thus did Esther address her brother. "They won't hurt me."

"Kamino, Ru-hamabu. A-mapu-i?" Vahitai seemed to question the heir apparent. He pointed to Esther. "You see this girl?"

The obese one nodded with all four of his chins.

"Fhu-apalu, mirada. T'ulli? You take girl for wife?"

"Uh-huh."

The witch doctor turned next to Esther. *"Fa-apalu, mirap, ul-hamelei?* You take prince for husband?"

My mermaid actually managed a brave little smile. "No. That cannot be. I am already betrothed to another."

Ru-hamabu: "Is good? I kiss her with mouth?"

The aged priest, instead of answering, whirled about to command his devotees: *"Uk-a-mani pa-ulalu! Aliki!"*

At once the savages dashed to the pool of fire and dipped their staffs into the bubbling lava.

Meanwhile, I stood in wonderment. *Betrothed? To another?* Was Miss Esther speaking in the ancient manner of our Jewish Queen, who was surely wed, in her heart, to Heaven's King? Or did she mean that, having just saved a certain person's life, she was bound to him forever and, in the vernacular, vice versa? Was Goldkorn the groom? Such rumifacations were cut short by the chilling cries of the dancers, who were now circling the iron pot with the burning staves in their hands.

"You become *Be-ak-adua.* Princess for our prince." Vahitai held up his spear for all his people to see. "Otherwise light fire."

What a terrible decision for the espoused Esther. Tears streamed from both of her eyes. "Oh, God!" she cried. "Help me! Show me the way."

"Don't let him touch you!" cried her sibling. "Tell them *No!"*

Esther: "Oh, Rick! Rick, my darling!"

The father: "Never mind us. Remember: we are about to go to a far better place!"

The rubbery royal: "Give kiss! Give kiss with mouth!"

Esther: "Dear God! Won't you give me a sign? What should I do?"

Bow-wow-wow-wow! So cried, in the common tongue of canines, every dog in the village. They were in full pursuit of the strange white man, a five-foot-fiver, who was dashing at high speed from the edge of the forest to where his inamorata was bound to the sapsago tree.

"Stop! Stop at once!" I cried, waving my arms as I ran.

"It's you!" cried out with joy the Queen of the Jews.

"Who is this?" demanded the swarthy Vahitai.

"Ouch! Ouch!" I answered, kicking aside the sharp-toothed terriers. "You must not make this marriage, Herr Doktor. Release those prisoners at once. It is definitely forbidden to eat human people."

Instead of replying, the high priest turned about, looking over his shoulder, which caused his feathered spear to dip down. That was the signal to ignite the faggots. Not with a whoosh but with a wump, as if some person had shaken a sheet or a blanket, the entire pile of kindling burst into flame.

Eeeee! The scream came from Miss Esther.

"Oh! Oh! Oh!" howled the two condemned men.

Leib Goldkorn knew he had to act fast. I raised my Revolver and aimed it between the witch doctor's eyes.

"Gun! A gun!" cried the rotund Ru-hamabu.

I motioned toward the prince. "You must order him to untie Miss Esther."

Vahitai barked his command: "Ur-mukalalie! Puta! Aliki!" A score of savages dashed toward me, their spears like the poles of vaulters approaching the hurdle.

"Gott! Forgive me!" I cried, and pulled the trigger. Nothing occurred. I pulled it again. There was only a clicking sound. "Ha! Ha!" I laughed. "I have wet my powder."

The aborigines surrounded me, the points of their weapons actually pricking my skin.

"Hey! Hey! Get us out of here!"

"What's going on?"

The poor Caucasians! Flames were licking up the blackened sides of the kettle. This was not the time for a disputation. I raised my Rudall & Rose to my lips and inhaled a full draught of air. But before I could exhale, one of the natives swung his spearpoint and knocked the instrument from my grasp. There it lay, mute in the dust.

"*Mak-aru, ka-kai!* Seize him!"

The painted tribesmen gave a shout and fell upon me. They pushed and poked at my body, stripping from me my Lloyd Brasileiro double-breasted, my shirt and undershirt, and my bosun's boots. They even pulled from my wrist my Bulova watch. Naked except for the score of my opera and the loincloth of my drawers, I was hoisted into the air.

Here was a dark moment for the members of the white race. Poor Miss Esther was slumped asobbing against the sapsago tree. Her father and brother were calling to their maker for assistance—*Help! Goddammit! Get us out of here!*—and I, gripped firmly torso to toes, was being carried like a trussed boar to the flame-enclosed vessel.

"*Va-emakalaylu!* Throw him in!"

Just then, as the natives lifted me over the iron rim and it seemed that Leib Goldkorn's numeral was, as Americans say, up, I noticed one of the paint-covered priests holding my watch to his ear and rapping it with his knuckles, so as to allow the trapped spirit within to depart. The Bulova! The time! I had a sudden inspiration. I knew what I must do.

"Wait, friends! You are making an error! My God is a great God. He will be angry. He will take the sun from the sky!"

Of course I was referring to the eclipse—the one that had been predicted on the nautical chart of the Nipponese. It was due to arrive, if I remembered correctly, at the hour of two. There was no way I could explain, as Professor Pergam had once done to his students on the Türkenshanzplatz, how the moon in its travels moved between the sun and the earth. I used instead words that such folk might understand: "He will turn the day into night."

The natives paused. I could feel, in their hands, their fingers, a slight trembling.

Vahitai: "Aitutaki will make more fire! He spits fire from mouth."

Ah, there was not such a great difference between the primitive and the professor. When the one spoke of umbras and penumbras, the other—that red tongue, the smoking cone above me—spoke of a volcano.

"Why do you wait?" demanded the high priest. "*Emakalaylu!*"

Once more, in those dusky fingertips, I felt the tremor of indecision. The whole of the tribe craned their heads upward. There bright Phoebus, as Pergam would term it, shone in the clear blue sky.

"*Aliki!*" shouted in unison the priests of the tribe, and, turning from the cloudless vault, they hurled me into the crowded vat.

The first thing that caught my attention was that I was of a sudden completely wet. H_2O! The element of water! Tiny bubbles were wobbling up from the bottom of this tepid liquid, while wisps of steam wafted from the top. "Ha! Ha!" I exclaimed to my two companions. "We have here a sitz bath."

"*Amolo-lu-lo. Kuko-a-monga. Uniki!*"

No translation provided—though it seemed certain that the evil Vahitai had demanded more fuel for the fire, since the natives came running with armloads of foliage and brush. Evidently this tribe, in practicing its cannibalistics, preferred to devour its victims boiled. Already the bottom of the cauldron was too hot to touch with our feet. Miss Esther's relations, tied by the wrists and ankles, were thrashing and squirming and uttering the sort of imprecation that in the Vienna *Tageblatt* would be indicated by either dots or a dash.

"Psst. Don't worry, fellows. There's going to be a total eclipse. In just one minute. Look up! Look!"

But for some reason the bright plate of the sun shone the same as ever, without the slightest chip in its rim.

"*Bow-wow-wow!*" The mongrels and mutts were racing about our pot in great excitement, having undoubtedly formed in some part of their minds an expectation of scraps. Now the tiny bubbles were growing larger and bursting about our armpits. What inhumanity! Even an unfeeling lobster is dropped into water that has already been brought to the boil. The face of Esther's father was now as red as the shell of one of those crustaceans. Her muscular brother was beating his head against the side of our circular coffin, perhaps in the hope of bringing on a state of non-consciousness. I peeped over the rim.

"Hola! You there! *Ja!* The gentleman with the Bulova watch. Would you be so kind as to give me the time?" But the barbarian only licked the back of the timepiece and threw it upon the ground.

I drew back. The freshly fed flames roared up the sides of the pot, which had taken on a reddish hue. Sweat drops sizzled on the griddle of my forehead. And still the sky remained without a shadow, and the sun shone on like an untouched disk at the top of a strongman machine. I looked at my fingers. Heavens! They were as plump as blood sausages. Little dots appeared before my eyes, as if the fluid within them had begun to effervesce. "Oh! It's killing me!" cried the stewing sibling, with his black, blistered tongue.

Just then I heard a noise, a kind of clanging and scraping; when I glanced out from beneath my poached eyelids what I saw filled me with indescribable anguish. Knives! Butcher knives! Paring knives! Machetes! The tribe was not even going to wait until we were done. The next words I heard—would they be my last?—were the worst to reach the ears of any civilized man.

"Cut!" That was the witch doctor's command. "Cut! Cut! Cut!"

I closed my eyes. I stopped treading water. Better to drown, to die, than be dismembered.

"I said *cut!* What's the matter with you? Cut, goddammit! Cut!"

That was not the voice of black Vahitai. I opened an eye. Two men, white men, were striding across the clearing toward our kettle. The Jew Cummings! Zanuck, the Gentile!

The Fox King: "Damn it, Irving! You wasted two thousand feet of film. At fifteen dollars a foot!"

"But D.F."—this was Katz-Cummings—"I figured it was all part of the script."

Zanuck held up his mallet for polo. "Untie that girl," he ordered the awestruck tribe. "And get those men out of the pot." His staff, it seemed, had more power than Vahitai. The natives dashed to the sapsago tree. Others reached gingerly over the edge of the cauldron. First they hauled out the bearded old man, then the young one. The Fox King was still fuming.

"We've lost the whole fucking morning, for Christ's sake! It's not just the money. To hell with the money! I've got Esther on loan from Mayer. He wants to put her in a Andy Hardy. I've only got three days left to make her a star."

Katz-Cummings: "Sorry, D.F. I don't know how this could happen."

"Who is that guy? Who let him in here? Get him the hell off my set."

"Ha! Ha! Greetings, Herr Zanuck! Here is Leib Goldkorn. Graduate of the Akademie. It seems that once again we have crossed our paths."

There was a pause. The face of the Fox King turned into a shade of what I believe is called ultramarine. Then—was this possible? Or only an hallucination brought on by heat prostrations?—the man's entire head lifted an inch from his shoulders before settling upon them again.

"Him! It's him! I'll kill him! I'll murder him! You—!"

This was addressed to the aborigines who had just started to lift me, wet and steaming, from the depths of the cauldron. "Put him back! Back! Back! Back! Get more logs!"

The next thing I knew I was once again in the seething soup. My heart beat for another half moment. I heard, as if from a great distance, a scream and human shouting. Then my blood came to the boiling point, and whether I was now under the water or floating like a turnip upon it I could not tell, since the whole world had gone black.

"What is this? Jesus H. Christ!" That voice, clearly that of a Christian, came from the fat figure of Ru-hamabu.

"Oh, Darryl! Hold me, honey." And could that really be Miss Esther? "I'm frightened."

"Dak-a-ri! Jina-ton-iki! Bati!"

"Cummings! Where the hell are you? I can't see a thing!"

"Neither can I, D.F! I'm blind as a bat!"

Then the human speech was replaced by all manner of animal noises. First a roaring, like a lion or tiger; and then much chittering and chattering from monkeys and chimps; and finally a mournful wailing from all the village hounds. This was followed by the strangest sound of all—from above, below, on every side, a kind of chirp-chirping, as if a chorus of millions were singing in the key of G.

"What's that, D.F?"

"I don't know."

"Neither," said Esther, "do I."

But I did. With my last strength I called out to those on dry land. "Ladies and gentlemen! Here we have a natural phenomenon. It is *die Grillen*. Yes, the song of *die Grillen*. Look upwards. Do you see?"

I turned my own gaze toward where the black sky was filled with uncountable numbers of tiny winking lights. "Poor *Grillen*. Poor crickets. They too have been fooled by the stepping forth of the stars."

"An eclipse!" cried the Fox King! "An eclipse of the sun!"

Katz-Cummings: "An eclipse? Is this some kind of rewrite?"

"*Amabulu! Boola-bu! Alla-aliki!*" With those words the South Sea Islanders seized me once more by my shoulders, my waist, my arms. They hauled me upwards and set me adrip upon the land. A cool breeze, a night breeze, blew across my smoking body. I looked around. I could just make out that all the members of the tribe—save for Vahitai—were bowing down before me, just as they had once done before their god.

"*Amabulu! Amabulu!*" they murmured in reverence. "*Abu-bulu-ama!*"

"Ha! Ha! It's just got to do with, you know, orbits."

Now a shadow moved toward me. What was this? Who might it be? I could smell the aroma of orchids. Next I felt their cool petals touch my parboiled chest, just as, against my May Co. cottons, I felt the soft silk of a sarong. Out of this darkness, from teeth as white and bright as bathroom tiles, came a flash; and the next instant two lips—they belonged, of course, to the Jewish Queen—pressed with a hint of tongue twists against my own.

"*Abu! Amabulu! Amabulu!*"

By now even the voices of the women and children had taken up this chant. The beat of the tom-toms repeated the rhythm.

"*Abu! Amabulu! Bula-bu!*" Into the jungle and up to the darkened sky went the strange-sounding words. *"Abu! Bu-aba! Gold-korns! Bula-bu Goldkorns!"*

How long has it been since I have passed water? Not counting the wee misfortune at the shop of the brothers Glickman. A whole day. A portion of the night. This is for Leib Goldkorn a definite achievement. But there can be no further delay. The bladder bag feels to me the way a swollen udder must to a Holstein cow. The Steinway Restaurant WC, both men's and women's compartments, is located at the bottom of the staircase, below the level of the street. Here have I in happier days moved my bowels, following which I laved both hands with liquid soap and dried them on a perpetual towel or, after the Stutchkoff era, squares of paper. Here too one might stand at the porcelain gully, with its lively little rivulet, while to the one side Mr. Margolies mumbled to himself words of encouragement and, to the other, Mr. Mosk shot burst after burst without use of hands. With eagerness I push through the crowd of dancers and start down the curving steps.

GENTLEMEN, *to the left.* Then why, when I push open the portal, is the room filled with ladies? "Ah, *Entschuldigung!*" I cry, throwing one arm over my eyes to avoid a sighting of bloomers. "Many pardons!" Impossible not to hear, however, the sighs and groans of those attempting a defecation. After all, I am only human: why not a peek? All about me are twenty members of the weaker sex, each of whom is straining within her own doorless cubicle.

"Oh! Oh! Oh!"

"Yes! It's such a big one! Yes!"

"Don't stop! I'm almost there! It's coming!"

With these and other exclamations the females cheer on the progress of their stools. Some, I note, hold reading matter—undoubtedly novels of romance or adventure—before their eyes, while others, as an aid to digestion, inhale the smoke of cigarettes. But what, pray, are those wires that extend over their heads or the small disks suspended before their mouths? And why is it that this lady, and that lady, indeed each and every Fraülein and Frau, is fully clothed? Even modesty may be taken too far.

I can't wait to hear your voice, Stud. Are you ready for me? I'm hot and wet and ready for you.

Familiar endearments. Where have I heard them before?

If you aren't man enough for me, or not eighteen, hang up right now.

Of course! The telephone! These are Bell operators. No, no! The Fone Fancies! I am in the House of Pain and Pleasure! But in this room of dowdies—Mr. Flynt, I fear, has been guilty of a false advertisement—there is no sign of Miss Crystal Knight.

To the right. If ladies are in the gentlemen's WC, perhaps the gentlemen are in the ladies'. In spite of weak illumination, I discover that such is the case. For here is row after row of moustachioed men. All eyes are focused upon the far side of the room, where there is depicted an allegorical scene in which a frizz-haired maiden offers her bum zone to a horse.

Odd: it seems that each member of the audience is a woodwinder. For on every man's lap, along with his foul-weather macintosh, there seems to be an upright ocarina. Odder still: on the stage the performing pony has also in his possession either an *oboe d'amore* or full-sized bassoon. Music lesson? No! No! The truth dawns upon me. Here the rules of nature are being turned upside down. Instead of a human mounting a quadruped, the quadruped is mounting the human. What wickedness! Like Sodom and Gomorrah! The sin of Catherine the Great!

"Siddown, will ya?"

"Pardon. I have come here in error. I was seeking merely the lavatorium."

And seek it I still must. Was there not, on the upper floor, a private cabinetto attached to the Stutchkoff apartments? I remember that, while breeding with the widow on the Sealy, I glimpsed through an adjoining doorway the promise of porcelains. Up I climb, past the fiesta on the first floor, and step by step approach the second. As I rise I feel the weight of the bladder bag stretching down, as if that sack has been filled with stones. At last the topmost floor. Before me lie a number of corridors, all at right angles to one another, and each with a series of tightly closed doors. Down which resides the mate of the late Vivian Stutchkoff? Impossible to recall. I have no choice but to plunge forward and knock on every portal.

Friends! Nothing in my childhood in the town of Iglau, and not even the Vienna of the sophisticate Schnitzler, has prepared me for what now greets my eyes. Only the Jews who dwelt in Babylon could have imagined such a spectacle. Men consorting with men, that is what I discover behind one door; and women in dalliance with women, that is the hijinx behind another. It is as if the Book of Leviticus had never been written. On I stagger, down yet another hall. Here is a room with a priest, or perhaps a cardinal, holding a youngling upon his knee; and here is another containing a definite gynandrite. Am I awake? Is this a dream? I stumble first left and then right along the gauntlet. One brunette-haired lady is conducting a urination upon the body parts of another. "Hi," speaks the shameless damsel, "I'm Shelly." Says the victim, "I'm Joy. Want to join in?" Strange to say, my own need for such a voidance has utterly disappeared. I have now but a single motive: to flee this wickedness. But I have lost my way in the maze. More doors beckon on every side. Animalistics! Orgiastics! I am lost in a land without taboos! Paraphilias, eroticomanias, fetishistics, too! Urnings and priaps and the sin of Onan! There is no end to these foibles. Ah, a whole room for hernias! Another for pedicures! Is there truly no escape? I break into a trot. Look, surely that is the Sun King, Louis Quatorze, and that a pasha with his harem. Heavens! A coffin! A casket! Can it be? Yes! Here is the infamous case 23 in the pages of Herr Doktor R. von Krafft-Ebing, in which a sergeant took for his amoreuse a human corpse! Mad! I shall go mad! There is no way out!

Was ist das? An open door. A light. The one at the end of the tunnel? Yes! Ahead is the abode of the Stutchkoffs. I move forward, only to hear, behind yet another closed door, the sound of voices:

Schwein! Schweinhund! Ich werde dir Respekt bringen!

I pause.

Ja. Schlecht mir. Ich bin ein yiddischer putz.

These last words: are they not in the long-forgotten tongue of my folk? How can I resist such pleasantries? Cautiously, I turn the wooden knob. Silently, I enter. Help! Oh, help! Compared to the abomination I now see before me, the entire abecediary of vice, from Aphrodisiasm to Zoorastry, was but what our English friends call a brass farthing. Oh, whisk me away to the Nancy boys! Anywhere, anyplace, but in the same room with this Hauptscharführer SS and the skull and the bones upon his cap.

Poor Leib Goldkorn! In the lair of the beast. Paralysis in the feet, paralysis in the tongue. Is my worst nightmare about to come true? Am I to suffer the fate of my people? What a brute is this, with, on his face, a thick-lipped sneer. A leather coat, a leather vest, and, shining like motor oil, trousers of black leather, too. On the floor before him, an abject Jew, with sidecurls and skullcap and a caftan already in shreds from the whip blows. Even as I watch in horror, this instrument of torture falls across my co-religionist's back.

Mehr! Mehr! Schlug schwehner.

Hit harder, that's what the Jew is asking, he does not want mercy. The *Hauptscharführer* is happy to oblige. The whip swishes once more through the air, and swishes again, like the hiss of some terrible serpent.

So! Nimm das, du dreckiger Jude! Und das!

What should I do? Flee? Or, armed with my Revolver, fight? Caught between these two alternatives, each of which seems to have seized control of a separate lobe of my mind, my body makes the decision by releasing three liters of urine; this runs down the twill tube of my trousers and spreads like a yellow map of Europe across the polished wood floor. Aghast, I can only watch as the Gobi Desert, that age-old boundary between the Russian peoples and the Mongolian hordes, creeps past the crouching Jew all the way to the jackboots of his oppressor.

Jackboots? There are no boots at all, only a single bare foot with five painted toes and one bright red, high-heeled shoe. What have we here? Case 129, the Hungarian who wore ladies' hose and ladies' gloves? Or the Countess, case 166, who in her high collars and watch fobs and even celluloid spats, dressed more like a Count? Transvestitism, friends! Off comes the rawhide jacket, off the rawhide vest. A zipping sound and the trousers collapse to the ground. Now the peaked cap with its death's-head insignia is tossed onto the pile, allowing glimpses of golden hair, like bars of butter. Here, within a brass-studded halter, are two milk breasts. Also a pelvis, with girdle straps. Flesh folds. Skin wrinkles. *Gott im Himmel!* It is Miss Crystal Knight!

Do you think, ladies and gentlemen, that the sight of my sweetheart, with pasties, fills my heart with joy? Is there naught but good cheer now that the arduous search is done? *Au contraire!* Sorrow assails me, and indignation, and soul-sickness, too. Why, Mr. Goldkorn, so glum? After all, until this moment I believed my paramour to be chained in a dungeon, where even her meager ration of bread and water was stolen by the sharp-toothed and sharp-clawed rats. Oh, that chamber of torture would be a paradise compared to this! What is the worst the Germans have done to the Jews? Enslaved us? Put us in ghettos? Beat us and starved us and burnt us in ovens? No, no: that has been our lot since Haman, since Pharaoh. The worst accomplishment of the Nazis is that they have turned us—with our godlessness! our cruelty to fellow Jews—into themselves.

"Ah, Madam Knight!" These words I pronounce aloud. "What have they done to you?"

The enchantress whirls round, causing a perturbation among her mams. The Yiddish speaker leaps upward.

"What's going on? I paid for an hour!"

But I hear nothing, see nothing, feel nothing. I am consumed by a single desire: to rescue from degradation my inamorata.

"Please! Please! I am begging!" And indeed like a beggar I fall before her on my hands and knees. "Don't walk on him! Walk on me!"

I lie like a polar bear rug in a daze of amazement. Miss Crystal—see how the shod and unshod feet draw closer—seems about to respond to my plea.

"What's going on?" demands the former victim. "It's only a quarter to ten."

"Out! Out if you please, sir! Take notice: I have here a repeating Revolver."

"Jesus!" With that exclamation, meant in a non-denominational manner, the gentleman departs. Slamming behind him the door.

Now Madam Knight raises above me the blood-red pump.

"Do not hesitate, my dear! Crush me! The way you would crush a worm. Yes! *Ein Wurm!*"

Now what I have long desired comes to pass. The bare foot trods on my dorsals, and the heel of the shoe, like the blade of a knife, sinks deep into the tenderloin.

"Ouch! Oh! Wait! Stop! It hurts!"

But the torturer seems to take encouragement from my cries. "So! The Jew feels pain! He begs for mercy!" After which words she plunges the dagger point once again downward, between two baby back ribs.

"Ow! Ow! It is agony!"

"*Schweinhund! Wurm! Ein jüdischer Wurm!* I will cut you in two!"

And now the whip whistles, slashing straight through the cloth of my chauffeuring jacket and into the flesh below.

"No! Not a worm! And not a Jew, exactly. I mean, here is a Graduate of the Akademie."

A pause. The whip hangs limp. The feet withdraw and I hear not the voice of sharp command but the tobacco tones, so low and husky. "Hold on a second. Academy? You've been here before—"

"No. Correction: yes, but many years in the past. As the Bechstein artist. Steinway Quintet. Trained, however, in woodwinds. Also glockenspiel."

"It's funny. I'd swear I've heard your voice."

"Explanation: we have had upon the Bell telephone a chinfest, during which you have described to me your unhappy life—the rodents, *ja?* Also, in the water trench, the reptiles."

"*Larry!* Is it you? Larry?"

"Ha! Ha! You have led me the merry chase."

"But how come, if we only talked on the phone—how come you look so familiar? There's something about that mouth. Those lips—"

"This is caused by blowing since youth upon a non-reed instrument. But I can say, Madam Knight, the same words to you. There is, in the blueness of those eyes, the blondness of those head hairs, a familiarity. Why? Because I have long ago made your acquaintance in the pages of a certain gentleman's rotogravure."

"Oh, no!" With a cry of abashment Miss Crystal throws her hands over her eyes, a gesture so childish—does she really suppose that if she cannot see, others cannot see her?—that for an instant she regains for me all of her lost schoolgirl's charm.

"Please, there is no reason for mortifications. We are in a fashion old friends. Like a fond uncle I remember you as a fledgling. The absence of eye-kohl. Breasts like *Makronen*. Wee almond delights. Also creamed flanks. The innocence, the spirit, of a maid of thirty."

Have I said an improper word? Suddenly the nymph is transformed once more into the Nazi. *Crack!* That is the sound of the lash, curling through the air. "Okay, Larry. You're not the first one to make a date on the phone. What do you want to be? My horsie? My kike? Or my slave?"

"Your slave? *Nein! Nein!* Your savior! Together we shall make from this prison an escape. Do you not remember my words? How we shall flee to the Avenue Columbus?"

"But you said you were a worm. You wanted me to walk on your back."

"That was only a test—to see how far a Jewish woman had been made to fall. Now I am more determined than ever to free you from the tyrant. The evil Hans Maltz!"

"What do you mean, *Jewish woman?* What makes you think that?"

"But did you not inform me in our heart-to-heart of double Ds? Is this not an ethnicity?"

Here she turned both eyes—admittedly, blue ones—upon me. Her lips spread in an unhappy smile. "To tell you the truth, I don't even know."

Could such a thing be? In infancy, in Iglau, before I knew whether I was a male or a female gender, or perhaps some species of frog; yes, even before I knew I was a subject of Franz Joseph, his *apostolische Majestät,* I knew I was a Jew. "Of course, Madam," I say, "you have not the advantage of circumcisions."

Before my companion can reply, there is a loud knock upon the door. Maltz! The despot! I reach for my weapon. Then the portal swings open and the head and torso of a man—he is wearing a green paper cap and a gown of green-colored paper—thrust into our chamber. "Here I am! Your incurable patient. Is nursie ready?"

This time it is Miss Crystal who slams shut the door.

Goldkorn: "Madam, we have no time. He will report to the tyrant. How to escape? The window? Is there a bed? We might descend on the bedsheet. Come! Come, my dear! We must flee!"

Madam Knight: "No. Stop. I want you to tell me. Tell me again."
She is motionless, her nearly nude nates against the doorframe.
What's this? Tears? Tears from those possibly non-Jewish eyes? "Tell
me," she repeats, "the way I was—*then*."

"*Mit* pleasure. No lipstick on lips. An A cup. Total poundage?
Forty kilos, in my estimation."

Now the tear stream flows on each cheek. She raises a hand for
silence. "No. Don't say any more. I was a different person. Different
even from what you saw in—you know, in the magazine. Yes, with a
white throat, with a little ankle. Untouched, Larry! Unspoiled!"

I can speak not a word. From below, as if from some hellhole at
the earth's center, comes the jungle beat of the tom-tom's, as the devils perform their dance of the damned.

Madam Knight: "Now look at me! Look at me, Larry! What do
you see?"

"You are in my eyes, Madam, a dazzler—"

"Ha! Ha! Ha! Aged fifty-three!"

I reach upward and remove my motoring cap. "*Voilà*, my dear."

For a moment she stares, non-comprehending. "What, *voilà*? I
don't get it."

"Do you not see? The hairlessness? The ear tufts? The spots of
liver? You have before you also a non-spring chicken."

The next instant her arms make an encirclement of my torso and
her lips touch one cheek and then, like a Frenchman, the other; following which, more in the Italian manner, she applies the force of
suction to my tongue.

I know full well that I am on Rivington Street. This cannot be the
Kärtnerstrasse. In other words, here is a moment from real life and
not a scene in a cinematograph. Then why do I hear the sort of invisible orchestra that, as in a kino, prompts us to feel excitement or
sadness, or to chuckle at the humorousness of human endeavors? Is
this not the duet of Brünnehilde and Siegfried rendered upon a—a—
a Rudall & Rose! It is the Number Two Finisher! "Hans Maltz!" I
exclaim. "Do you hear him? He is playing my flute!"

"No, no, Larry, love. That's Harry Schwartz. He runs things for
Hilda."

"Schwartz! That is his *nom de plume*! I remember! He is the consort of Madam Stutchkoff. Oh, Madam Knight—may I call you Miss Crystal? How much we have in common. I, too, was once held a hostage in this same Steinway Restaurant. And now the two of us share the same foe. He is the arch-fiend, the Prince of Darkness, bane of my existence."

"Oh, I don't know. Harry's not so bad—"

"A war criminal! A Haman! A—excuse my asking: what are you now doing?"

"You took off your hat. I'm taking off your coat. Don't you get tired wearing it even when you're not driving people all over town?"

"Driving? I am a non-driver. Ah. The motorman's costume. The time has come for a confession. I am not, Miss Crystal, the person I seem—"

"Want to know something? I'm not either. Crystal's not even my real name. It's just for show."

"Really? Not Crystal? Well, I, too, am a non-cognito. This uniform—oh? Are you also removing my Arrow shirt? Ha! Ha! I am skin-sensitive: this uniform is my disguise. Now you see them. My hirsute shoulders. An affliction almost from birth. If only this growth could by miracles of modern medicine be transformed to my head. Where are you going? Don't leave me! Oh: a Murphy-model bed. A space saver. You wish to seize forty winks? It seems you are unlacing my Thom McAns. These are my own wardrobe items. Oft resoled. Ha! Ha! Yes! Heel lifts. I am a five-foot-fiver. I ask your pardon. I am not a darner. And Madam Goldkorn even in the palm days of our marriage was not an expert at repairing the holes in my—ha! ha! ha! A ticklish zone: in my socks. *Bow wow! That's my dog Tide. He lives in there, too!* Advertisement, on the Philco, for this brand of shoe. What? Also the dungarees? But I have not brought pajamas. Oh. Ah. I have not in my connubial life experienced such nibbling upon the nipples. Definitely a sensation. Very well: off with the breeches!

"Wait. Halt, Madam. I must first make a further confession. I am not the paragonian you think I am. This is, to be frank, honey, yet one more thing we share. I, too, and in this same Steinway Restaurant—what? Lift my left leg? *Eins, zwei,* and a little hop: I have had once an escapade. I am ashamed to tell you at whom I aimed Cupid's bow. Hildegard Stutchkoff! Yes! And I was at the time a completely married man! Philanderer! Adulterer! Libertine! I cannot deny it, my Cleopatra: there was a near penetration. What now? What next? Those are my S. Klein elasticized drawers. An heirloom item. Difficult in this non-boxer era to replace. Note the Western motif. Buckaroos. Flying sombreros. The old corral.

"Perhaps I might remove with your permission the halter about your mams? What? Here? In the back? Ha! Ha! Such fumble fingers! Now! There! Goodness, how they tumble down! No, no: do not hide them! To me they are a gift—yes, hanging downward like the holiday stockings that pious Christians attach to their mantels. Bulging! Yes! With bonbons! With Tinker-type toys. A touch. A mere hand touch. Ah! *Pardonnez-moi!* I see that my kosher-style has burst from overeagerness through the cleft in my drawers. Ha! Ha! We need a cowpoke for this Texas-type bull. Here you see the handiwork of Rabbi Goldiamond. A sign of the Covenant, according to the myths of our people. But how is it you do not know whether or not you are a Jewess? Wait! Let me guess! You are an adoptee? No? Stolen from birth! So, even that is between us another mutuality. I know what it is to lose a daughter. Your poor mother! Poor father! Ours was a non-starter: that blue little face, the little blue arms, two open blue eyes. A breath. And gone!

"These straps, my Venus. Do they not chafe the pubics? We could, you know, remove them. Do not think I am a sodomite! No, no, no! Those gazettes were read upon doctor's orders! This is an unusual and gratifying experience: to have the breathings of a handsome woman blown into the ear. Once a year! November 9th. My date of birth. To encourage a pollution. In my latter years I must rise for urinations many times in the night. There! All undone! Well, well. A surprise in the nether lands: so we are a fiery redhead. And above? You are perhaps the twin with the Toni? In the days of my youth my hair was rubicund too. A further bond between us.

"Time for the nap? You on the bottom and Leib Goldkorn on top? Like the missionaries at play in the mission. Of course, since you know I have sired a daughter, it is only logical to expect that I have experienced a defloration. I am certainly aware in matters of bawdiness what I must do. Here? It goes here? Or in this one? Ha! Ha! Almost an error on my part. Let us make another attempt, my Helen of Troy. Do you doubt Leib Goldkorn's expertise? I direct your attention to the dressing room of the Tivoli Jewish Art Theater. The sight of garter trolleys! The scent of orange blossom perfume! Perforation achieved: November 13th, 1942. A definite conception. Birth of daughter—alas, it was also the day of her death. 6/7/43. At the same Tivoli, transformed into the Cine Palace. Ah. There. A little wider, *s'il vous plaît*. A little higher, too. Ah! Ah! I am having a *Sensationslust!* Ingress! Almost a centimeter! What? Why do you make a fidget? You mean, that is your birthday, too? A Gemini, eh? Also, 1943! *Incroyable!* What a coincidence! Oh! Oh! I am feeling peppercorns! Our doctor's name? M. Goloshes. He took in kindness the wee babe away. *You* were raised by a Goloshes? *Milton* Goloshes? Wait! Oh! *Mein Gott! Gott!* This is a tragedy written by the Greeks! Your name, Miss. Tell me! What is your name!"

"Martha."

At that very moment there is a shrill whistle, as if the proximity of the two Goldkorns—the father staring into the daughter's blue eyes, the daughter into the father's brown ones—has set off an alarm. There are shouts of outrage. Cries of dismay. Shrieks, even, of terror. Naturally there can be now no question of conjugals. We each leap from the Murphy. Too late! The voices are moving into the stairway. We hear them echo through the halls. Once more the whistle's shrill call.

"It's a raid! Nobody move! This is a raid!"

4

As the Fox King told us, he possessed the services of the Swan of the Surf for only the first week of December, 1941, which meant he had only three days left before returning her to the Lion of MGM. But he could not shoot even one "foot" of film without the approval of the Bula-bu, the Great God Goldkorn, before whom the native folk of the island now bowed down. Yet even a god may have problems. How, in such a brief period of time, could we transform this South Seas adventure into *A Jewish Girl at the Persian Court?* Luckily, the score of my life's work had survived parboiling intact. With the help of the eponymous Esther—how diligent, my gorgeous guppy, at duplicating with paper and pencil those endless sharps and flats—we soon had enough copies for Señor Cugat and each member of his orchestra: yes, Cugat, that Carib, Miranda's admirer, and by a fate twist also on loan from L. B. Mayer.

As for the drama itself, our method was to build on the photoplay my people had already learned. Thus the Christian-type cross on the burning chapel was replaced by a Star of David, and the former worshipers of Aitutaki were converted into the most devout of Jews. Esther's father, in real life a Mr. W. Pidgeon, played the part of her cousin Mordecai. Mr. Victor Mature, formerly her sibling Rick, was our Ahasuerus, the manly King of all Persia, in spite of the fact that from his pectoral section hung a pair of not unappealing mams. And the sable-skinned Vahitai? There was only one role which, grinning and gleeful, he desired to have:

> These Jews! I'll uproot them—stem, pistil, and stamen
> For I am the son of Hammedatha the Agagite, a.k.a. Haman

Even the mighty volcano—in fact made of paint, pasteboard, and plaster of Paris, which explains how the portly Prince was able to wade through the lava unharmed—had a part to play in the eyes of the downtrodden children of Israel:

> O, look! Have faith! Take heart for the fight!
> There is the cloud by day, the pillar of fire at night

By day, indeed, and by night—that's how we toiled, from Katz-Cummings in his canvas-backed highchair down to the lowest of my subjects, who turned themselves into footstools, upon which their Deity was obliged to take a seat. One by one the scenes of the grand opera unfolded before the camera's rapidly blinking eye. Everything that Madam Henie had performed on ice, Miss Esther now enacted on top of water. The Dance of the Virgins actually takes place beneath it, the dark-hued maidens twisting and turning like sea trout, their legs kick-kicking, their firm swimmers' buttocks—from which, surely, we derive the word *natatorium*—thrust upward with provocation, and little silver bubbles ascending from their smiling mouths. When the Persians, actually Papuans, threatened the jaunty jewfish, Mr. Mature, appropriately doing the breaststroke, declared his intentions:

> Hold! Hands off! Do not molest her!
> Of all these mermaidens my bride will be Esther!

Only Vahitai refused even to dip a toe into the watery element:

> What? Am I a perch, a flounder, a kipper or salmon?
> I'll do my deeds on dry land, or my name isn't Haman

Thus did he approach the water balleteers with, in his hand, a vial of venom:

> Shall I drown all my foes in a terrible flood
> So Jews and Jewesses will stick in the mud?
> Or shall I with cunning open the dike
> Goodbye to every Yid, Hymie, and kike!
> No! I must screw up my moxie, and then
> This potion will remove from water all oxygen

Terrible vision! Poison for the *poissons!* Even though I knew we were only filming a movie, the tears sprang to my eyes as I watched my fellow Jews gasping within their giant fish bowl. They clutched their throats. Their eyes seemed to bulge from their sockets. They even turned bluish, as if inhaling some invisible gas.

"Help! Help them!" I, from my spot on the sidelines, declared. Too late! Had something gone wrong? Half the Hebrews were floating belly side up; the rest were sinking toward the bottom. Vahitai—the Haman, the Hitler—had won the day!

Just then the Cugateers began to play a Leib Goldkorn scherzo for shimmering strings, while, at the bottom of the transparent tank, the shell of an outsized oyster slowly opened, revealing the pearl inside. Not a pearl! Silver-suited Esther! She opened her arms, made a saddle arch, and then floated with the sole of her right-hand foot against her left-hand thigh. Never once, in spite of the thousands of pounds of pressure, did the fixed smile leave her face; her teeth gleamed like a garage door that had come down on the little red roadster of her tongue. Then she turned and, trailing bubbles like thoughts in a cartoon, swam to her people—touching this one with a finger and that one with a toe. And wherever she went the drowned Jews revived. The daughter of Abihail was breathing into them a magic elixir. Up rose her people, smiling, wig-wiggling, higher and higher, until they broke the surface in lusty song:

Alive! Alive! There's no need for an inquest here
We have been saved by our own dear Queen Esther!

Nor were the swimming Semites content to remain on the surface. Like some prehistoric mammal, a missing link, a lumbering lungfish, they crawled from their lagoon and seized their tormentor upon the shore. Esther embraced Ahasuerus and demanded justice for her people. Mr. Mature flexed his mammalia:

Just as he intended these Jews to slaughter
Build up the fire, fill up the vat
So shall he die surrounded by water
He shall see what his deeds begat

Chorus of Israelites:

Cook him like a carp, bubble him up in a brew
Skin him like an ocean sprat
We'll soften that hard heart in a stew
Even if he's not strictly kosher, glatt

Thus began the great Purim celebration that would be completed on our third and last day of filming. With what excitement did I await that moment. How quickly the time flew by: Action! Cut! And once again, Action! Even the Fox King seemed content with the pace of our work. Each night we threw ourselves down for two or three hours' sleep before rising again the following dawn. Sleep? How could I sleep? Was not my masterwork being recorded for posterity? Would it not be shown in the Pantages and the Roxie and the great cinema palaces throughout the world? Alas, the one theater in which *Esther: A Jewish Girl in the Persian Court* would never appear was the Kruger Kino, where I had experienced so many fantasias as a youth. Yet the thought of this exception filled me with pride: the Jews, who were no longer permitted to enter that kino or any other within the Reich, were about to be saved. Surely in the days following our Grand Premiere, brave soldiers and sailors would march forth on the land and sail forth on the sea to liberate the Israelites, just as goggled pilots would swoop down upon their tormentors from behind the cloud puffs that filled the air. Who was that merciful and avenging god who had brought this about? It was I! None other than I! Patience, my people. Lord Leib comes!

It was with such thoughts as these that I stumbled into my grass-type hut in order to obtain the proverbial forty winks. "*Abulu-bu, boola,*" drowsily murmured my half-dozen wives. They lay, in the moonlight, the way that slick-coated sea lions recline while abask in the sun. I stepped carefully among them, as a farmer might amidst his field of aubergines, and sank down into the hibernating harem. At once my six spouses rolled toward me their maroon mammalia and, thus pillowed, I entered the kingdom of Morpheus.

"Oh, Leibie. My Leibie. Are you asleep?"

Who spoke such words? Surely not one of my squaws.

"Can you hear me? Can you feel me? What about this?"

Once—the year was 1925—I experienced in my sleep a visitation from Miss G. Ederle; rather, I saw the photogravure of this nymph that had appeared that day in the *Tageblatt*. She wore the same costume in which she had just crossed the Ärmelkanal—a one-piecer, which, through salt-water shrinkage, revealed to the practiced eye the precise location of the human paps. Instantly I found myself covered with an effusion, as if I too had emerged from a dip in the sea. Was this another such dream?

"Wake up. Wake up, Leibie. It's me."

What was that gleaming light? Like beams from a headlamp. I

opened an eye. Yet I seemed still to be dreaming; for what I saw, as if myself immersed in the English Channel, were the chalk cliffs of Dover. A second eye. Miss Esther! The moonlight ablaze on her teeth!

"Oh, Leibie, hold me. Take me in your arms."

"But Madam. My little anchovy. I thought you were a D.F. Zanuck property."

"Darryl? He's all right. But none of his tricks can match yours. Oh, Leibie. Your magic takes my breath away."

I could see, in the darkness of the night, the darker flesh of my consorts, like that of a hippo herd hip high in the Congo. They stirred but did not wake. I felt a five-fingered hand reach between my cutlets and fasten upon my vegetative part. It sprang forth to sniff the air.

"Magic, my pretty Pisces? The magic is in your prestidigits."

"Tell me," she urged, not slacking her manuals. "I'll do anything if you tell me. How do you do it?"

"But, my deft dolphin, there is really nothing to it. Here we have a completely non-voluntary phenomenon. Ha! Ha! Like the salivation of the wolfhounds at the sound of the dinner bell."

"No, no, no. The trick. You know, the way you make the sun disappear. I've never seen anything like it. One minute it was day, the next minute night."

I felt, at her chafing, a sensation of warmth, followed by a bubbling in the depths, like a fondue. Then I noticed an odd thing. Beyond our hut, with its sounds of breathing, the entire encampment had grown perfectly still. Deduction: our cricket friends had stopped their singing. And that, in turn, could mean only one thing.

"Abra—in the words of the Baal Shem Tov, ha! ha! ha!—cadabra!"

Cock-a-doodle-doo! came the answering call, followed by a lone sunbeam that worked its way through the thatch above us and flashed upon my partner's bicuspid. Without a second's delay we heard a human cry: "Places everybody!" It was the voice of Katz-Cummings. "On set! Everyone on set!"

Esther was the first to gain her feet.

"Wait. Please. My gudgeon. I have need of further fluctuations."
But she only stared at me with widening eyes. "Oh, Leibie! My
wizard! You did it again! But backwards! You just turned the
night into day!"

Or, as Homer, a Greek, has written, *Came the dawn.*

And what a joyous one it was! The nuptials of Esther and Ahasuerus, the holiday of Purim, and the final victory over the evil
Haman.

There is our enemy, tied up with knots
He's the main dish in the Feast of Lots

So sang the chorus of Israelites, pointing first to where, in
ropes, Vahitai stood close to the steaming kettle; and then to the
volcano, from whose cone there bubbled and burbled a crimson
stream:

Hot tea? Potage au tomate? A brew from the bean of java?
No! It's the bride! Our Esther! The Queen of lava!

Then out of that same fiery mountain there appeared ten,
twenty, thirty laughing lasses, each in a skintight bathing costume, holding, in lieu of a lei, a bouquet of sparklers. Two by
two, these bridesmaids slid down the flaming flanks of the volcano, creating twin trails of fire. Now Esther appeared in a daring two-piecer: a wisp of wool below, a twist of taffeta above,
with the whole of the porterhouse exposed. There was a sudden
beam, like that cast from a lighthouse lantern, and smiling she
too came down that flow of lava the way a skier might plummet
down the snowy slopes of the slalom.

Oh where are the lads who have promised to marry us?

So sang the neptunettes as they sidestroked within the pool of
molten minerals.

Look! They come! Led by the great King, Ahasuerus

From the top of the sapsago tree came thirty native boys, clinging to thirty jungle vines. Down, down, down they swung; and then, up, up up, until at the apogee they released their holds and, arms outflung, loincloths aflutter, dove into the torrid tank. It was then that the King appeared on the tiptop branch; falling faster, flying higher, than any of his subjects, he too disappeared into the burning lake.

For a minute, for two minutes, the Cugateers played a Purim potpourri. Finally, after three such minutes—could even a diver for pearls hold his breath for such a long spell?—there was a disturbance at the center of the pool. Up rose a pillar of fire, with flames as gaudy as ostrich feathers stuck to a hat; at the center of the conflagration stood, bosom to bosom, Miss Esther and Mr. Mature. Now, the mermaids and myrmidons also appeared, their heads underwater, their legs swaying in the open air.

Esther (embracing Ahasuerus):
   Progress among mankind is slow, even glacial
Ahasuerus (embracing Esther):
   Oh for a world in which all men can play tennis or
     rugger or golf
Esther (about to be kissed):
   We'll set the example through our love interracial
Ahasuerus (bending toward her):
   Once we've rid our planet of Hitler, Adolf

Chorus:
   Einstein, Columbus, Meyerbeer, Freud
   Such contributions you can't avoid
   Above all a notion to which all men give the nod
   A burning bush, a whirlwind, the idea of one God

Admission: tears of triumph filled up my eyes. Yet even through that prism I saw one item amiss. Haman had somehow loosened his bonds. Not only that, he had seized one of the burning logs beneath the kettle and was starting up the volcano's steep incline.

L.G.: *"Wait! Vahitai! Do you want to cause a riot?"*

Katz-Cummings: "Quiet on the set! Quiet! Quiet!"
Zanuck: "Goldkorn! I knew we should never let you alone."
L.G.: "Majesty! It's Vahatai! He's climbing up to the cone!"
Indeed, by that time the former witch doctor was well along the flanks of the volcano, the flaming torch in his hand.
Katz-Cummings: "Stop him! Don't let him get higher, jerks!"
D.F.: "That volcano is stuffed full of fireworks."
Esther: "Oh, no! Oh, golly!"
Mr. Mature: "He'll ruin our grand finale!"
D.F.: "Keep filming! Keep shooting! Don't stop! Don't cut!"
L.G.: "Don't worry, chaps! Ha! Ha! I'll stop that nut!"

Do not be surprised to hear that I—remember at that time only one month over the age of forty—was already bounding like a bodybuilder up the side of the mountain. Upward I leaped, ever upward, past plaster boulders and pasteboard rocks, in and out of the fast-moving stream of mock lava. Above me, the dark-skinned Vahitai had paused for breath. I stopped as well. Far below I could make out the native swimmers forming kaleido-scopic patterns of mams and gams, while snatches of my own melodies rose through the whistle of the wind. I called up to the panting Papuan:
"Please, sir, I beg you: don't climb any more."
For a moment longer Vahatai lingered, grinning:
"Sorry to disappoint you, meu caro senhor."
Then he was gone, making a last desperate dash to the sum-mit. I stood, stunned, staring at the retreating figure and his fire. Senhor? Senhor? For a horrible instant I thought I must drop in dizziness all the way to the earth. This man, so squat, so swarthy, was no South Sea Islander. Here was a Rhythm Boy! Felipe! Gestapo member! The very one who had blown a dart into the flanks of Madam Milanov! Now I knew—oh horrible thought—who was the seclet agent. He, it was he, who was going to signal the waiting foe.
With new strength, and new purpose too, I threw myself into the chase. The course of history, the fate of mankind, depended upon Leib Goldkorn.
"Stop! Stop! You traitor! You spy filled with guile!"

To my amazement, he did stop, but only because he had reached the lip of the smoking crater. He raised the torch high.

"Viva o Hitler," he shouted, "Hitler, heil!"

I lurched forward and managed to grasp his waist with my arms. We wrestled there face to face above the abyss. First I had the advantage and got my hands about his throat. Then he brought his kneecap rudely against my gonadium, at which I dropped to my knees at the very brink of the precipice.

"So, Judeu, now you cry, you weep, eh?"

"Have mercy, spare me, my dear Felipe."

The callousness! The cruelty! Instead of taking pity on a helpless foe, he thrust the burning brand directly at my prostrate form. At the last instant I rolled to one side, simultaneously seizing the fiery branch. The Rhythmaire backed away, his thick lips atremble. Now it was he who tottered at the edge of the smoking pit. I stood, weapon in hand.

"Ha! Ha! I am not singed. Not one hair is burned."

"Faz favor. Faz favor. The tabelas are turned."

Then, to my horror, he charged straight at me. I hurled the torch. He ducked. The flaming log went end over into the crater. Instantly there was a detonation, and ten thousand stars shot over the rim. What a display! Pinwheels, clusters, red-hot squibs. Incendiaries shot a hundred feet into the air and burst into smoke and flame. Rockets trailed sparks high into the sky before exploding into whirling fragments of fire. Out of the huge smoke cloud came a storm of embers and ash. Anyone looking on, from land or sea, would have thought a long-dormant volcano, a Krakatoa, a Vesuvius, had come to life.

Both Felipe and I crouched down, covering our heads with our hands. Five minutes went by. Then ten. How long could such pyrotechnics continue? I took a quick glance at my Bulova. Eight minutes past eight. But the eruptions did not abate. If anything, they only increased in intensity. The fulminations grew louder. The very ground shook beneath me. The columns of smoke, like one of the Great Goldkorn's magical tricks, had dimmed the face of the rising sun. If I did not know better I would have thought that the fierce god Aitutaki, intent on revenge, was with these concussions bringing an end to the world.

Finally, my antagonist got to his feet. He was gazing off to the east, over the crest of the neighboring hilltops, toward a sliver of the silvery sea.

"Meu Deus!" he exclaimed. "Olay!"

"*What chaos,*" I responded, standing as well. "Oy veh!"

It seemed to me that the whole earth was in flames. Out toward the sea thick smoke, black smoke, curled as high as the clouds. Shells continued to fly upward, bursting with tremendous reports. Here was something new: yellow canaries were flitting everywhere through the sky. Not canaries! Aircraft! Now, on the breeze, came the sound of distant sirens. It was like the wail of a million men in pain. Suddenly a stray warplane roared by our volcano—there was the face of the pilot, merely a boy, with a scarf of checkers tied under his chin—and released a bomb that tumbled downward and blew the set of *Esther,* along with the cameras and canisters that contained *A Jewish Girl at the Persian Court,* to countless smithereens.

"Mr. Felipe, what is happening? Will you tell me, please?"

But within my breast I already knew what a blight that, with a single terrible torch toss, Leib Goldkorn had brought to the world.

"Maravilhoso! *A raid on Pearl Harbor by the Japanese!*"

"A RAID! A RAID!" The cries are everywhere now. Hip-hopping, I pull on my twills—trousers, jacket, oversize cap. Miss Crystal, my little maid Martha, dons a two-button robe. I hold my McAns in one hand; she has but one boot on her foot. Together we rush through the door. Pandemonium reigns in the hall. Men and women, dressed and undressed, are running this way and that. They scream. They shout. Is it a pogrom? Are these Ukrainians? Up the stairs on the left come three helmeted policemen, blowing on whistles and waving their clubs. "Halt! Halt!" they command. But no one heeds. I race off down the corridor in the opposite direction, pulling my dear daughter by the hand. Suddenly a door opens and a beautiful woman, a redhead, with a beauty mark on her cheek, rushes out to accost me.

"Sammy! For Christ's sake! Get me out of here!"

"Sorry, Miss! Ha! Ha! Mistake in identity."

"What the hell are you talking about? It's me! Rudy!"

With that the beauty removes both her hairpiece and mole.

"Mayor Giuliani!" Crystal cries.

"Right! Hurry up, Sammy. Get the car."

Now I too take off my head covering. "You see? I am not Mr. Sam."

His honor throws up his hands in surrender. But I know that it is I, Leib Goldkorn, that these minions of Morgenthau are determined to capture. I drag Madam Knight, limping on her high, sharp heel, down the hallway toward the little line of light that shows beneath the very last door. No need to knock. We burst across the threshold. Inside a little grandmam is rocking in a chair, next to a recliner on which lies a wee wizened grandpap. In spite of age, the wrinkled skin, bosoms that sit like twin tots on her lap, I recognize the woman. Madam Stutchkoff! Former beloved.

"Mr. er—Mr. ah—" she pipes, squinting through what must be failing eyes.

"Goldkorn!" says her companion. I whirl. The shrunken man, a palsy patient, stares up at me from beneath two gray-haired spit curls. His withered lips spread in a gap-toothed smile. Herr Maltz! Hans! Number Two Finisher. At once I fumble for my *Revolver* but realize I have left it in Crystal's chamber. No matter. I can strangle this Nazi nemesis with my bare hands. Strangle him? It seems that with a single woodwinder's breath I could blow him into so many fragments of dust. What's this? Pity? Forgiveness? No. Fellow feeling. For what must he see, with those clouded eyes, as he looks up at the remains of Leib Goldkorn?

"The flute," I declare. "The one from the prawnshop. The Rudall & Rose."

With a trembling hand he points to the top of the nearby bureau. *Voilà!* My silver-plated instrument. I seize it. Time now to leave. But there is, from this room, only one exit: the same door through which we entered. With a last glance backward—farewell to these two little dolls, old love, ancient enemy—I lead *meine liebe Tochter* back the way we have come.

At once the policemen see us. They are in their gumshoes racing straight down the hall. Trapped. No escape. I wave, as if it were magical, my woodwind wand; and to my amazement a miracle does occur. A door on the left opens wide and out of the darkness a familiar voice says, "Mr. Goldkorn. Quickly, please. This way."

Who is this? Straight hair, shy smile, Asian-style eyes: the Nipponese cleansing lady! "Can it be?" I ask, as we accept her invitation into the room. "Have you followed me even here?"

"There is no time for talk." With a pretty little finger she gestures toward the window. "You must go outside."

We dash, as Rabbi Rymer might say, to the sash. A fire escape! A ladder to the ground! "Don't wait!" commands the Japanese janitress, throwing the bolt on the door behind her. "You have only a moment."

Perhaps not even that: for the policemen are already pounding on the portal. "Open up!" they bellow. "In the name of the law!"

But my darling daughter has already climbed over the ledge and is making her way down the iron ladder. Clutching my flute, I follow. In the rain and the dark of night we descend toward the alley at the side of the building. All there seems quiet and still. Miss Crystal arrives at the last rung and drops to the ground. A minute later I drop down too. "We are safe, my dear," I announce, and with relief embrace her.

"Hands up! Don't move! You're surrounded!"

Lights blaze all around us. Behind the illumination, a wall of blue. A score of policemen, each with a pistol in hand, step forward out of the gloom. The gig, to quote the slang saying, is up.

"Don't shoot, constable! I confess! I took the wallet! Yes! Yes! It's shameful. Poor Fingerhut, *père!* I have no excuses! I have robbed a human corpse!"

The gendarmes close in. They seize me by Sammy's collar.

"One minute, officer." That is the voice of the Hotel Plaza employee. Now she too leaps from the ladder to the ground. From about her neck she holds forth a small square of paper; the plastic in which it is enclosed gleams in the light.

"Press pass," she announces. "*New York Times.* Book department. These two are with me."

5

WE ARRIVE, MY Martha and I, at the Museum of Nature some time before midnight. All about us are the unending mists. We turn west and walk—is my arm in her arm, or has she placed her arm in mine?—toward the Avenue of Columbus. "Dad—" These are the first words she speaks. Let me repeat the three letters: "*Dad*, who was that woman?"

"That was, in my opinion, Miss Michiko. The Kakutani. After all, only one-half a Finn."

"And why did she save us? Is she sweet on you or something?"

"No, no, no, no. *Pas du tout*. She has done this, my dear, for art."

"And is what you say true? I won't have to go back? No more chains? No more clients? I'm getting, you know, a little old for this line of work."

"No. No return. You shall live with me five stories in elevation. High above the hoi polloi. We shall look down, my child, from this aerie at the comings and goings of men and women—their graspings, their busyness, their hot pursuits. Oh, the baubles! The toys! Their poor lives of flesh. I shall on occasion open a Campbell's. Not only that: as we laugh at foibles or discuss one with the other the works of let us say Victor Hugo, we can partake of a chicken pot pie."

"Oh, Larry! I'm so happy!" So saying, she stops at the avenue and, with one arm trustingly about my waist zone, she reaches to her ankle and removes her bright red stiletto-heeled shoe. This she deposits in the nearby receptacle for trash. Keep New York City Clean, ha! ha! ha!

"Dear Martha, *mein kleines Kindlein*: I am experiencing happiness, too."

Fatal words! Best never uttered. For at that moment I see the flashing lights of an emergency-type vehicle that is parked—heavens! On 80th Street! In front of my very own door! We hasten southward one block. In my mind are dire imaginings: floodwaters pouring from the fifth-floor windows, collapse of roof shingles, a stovetop detonation. And tied round my heart, dragging behind each of my footsteps as an anchor might from a vessel at sea, is a heavy burden of guilt: for in my recent dream, that fantasia of filials, there has been no thought of dear spouse and doting dam. Clara! It is worse, that mental expungement, than actual murder.

Number 130. All seems normal. All seems calm. But our journey to the top is akin to a trial by fire. On landing one, the familiar odors of cabbage and *pieds de cochon*. "Pardon, *meine liebe Tochter*. An explanation: we have not in this building an exclusively Hebrew population." Landing two: Fingerhut, *fils*. Red of face. Distortion of features. "Goldkorn! The rent! The payments! I've got a notice! You're out first thing in the morning! Out on your ear!" Onward, upward, along this *via dolorosa*, to where, on landing three, Bowswer stands snarling and snapping, as if he were possessed of teeth. "One moment, Missy: I must now hum the bars of the *Tannhäuser* overture." Level four? A respite, on which, as automobilists pull to the side of the road at designated spots of rest, those making this ascent may pause for breathlessness. Fifth floor. The cabinetto. No sooner have I with a face blush noted that it is here that we make our ablutions than the door flies open and Madam Schnabel, in deshabillé, bursts forth. "So, Mr. Goldkorns! Such a bon vivant? Engaging in carnalizations?"

"Oh, hello, Myra." It is the former *Hustler Review* model who speaks these words.

"Ha! Ha! So the ladies are acquainted?"

No answer. My neighbor has with a door slam disappeared once more into the WC.

After all, a landlord, a boxer type, the coloratura: these are the normal challenges one must meet upon the gauntlet to apartment 5-D. But what next meets my eyes is without precedent. The door is open! Wide open! I walk with briskness to the spot. What has happened is all too clear. My books, the myriad volumes of *Goldkorn Tales,* have absorbed the water that poured owing to Fingerhut negligence into our apartment. What were once neat columns stacked floor to ceiling are now enormous gray mounds, like so many sodden haystacks that dot the farmer's field. Unreadable runes! Moldering memoirs!

"Is anything wrong, Pop?"

"No, no. *Entréz! Entréz!*"

She does so, padding forward on her unshod feet. "It needs work," she declares, upon looking about.

But I am already stepping around a sierra of sagging spines. "Yoo-hoo! Miss Clara? Are you awake, little mouse? I have for you a surprise." From the Posturepedic, upon which my yokemate is sleeping, no response. Bald spot, naughty nightie, the teeth in a tumbler.

I turn to *mein kleines Kindlein.* "Come, come, my seedling. Do not on such an occasion be shy." Mistress Martha now joins us, standing coyly, like a schoolgirl, thumb hooked in thumb. "My eye's apple, may I introduce the former Clara Litwack?"

Our joint legacy moves closer, then falls to her knees. "Hi, Mom. Hello, Mommy. I'm so glad to meet you. She doesn't say anything." These last words are addressed, in tones of concern, to me.

"Wake, wake, Madam Goldkorn! Arise, my helpmeet. This is our little one. You remember? At the Tivoli? The poor blue babe? Look how she has become a strapper!"

"Mommy! Mommy! What is the matter?"

"It's nothing. Nothing. A slumber, you know. Because of the dropsy. Up, up, Madam! Awake!"

Alas, the only sound—it doesn't come from the mattress but from behind a pachyderm pile of rotting remainders—is a stifled sob. What person is there? With a quick step I round the barrier and see, huddled in the corner, a weeping figure. "Goloshes," I cry. "M.D.!"

The doctor looks up, teardrops shooting from his bespectacled eyes. "You have killed her!"

"What do you mean, sir? My lifetime companion? This is only a catnap—you know, a kind of coma."

The physician with spryness—he is not even a man of eighty—leaps to his feet. "She's dead! My Clara! Monster! Murderer!"

I return *post haste* to the Posturepedic, where the offspring, pale now, and trembling, stares wildly. "What's happening? Momma! Why won't she wake?"

The truth is, my better half does look, about the chin whiskers, a little blue. I take her hand and deliver a sharp knuckle rap. "Miss Clara! Honey! *Honigkuchen*! Speak! Would you like a Slim Jim? Aha! Look there! A definite lip curl!"

"A reflex." That is the diagnosis of Dr. Goloshes, who now pushes to the other side of the bed. "There is no breath. No pulse, either."

Then the erstwhile Fone Fancy begins to declaim. "Can this be? Is it you? Milton? After all these years?"

"Martha! Child! I have not seen you since you eloped with—what was his name? Bibelnieks?"

"Wait! None of this is possible. Miss Litwack! Madam Gold-korn! When I left her this morning she was in fettle. Cute, ha-ha, as a button."

Dr. G: "Yes, this morning! It's a confession! What time, exactly, did you leave?"

L.G.: "The time? In the *ante meridiem*? What does that matter? Maybe it was actually in the afternoon."

At that, the licensed practitioner leaps toward the Frigidaire, flings it open, and takes from the garden crisper the needle for hypodermics.

"Uh-oh."

"Look! Do you see? Full! It's full! You forgot the injection. Forgot? It's on purpose. It's murder. It's criminal neglect."

M.G.: "No! It can't be! Poppy! How could you?"

"It's a mistake, more or less. I had to go to Rivington Street. Goloshes, I had no choice. My daughter was in danger. Look! I saved her! Isn't she a peach? I couldn't be in two places at once. It was a decision, like in the Talmud."

"Your daughter! *Yours*? You fool! She doesn't belong to you."

"But you must remember. The Tivoli Cine Palace. June, 1943. *Happy Go Lucky,* a world premiere. *A Musical Cruise,* these were the words upon the placard, *That Chases the Blues.* Here the bride of L. Goldkorn gave birth. There can be no doubt. M. Martin. R. Vallee. B. Hutton. Also D. Powell. *A Tropical Trip that's Really a Pip!* The screams of the newlywed. The pant-pantings. I thought she was having a catarrh. You, sir, the medical student, were seated by chance, or let us say by providence, two rows behind. It was your skilled hands that brought the urchin—so small, so blue, a prematurity—into the world. Can you doubt that this is the neonatal who stands before you now?"

"*Premature!* She was almost three weeks *late.* By *providence? Chance?* You think that's why I was in the theater? I had been following her everywhere. I should have married her. Oh, poor Clara! You poor woman! Your unhappy life!"

"But how can this be? I thought there was a penetration. We had uttered our spousals."

Just then two men, one at either end of a stretcher, enter apartment 5-D. Dr. Goloshes points to the Posturepedic. The attendants walk to the spot and roll with rudeness the one love of my life onto their canvas sling.

"I don't understand. I am in a cloud of confusion. Do you mean it was Pepi Pechler? He came to the Hotel Plaza. He was definitely the best man."

"No," says Goloshes. "He wasn't the father." With that he gives a signal to the two intruders, who, their burden between them, make their way to the door.

"Stop! Stop at once! Where are you taking this woman? She is my wife!"

But they are through the portal, down the hallway, out of sight.

Goloshes—what a fine-looking youth he was, a ruddy type, with freckled spots in the non-Jewish manner: this Goloshes holds his arms out to my sole living relation. "Martha. Won't you come?"

Wordlessly, she gives a nod.

I seek to interfere. "But what about Victor Hugo? The corn chowders? You were to be the comfort of my golden years."

"You should have thought of that, Mister, when you forgot to give my mother her shots."

Out she goes, my Martha, stepping through the last remaining puddle, leaving on the wooden floor an impression of a foot—a high arch, a rounded heel, the dots of the digits—that lingers a full minute, and then a minute more, before dwindling into the air.

Who knows the time? Deep now in the night. The darkness before the dawn. Impossible, lacking a Bulova, to determine the hour. Naturally I do not partake of the pallet where of late my helpmeet lay. Upright, then, upon the Windsor type. Or pace-pacing the wooden floor. No Philco for entertainments. No Admiral. Not even the Sunbeam, should one wish the diversion of the lurch of toast. Poor Goloshes! He himself has fallen victim to the same Uncle Al from which he sought to save me. The capital of Missouri is not, as commonly believed, St. Louis, but Jefferson City. Hawthorn, the flower. Poultry, grains, livestock, fruits. I am certain that it is a prolonged bachelorhood that has driven him into madness. What could the lonely doctor know of the joys of married life? The walk, one day, in

Riverside Park. The way, in the Horn & Hardart, I would leave a small *pourboire* for the table sweepers, only to have the lifetime companion in frugality remove it. The occasions when weary she allowed me to remove her shoe. No need to mention the Magic Chef and how it sits waiting. The wide white door, like a philosopher's brow. Within? Within we see restored the little blue flame, like the portrait of a human soul. Is that you, Miss Clara Litwack? Skipping and dancing? Or have we here Madam Henie? Madam Miranda? Are you dancing there, too? Wait. Moment. What of Miss Esther? To the best of my knowledge the *Herald Tribune* never carried the story of that great star's demise. Still living, then? Ah, that Pepsodent smile. Might I still take pen to paper and by that method tell her how much I admire her line of swimwear? Signed, L. Goldkorn. A friend from youth. It is not altogether impossible to receive a reply. Thus might occur a correspondence. A critical discussion of filmics, from the Hardy feature for Mr. L. B. Mayer to the excellent *Dangerous When Wet*. The way, in *Pagan Love Song,* you wrapped yourself in a sarong. Do you recall how, on our own enchanted island, I played a rhapsody upon the flute? I have the same instrument now. A genuine Rudall & Rose. Listen: I shall begin a S. Romberg selection.

TWARPF-TU-TU-TWAPFT!

That? That is merely the sound of the neighbors; they wish to remind us of the lateness of the hour. Let us move our recital to the open window.

TWANK!

Look: the mists at these notes seem to hasten away.

TWUUPT!

Yes, at my melodies even the rain and the drizzle come at last to a stop. End of the forty days. End of the forty nights. Time to send out, in search of a new life, this dulcet dove.

THRRRPT!

There! There! How the clouds flee! *Mein Gott!* How they part! Such is the power or music. Of magic! *Abra*— Do you see? Do you see? Are those not the stars? *Cadabra!* Ah! There you have it, rising higher and higher, the half-filled orb of the moon. Soon, soon, before one can say J. Robinson, your Leib Goldkorn will turn this blackest of nights into day.

   Abracadabra! Ha! Ha! Ha!

   Abracadabra, my dears.

Leslie Epstein was born thirty-seven years after Leib Goldkorn and has been gaining on him ever since. He was certainly alive and kicking when Leib arrived in Hollywood, since his father and uncle, Philip G. and Julius J. Epstein, had already established themselves as legendary screenwriters (*The Strawberry Blonde, The Man Who Came to Dinner, Yankee Doodle Dandy, Arsenic and Old Lace, Casablanca,* and some fifty others) and wits, mostly for Jacques Warner, never for D. F. Zanuck. Epstein left Hollywood for Yale and Oxford on a Rhodes scholarship, and has published seven previous books of fiction, most notably *King of the Jews,* which has become a classic of Holocaust literature, *Pinto and Sons, Pandaemonium,* and of course *Goldkorn Tales,* many copies of which still exist. His articles and stories have appeared in such places as *Esquire,* the *Atlantic Monthly, Playboy, Harper's,* the *Yale Review, Triquarterly, Tikkun, Partisan Review,* the *Nation,* the *New York Times Book Review,* the *Washington Post,* and the *Boston Globe.* In addition to the Rhodes scholarship, he has received many honors, including a Fulbright and a Guggenheim fellowship, an award for Distinction in Literature from the American Academy and Institute of Arts and Letters, a residency at the Rockefeller Institute at Bellagio, and various grants from the NEA. For many years he has been the director of the Creative Writing Program at Boston University. Having sent his own three children off to college and beyond, he lives with his wife, Ilene, in what suddenly became a very neat condominium in Brookline, Massachusetts.

Available in Norton Paperback Fiction

Andrea Barrett	*Ship Fever*
	The Voyage of the Narwhal
Rick Bass	*The Watch*
Simone de Beauvoir	*The Mandarins*
	She Came to Stay
Wendy Brenner	*Large Animals in Everyday Life*
Anthony Burgess	*A Clockwork Orange*
	Nothing Like the Sun
	The Wanting Seed
Frederick Busch	*Harry and Catherine*
Stephen Dobyns	*The Wrestler's Cruel Study*
Jack Driscoll	*Lucky Man, Lucky Woman*
Leslie Epstein	*King of the Jews*
	Ice Fire Water
Montserrat Fontes	*First Confession*
	Dreams of the Centaur
Leon Forrest	*Divine Days*
Paula Fox	*Desperate Characters*
	The Widow's Children
Carol De Chellis Hill	*Henry James' Midnight Song*
Linda Hogan	*Power*
Janette Turner Hospital	*Dislocations*
	Oyster
Siri Hustvedt	*The Blindfold*
Starling Lawrence	*Legacies*
Bernard MacLaverty	*Cal*
	Grace Notes
	Lamb
John Nichols	*The Sterile Cuckoo*
	The Wizard of Loneliness